GODCHILDREN

GODCHILDREN

A NOVEL BY

CHARLES CASEY MARTIN

VIKING

*The author would like to thank
the Great Midwestern Ice Cream Company, Iowa City, Iowa,
and the Bagel Deli, Northampton, Massachusetts,
for generous grants that aided in the
completion of this manuscript.*

▼▼▼▼▼▼▼▼▼▼▼

VIKING
Published by the Penguin Group
Viking Penguin, a division of Penguin Books USA Inc.,
40 West 23rd Street, New York, New York 10010, U.S.A.
Penguin Books Ltd, 27 Wrights Lane,
London W8 5TZ, England
Penguin Books Australia Ltd, Ringwood, Victoria, Australia
Penguin Books Canada Ltd, 2801 John Street,
Markham, Ontario, Canada L3R 1B4
Penguin Books (N.Z.) Ltd, 182–190 Wairau Road,
Auckland 10, New Zealand

Penguin Books Ltd, Registered Offices:
Harmondsworth, Middlesex, England

First published in 1990 by Viking Penguin,
a division of Penguin Books USA Inc.

1 3 5 7 9 10 8 6 4 2

LIBRARY OF CONGRESS CATALOGING IN PUBLICATION DATA
Martin, Charles Casey.
Godchildren: a novel / Charles Casey Martin.
p. cm.
ISBN 0-670-82663-4
I. Title.
PS3563.A723272G6 1990
813'54—dc20 89-40417

Printed in the United States of America
Set in Primer

for Teri

CONTENTS

If I could I surely would,
Stand on the rock where Moses stood.

— from traditional blues

PART ONE

WHEREABOUTS

1

Aaron Dodge would've packed on Wednesday. But late Tuesday afternoon a bank robbery occurred at the credit union. The incident, the
way the fat man heard it described later, began like this. A man with
a bush of kinky hair parted in the middle walked into Camel-Op Natural
Foods Co-op. No shirt. No shoes. Six-inch sideburns that angled backward, ending underneath his earlobes like sloppy "J"s. After helping
himself to one of the grocery sacks near the bulk bins, he started to
fill it with cashews, using his hand instead of the aluminum scoop.

While customers and personnel took turns making sure that he
didn't snack on the nuts before having them weighed, a second man,
who might or might not have been an accomplice, wearing a palomino
leather coat and expert-slope sunshades, revealed a pistol of convincing
caliber, unzipped the Ciao shoulder bag he was carrying, and let the
teller in charge of the credit-union window figure out the rest on her
own. His presentable appearance allowed the holdup man to escape
without attracting suspicion, either from the volunteers stocking
shelves in the grocery aisles or from the Camel-Op staffers on duty at
the lunch counter and at the checkout. He walked right past them,
out of the store, and was never identified, never apprehended, and
never seen again, except in various incarnations of his hairstyle and
wardrobe that breezed through the co-op daily.

The Alternative Bandit, people at the Camel-Op lunch counter were calling him on Wednesday morning.

"He was probably hopped up on styling mousse or something," a friend said to Aaron Dodge, and the fat man answered with an agreeable shrug: "A guy's cats have to eat."

"American Express wouldn't wait another day," somebody else ventured. "The word was out on the street. He had to do something."

And so the fat man didn't pack on Wednesday. Or on Thursday or Friday. Or in February, March, or April. But Aaron Dodge did intend to move. Absolutely. His plans hadn't changed.

"Don't go," Bob the Brush advised him one afternoon in early May.

According to his friend, the car Aaron Dodge drove would never pass inspection in any of the states he'd mentioned so far. He'd need a whole new wardrobe. Did he really want to crate and ship everything in his workshop? Junk or sell all the cripples stabled in the stalls behind his complex? Moving would mean locating a trailer. Messing with the hitch and light setup. Listening to improperly packed kitchenware clink at him for two thousand miles. They'd practically covered the napkin they were writing on with objections when Lulu interrupted to refill their coffee cups.

"You fear involvement, Aaron Dodge," she told the fat man. Like a number of his friends, Lulu had an advanced degree, a restaurant job, and nobody to share her ideas with.

"I've been watching tv," she added. "More than I should, probably. Anything from cartoons to the late, late show. Anything with a plot, so-called." She drew quotation marks in the air with her fingers. "And I think I know why you're so unhappy. Why we all are. People our age."

"Wait a minute," said the fat man. "Who's unhappy? Bob? You unhappy?"

"Listen to her," said Bob the Brush. "Lulu's a true scholar. She wouldn't say it unless somebody else had said it first." His friend Bob the Brush frequented Camel-Op because it was a place to find a healthy argument. Also, at least in the beginning, he'd assumed he stood a good chance of "scoring some liberated pussy" here. He was called the Brush not just because of his anachronistic haircut, but also because of his job. He clerked in the paint aisle of a hardware-and-home center in a nearby mall. Aaron Dodge's workshop was crowded with supplies and machinery purchased with the help of Bob the Brush's employee discount.

"It's this incredibly simple statement," Lulu said. "But so hard to believe. What we saw on tv just does not exist. Those families. Those heroes. Those loves. And what about the *pace*? Quick resolutions. Sequential, plotted action. I worry about it. A lot. Ordinary, everyday life is such a disappointment in comparison."

Aaron Dodge heard the sound of diesel-engine clatter outside—a semi downshifting and pulling into the lot. Bob the Brush heard too, it seemed. Pressing his palms against the countertop, he raised himself far enough off his stool to see out the front window.

This part of the city normally didn't host much truck traffic. And the occasional trucker that did exit the freeway usually ate at some franchise place, not here. The fat man had sat beside them at Sambo's or Howard Johnson's and listened to their complaints. The short stretch bisecting Phoenix was the only uncompleted section of I-10 between Jacksonville and Los Angeles.

"Ordinary, everyday life," Lulu said, rearranging cubes in the ice well with a silver scoop, "lacks any sense of directedness. Ninety percent of the time we're waiting. Which of our timid, anemic actions will take on a—what do I want to say?—a sudden, unexpected significance. That's why I'm excited by this move of yours, Aaron Dodge. On a number of levels."

The truck driver looked like a truck driver should look. You know. The gut, the broad forearms, the vest with no shirt underneath. Pimples on his face and shoulders the size of a ballerina's tits. He sat down at the counter. Inspected his surroundings with a blank expression.

Once, Camel-Op Natural Foods Co-op had been located on Camelback Road. Thus the name, whose origins Aaron Dodge sometimes wondered whether anybody but him remembered. In 1985 an L.A. basketball team called itself the Lakers, and a Utah team the Jazz. Native North Americans were still known as Indians. In such an era anybody who expected much from a name was going to be disappointed. New Mexico, New Jersey, New Hampshire, New York. What was America, after all, but a relocated franchise? As a business, Camel-

Op, an organic grocery, luncheonette, and credit union, functioned with the good-natured inefficiency of a grade-school civics project. But it was a place where clean karma, cosmic vibrations, and expanded consciousness were available, along with soy grits, mung beans, bulgur, and Little Bear's Breakfast mix, in bulk. Pilgrims claimed its aura was visible for miles. A sign near the front entrance identified it as a nuclear-free zone.

"You're a marketing representative," Lulu was saying when the trucker arrived. "Air travel is a normal part of your routine. But then one day your plane crashes on top of a mountain in Alaska. Your life changes. Would you like to see a menu?"

"Please, ma'am."

"Coffee?"

"No thank you."

"Suddenly you're thrown into an unfamiliar context. Faced with the urgent necessity to proceed directly, by the most immediate, efficient path, to a goal or destination."

The stranger glanced from his menu to Aaron Dodge, from Aaron Dodge to Bob the Brush. "Must be true," Bob said. "They gave her an A on it."

"The hero inserted neatly and dramatically into a new and threatening situation. The *Tarzan Goes to New York City* plot, you might call it. I'm sorry, sir. We ask for no smoking."

The stranger put away his Carltons.

Shut his menu.

"Interesting thesis," he said. "But the Tarzan film presupposes a voluntary entry into this new environment. Something your initial example, the sales representative stranded on a mountaintop, doesn't imply."

Lulu brought a stick of Carefree out of her uniform pocket.

Unwrapped it.

Folded it into her mouth and stared calmly at the stranger on the other side of the counter. "Doesn't matter," she said. "The point is, both find themselves in, I guess you'd say, peril. Willing or not, both become adventurers. Will Tarzan's primitive savvy do him any good at rush hour? Can the salesman's skills, developed in the 'burbs, perfected in corporate boardrooms, at Holiday Inns, serve him with any validity in a blizzard or avalanche? Ready to order?"

Gazpacho.

Sprout-and-cucumber salad.

Iced tea.

The stranger, it turned out, had studied literature and theology at the University of Utah. GI Bill. Graduate school. MLA job list. Beacon Transfer and Storage.

"Red Zinger, Lemon Mist, or Camomile?"

"Zinger. But what happens if this adventurer doesn't happen to be a good guy? What if he's a villain?"

"Or she," said Lulu.

"Sorry. Or she."

"Lulu's a feminist," said Bob the Brush. "Watch out."

"But not one of the strident ones," she said.

"The reason so many women get to be feminists," Bob told the stranger, "is that it's one of the few ideologies involving a distinction simple enough for them to grasp."

Lulu held up a finger. "Grasp this, numb nuts." She ripped the ticket out of her pad and pinned it to a wheel on the ledge separating her from the cook.

"An intruder, you mean? If you mean an intruder, then we're totally finished with Tarzan. Now we're watching *The Invasion of the Ant People* or something. Instead of an adventurer, the hero is a defender. It's"—Lulu consulted the clock on the wall behind her—"six-oh-seven on a Friday afternoon in May. Ant people swarm through the streets, carrying off sorority chicks in Tempe, tearing cowboys from behind the steering wheels of their king-cab pickups in Dysart and Chandler. The question now is, how strong are my defenses? How reliable are my strategies and traditions? Values, virtues, family, friends? Are they truly dependable?"

Thoughtfully, Lulu pressed the cap of her ballpoint to her lower lip. "The pace may be different. But as far as plots, that's it. Tv and everyday, ordinary reality are the same. Pick one. Invader or defender. Adventurer or preserver. All of us—and I really believe this, I guess—have to ask ourselves at some point, 'Which am I? If I'm a defender, is what I'm preserving worth preserving? If I'm an adventurer have I developed abilities which will sustain me in a hostile environment? Realistically, what are my resources?' It matters. A lot."

The four of them were silent a while. Stools creaked. Fingernails tapped against coffee cups. Presumably, inward decisions were made. Sides chosen. Finally the bell on the ledge behind Lulu pinged. She collected the stranger's order. Served it. Lifted a pot off the hotplate in back of her.

"No more for me, thanks."

The fat man sealed his cup with the flat of a hand.

Climbed off his stool.

Later, as he drove up 35th Avenue, he reached for his sunglasses, hanging by an earpiece from the visor, and switched on the radio. A professionally enthusiastic woman informed him that it was hot outside, guys and gals, managing to work call letters into the report at least three times, as an adjective, a noun, and a verb. July hot, not May hot. Hot enough to singe the fuzz off a tennis ball. The upcoming weekend she also claimed on behalf of the station, plus any fun he might be planning to have, with the bold and jolly charm of an explorer seizing a chain of islands in the name of the queen just prior to slaughtering its inhabitants and enslaving their children. Guys and gals.

KKGB. A pet name Aaron Dodge had given it and its Top 40 competitors here in the Valley of the Sun.

A move. An invasion. An adventure. The possibility seemed exciting again after talking to Lulu. He knew where he could get his hands on one of those trailers that look like the amputated bed of a pickup. He'd trade the soundest of his disabled vehicles for it, a gray Buick Skylark with a stuck valve, and sell everything he couldn't haul. Lulu was right. He didn't feel at home in the 1980s. He'd been depressed lately. Like since about 1977. Unappreciated, exhausted, and ignored, he felt like a vandal who'd written all his best graffiti in chalk. A lot of his friends said they felt the same way.

The fat man arrived at his West Phoenix apartment village just as a sennet of electronic bugles interrupted the KKGB announcer. Clattering ticker tape in the background underscored the bulletin's urgency.

Tornado? Assassination? Nuclear war?

Much earlier on that bright, hot Friday in May, in a suburb northwest of where the fat man lived, a little girl had disappeared while delivering morning papers for the Arizona *Representative*. She'd last been seen riding a bike with motocross handlebars. Wearing a purple-and-gold

Phoenix Suns t-shirt. Turquoise gym shorts. Socks with three-colored bands. Tennis shoes with Velcro straps instead of laces. If you had information to offer, you were supposed to call a toll-free number, 1-800-KID FIND.

Her name, the newsman said, was Mary Vanessa Singer.

2

▼▼▼▼▼▼▼▼▼▼▼▼▼▼▼▼▼▼▼
▼▼▼▼▼▼▼▼▼▼▼▼▼▼▼▼
▼▼▼▼▼▼▼▼▼▼▼

Home, the fat man served himself dessert and plugged in the tv. Adjusted its tinfoil flag and turned up the volume with a pair of pliers. His program didn't air till seven. Half an hour. Meantime he'd catch a nap. Or maybe there'd be a news flash concerning this lost kid, Mary the papergirl.

Though he hoped to sleep, he wasn't as interested in the actual nap, the rest, as he was in waking up afterward. There was this alarm he'd devised, which he wanted to try out. He set it for just before seven, keeping an eye on the screen as he tinkered. The alarm was more of a mental than a mechanical experiment—an automatic day/night crime-stop timer, connected, instead of to a lamp, to a tape player that held a cassette on which were stored, among others, the nightmarish sounds of a dentist's drill and a ripsaw encountering nails in a knotty plank. He'd tested practically every device sold—snooze, whisper, light, pulse, ring, bleep, and even smell alarms—and he'd discovered that of all the senses the sixth was most responsible. The more obnoxious and nerve-jangling the sensory experience that awaited you on the other side of oblivion, the more likely you were to wake up ahead of schedule to avoid it.

The tv his lullaby, he sat upright on the sofa, arms folded across his stomach, and shut his eyes. If you weighed two-fifty or over, you could count on hearing your name mentioned regularly in connection with some animal, and Aaron Dodge emerged from such comparisons with greater dignity than many men his size. Appearing more bearish than toadish or piggish, he snuffled and sighed. His big hands fidgeted. His lids twitched. His heart palpitated. Ten-cup-a-day users don't normally sleep in the daytime, and not that well at night, and when they do, caffeine produces psychic distortions that would make the state unrecognizable to those used to associating bedtime with relaxation. The semialert condition the fat man entered wasn't sleep, though he came to when it was over, and, though its patterns of logic disqualified it as ordinary thinking, it wasn't exactly dreaming either, but instead the agitated product of a serious coffee jones coupled with whatever he'd happened to be thinking about last. Which today was his move. That and this little girl. Her and her papers. Mary. Along with her name, four inevitable lines of children's verse occurred to Aaron Dodge as he sat in his living room waiting for the shakes to recede.

> *Mary had a little lamb,*
> *Its fleece was white as snow.*
> *And everywhere that Mary went,*
> *The lamb was sure to go.*

It was one of the nursery rhymes that he and his friends grew up listening to. A favorite of theirs. Maybe because it applied so well to the lives they would lead. As they grew up, everywhere that Aaron Dodge and his friends went, prosperity, publicity, and pandemonium were sure to follow. Because Aaron Dodge and his friends were part of the largest generation of Americans ever to inhabit their country. A Baby Boom, it was called.

Aaron Dodge and his friends. Mary and hers. Their whims created industries and their annoyances bureaucracies. Their story made a great nursery rhyme, and an even better fairy tale. Mary, born during a time when everybody wanted children, naturally stayed a child for as long as she could. The industries and bureaucracies that followed her everywhere slowed Mary down. Meanwhile her little sister, born during a time when parents wanted fewer children, also obeyed her elders. She grew up so quickly that she got there ahead of Mary.

Not that there weren't people the fat man's age who grew up to be wealthy, optimistic, confident, powerful, and satisfied. Plenty did. But what seemed—at least if you were one of them—like an entire generation of thirty- or forty-year-olds, reared in the 1960s, found themselves twenty years later—suddenly without money, without insurance, without families, without heroes, and with opinions instead that everybody else thought were quaint, dated, or crazy—working for people ten years younger and wondering what to do next.

"We're experiencing a metamorphosis," the fat man liked to tell his friends. "Something like what a steak dinner goes through on its way from the table to the toilet."

Dodge was. But "Aaron" wasn't the fat man's real name. His friends had corrected it for him back in high school, when Aaron Dodge, then a skinny teenager, started his own repair business. Reasonably talented, erratically trained, but endlessly enthusiastic, he wasn't sure what exactly he'd be repairing. So for the time being he gave his business an all-purpose nickname. Aaron's Enterprises. He chose "Aaron" so that his listing, if he ever made enough money to afford one and if he ever decided what to specialize in, would appear first under its heading in the yellow pages. He never made the money. Or the decision. But one of his high school friends started calling him Aaron and pretty soon they all were.

West Phoenix. East Phoenix. Tempe, Glendale, Mesa. His listing in the white pages had changed regularly since then. His enthusiasm had moderated some. His weight had doubled. And meantime he'd watched the city of Phoenix grow along with him. And grow. And grow. Between 1970 and '80 the population doubled. In the wintertime there were even more people—tourists and half-year residents. What had once been the entire population of Michigan eventually resided west of the Rockies, with Ohio on the way.

Vanity, materialism, superficiality, self-delusion, and casual greed. Make no mistake, the fat man could tell you stories. His cynicism was pure, his disenchantment total. His situation might've seemed pathetic if he hadn't kept a sense of humor about it. If he hadn't had friends to share it. Wherever, whenever they assembled, his could be found among those well-fed, all-weather, all-American faces indigenous to diners and ungodly hours of the night. People who never sleep. Whose coffee cups the waitress refills without asking. You know. Bob's Big Boy, Perkins, Humpty Dumpty. Phoenix was full of the fat man's friends.

Friends, yes. Girlfriends, no. The fat man was a bachelor. By nature, by inclination, by resolve, by God. He lived like a bachelor, he ate like a bachelor. He'd invented a set of kitchen guidelines, unwritten but nevertheless observable, that he lived and ate by.

Always cook dishes that last more than one meal.

Whenever possible, cook two or more dishes in the same pan, either simultaneously or sequentially.

Eat from the pan you cooked in.

Eat with the utensil you stirred with.

Cook in a pan that you can not only eat from, but also refrigerate leftovers in, heat up leftovers in, and eat from again next time.

If you must eat a meal from a plate, simply refrigerate your plate and fork afterward, and reuse them next time along with the leftovers.

Drink water. That way you won't have to wash the glass.

Or, better yet, beer.

More than an eligible bachelor, more than a confirmed bachelor, Aaron Dodge was a man supremely well equipped for loneliness. That's what his friends said about him. They were always asking Aaron Dodge who he was seeing. Who he was with.

With. Whatever they meant by that.

His car didn't help matters much. He drove an unexotic, odd-looking cross between a pickup and an auto, built by Chevrolet and called an El Camino. Manufactured without a back seat and temporarily lacking a front one on the passenger side, the El Camino simplified Aaron Dodge's romantic life considerably. He planned to reupholster the missing seat and replace it, but meanwhile all the cargo he could fit into the extra cab space appealed to him more than a majority of the passengers a seat would've made room for.

You need a relationship, Aaron Dodge, his friends would tell him. Physical affection, don't you miss it? When I do, I cut both ends out of a can of corn and pack it with raw liver, he'd tell them—referring to a popular invention he'd introduced to his West Phoenix neighborhood at the age of eleven. His friends accused him of hiding behind a macho façade of aggressive self-reliance.

They couldn't believe the apartment he lived in. Two bedrooms, no bed. Aaron Dodge slept on a couch, because the bedrooms were crowded with inventions more important to him than a bed. Inventions, literally. Aaron Dodge's apartment was full of them. All his own. Ideas that had succeeded, ideas that hadn't, ideas that might. In fact, the couch Aaron Dodge slept on was his own idea. An Aaron's Enterprises design. The back cushion and seat cushion could be separated and stacked, with the wooden arm-rests and legs for support, to produce two comfortable bunk beds instead of one uncomfortable double. It and inventions like it caused Aaron Dodge's friends to accuse him of booby-trapping his romantic future and creating conditions that perpetuated a lonely bachelorhood. I'm not lonely, Aaron Dodge told them. Just not married, is all. The dilemma of the bachelor, he'd discovered, was similar to the dilemma of the inventor. How do you share something original and useful but at the same time retain full rights to it yourself?

The fat man, it could have been argued, was not attractive in the traditional sense. His brand of sex appeal had enjoyed brief popularity in the mid-'60s to '70s, back when people still maintained utopian illusions. One being that wit, charm, and intelligence didn't have to be calculated in inverse proportion to pounds, or according to a golden mean established courtesy of GQ ads and photos of stick-figure females, their cheekbones accentuated by extracted molars, their menstrual cycles perpetually bewildered by starvation.

A remote time.

A deluded faction of society.

Literally and unapologetically, Aaron Dodge embodied in his appearance that previous era, from his long ponytail, often sleek and nearly radiant after one of his prolonged baths, to the well-made Mexican sandals of dark leather he wore on formal occasions year-round, and which he could get you a hell of a deal on from this friend of his down in Nogales if you were interested. Because of this, he tended to evoke the dormant attitudes of that gentler, more compassionate period, even in those who'd only experienced it in the form of rumors, flashbacks, or cheap trivia. And so the fat man never found himself without friends, and only rarely (and then more likely as a result of his reclusiveness than his looks) without a romantic prospect. Often someone surprisingly attractive—in the traditional sense—compared with the matches his friends still occasionally tried to concoct with his welfare in mind.

Safely past the age of twenty, when you marry because that's what your parents did, and past twenty-five, when you get married because all your friends are, and past thirty, when you do because pretty soon nobody will have you if you don't—safely into his thirties, Aaron Dodge had only three words to say to the prospective brides—plump, perfumed, desperate—that his friends kept trying to breed him to.

No.

Fuck.

In.

Way.

People in Phoenix hadn't always been like this. Aaron Dodge could remember a time. He'd first noticed the beginnings of a change in the mid-'70s. The Bicentennial. Jimmy Carter. Then in the '80s the state officially recognized the transformation, replacing its familiar license tag—evergreen numerals on a sand background—with one the color of imitation black-cherry soda. Three Mile Island. Ronald Reagan.

Nobody you met there, it seemed—Aaron Dodge and all his friends included—had actually been born in Phoenix. He was born in Galveston, Texas—where they have all the hurricanes—and moved to Arizona when he was eleven, along with his mother and a man named Earl Mathias, his then current father. His mother had married Mathias, a high school biology teacher, soon after her first divorce, following their return from a tour of the Holy Land sponsored by a local tv station. Her first husband, Otto Dodge, had been killed in a gruesome industrial accident when their son was still in grade school. Her second, a big mistake, had admitted to bisexuality after a year of marriage. Like her adopted home, Esther Dodge would remain throughout her stay there a conspicuous but resigned victim of twentieth-century trends.

When the three of them arrived in Phoenix, they found a yellow-and-green Mayflower van or an orange-and-silver U-Haul in every second driveway of the housing development that would be their home. They lived on a street called Encantero Drive, at the end of which the faint outlines of a golf course were visible, indicated by tufts of freshly sown bermuda and rye grass, and palm trees transplanted fully grown and propped at a slant with two-by-fours. He attended a grade school named for a variety of cactus, and later a high school whose name honored the memory of a Spanish conquistador. The neighborhood, a subdivision called Sunset Shadows, was so new that there were no mailboxes, and snakes would crawl out of the desert to sleep in the shade of the fences.

One day Earl Mathias brought home a younger man who wore a hand-tooled leather visor and a golf shirt with "The Arizona Representative" printed in Biblical lettering over his heart. He sat on the living-room sofa, leaning forward, his hands clasped between his knees, and spoke earnestly. Emphasizing the sense of pride and responsibility a job would instill, the health and high spirits promoted by outdoor activity, the organizational and financial challenges represented by after-school employment, and the bonuses, premiums, trips, and prizes he could win, the young man, whose name was Brad Moe, offered him the opportunity to become one of the first carriers in the territory.

After that, every day at sunrise, he pedaled to the corner—his corner: Encantero Drive and Canyon Creek Court—and collected his draw, a wired bundle of Arizona *Representatives*. After school, one day a month, he billed his subscribers.

It was while straying briefly from his assigned daily route that he discovered, near a street so far indicated only by ribboned stakes, the ruins of a building in whose adobe bricks could still be seen the shallow handprints of Indian slaves who'd formed them, and in whose east wall voids a finger deep indicated where prisoners had stood at dawn to be executed. In a dry riverbed he uncovered a burlap sack that held the bones of six kittens, their skulls, and the rock that had drowned them. He grew into a resilient, self-reliant, sleepy teenager whose good-natured cynicism was no match for the headlines that inked his fingers every dawn. His disenchantment was certified by the names of the era's villains. Oswald and Ruby. McNamara. Westmoreland. Starkweather, Speck, and Manson. Daley. Agnew. Wallace and Maddox. Sirhan. Ray. Calley. Nixon.

And Earl Mathias.

A man named Al Blodgett, who brought with him a portable tv set, a bag of golf clubs, and suitcases containing polyester flare-bottom slacks, V-neck shirts with penguins on the breast, and wide white belts with double rows of chrome eyelets came to live with him and his mother in the house on Encantero Drive.

He turned sixteen with a new father, his fourth.

You weren't officially a Phoenix resident until you reached that age, because till then you couldn't drive a car legally. He bought his first, a black '58 Volkswagen Karmann-Ghia, with money his route provided. He and a girl named Corazón Inez Hidalgo lost their virginity together in a sand hazard on the twelfth fairway of the golf course down the street, which had been given the name Desert Lakes.

Along with the unknown qualities contributed by his father, he'd inherited from Esther Dodge a recklessness responsible for the half-dozen divorces that would complicate her life, but also the determination that would convince her to marry that many times plus one. The result was a disposition that made overhauling, renovation, tinkering, and invention inevitable natural impulses. He was always fixing his friends' Barracudas, Novas, Chargers, and VW buses. He ran the light board and repaired amps and mikes for Brad Moe, who'd given up his job as a route supervisor to start a band. In those days he was a tall, skinny kid, always pulling up his Levis by the belt loops when he walked, and preceded by an enormous, bony nose with a permanent smudge beside it, renewed each time he brushed his shoulder-length blonde hair from his eyes with a greasy knuckle.

Since Al Blodgett's arrival, he rarely went home between school and bedtime. If he bothered to eat supper, it was usually an omelet at the Hobo Joe's near Sunset Shadows, where all you had to do was transfer a brass bushing from your pocket to the counter and there'd always be somebody around who'd scoot his ashtray and coffee cup a stool closer and ask was it a seven-eighths or a thirteen-sixteenths. One night a blonde waitress named Cody, older, and new to Phoenix from California, handed him a crescent wrench and said please, the CO_2 cylinder that fed the Pepsi and Sprite machine had discharged, and a conversation began that ended at Cody's unit in a West Phoenix apartment village, on a recent invention called a waterbed. These disenchanted people, who ate supper at midnight and drank coffee till dawn, became his friends.

That was in 1969. The government had announced a new strategy for inducting nineteen-year-olds into the armed services. A yearly lottery. Beginning that August, every summer the selective service would make permanent enemies of tens of thousands of American teenagers and their birthdays. Aaron Dodge and boys his age had two years to anticipate the drawing that would decide their futures. Twenty-four months to consider a response.

On a portable color tv given to him as a bribe by Al Blodgett, Aaron Dodge watched that first draft lottery. And saw the decade's other events inject their venom. Protests, mobs, demonstrations, riots. He remembered how, for him, the decade had begun much differently. In black and white, on a set in their second-grade classroom, he and his friends had watched an astronaut, after numerous delays and countdowns, launched into earth orbit. In seconds the rocket was so far away that cameras could barely track it, and the subtle adjustments necessary to keep the missile in the center of the screen resembled the effects of an earthquake.

The young decade, and similar Texas classrooms, had provided a *crisis* in Cuba, a *tragedy* in Dallas, *turmoil* in Asia, Africa, the Middle East. And one, untelevised memory that belonged to no one else.

Otto Dodge died in 1960, when his son was eight years old, in a Galveston Island grain elevator that blew apart with such force that the body count had to be determined by consulting a work schedule, then revised accordingly after contacting the families of employees whose shifts were supposed to have coincided with the disaster. The remains recovered couldn't be assembled in any conclusive way and kept adding up to different numbers. Aaron Dodge remembered how, as a boy, already with the instincts of an inventor, he'd immediately understood the physics of the calamity. Hazardous concentrations of dust, friction between particles, a monumental chain reaction. Basically, topsoil carried to the elevator by the megatons of grain stored there had turned the silo into a stick of dynamite. The explosion, resounding across the island to the windows of his school, shook his view of the outside, from that day to this, in ways he preferred not to think about. But, looking back from the '80s he had to admit that the catastrophe, occurring as it did at the turn of the decade, and as a result of a violent uprising by otherwise inert and invisible coconspirators, seemed mercilessly prophetic of what the future held for him and his tiny classmates.

You fear involvement, Aaron Dodge.

Some accusations you get tired of listening to. Even when friends do the accusing. So you decide, "No more for me, thanks," seal your cup with the flat of your hand, climb off your stool, and call it an afternoon. Or a week. Or several. Which is exactly what the fat man decided on the bright, hot Friday in early May when Mary Vanessa Singer disappeared. He didn't show that night, or the next night, or the next—not at Denny's, at Kountry Kitchen, at Bill Johnson's Big Apple, or at Camel-Op. His friends must've wondered.

Anybody seen Aaron Dodge? What's it been? Two weeks? Three? Why, a fella his size, he could a had a heart attacked or something, knock wood. We ought to one of us pick out a nice card to set there by the register for people to sign.

Wonder where he's been keeping hisself? That rascal.

The fat man went to his kitchen for a spoon and a quart of fudge ice cream. He sat in front of the tv and pried the lid off the carton. The alarm had operated perfectly. That is, hadn't operated. He'd opened his eyes in time to disarm it before the next cut on its soundtrack—a recording of that awful, prolonged female screech that greeted the Beatles on their first U.S. tour, twenty years ago. He stomped the floor. Whipped the antenna back and forth. Smacked the side of the set. The picture disintegrated into a frenzy of leaping diagonal stripes.

So far the annoyances had been minor ones. But then Aaron Dodge didn't need much encouragement to generate a desolate mood. He was an inventor, he could do a lot with a little. A couple of aggravating memories, and then the lost papergirl he'd heard about on the radio today on his way home from Camel-Op. To Aaron Dodge they were like the atmospheric motes around which hailstones form. Or was he thinking of snowflakes? Or comets? Maybe he had it wrong meteorologically speaking, but emotionally he recognized a shitstorm when he smelled one coming, and was doing his best to stay clean. It was easy to avoid remembering in a place where you'd lived for twenty years and where you intended to live for twenty more, but decide to leave a place and suddenly recollections animated everything you looked at with irritating significances.

The tv for instance. It was the same '69 model portable his stepfather Al Blodgett had given him. Nowadays it required an indeterminate amount of coaxing—on days when it would operate at all. He wedged the selector between channels and waited. The zigzags hadn't altogether disappeared, but the audio asserted itself boldly behind a faint sizzle.

La Low-tay-REE-yah!

Low-tay-REE-yah!

Low-tay-REEEE-yah!

The picture consolidated abruptly. Demented jade eyes. Lavender skin. Aaron Dodge side-armed a paperback. Colors modulated wildly the length of the spectrum and back before stabilizing.

Bow-NAHN-sah!

Five minutes of undiluted media frenzy, the *Jackpot Jack Show* occupied the Friday slot between local programming and prime time. A whore taking cuts in communion line. An outrageous and undisguised offense to moderation, propriety, dignity, and good taste.

Aaron Dodge watched religiously.

Played when he could spare the buck.

Jack energetically spun the wheel of fortune. Moan-you-maiiiin-teal! Then rescued a sequence of hot-pink, lime, and lemon Ping-Pong balls from a turbo-charged Plexiglas aquarium—Meel-you-naiiiiire! The game was pick-six, but by three the fat man was already ripping up his computer-generated chits. Dropping them in the trash. Walking, disenchanted, to the kitchen.

When he opened the icebox door it spoke to him. *Quid vee ding your vace you vad big.* One of his inventions. He'd removed the chip from a greeting card that played "Happy Birthday" when you looked inside. With the help of an engineer at Honeywell, a friend, he'd reprogrammed it to insult him for snacking.

A takeout bar-b-q's lucky phone number. Winning parlays suggested by the plates of significantly parked vehicles outside a brightly lit convenience store at 3:00 A.M. Bar codes off the labels of his favorite foods. None of the reliable combinations had been paying off for the fat man. He was tired of the Promised Land. Land of Milk and Honey. Lately he suspected caramel coloring. Cartons exhibited photos of abducted children. An "Apartment for Rent" sign, hand-lettered on the lid of a to-go pizza box, was posted to a young citrus tree on the strip of lawn in front of his unit.

An average Friday evening would've included the lottery payoff extravaganza, plus maybe one other tv show. Then the fat man would've

Tulane unclipped a pen from inside the neck of his t-shirt. Placed it on the fat man's side of the table.

He pretended to keep reading for a moment longer, then looked up. He signaled the bartender with two fingers. Pointed back and forth between their empties. "That Ernesto? Who's Ernesto?"

The bartender delivered beers. "Hi. I was just asking Tulane here who Ernesto is?" He waited silently for one of them to pay, then silently returned to the register with Aaron Dodge's money.

"What you say, man?"

"Tulane, I'm moving. I doubt I'll be in town but about another month."

"I know you done lived in the Phix twenty years, Jack, where you going all of a goddam sudden? Hell, I got to I can call you ass on the telephone, man. I don't see nothin' here says we boaf of us have to live in the same town no how. Man, come *on*. You got to do this for me."

"Couldn't you—"

"You *it,* man. How many responsible white fuckers with a job you think I know?"

Aaron Dodge hesitated. Eyed the snack items near the stairstep shelves of liquor behind the bar. Slim Jims. Planter's. Rold Gold.

"This place have a pisser?"

Wearily, Tulane aimed a finger in the direction of a dim hallway, at the end of which Aaron Dodge discovered a rear entrance. He let himself out, into the alley. He knew only one lawyer, a patent attorney, a friend of his. He found a payphone and dialed. At first Max showed a reluctance equal to any doctor's at being asked to prescribe over the phone. Then the fat man explained his predicament in more detail.

"Ernesto's?" said Max. "You're kidding, Aaron. Isn't that one of those places down there that claims to be where Miranda was stabbed?"

"Claims?"

"Ernesto Miranda. Nineteen seventy-five. Murdered in a bar right here in Phoenix."

" 'You have a right to remain silent?' That Miranda?"

"You're in a scuzzy South Phoenix dive, Aaron. This is a nineteen-year-old kid. With an arrest."

"So you're saying . . ."

"I'd cover my ass. With both hands. But of course it's up to you."

It was nearly dark out, but still a hundred degrees or better, when Aaron Dodge retreated up the alley behind Ernesto's and crossed the parking area. An area some of Phoenix's unluckiest residents must've passed through before him. Drug dealers, consumers, cops on the take. Uninsured motorists, prostitutes, pimps. Tulane Wiggins. They'd all stepped over, past, or around it, but Aaron Dodge, naturally, stepped squarely onto a molten glob that yanked his rubber sandal completely off his foot.

Until you've lived in the desert, you underestimate what sunlight can do to a wad of chewing gum.

"Goddammit!" he whispered, then hopped back to the shoe and wiggled into it. When he lifted it to inspect his problem, it stayed attached to the ground by stringy pink rubber bands. He tried dragging the sole across the asphalt, which only spread the stickiness more evenly across the rubber. He hobbled over to the length of curbing the El Camino was parked against and scraped his heel on the edge. His foot still felt like it was sending down tender roots when he took a step.

"Fucker!" he whispered, and kicked the gummy thong, soccer-style, halfway across the lot. It landed with a slap, skidded, and rolled under the front tire of a van backing out of its stall. The shoe stuck to a tire, which carried it—flop, flop—for a few revolutions and dropped it near the lot exit.

"I help you? Lewis?"

Tulane Wiggins and the bartender stood in the doorway of Ernesto's, watching the fat man.

"Sure. Thanks. I was just . . ."

Tulane retrieved the sandal and helped him on with it. He lifted his bare foot the way a horse offers its hoof to be shoed, at the same time resting his forearms on the roof of the car for support. "Damn!" Hot as a skillet. He backed ungracefully away, tottering on one foot, lurching cumbersomely the way large people do when removed from familiar surroundings, their choreographed gestures suddenly unavailable to them.

Tulane passed him the affidavit and pen. The fat man sat in the El Camino's driver's seat, its only seat, and, using the door of the open glovebox for a table, signed the court document. It wouldn't've squared with Aaron Dodge's twenty-year-old conception of himself to do otherwise.

Tulane grinned. Admired the signature as if it were a hero's autograph. "You got my gratitude, man, for this here. That's no shit. Whew! Thank *you*, man." Tulane unhitched his bicycle from the gas meter behind Ernesto's, mounted it, and rode away, waving.

On his way uptown, Aaron Dodge stuck to the brake pedal every time he stopped or slowed down. He knew he'd spend the rest of the weekend, at least, peeling himself loose from every step he took.

He parked in front of a long, narrow cinderblock building whose sign, even though it was located between a Jiffy-Lube and a Valley Bank branch, identified it as the Kopy "Korner." Inside, lit by rectangles of eerie fluorescence embedded in the ceiling, a man with the same off-white complexion as the shrouds of nearby Xeroxes and IBMs fed a self-service machine with robot efficiency.

"Boxes?" Aaron Dodge asked. "I need some of those heavyweights they ship paper in. Many as you can spare."

The store monitor, Wendy, wore a tangerine smock. Wendy Wendy, Aaron Dodge and his friends called her, in recognition of the duties she performed here. Her hair, except for a stumpy braid at the nape of the neck, was short and uncollated. She had on mismatched earrings—one a teardrop prism, the other a tiny silver jet. She asked him to watch the register and returned from the rear of the store with a carton under each arm. "Two help any?"

They'd attended the same high school at the same time, back when she was Wendy Winston and he was Lewis Dodge, but neither of them realized it till the day he brought in the paperwork for a patent application that had to be typed in infinituplicate. The patent, typically, was rejected, but Wendy Wendy might easily have reached a more favorable decision. If only he hadn't been a diehard bachelor. If only she hadn't been one of those women. Driven by a suicidal belief in either hope or destiny, they return at the end of—or, just as often, in the middle of—every new romance to the same man. Bart was this one's name.

"You won't believe what I just did."

"Oh, good. Gossip. Let's hear."

He told her about Tulane.

"Really? What was he in for?"

"That's parole. This is probation."

"Oh. Right. How much was it?"

"That's bail. Probation is something else. Can you believe I did this? Me?"

"Now I remember. Probation is like when it's a first offense. They let you off easy."

"Judge Nathan Pollard III. How's Bart?"

"Fine. We're not, you know, seeing each other right now. We're still friends, but . . ."

Why was it? The wide-eyed, fragile, quiet women, timid as forest creatures, ended up with musclebound, stupid, loud, and dangerous men. Jungle animals. The outgoing, earthy types pursued stringy, bearded, awkward fellows. Intellectuals and gun collectors. Vegetarians and alcoholics. Birth control, pregnancy leave, midwifery, visitation rights. All of Aaron Dodge's friends had two or fewer children, but all the children had six parents apiece.

Wendy Wendy passed originals through a machine half an atom-smasher long and stacked them on the counter, doubled, still warm. As they proliferated, Aaron Dodge inspected one, a handbill. It requested information leading to the whereabouts of a number of children, pictured. Among them, already, was a photo of Mary Vanessa Singer, the missing papergirl. Wendy Wendy said she'd talked the store manager into providing copies free of charge to aid in the search. Hers had to be the purest form of human kindness Aaron Dodge had ever run into, untainted by any inkling of the complexities, or even the fundamentals, of most issues. Amnesty International, Greenpeace, NOW. Wendy Wendy supported so many that she tended to mix up her causes. As she sorted, haste or distraction occasionally caused her to refer to the lost children as "hostages."

"To me it sounds like—I don't know—a neat thing. What you did."

"I didn't ask to do it."

"Just the same. It was—whatever—nice, you know."

"Maybe I can get out of it." The fat man shrugged, rocking from foot to foot. The store's hairless, weatherproof carpeting adhered to his shoe if he stood still for more than a few seconds.

"How's Bart?"

"You asked that."

"Did I also say I was moving?" He nodded in the direction of the boxes.

"You found a cheaper place?"

"No. I mean leaving town. Relocating."

"When did this happen? How come nobody told me?"

"Got up one day, ate breakfast, gave the landlord my notice."

"Where'll you go?"

"Prescott, maybe. Sedona. Flag."

"Escape the heat, huh? Listen. Before you go. Give me a call. We can, you know, get together."

The fat man discovered something about empty boxes that Friday night. They were hard to come by. He tried the convenience food stores, all-nite chains you go to for a job if you can't make it in dishwashing or valet parking. From behind displays of *TV Guide* and throwaway watches they greeted him—gawky men with crooked mustaches and complexions like the least-cooked portions of an undercooked omelet. You know. People nobody will miss when they're gunned down in a holdup while eating lunch at 4:00 A.M.

Boxes?

Wow.

Shit.

You mean like that I could give you?

Now?

The supermarkets had closed by then. Though with supermarkets it was hard to tell. The lots looked emptier and the lights dimmer, but evidence of activity never completely disappeared. Basha's. El Rancho. Alpha Beta. In back, near the piled dairy crates, the giant scarred beam where semis docked, he located an employees-only entrance. Always the same boy, a white apron, a feather duster in his hip pocket, answered the fat man's knock.

"We break down all our cardboard, sir. Sorry."

Flattened bundles lay nearby on the stockroom floor.

"What would you charge me for one of those bales there? The recycler that buys them off you, what's he pay?"

This time the boy in white was a girl. She shrugged, seeming to accept his invasion without suspicion, without anger. "Shit, mister. You want one? Take it."

Before bedtime that night, Aaron Dodge rebuilt a stomped carton or two, driving in staples with a power gun and crimping the points of each with the needle-nose pliers he used to tune his tv set. Del Monte. Heinz. He'd resurrect the others tomorrow. For now he filled the bathtub. Climbed in. Submerged himself, except for his matterhorn of a nose and the roundish islands of his knees and belly.

They arrived most often at times like this. In the quiet hours after midnight. Alone. Broke. Disenchanted. Maybe he'd spent too much time reading New Age literature on the pot in Camel-Op's public restroom, but Aaron Dodge believed it. Knew it. You couldn't visit them, but they could visit you. Not only visit, impose upon.

Physically, travel could be intimidating, even in a decade offering cruise control and super-saver fares. Physically, you were protected by expense, inconvenience, and grueling distances from friends who might be planning to drop in unannounced. But not mentally. Not emotionally. A stray thought, an uninvited memory, and there one of them stood. Hi. When do we eat? I'll take the bed, you take the floor.

This time it was Herschel Wiggins. When he walked into Aaron Dodge's bathroom at 2:00 A.M., Herschel wore a shimmery Kansas City Royals warmup jacket, a V of bare chest separating the "y" and the "a." White pants and shoes. Hair buzzed close; the part a thin scar. He hung his boom box from the clothes hook on the back of the door.

Chicken.

Shit.

Mother.

Fucker.

Leave my brother sit in niggertown while you try sneak you fat ass thew the back door. Man, what you usin' for balls? I never knowed nobody so big around as you could be so full of nothin' inside. And nex' you go try book out a town on top a it all.

Underwater, Aaron Dodge waited for Herschel to turn down the volume and say it. But Herschel seemed to be speaking in a calmer voice. Saying something Aaron Dodge couldn't quite decipher. He lifted one hand out of the water, indicated the radio, and moved an imaginary knob a notch to the left with a dripping thumb and forefinger. Herschel punched the silence button to accommodate him.

I say you look at any tv this week? he said. Sis o'clock news, maybe. Or ten o'clock. You watch lately? They talk about it goin' to happen Sunday, man.

Herschel Wiggins' name was on the big monument in D.C. The black granite ditch that people kept wanting to put up bronze apologies near. Herschel was killed not by VC or NVA, but by a white man from the West Coast. The result of a gambling dispute. That was the way Herschel told the story, always giving you time to form a judgment, plenty of opportunity to condemn, before supplying the critical information. The man's name, Nixon, and the game he ran, a lottery.

Sunday. Now don't you forget.

Herschel brought something out of his jacket pocket, curled an index finger around it, and fired it at Aaron Dodge with the flick of a thumb. It skipped once on the water and floated. A Ping-Pong ball.

Weckome home, Aaron Dodge. Weckome back.

They had a toll-free number you could call, 1-800-WAR DEAD, and they'd tell you whether somebody's name was carved in the black granite or not. That's how he'd eventually found out about several friends. But Herschel was the one who kept showing up unexpectedly. Renewing the friendship. Memories, mostly bad.

August 6, 1971. A machine like a popcorn popper in a movie-theater lobby circulated numbered Ping-Pong balls. Aaron Dodge watched as a green cuff with yellow braid picked another bingo birthday from the vacuumized hole. The official fingers added the ball, date facing, to a row of others lined up on chrome rails.

Four April followed 16 October.

Christmas came near the beginning.

He thought of buildings. Ones so valuable or historic that experts systematically pry apart each wall, number each brick, and reconstruct them someplace else. He was watching something similar happen to the house he was born in. It was being moved—a day, a brick, a Ping-Pong ball at a time—from its original address, and reconstructed at a more convenient location. But the way it was being put back together was unforgivable. This house was noplace he'd ever be able to live again.

Aaron Dodge didn't like to talk about it. But this is how his war story began.

For hours following Herschel's departure, the fat man didn't move, except to open the drainplug, then the hot water tap, and regulate depth and temperature. He still lay in the same position when, near dawn, he heard a knock at his front door. More like a thud, really— diminished by the water between him and it. The official arrival of Saturday.

Not bothering with a towel or robe, he retrieved it from his doorstep, spread it open on the kitchen table, and began to study it. Who'd terrorized whom? Who'd put x-tra-strength cyanide in what? Which group would claim responsibility? If Herschel said there'd been a story in the news, he believed.

A prominent article told how the little girl, Mary Vanessa Singer was being searched for by family, friends, and volunteers in the neighbor-hoods near where she'd last been seen, and in the desert west of Phoenix. He scanned headlines and photo captions until another item invited his attention. It was brief, since the event it concerned wouldn't actually occur until tomorrow, Sunday. It described preparations, an-ticipated reunions. Evidently a celebration, a parade, would be held this weekend in Washington. Whoever planned ticker-tape parades had planned this one to welcome home veterans and to observe the tenth anniversary of the war they were being welcomed home from.

What's your rush? Aaron Dodge asked the front page of the Arizona *Representative.*

It was a ceremony, and apparently Herschel thought Aaron Dodge fit right in. Even though he hadn't earned the belatedly heroic cre-dentials that these veterans with confetti in their hair would be able to claim, the fat man, like them, had had to live with public opinion, and with private ones. His own, slow ceremony had lasted a decade or more. He'd had to reconstruct a welcome home, one strand of ticker tape at a time.

Aaron Dodge didn't like to talk about it. Or read or think about it. He returned to the bathroom. Climbed in. Submerged himself, except for his matterhorn of a nose, the roundish islands of his knees and belly. He did wonder, though, about those Ping-Pong balls. Three hundred and sixty-six of them. Where were they now? He'd sure like to own the one with 15 August printed on its face. A war souvenir. Stored someplace in the basement of the Pentagon, he bet. In egg cartons, probably.

A decade and a half earlier, at age nineteen, Aaron Dodge knew probably a dozen or so older boys, graduates of his high school, who'd been drafted or who'd enlisted. Mostly acquaintances. Few of them close friends. Ruiz, Rivera, Washington, Dupree. They'd come home with everything from citations for valor to bad paper. Having lost anything from their legs to their virginity. To become everything from addicts to entrepreneurs. He sat down with some in junk-food palaces or poolrooms, with others in their offices or between classes in college unions. They all told him pretty much the same thing.

If I was you, man . . .

"Give me one good reason why I should go," he asked Ray Lowhaefer, his mother's latest husband—number five.

Lowhaefer sat in a brown recliner, wearing just a pair of boxer shorts, the tv screen haphazardly illuminating his hairy belly, bare feet, and distorting his puffy face. Esther Dodge sat across the room, leaning past an arm of the sofa, extending the magazine she was reading partway into the parallelogram of light spilling onto the living-room floor from the kitchen.

"You'll be safeguardin' the 'merican way a life," said Lowhaefer.

Avoidance, resistance, evasion, desertion. Aaron Dodge studied the alternatives. And on the day of the lottery broadcast, as he sat before his tiny color portable to receive a number, he was confident. His draft board might think they were plotting his future, but really they were only planning his menu.

Twenty-one February. Thirty November.

A quart of 31 Flavors Jamoca Almond Fudge waited in the freezer. And he intended to eat it all. Sooner or later. As a dessert or an appetizer, he didn't know yet which. Seven June. One April.

He'd graduated by then. That June he'd moved out of the house on Encantero Drive, into a rental in a trailer park near Glendale Community College, where he'd enrolled for the fall semester. Cody, the blonde waitress he'd met at Hobo Joe's, was his steady companion. Today, though, he'd asked Cody to stay away. Not to visit or to phone. Later maybe. And only if the lottery telecast provided an occasion for a party. Twenty February, 31 July.

She came anyway.

By then he'd finished the ice cream.

He'd located some leftover lasagna. Half a loaf of bread.

"You don't look too upset," she said, and hugged him. He smiled. Wiped the last of the sauce out of the bottom of the pan with the heel.

"You won't go. Will you?"

They smoked some homegrown that night, and one of them came up with the idea of putting the dates together in the order they'd been drawn. They drove to Standard Brands and bought a pint of lacquer, and to KDKB Studios, where the DJ let them Xerox the official order of finish.

Back at his trailer, they took down a mirror and posters and started to paste dates, numbered squares from a cheesecake wall calendar of Aaron Dodge's, onto the masonite paneling, getting a little higher off the open can of lacquer as they did. They also cut the calendar girl apart—Miss Phoenix, Miss January to December—and plastered her back together at random. A tit for a foot. Her wig where her bikini bottoms belonged, and vice versa. She looked like she'd enlisted in Aaron Dodge's place and come home the unlucky way. Cody was afraid too.

"Aaron, you won't, will you? Go?"

At first Cody and his other friends blamed Aaron Dodge's overeating on worry. At breakfast, while stirring the batter for pancakes or French toast, he'd eat donuts and children's cereal and drink chocolate milk. He'd tip a plastic bottle of Log Cabin, aim for his gullet, and squeeze. Macaroni-and-cheese dinners, submarine sandwiches, whipped cream, pastries. Throughout the day he'd sip an elixir, guaranteed to increase bulk, that he'd ordered with a coupon from a weightlifting magazine. Hamburgers, fries, shakes. Pecan pie à la mode. In restaurants he'd disgust his friends by tearing into sugar packets and downing their contents like shots. Cheesecake, pizza, soft drinks. And beer. Lots of beer.

He went to the house on Encantero Drive for advice. His mother sat quietly, neutrally in front of the television while Ray Lowhaefer urged him to serve. Comply, accept responsibility, be a man. There was a bonus for enlisting. Aaron Dodge recognized the pitch—the same one he'd delivered in a number of living rooms, while sitting across the coffee table from the parents of a prospective paperboy. Cody and the rest of his friends had also been encouraging him. Leave the country, Aaron Dodge. Canada. He tacked a map of the U.S. on a wall of his trailer, near the découpage he and Cody had assembled. By accentuating with a black marker its lines of longitude and latitude, and numbering them in increments of ten—pounds increasing north-ward, days increasing eastward—he turned the map into a sort of graph. The rate at which he gained would create a new highway, climbing northeast from Phoenix, latitude one-seven-five, to the Ca-nadian border, whose latitude in total pounds equaled three hundred. Interstate 4-F, he called it. Destination, Fat City.

In red he opened daily a new section of road, angling raggedly. Size soon began to change Aaron Dodge's life. Near Denver he had to park his Karmann-Ghia and buy an American-sized car. Then, in Iowa, Cody's physical safety started to require rerouted attempts at sexual access—an inconvenience they both accepted, assuming the obstruc-tion would be temporary. On crossing the Mississippi, he discovered that added weight had created new employment possibilities. Barroom bouncer. Santa Claus. In Chicago he replaced, for the second time since August, the forty-watt bulb that lit its interior each time he opened the door to his icebox. Sitting in a booth in a truck-stop diner overlooking Lake Erie, he decided it would be necessary to drop out of college and devote himself to full-time gluttony. Astraddle a foul commode in a doorless stall at a rest area someplace on the desolate American highway, he reached the conclusion that a feast is not always a celebration.

According to his homemade fat graph, he was someplace in Penn-sylvania the day he received the registered letter. Greeting. Happy birthday to you. By then he was single-handedly supporting chains of supermarkets and personally guaranteeing the success of restaurant franchises. Thanks to his wardrobe needs, textile mills and clothing outlets flourished. Large segments of the national economy depended

solely upon his massive consumption of material goods. Aaron Dodge
was fat.

On the morning of his preinduction physical he ordered a last breakfast—blueberry waffles, biscuits and gravy, potatoes, a chocolate
shake—at an International House of Pancakes. Thirty-six hours earlier,
fueled by a pint of Kahlua, a four-pack of Guinness stout, and enough
pasta to fill a laundry basket, he'd crossed the border near Niagara
Falls. When he explained his military status, the I-HOP waiter gave
a thumbs-up salute, tore the check in two, and with a proud smile
touched his own, uniformed stomach and said, "Three-oh-seven."

His lottery number, not his weight.

He didn't like to talk about it. But in Aaron Dodge's war story one
confirmed tragedy had been recorded. He remembered the two of
them, him and Cody, partway through his journey to Canada, standing
together in Camel-Op, facing a wall of shelves filled with gallon-size
jars on the day she decided she was pregnant.

Cody. Slender, blonde, beautiful. And California, strictly California.
Just a girl who couldn't say, like, you know, no. Conventional upbring-
ings often seemed exotic to Aaron Dodge. Cody's had been affluent,
presided over by two parents (and so far the same two), whose concern,
or whose tolerance at least, had survived their daughter's rebellious
pilgrimage out of state. The monthly checks that kept arriving to
supplement Cody's waitress salary permitted him to observe, when
she occasionally let her radical political views degenerate to self-
righteousness, that he'd never known her to let an enthusiasm for the
violent overthrow of the government upset her bank balance. Till lately
she hadn't minded such teasing. In fact, earlier that summer, before
he started gaining, she'd asked him to move in. He said yes, but
procrastinated. He wasn't ready yet to go halves on shag carpet,
houseplants, cats, central air, and a lease. He was keeping a brick or
two in the toilet tank at his place at the time to save a few cents a
flush on the water bill. Cody had kept asking and he'd kept saying yes
till finally she got the message.

Standing together before the shelves in Camel-Op, the rows of labeled jars, they first looked under "B," then "K." The jars were lined
up in order—"A" to "Z." "A" to "Y," actually—allspice to yarrow—since
there apparently were no common herbs or teas whose names began

with "Z." They finally found it under "C." Black cohosh. Lulu or one of their other hundred-percent-organic friends had told them about the remedy. They bought some gelatin caps, and Cody, that night at his kitchen table, stared across at Aaron Dodge, placed the first capsule on her tongue, and swallowed it along with a gulp of tea brewed from the same herb.

That weekend he and Cody drove to the coast to escape the heat. They'd agreed on the trip before Cody missed a month, and decided not to alter their plans. He didn't count how many she took, but on the way she kept reaching inside the glovebox for one from a baggie full of the capsules, glancing over at him, then curling her tongue around it and swigging from a canteen. They arrived in San Diego after dark. The inns were full except for some sixty-dollar rooms at a Sheraton. Fuck that. He wasn't about to spend thirty bucks for half a bed. Cody rented the room for herself and he slept, or tried to, alone in the car, using a beach towel for a pillow, parked in the lot of the all-nite diner where they'd eaten dinner.

In the morning, his backbone permanently reconfigured, he ate eggs and drank coffee with Cody in a booth at the diner. He was a cheap bastard. She was a spoiled rich-bitch. She took a capsule with the ice water the waitress brought.

On the way to the ocean, they stopped at a motor court called the Pompeii and asked them to hold a room. At the beach he mostly slept and ate. Cody read a book on out-of-body travel. They walked the shoreline in opposite directions. In the room that night, sunburn radiated pinkly from Cody as they made a silent, fiercely competitive variety of love they were both too young to be familiar with.

At his trailer, a week later, she miscarried. She didn't want him to look, but he did. In the clotted, bloody mess he searched for something recognizable. A finger? A tailfin? He didn't know what. After three flushes the water was still orangish. Threads and pinpoints of blood floated up. Not till he took the bricks from the tank did everything stay down.

He lent her the black Karmann-Ghia. Cody sublet her apartment and drove to California. To stay with the family for a while. To think. They exchanged letters, how many he couldn't say—just that he wrote her one more than she wrote him. Aaron Dodge suspected, and would always suspect, that his increased size figured as prominently in their breakup as the pregnancy.

"It's just as well, I guess."

Ray Lowhaefer's reaction, the night Aaron Dodge told his mother about the medical deferment. She'd asked him to stay for supper. They were eating. "Those boys are about to mess around and lose this thing over there anyways. Wished I was thirty years younger."

"Ray was in the war, you know," Aaron Dodge's mother said. "He fought in the Pacific."

"Must've got awful wet."

Lowhaefer put down his silverware and stared at Aaron Dodge. Aaron Dodge stared back. Lowhaefer stood up, clenching both fists. Aaron Dodge did the same. They faced each other across the supper table— his battlefield. A prolonged silence, then Ray Lowhaefer rested his palms on the tabletop. Looked down at his plate. Started to chew again. His chair creaked as he lowered himself into it.

It was at that moment that Aaron Dodge realized for the first time that he was nineteen, going on twenty. And that he was a very, very large young man.

A woman, her long blonde hair tied back with a peg and a square of leather, walked into the fat man's bathroom. The t-shirt she was wearing—with "Camel-Op Natural Foods Co-op" printed on the front— wasn't as noticeable as what she wasn't wearing underneath. She unbuttoned and unzipped her cutoffs, which fell to her ankles as she sat down. Aaron Dodge heard—from underwater—the sound, like a far-off dishrag being wrung out, that women make when they pee.

Hi. I just happened to be passing by.

Water distorted what he could see and what he could hear. Underwater, he had to listen some and do an equal amount of lipreading.

Mind if I use your bathroom?

Without lifting his head out of the water, the fat man gave his permission.

He hadn't contacted any of his friends in weeks. Not since the day he'd read about the welcome-home parade held ten years too late. He'd been staying at home, watching tv, drinking beer. He'd been thinking, and trying not to. He'd been living underwater. In the past. His apartment smelled like the inside of a thermos. And Aaron Dodge looked like he'd crawled out of the gap between the stove and refrigerator where people keep their old grocery bags. Just his matterhorn of a nose and the roundish islands of his knees and belly showed above the waterline.

Cody stood up, tugging her cutoffs past her knees, her thighs, her hips. She buttoned the button and zipped the zipper. She flushed, dropped the lid to the pot, and sat down. Aaron Dodge shut his eyes.

Cody was back up instantly. Or at least the fat man supposed so, judging from the volume of what he heard next. Even though he was making no attempt to listen, Aaron Dodge knew what Cody was telling him with such conviction.

Where have you been? We've been worried about you. Don't you care about anybody but yourself? You're getting very strange, Aaron Dodge. Stranger by the day. And what about the chemicals in this water? Do you have any idea what you're doing to your skin? Even nuclear submarines surface once or twice a year, you know. Even whales do. Even hippopotamuses. You need somebody, Aaron Dodge. You can't be without anybody forever. Aren't you ever going to admit that?

She'd actually said all those things to him at one time or another. Most of them more than once. And so had his other friends. He heard a thump as she kicked the side of the tub.

Then he felt her breath on his face. Her hands in his hair. She yanked—or shoved. Her elbows pressed against his shoulders and chest. He heard splashing, yelling. He couldn't tell whether she was trying to hold him under or above water, but he didn't resist.

When she was gone, Aaron Dodge flipped the chrome lever with his toes and opened the drain. The water tickled his scalp and crotch as the level descended, until an echoey sucking noise told him the tub was empty. He lay there on the cold porcelain, face up.

3

Aaron Dodge lay in bed. Looked up.

So different from Cody.

That's what he'd been thinking, lying awake the past hour.

It was called a Bunkport, the combination bunk beds and davenport that he'd invented and which he hoped to patent or at least market. He looked up, at the underside of the Bunkport's top bunk, at the slight roundish sag in the mattress. She must, he thought, be sleeping on her side. As he examined the soft protrusion caused by her hipbone, he refused to measure other effects. Lasting or temporary. Mental or emotional. He didn't feel healthy enough to face them this morning. This week. This month.

Just a head cold. Everybody gets one once in a while. You stay in bed a few days. You buy capsules full of tiny, different-colored medicine beads to combat unpleasant symptoms. You'll feel better by next week. Nobody worried about calling in sick for a day or so due to a cold. But Aaron Dodge was one of the few people he knew who could be equally stoic about his mental health and emotions. You wake up one morning and your brain refuses to think or your heart won't break or soar. You get up, go to work, eat, walk, talk. But something inside you isn't participating. Quit worrying. That's what Aaron Dodge always told himself when his mind or his emotions deserted him. You're only suffering from mental sniffles. Or emotional flu. All your brain and your heart want is to stay home in bed, numbed with drugs, till they feel a little better. So don't panic. Don't assume it's cancer.

Aaron Dodge didn't panic or assume. He decided to decide later, when his condition improved, what he thought and felt about her. His bunkmate.

Aaron Dodge carefully climbed out of bed and dressed slowly in the dark to avoid waking her. He smoked a joint in the bathroom and in the kitchen took a vitamin with a swig of milk. The sun wasn't up yet when he let himself out the front door. With the help of a pole light in the apartment-house lot he found the right key, unlocked the car, and started it. Congestion, chills, fatigue. In spite of his symptoms, he decided to jog that morning, as he regularly did, in his yellow El Camino.

At three-hundred-some pounds, Aaron Dodge didn't resemble a dedicated runner. But that was only because his were mental and emotional rather than physical morning workouts. For a few minutes every day, so he wouldn't forget how, Aaron Dodge tried to think about something. Anything. Likewise—and again on a daily basis—he attempted to feel love, jealousy, anger, joy, grief, or some other strong emotion, since those muscles could atrophy also. It was a policy he'd instituted at some point during the 1970s, he couldn't remember the exact year, when he realized he hadn't cared passionately about a person other than himself or concentrated on a single idea for more than the length of a tv ad since early in the decade. He was no fanatic athlete. He continued to keep his inner faculties in respectable shape only because he enjoyed the exertion and found exercise relaxing.

His body was another matter. So many people in Phoenix were slim, brown, muscular, and energetic. Aaron Dodge was, he was the first to admit, huge. I'm so huge they tie red flags to me when they take me out. So huge I show up on tv weather radar. Robust, his friends told him. Huge, Aaron Dodge contended. Aaron Dodge took care of his mind the way his contemporaries took care of their bodies, and his body the way they took care of their minds. Aaron Dodge ate indiscriminately, drank beer after beer from cans fitted snugly into Styrofoam sleeves, deprived himself of sleep, read in poor light, elevated his blood pressure with coffee and marijuana, and refused medical help during illnesses. His mind, though, was fit, and moderate exercise had increased his heart's sentimental efficiency.

Because he gave his intellect plenty of rest, and never pushed his conscience beyond reasonable limits, friends often accused him of goldbricking. They didn't always take his colds seriously. Some even denounced him as a chronic malingerer. But always, and just when he knew he'd exasperated them beyond patience, he'd rise from an extended bath, dry himself, and amaze them with a feat of spiritual strength equally past comprehension.

But his friends' opinions weren't the ones that occupied his mind as Aaron Dodge, doing forty-five in a thirty-five zone, headed north, ignoring stoplights, on deserted Phoenix streets. After all, what were their minds doing while his was out jogging at dawn? It was another doubt instead that pursued him as he ran. Like people must wonder who swim laps endlessly, or who regularly labor along the shoulders of highways in sweatsuits and expensive shoes, the fat man occasionally wondered what he was in training for. Like those who lift weights at Nautilus spas must, and those who enroll in Tae Kwon Do courses at the YMCA, he sometimes doubted how reliable his sensibly acquired skills would be in an actual emergency. Would he mentally choke? Or emotionally pucker? Was he, morally, no more than an armchair athlete?

This was the route Aaron Dodge's thinking took that morning—the morning he woke up underneath (because he was too broad and his bed was too narrow to allow him to wake up next to) the only nineteen-year-old since Cody that Aaron Dodge had spent a night with.

She lived in an adjoining apartment in Aaron Dodge's complex on West Indian School Road—a building painted the color the bottoms and sides of swimming pools are painted to make the water in them look blue. Her blow-drier was forever interfering with his tv reception. Until one day he pounded on the wall and the noise stopped. After that, all he ever had to do was pound and the noise always stopped. So promptly that he soon stopped pounding. He didn't want somebody that nice going out with wet hair and maybe catching something. He had a temper and would sometimes punch walls and doors for reasons that had nothing to do with her. Later she would admit that when he did she always froze and held her breath, wondering what she was doing that she should stop.

She drove an old pink Mustang, or so he discovered when she knocked on his door one morning and told him it wouldn't start. She had a fresh, open, lively face—the look of somebody who hadn't committed any of the really major sins yet. She even wore her hair in pigtails. They bounced carefreely against her chest like curtains sucked out an upstairs window by a breeze.

"Does it sound like the battery?" she asked.

"Quit grinding it," he said. "It'll flood."

He loosened the wing nut, lifted off the breather, and told her to try it again while he choked the engine by holding a hand over the carburetor. The engine caught and roared.

He changed the points and plugs in her pink Mustang and timed the engine with his strobe. She told him she owed him a dinner some night. Her name was Kennedy.

Kennedy St. James wore inside-out sweatshirts, always with the necks ripped out of them so that they slipped nonchalantly past a shoulder, revealing one strap of either a sleeveless grandpa-style undershirt or a darker leotard. She also wore baggy pants that didn't quite reach down to her socks, dainty white socks that didn't quite reach up to her pants, and white sneakers with pointed toes. She carried a nylon backpack instead of a purse, and instead of a backpack she called it a "book bag." It and the parking sticker on the windshield of her pink Mustang identified her as an Arizona State commuter student. Interior design. Commercial art. Maybe fashion merchandising or city planning. He wasn't sure he trusted her.

And he knew he didn't like the friends she invited over. Not that he'd met or even seen any. But anybody with a name like Kennedy St. James could have only one kind. He saw Firebirds and Camaros with automatic stickshifts. And visors and golf shirts with Greek letters printed on them. He heard Memorex rock 'n' roll played too loud through open windows, in a desperate attempt to make it sound authentic. He detected, flowing from open mouths, opinions injected directly into closed minds through orange foam-rubber mushrooms connected to earphones, connected to cassette cartridges, connected to Duracells, without ever having passed through a brain. Kyle, Cameron, Nathan, Chad, Sean, Jason. Aaron Dodge recognized them. They were the ones who, by not joining the Peace Corps, not spending twelve years in college, not hitchhiking coast to coast, and not living through or dying in a war, had rocketed into premature adulthood instead, making slaves of Aaron Dodge and his friends.

Over the next few weeks she reissued her invitation to dinner whenever they met in the parking lot or laundry room. She kept asking. He kept saying yes. But she never got the message.

She was cheerful, polite, healthy, likable, articulate, refreshing, and—there was no substitute for the word—nice. She never said "like," "you know," or "uh." Never said "I go," "he goes," when she meant "I said," "he said." Never said "exscaped," "supposably," "Can you give me a pacific example," or "new cue lur war." She didn't need to lose weight, didn't have hair that hadn't been cut in over a decade, didn't have a scraggly mustache, or unevenly distributed inert substances where teeth belonged. She didn't have a complexion like a used flashbulb. Aaron Dodge, who insisted he did, was totally intimidated by her from the moment she knocked on his door.

"What a wavehead," he told his friends, retreating behind a macho façade of aggressive self-reliance.

He did wonder, though, why she drove an old pink Mustang with Arizona rather than Michigan, Ohio, or Pennsylvania license plates. She'd told him she was paying nonresident tuition, so why wasn't she back home for the summer, leeching off her parents till September, the way all college students did? He also wondered about those sweatshirts. Did she buy them ripped or rip them herself? Did the rips cost extra? Nowadays were they selling sweatshirts with unripped collars as factory seconds? He wondered. But not enough to climb out of the bathtub and answer the door when he heard a knock that might be hers.

Not until, on a 115-degree afternoon late in May, Kennedy St. James told him a joke. "Do you know how Lady Diana is like a Tampax?" she asked him in the apartment-house lot. Aaron Dodge, who did know, looked at her suspiciously and asked: "How's that?" "Both of them," said Kennedy St. James, "are stuck up cunts." And Aaron Dodge, for the first time since May 7, laughed. That night he answered the phone. He threw away yesterday's leftovers and cooked a fresh meal, which he served himself on a plate instead of from the pot. He spent only a half-hour in the bathtub because, submerged, he'd laugh and suffocate himself with bubbles.

Not that the joke was all that hilarious. But the fat man recognized it. The joke was one he'd originated himself, back before he went underground—or underwater—earlier that month. During his retreat it must've been circulating, passing from cashier to customer, barber to bartender, until it reached Kennedy, who completed the circle by returning it intact to Aaron Dodge. Aaron Dodge was an inventor. There was nothing he loved more than creating something, then watching from a distance while somebody else, a stranger, used and enjoyed it.

At five-thirty Aaron Dodge parked the El Camino in front of a disenchanted cinderblock building located between a Payless Shoe Source and Bayless food store on West Olive Avenue.

Inside, he found an unoccupied stool and turned the capsized cup on the countertop in front of him right side up in its saucer.

"Where've *you* been?"

"Hiding."

"What from?"

"Me."

"That's kind of against the laws of physics, isn't it?"

"I got me a sharp lawyer."

Amid the dishclatter, overlapping conversations, laughter, and adjusting of newspapers, Lulu filled his cup and took his breakfast order.

"Pass me the horoscopes, will you," somebody shouted.

". . . solidarity," somebody else declared.

". . . divestment."

"So you're back. How come?"

"Hiding."

"Again. What from this time."

"Her."

"That I understand," said Lulu.

Lulu was a cackling, gum-snapping, wisecracking redhead. With important modifications. Her hair color was natural, her gum was the healthy kind, and when Lulu used the word "honey" she was referring to the actual substance, not addressing a customer. On a given weekday in 1985, what was left of the '60s counterculture could usually be found seated at Lulu's counter. Present today were a number of the fat man's friends.

Brad Moe was there, sporting a fresh haircut. Do, rather. He looked like he'd been asleep in the yard when somebody came through with a weed eater. Lately Brad managed a New Wave band and called himself Agent Orange. Bob the Brush, with his more conservative hairstyle, sat in a booth below some spindly hanging plants with La Shorty and El Holmes, a gay couple who worked at the fat man's favorite Mexican place. He saw Wendy Wendy too, wearing sweatpants with the elastic at one ankle turned up to create a temporary pocket suitable for securing her house key and breakfast money while she jogged. Of many an alliance sworn to in the 1960s by Aaron Dodge and his friends, compromised in the '70s and betrayed in the '80s, a membership in Camel-Op Natural Foods Co-op was the only surviving evidence.

His breakfast arrived. Buckwheat cakes and guava juice. Aaron Dodge had decided exactly what he'd say to her the next time he saw her. Then, by the time he finished eating, he'd made up his mind not to say anything. Lulu slid the check underneath the edge of his plate. On the back it said *Thank You!* and in smaller print *made from recycled paper*. By then Aaron Dodge had determined he'd avoid her completely.

Lulu refilled his coffee cup from a lime-encrusted glass pot quarantined on a hotplate a shelf away from the ones containing decaffeinated blends and water for brewing teas.

"So who's this you're seeing?" Lulu asked.

"Nobody."

Wendy Wendy set down her cup and the little chrome pitcher with her tea bag in it and spun onto the stool next to him. "Who, Aaron Dodge?"

"Just another piece of strange," said the fat man, "about to get too familiar."

Lulu answered with a polite pause.

"This may be some kind of summer fling for her. But for me it's practically statutory. If not pedophilia."

"Young, I take it?"

"Young? Does Fernando Lamas play gigolos? She'll want to take up with somebody her own age once her friends get back from summer vacation. Travis or Todd. Shane."

"Possibly."

"I'm too old for her. I'm old enough to have buildings and bridges named after me."

"An age difference can complicate a relationship, true."

"Who knows what she sees in me? Just lonely probably. Desperate. First time away from home. Must have a fat uncle or something."

"Quit saying that about yourself," Wendy Wendy said.

"It's the truth. I'm so fat an Alaskan could haul me around in the bed of his pickup for traction."

"Be that as it may," said Lulu. "You're still an awfully attractive fellow. In your own way. Ask anybody."

"Besides," said Wendy Wendy, "haven't we progressed beyond those kinds of shallow perceptions? Am I wrong or was there a social revolution in this country less than twenty years ago?"

"Might as well've been a thousand," said the fat man.

"When you say she's thin, Aaron Dodge," Lulu said, "how thin is thin?"

"I don't mean compared to me. I'm saying one-ten, one-oh-five. I could bench-press her fifty times at least."

"Jesus," said Lulu. "Don't bring her around here. I refuse to have anything to do with someone that thin."

"Congratulations, Aaron Dodge," said Wendy Wendy.

"This is scary," said Lulu. "Do I dare even suggest it? That a few of the values I once believed in actually rubbed off on someone from a subsequent generation?"

The fat man had considered this same explanation for Kennedy's evidently unprejudiced view of him. Maybe the twenty-year-old events and impressions he and his friends remembered had survived after all, to influence nonparticipants. Maybe Kennedy St. James represented a new, mutant species of youthful idealist, with an unselfconscious enthusiasm for principles supplied by others. Sort of like when a poor man struggles his way to wealth, and it's his children who take the luxury for granted while he keeps pinching pennies.

"I just figure I should be honest with her about my shortcomings is all," said Aaron Dodge.

"You're very responsible," Lulu said.

"I was a paperboy."

"Then it's no wonder."

———

At home the next day, while standing at his workbench in one of the bedrooms, he heard a timid knock.

All his friends knew the door was open, so Aaron Dodge ignored the interruption. He more than ignored it. He slammed cabinets, turned on the tv, ran bathwater. Just so nobody got the idea he was hiding. After a safe wait, he nudged a front curtain aside and looked out.

The tub filled past the overflow return, activating a float valve that automatically impeded water flow. Another of the fat man's unsold inventions. He took off his clothes. Climbed in. Slid under. Her? he asked himself. Again? Maybe she was lonely but not the type to peddle her ass at Minderbinder's or the other singles dungeons. Between semesters at the university . . . the usual outlets for meeting people closed off . . . a summer-long gap in her social calendar to fill. It made some sense. But right then he didn't want to talk about it.

That afternoon, while peering into his icebox, mentally blueprinting a high-rise sandwich, Aaron Dodge heard the knock again. The door creaked open. Creaked shut.

"Anybody home?"

"In here," he said, "the kitchen," and shut the icebox door.

Later, still naked, they lay close.

Kennedy in her bunk.

Aaron Dodge in his.

Now was the time, he told himself. He had to ask her. The first night he'd been surprised. And grateful. Now he was suspicious. He prodded a bulge in the mattress above. "Kennedy? You aren't, are you? A vir—"

"—gin? Yes, I am. All right, maybe not by a purist's standards, but by my own, Aaron, yes, I am. And I hope you'll respect that. For now."

The satisfied victim of a series of oral and manual diversionary tactics designed to salvage the ruins of her honor, Aaron Dodge felt free to speak openly. "Look," he said. "Listen. Okay? I don't expect this to work—"

"—out, I know," she said. "You don't have to." Electric fans, three of which he'd brought into the room and aimed at them, hummed furiously. "But do you want it to? Work out?"

"Sure I do. I mean no. I don't. I don't do that any more. I never want anything to work out. Because I know it usually won't."

She leaned past the edge of the mattress, so that from below he could see her face, upside down. "You mean you don't hope for stuff? You never dream?"

"I stopped."

"When?"

"Can't remember. Exactly. I guess you could say I'm a little dis—"

"—appointed?"

"Not exactly. More like dis—"

"—illusioned?"

"That too. But I was going to say dis—"

"—couraged?"

"Enchanted."

"Disenchanted." Kennedy St. James tried the word out, but it didn't sound right coming from her. "Disenchanted," she said again. Then: "Aaron? Can I come back again?"

"If you want."

"But do you want me to?"

"Nope."

"Then you want me to stay away?"

He thought about it. "I don't know," he said finally. "Ask me later." The fat man didn't believe in dreams any more. But some days he was only an agnostic in that respect, not an all-out atheist.

He and Kennedy collected scattered articles of each other's clothing, traded appropriately, and dressed. "I still do owe you that dinner, remember?" said Kennedy.

"I'm not really all that hun—"

"—gry, all right," she said. "But I am. Will you drive me? The car's making a noise. Maybe you could listen and tell what's wrong."

There actually was a noise. The muffler. Aaron Dodge stopped at a supermarket, bought a roll of tinfoil, and temporarily plugged the exhaust leak. He thought of taking her to La Cuchara Grasosa for a plate of La Shorty's green chili and an El Holmes margarita but instead chose a glittery chain-food place.

Dining in public could be a humbling experience for a person Aaron Dodge's size. And a trial for his companions too. In the 1980s a fat man accompanied by a healthy, trim girl like Kennedy often received the kinds of glances once directed at racially mixed couples in the Deep South during the years of the Freedom Rides. Kennedy, though,

seemed indifferent to any attention they were attracting. The hostess
seated them. A table close enough to the door to minimize the disturbance caused by his entrance, but not so near that he'd frighten away
prospective customers. When Kennedy did finally acknowledge the
reaction they'd received, it was only indirectly. And with a commend-
able amount of discretion, Aaron Dodge thought. She waited for the
waitress, dressed in a gaudy flamenco skirt, to take their orders. Then
she asked casually: "Guess how come I noticed you, Aaron. What do
you think first impressed me?"

"What?" he said neutrally. Lots of men made it a rule never to be
first to say, "I love you." With Aaron Dodge it was: "Never be the first
to say 'fat.' "

"So many of the people I grew up around—no practical abilities at
all. I could tell you knew how to do things. Every time I saw you, you
had a tool of some kind in your hand. When people said you were an
inventor, I was fascinated."

"People?"

"At the apartment complex."

"Oh, you were stalking me," he said good-naturedly.

"It's not all that big a place. And you are my next-door neighbor. I
was aware of you. How's that?"

He nodded. Situations such as apartment living, that promoted fa-
miliarity, always treated fat people kindly. Aaron Dodge had discovered
that in those circumstances frequent exposure tended to diminish the
importance of looks. After new acquaintances recovered from the initial
shock, their discomfort or their outright revulsion would gradually
dissipate, and might even come to resemble admiration. The assumption may have been: anybody this unconcerned with his appearance
must have something exceptional going for him in another area of his
life. Your weight struck them like Einstein's hair—proof of distracted
genius. Besides, Aaron Dodge wasn't exactly repulsive in spite of the
way he talked about himself. Though certainly no athlete, the fat man
led a frequently active life when he wasn't anchored in his tub or
immobilized behind a beer or coffee mug. Inventing could be a sweaty,
strenuous undertaking at times. Lift and carry, load and unload, assemble, break down, and reassemble. He often found himself working
with devices stalled in a stage of development requiring an immediate
investment of manpower in exchange for the eventual realization of

mechanical potential. Because he didn't happen to quiver when he walked or spread out like tons of curdled yogurt when he wore shorts, this entitled his friends to use words like "solid," "powerful," "brawny," "imposing" to describe him. Though he recognized flattery when he heard it, he also understood what they meant. He bore his weight with a certain amount of pride, knowing he'd gained it for what had once seemed legitimate purposes.

Kennedy appeared so at ease, so unpreoccupied with his physique, that he began to wonder if she had, after all, noticed the impression they'd been making. "I hope this isn't uncomfortable for you. You're probably not used to being—let's say 'observed.' "

Kennedy laughed. She carefully placed her fork alongside the other utensils by her plate. Aligning and realigning them, she said quietly, without looking up: "Aaron, I hate to be the one to tell you. But these people aren't staring at you. Didn't you notice who came in at the same time we did? They're sitting right over there."

"Where?"

"Don't look. Over there by the plaster Spaniard. It's the Singers. The parents of that little girl that—"

"I know. The papergirl."

"I've seen them on the news. It's really terrible. I feel so sorry for them. Listen, pretend you're looking for the bathroom. You can walk by their table and—"

The fat man indicated disapproval with a wince.

"That was stupid," she said. "I'm sorry."

It was as close, that first meal they shared, as either of them came to a direct reference to his weight. Curiosity? Probably. Misgivings? Likely. But if so she kept them to herself, as gracious in this respect as she'd been in dropping her morbid fascination with the Singers the minute he'd objected. All the evidence suggested that Kennedy enjoyed his company. Liked him. Didn't care that he probably outweighed most of the refrigerators her family had ever owned. Was it possible? A woman this sensitive? At her age? In 1985?

Just in case it wasn't, the fat man ordered sensible portions. Limited himself to one beer. Declined the sour cream. Only reordered chips once. Kennedy finished just half her combination platter. Typical female. But Aaron Dodge imagined a second, deeper meaning in the untouched rice and beans, the calorie-intensive tortilla she'd carefully eaten her way around. The leftovers seemed to reaffirm, in an intimate but unpremeditated way, his own self-imposed moderation, and he smiled across the table at her as he laid aside his napkin.

Now ought to have been the time. In nauseating tones, interrupted regularly by enraptured sighs—this was how new lovers were supposed to confide the details of their lives early in a romance. But Aaron Dodge resisted the inevitable sentimentality of that kind of exchange. His past. He didn't want to talk about it. Instead—to find out just how open-minded she really was—after dinner he introduced Kennedy to the city of Phoenix.

Most Western towns, he told her—while the Mustang idled in the last of rush hour—had one main street resembling every main street in Phoenix. A strip, it was usually called. An appropriately one-dimensional nickname for the matching rows of storefronts, a story high and a building deep, that faced each other across four lanes of traffic, stretching for miles, a stoplight at every other intersection. The strips were all alike—identical Muzak tapes spliced together in varying lengths. Jack in the Box, Circle K, Brake-O, Church's Fried Chicken, Exxon, Taco Bell, Radio Shack. Only an occasional oasis known as a mall interrupted. And a mall, Aaron Dodge explained—later, parked in a thirty-acre lot deserted except for the pink Mustang—was exactly the same as a strip, only confined to a one- or two-block area. Matching storefronts, a store high and a store deep, faced each other across an enclosed, air-conditioned plaza with a fountain, ashtray, payphone and instant-access machine at every other intersection. There were more convenience markets in Phoenix than fireplugs, he told Kennedy. More country/Western stations than hospitals. More pizza delivery vans than police cars.

Kennedy St. James was appropriately horrified.

Aaron Dodge kept quiet about the rest. The desert, the mountains, the sun. The good, cheap Mexican restaurants and the cars that never rusted out. He didn't mention the pink dust clouds, a hundred stories high, that tumbled out of the foothills on summer afternoons, followed by blue-black storm fronts sizzling with thunderbolts, charged with the steely smell of ozone, that lowered impenetrable curtains of rain, then passed just in time for grapette-and-orangeade sunsets. You could park on a dirt shoulder of 40th Street, against the chain-link fence at the east end of Sky Harbor, so close to an incoming DC-10 that it was possible to look up and read the instructions to baggage handlers printed on the fuselage. An hour later you could drive past farms and orchards on 151st Avenue, through corridors air-conditioned by alfalfa fields. Aaron Dodge didn't say so to Kennedy, but there was an undeniable beauty, especially in the summer and at night, to even the most objectionable aspects of the city, as he could've easily demonstrated by stopping the pink Mustang at a South Mountain Park scenic overlook and showing her how from that distance the municipal constellations outgenerated the heavens so spectacularly that it was hard to believe they owed their brightness mainly to Whataburgers, U-Totems, and Checker Auto Parts stores.

The fat man chose to keep Phoenix's most appealing features—and, out of habit, his own, too—a secret.

"I really like this place," Kennedy said. "The desert."

Home from their tour, they sat in aluminum lawn chairs chained to the fence surrounding the complex's polluted swimming pool, watching starlight accentuate oily surface swirls.

Aaron Dodge chuckled self-righteously. "Wait'll July. It gets up to a hundred and fifty degrees. Jets land and take off at the altitude of mosquitoes to keep from being melted by the sun. Naked demons shovel truckloads of gravel onto the roads at dawn, and by noon the stuff has sunk in like pearls into bottles of Prell."

Kennedy looked briefly uncertain. But only briefly. Already, as she'd climbed into the top bunk that afternoon, the fat man had noticed indications of a resoluteness he'd never have expected from anybody her age. A rear view had revealed the raw insignia that undeniably separated the full-time Arizona resident from the snowbird. An upholstery pattern branded into her thighs commemorated the moment she'd first slid innocently behind the wheel of her pink Mustang while wearing shorts.

Kennedy St. James was falling immediately and obviously in love. Aaron Dodge had been afraid she would. They all did. That's the way the West was. No newcomer he'd ever met could believe how big, how beautiful. Here, a mountain was a real mountain, not just a civilized hump. Huge, scarred, and treacherous, the desert did its best to keep its virtues hidden. But always its admirers made comparably dramatic efforts to locate them.

4

"That has sugar in it," said Lulu.

"I know."

"Refined sugar."

Aaron Dodge had just removed a sweet roll he'd bought at a bakery down the street from its wax-paper bag.

"I thought you were giving up white sugar."

"I don't think I ever said I was. I think it was you who said I should."

"You'd feel better. Lose weight. Eliminate mood swings."

"My moods don't swing. I feel like shit. Consistently."

"Addict. Junkie."

"Self-denial is itself a drug."

"Cut down. At least do that."

"Don't lecture me about abstinence. You're looking at a man who for over a month did absolutely nothing."

"Here. You'll get that all sticky." Lulu took the envelope he was about to open away from him. She picked up one, then the other of his large hands with her tiny, nervous ones and wiped them with the rag she used on the counter.

Aaron Dodge had come to Camel-Op for lunch. Also to open mail. But chiefly he'd come here to reinforce order. He'd been behaving uncharacteristically. Preposterously. It was important for a person about to institute sweeping change in his life to establish a routine.

With his pocket knife he slit the end of a long gray envelope and shook out the contents. A single folded sheet. Advice. From the syndicate.

Aaron Dodge was an inventor. But his major responsibility and the main source of his income was a four-inch-by-two-column panel that the Arizona *Representative* expected him to fill five times weekly. Located in what contemporary newspapers called their "Tempo," "Lifestyle," or "Now" pages, the fat man's contribution represented a synthesis of "Mark Trail," "Ripley's Believe It or Not," and "Hints from Heloise"—a light yet informative illustrated description of a patented or patentable device. He'd been able to sell the panel idea on the strength of his longstanding relationship with the *Representative*. Since then it had offended few enough readers to survive in regional syndication. In fact recently somebody had said that Aaron Dodge was Phoenix's official inventor in the same sense that an inoffensive and professionally wholesome lounge singer named Dolan Ellis was Arizona's Official Balladeer. He wasn't proud of the comparison. Or the job. The fat man had always wanted to be the kind of inventor who designed energy-efficient solar generators or engineered pollution-free waste-disposal systems. He dreamed of inspiring people. Instead he amused them.

> Tired of the covers of your spiral notebooks falling off before the pages are filled? Why not a convenient snap-on replacement like this one, invented by Bo Padgett of Arlington, TX.

He'd discovered a toll-free number you could dial, 1-800-PATENTS, which allowed him to fill a few days' worth of panels when his own ideas dissatisfied him.

The terse, congenial message from the syndicate informed him that he owed, as of the date the letter was postmarked, nine new installments of "Aaron's Inventory." Not that the fat man was behind. But, like all syndicates, this one required a substantial backlog. If you failed to keep up, even though you were already 'way ahead, you could look forward to mail. Phone calls. Visitors. The fat man folded the syndicate's letter and filed it in his wallet, where he'd have to confront it every time he paid for a cup of coffee.

Next he opened a generic-looking windowed envelope with a P.O. box for a return.

It is sometimes easy to overlook a statement or to forget payment
of a bill.

He'd received another just like it a week ago, addressed, like this one
was, to Lewis—spelled "L-o-u-i-s"—K. Dodge. A mildly threatening
allusion to an obligation never directly identified. The creditor's name
still didn't register, but the amount referred to, equivalent to one
month's rent, indicated that the warnings had likely been authorized
by the association of anonymous landlords that controlled his complex.
    "Look. They're saying I owe for an imaginary month."
    "Who?" said Lulu.
    "Them. The rental agency. The landlords."
    Lulu read the notice from the adjustment company. "You must've
forgotten to pay rent last month."
    "No, I didn't. And they're still holding my damage deposit too. They
invented it. Slipped in a thirteenth month on me. May, It, and June."
    Lulu shrugged. "Talk to the manager. Doesn't your complex
have one?"
    "I already did."
    The woman in apartment number one was a chubby housewife with
a skeptical frown who knew little about legal procedures, less about
electricity or plumbing. She'd been given a list instead—numbers to
call in case anything went wrong. He'd said nothing to her about the
thirty days' notice he'd phoned in. Well over a month ago now.
    The fat man still planned to move. As soon as possible. But the vets'
parade and the feelings it had resurrected, not to mention this girl he'd
met, had put him far behind schedule. There was a time for swift,
efficient, independent action, and a time to allow electronic and corporate red tape to unspool at its own haphazard pace. He figured a
week, minimum, for the manager to contact the property holders. Two
for the owners to isolate and verify the misunderstanding. Another
before they'd notify the manager, who'd then notify Aaron Dodge—if
she could find him. Meantime, mentally, he'd work on his tan. Emotionally, he'd lay out in the sun a while. Relax. He'd have time to pack.
Select his new home. Break the news to Kennedy St. James.
    "Maybe they sent some kind of implied consent form and you just
spaced it off. In with your gas bill or something."

"These people don't have anything to do with the utility companies. These are landlords."

"I never do read those inserts. Do you? They could be telling us anything. Or maybe it's some kind of surcharge, Aaron Dodge. An extra deposit like pet owners pay." Procrastination was the fat man's pet. And somehow he didn't have the heart to put it to sleep. Not immediately.

Sandwiched between junk-mail items from foundries, tool companies, and electrical supply houses the fat man discovered a postcard.

Dear Mr. Dodge:
I've been attempting to reach you for weeks, unsuccessfully. I'm concerned that you may have forgotten our scheduled meeting.

Who was Tulane's ghostwriter? The same man who'd called him Lewis on the phone a month before?

It is imperative that I contact you in order to fulfill the terms of my probation. Please meet me at Ernesto's on Friday evening at 8:00 P.M. Or, if this is inconvenient, please leave a message at the number included below.

"How's your girlfriend?" Lulu asked.

"She's not my— Turn that up, will you?"

Lulu adjusted the volume control on the stereo system that piped a local classical station to Camel-Op's patrons. Aaron Dodge had installed the speakers himself. The news was playing, and he thought he'd heard that name again, the news carrier's. Mary Vanessa Singer. "Listen," he told Lulu.

A runaway, some people said. Kidnapped, others insisted. So far the evidence didn't point conclusively in either direction. The police had been investigating a number of possibilities, which they preferred not to comment upon at this time. The city's heart had gone out to her, of course, and to her frantic parents. Which normally would've been enough to cause Aaron Dodge to sneer at the entire production. But he'd been secretly following the story, clandestinely hoping.

"Those are the ones they hardly ever find," Lulu said sadly.

"And if they do they wish they hadn't," the fat man added.

That afternoon he worked on a new invention and wrote checks to cover bills he didn't feel he could put off paying any longer. That night he drew an installment of "Aaron's Inventory."

> Cooks, you say your recipe calls for a tbsp. of cornstarch or flour but you just finished using the spoon to add vanilla or vinegar? Measure wet and dry ingredients with a single utensil, using this double-ended set, the brainchild of Eunice Pace, Groton, CT.

Later he slept for a few hours. Long before daylight he woke, got up, filled the bathtub. He climbed in, hoping to concentrate on practical matters. Finances. Kennedy occupied his thoughts instead.

She'd spent the night again.

Twice since she'd bought him dinner.

By now he'd given up trying to guess why. She was nineteen years old. To expect predictable behavior from someone so young would've called for an acrobatic leap of faith that Aaron Dodge was no more capable of emotionally than physically. Unless nineteen-year-olds had changed since he was that age, he knew Kennedy's nature must be volatile, not yet entirely formed. He, on the other hand, at thirty-three, was if anything as overgrown internally as externally—encumbered by the kind of tiresomely realized personality you got sick of encountering in people of his generation. Psyches evolved past a point of optimum efficiency. As an inventor he was familiar with the concept of aggressive engineering. All you had to do was take a look at almost any car on the road today to see the principle at work. Most of the personalities running loose up there—beyond the surface of his bathwater—operated as if they'd been built to keep psychoanalysts in business, just as most of the machines seemed designed with the best interests of mechanics in mind. So, with his overdeveloped sensibilities, Aaron Dodge tried to measure Kennedy's underdeveloped maturity, and forecast how long her interest would continue. If she was as inexperienced as he'd been at nineteen, and if, as he believed, the most you learned as you got older was how to vacillate with greater dignity between options less and less satisfactory and opinions more and more indefinite, then they were probably in for a short ride on a fast elevator.

As the fat man steamed, keeping just the usual anatomical features dry, he marveled at what youthful enthusiasm enabled a person to ignore. When Kennedy looked at him, she seemed to see a person entirely different from the one the physical evidence suggested. A person as thin as the next guy. Only occasionally did she attempt what he perceived to be a roundabout approach to the topic of weight, and even then, when he'd rush to defend himself, he'd generally discover his own paranoia impeding him.

"How did it first occur to you to make up your own jokes?" she'd asked from the top bunk the night before. "Were you a kid?"

He'd quickly surmised, or believed he had, the intent of the question: lonely childhood . . . pathetic fat boy . . . compensatory clowning behavior. "I started in grade school. Want to hear my first joke? 'How do you make a candle you can hear with?' "

"How?"

"Earwax. What did the millimeter say to the kilogram?"

"What?"

"Take me to your liter."

If she noticed his evasiveness, she didn't say so. He told her about the Texas Gulf Coast. Growing up there. Moving to Arizona. To hear him talk, you'd've thought his life story ended August 6, 1971, and began again the day he met Kennedy. He told her about the house on Encantero Drive. Esther Dodge. His paper route. Was this some sort of hopeless attempt to equalize their ages by eliminating everything that took place after his high school graduation? He hesitated there, on the eve of the most important years of his life, and circled back to the afternoon of his father's death. He manufactured a phony insight to explain an event he should've addressed simply and straightforwardly. "It's probably why I became an inventor," he said of the explosion that had claimed his father. "You know. Spare parts. Salvage. Construction. Creation. I've been trying to do the impossible. What I couldn't do back in Texas. Put a man back together again using substitute materials."

"Do you really think so?" Kennedy had asked, never more a gullible nineteen-year-old than at that moment. "That's really touching," he'd heard from the dark above him.

That's the biggest load of hippie shit I ever smelt.

Still as lean as could be, but gray-haired now, he walked into Aaron Dodge's bathroom. He took off his workshirt, khaki like his pants, and hung it from the clothes hook, then removed his wristwatch and wedding ring, which he left on the lid of the toilet tank. He started to wash up with the fat man's bar of Lava. Aaron Dodge watched from underwater. His narrow back. The outline of his wallet, buttoned into baggy trousers cinched tight at the waist by an old brown belt.

Otto Dodge.

You got no scruples whatsoever, do you?

If it had been possible to slide deeper into the tub, the fat man would've.

What can you say about somebody who'd pimp the memory of his departed father for a shot at some skinny teenage tail? People, they sure do change with the times.

Otto Dodge opened the medicine cabinet. Brought out the razor and shave cream. Shut the door again. Established eye contact via the mirror.

She's a nice gal. How would it be if you was to make a halfway effort not to fuck this one up? I mean let's face it—in the looks department your stock's pretty depleted. Maybe you ought to try and hang on to what little you got going for you. I'm talking about integrity. Character.

Otto Dodge rumbled. Growled. Spat, after a final, productive hack, into the sink.

You once had some of that, I believe. You and them longhair friends a yours. Least you claimed you did.

He shaved as he talked. Drew the skin tighter with his fingertips at a cheek, underneath the jaw. Eliminated swaths of lather.

I don't know. Any guy who'd swap soul-searching for pussy? Any guy who'd turn around and take a cold-blooded dump on his old man's grave? I don't know what to say about anybody that sorry. I truly honestly don't.

He glanced past a shoulder at the fat man.

Do you?

He slapped on handfuls of Aaron Dodge's rotgut aftershave. Replaced the gear behind the mirror. Shut the door. His tired eyes met his son's.

But there's ways you could make it up to me. Show me you deserve somebody as understanding as that girlfriend a yours. Prove something to me—and to yourself—if you're still able.

Otto Dodge reached for his shirt. Unbuttoned the pocket. Reached in.

Think about somebody besides yourself, why don't you? For once.

He flipped something—paper, it looked like, or cardboard—in Aaron Dodge's direction. It sailed, banked sharply, spiraled, and alighted on the surface of his bath. Aaron Dodge picked it up for a closer look. Squeegeed it with a finger. A postcard. He didn't remember seeing it in the mail he'd sorted at Camel-Op.

See that pitcher? Rekonize her?

The card supplied a caption: "Have You Seen This Child?" And a photo.

Otto Dodge quickly collected his valuables. Watch. Ring. Took his shirt and left the fat man alone to consider his advice.

Watching him go, Aaron Dodge shivered. Because his bathwater was cold by now. Because a lot of what his father had said was undeniable. It was Aaron Dodge who'd said, a year or so earlier, when a man in San Ysidro, California, massacred twenty-some people in a hamburger chain store, "Too bad it didn't happen at a Kentucky Fried. They could serve wings with black armbands." Natalie Wood and Rock Hudson jokes? The fat man had initiated his share. He'd turned, as Otto Dodge had implied, more than a little hardhearted over the past fifteen years. But his reaction to the papergirl's disappearance hadn't been a typical Aaron Dodge reaction. Not so far. He'd been paying attention to the reports. Not the kind of attention ambulance chasers pay to misfortune. His concern had remained private. Even reverent. If his friends noticed, they didn't say so.

Aaron Dodge knew that he possessed an inner faculty somehow attractive to the victims of tragedies. Fatal tragedies. Maybe Mary Vanessa Singer, in a gold-and-purple shirt, wearing tennis shoes with Velcro straps instead of laces, would walk calmly into his bathroom some night and tell a gruesome story. That she hadn't yet seemed encouraging. A barely perceptible indication of hope.

5

Until he met Kennedy, everybody in their apartment complex seemed to dislike Aaron Dodge, probably because his extra cars were always occupying the visitors' spaces in the lot. But once the two of them began to be seen together, he could sense his reputation improving. At least one person in every apartment seemed to owe a favor to Kennedy, who babysat, gave lifts, loaned money, and looked in on plants and pets as if some instinct compelled her. She was a wired and cheery girl who walked everyplace like somebody rushing a pizza home before it could get cold.

Both their apartments had air conditioning—window units—but neither of them could afford to run it. The hundred-plus days and correspondingly unbearable nights established their routine. They did a lot of after-dark driving, into the desert west of Dysart and Litchfield Park, into the Superstitions east of Apache Junction. At a Circle K they'd buy beer, gas, and diet soda, and at a Mexican restaurant takeout dinners packaged in Styrofoam. Their goal: drive until all containers were empty.

For certain necessities they did stop, and then a green bedspread protected them from the Mustang's ruined back-seat upholstery—rotted by Phoenix heat, crumbling. One was a fast and the other a fugitive color, so the sun quickly extracted all the blue from the cloth but none

of the yellow. Soon only the two of them could see that the yellow
bedspread was green.

On the green bedspread, Kennedy's definition of virginity evolved.
First *ejaculation* without *penetration* represented their legal maximum. Then he penetrated and the speed limit inside the Mustang rose
to *penetration* without *ejaculation*. Until one night he ejaculated and
Kennedy decided that the *ejaculation* that followed the *penetration*
had to have been *on purpose*.

That's how he discovered she was Catholic. In the process of shedding her religious beliefs, but noplace near the end of that process.
She still clung to a superstition common among the newly disenchanted. The beliefs I'm giving up are a lot more important than any
anybody else has ever disavowed.

"Kennedy, if you're going to indulge," he told her one night at his
apartment, "—if we are—then we're going to have to—"

"—birth control. I know. One of these days I'll just have to do it.
Make the commitment. I'm nineteen years old. Can't stay a virgin
forever. I know that, Aaron."

This was another habit of hers he wondered about. She finished his
sentences for him. "All I mean is, you better face up to it. It's an
important responsi—"

"—bility, yes, that's true." Not quite prompt enough to be clairvoy-
ance, not quite tardy enough to be ordinary repetition. Was she trying
to help? Agree? Argue? Was finishing somebody's sentences for them
an act of generosity or selfishness? "I know I—"

"I'm not sure you do know. If you did, I think you'd help me do
something ab—"

"—out it. You're right. I guess I would. And I will. I really will, when
the time comes." She even finished his sentences for him when he
was interrupting her.

Just when he thought most of the questions he'd had about her since
her blow-drier first jammed his cable signal had been answered to his
satisfaction, he met Kennedy's sister. One day he saw the pink Mustang pull into the parking lot of a fast-food place near where they lived
just as he, in his yellow El Camino, was pulling in the exit. Kennedy's
sister was a dark, frail, gentle-looking woman whose large brown eyes
held Aaron Dodge's with a look that whispered simply: Help. If she'd

been a car, she'd've had her hood up, flares out, and emergency flashers blinking. And Aaron Dodge, a repairman from his boyhood onward, found that look a difficult one to pass up. Why didn't he join the two of them for lunch? she asked. Her name was Laura.

The pink Mustang belonged to Laura and her husband. Which explained why the Arizona plates, when Kennedy still legally resided with her and Laura's mother in Illinois. Laura was two of the reasons Kennedy had decided to go to school at ASU. First, Laura's husband was a fighter pilot, stationed at Davis-Monthan Air Force Base outside Tucson, and it would be fun to have a friend and relative close by. Also, Laura's husband the fighter pilot had no intention of accepting the divorce Laura wanted, so it might be necessary to have an ally equally close by. Kennedy felt a special responsibility to Laura, she said, because she was godmother to three of Laura's children.

"Three of? As in 'a minority of'?" Clearly Laura hadn't escaped the Church's influence either.

They dumped the empty Styrofoam and cardboard on their lunch trays into a push-lid garbage box with "Thank You" engraved in its door and left the restaurant.

"What're you, breeding them to sell?" the fat man asked curmudgeoneously.

"Six in all," Laura said. Today they were staying with their great-aunt, who lived in Sun City, the retirement mecca west of Phoenix. Aunt Hazel, Kennedy called her, and pronounced it "Ont." Aaron Dodge realized then why Arizona had been growing so fast. Every family in Illinois had three representatives here.

He'd installed a new muffler and wanted to take the pink Mustang out for a test drive, so one weekend in July the fat man went with Kennedy to visit Laura and her husband. The trip to Tucson had a second purpose, diversionary in intent, which he discovered only after it was under way.

"Suspicious? Why would he be suspicious?" Aaron Dodge asked. Laura was nearly ready to ambush the World War III flying ace with a divorce announcement. Nearly but not quite.

"You haven't met this guy," Kennedy said. "He's always suspicious." Aaron Dodge had encountered the type. No way do you know anything I don't know. So I'll pretend to know things I only suspect you're thinking, just in case. Not only suspicious, also ruthless, arrogant, and possessive, according to Kennedy. Chauvinistic, selfish, demanding, and inflexible.

"You say 'possessive'?"

"Don't worry." Kennedy drew her legs underneath her and leaned into his shoulder. "You're with me."

Laura and her husband lived off-base, in a Tucson suburb, in a house not nearly big enough for six children. If such houses existed. Laura, preceded by a toddler and carrying an even smaller child, met them in the drive. They exchanged hugs and hellos. Laura attempted to transfer the younger child, a girl, to Kennedy, but she was having none of it.

"They always cry when I hold them," Kennedy said.

"If you think they cry when you hold them, you should see what they do when you drop one."

"He's fat."

"Brett! You hush!" said Laura.

Inside, Aaron Dodge was introduced to Brett's namesake. Six feet tall, blonde, tanned, muscular. Eyes the shade of those tank additives that automatically color the water every time you flush.

The older kids were at the neighborhood playground. Laura and Kennedy kept the others corralled in the kitchen. They drank coffee and gutlessly abandoned Aaron Dodge in the den with Laura's husband. During the next hour the two of them managed to budge a few conversational boulders—mechanics, athletics, nuclear war. Theirs was the exaggerated politeness of two men who neither expect nor desire to see each other again, and aren't altogether thrilled with this meeting either. Kennedy was right. Aaron Dodge sensed the tension. Someplace in this house a bomb was being disarmed. And not by experts.

"That's him," he told Kennedy as they drove home. "The man with his trigger finger on the stop/eject button at the end of the world."

All of July and into the stalled and suffocating days of August, Kennedy kept the fat man informed. She'd helped Laura locate an apartment for her and the kids. A lawyer, a private bank account, and a part-time job had also been arranged. The preparations concluded, a date was chosen. The husband would be away. Leading air strikes against the Navajo or something. The escape was set for, of all days, August 15. Aaron Dodge's birthday.

Kennedy kept asking and Aaron Dodge kept saying yes till finally she had to find somebody else to help Laura move.

Where are you?! Laura's important day! You said you'd help!!!

A quickly drawn circle containing three dots for a nose and eyes and an upside-down "U" for a mouth indicated Kennedy's displeasure. Aaron Dodge found the note taped to his door on the morning of the fifteenth, when he returned from a meeting at the law firm of Zuber, Zunkel, Yocum, and Yoder. It was the conference with Max Yoder that had caused him to overlook his promise to Kennedy.

Maxine was his patent attorney—fourth member of a law partnership that, according to Max, had voted one subzero Wednesday to pack up an executive suite's worth of Des Moines, Iowa, and transfer it to Phoenix, where, according to Aaron Dodge, the summer climate was uniquely suited to preparing lawyers for the afterlife.

Maxine was a scrawny, storkish woman with yellow teeth, disorganized hair, and a complexion that looked like it had been applied with a putty knife. She was enthusiastic but dignified, hopeful but pragmatic, articulate but reserved, courteous but relentless, and fairly easygoing for a woman with three clocks in her office. If you counted her wristwatch. Which she consulted frequently and conspicuously during the fat man's appointment.

"The t-shirts," Max said. "Terrific potential there, Aaron. Ideally, you'd want to secure a trademark. But, realistically, is it the kind of idea anyone would steal? We could file for copyright. What do you think?" Max was roughly his age, and, like many of the more successful members of their generation, she camouflaged her disenchantment with a dual response to every situation. She prefaced these contradictory opinions with tipoffs such as "ideally" or "realistically." The implication being that, while she understood your fanciful attachment to one option, you were a fool if you didn't choose the other.

"Move quickly would be my advice. Though it's your decision, of course." Max was talking about an idea for which Aaron Dodge had hoped to secure legal protection. It was based on the nauseating "I

Love New York" campaign currently being waged on every available surface in America—"New York" abbreviated and love understudied by a plump valentine. The fat man's alternative was similar conceptually but opposed philosophically. Above an "NY" in a typeface reminiscent of the original, it featured an "F" and a "CK" separated by a valentine that, in this case, represented an ordinary "U" instead of love.

"Risky," said Max. "But worth a modest investment. I wish you luck with it."

"Thanks, Max. For sticking my neck out like this."

Max adjusted the bracelet above her wristwatch, which was studded with hunks of turquoise the size of rivets. "The Bunkport. Now that's another matter," she said. "Here, I think we should do a search. Apply. Look for backers. Write to manufacturers. The whole nine yards, Aaron."

Aaron Dodge agreed, even though he'd be paying for the patent search, the applications, the phone calls, the letters, and the yards, all nine.

"I think you may really be on to something there," Max said. "And maybe with your exerciser too. Those health and fitness gadgets are *du jour* as hell right now. Though who can say how long that will last." The exerciser, another of his recent ideas, was a mechanical jump rope which consisted of a spool of breakable cord attached to a rotor mechanism he'd scavenged from the base of a kitchen blender. The cord spun at a height and speed controlled by the owner, who exercised by hopping over the whirling cord once per revolution. Aaron Dodge called it a JumPropellor.

Max held her left wrist to her right ear and listened—an optimistic gesture, since she wore a digital quartz. The fat man liked that about nervous habits. The way they lagged far behind technology. "Speaking of backers . . ." she said.

"You take care of it, Max."

"I can't, Aaron. You know I can't. They want to meet you. And they have a right to. I made the appointment for tomorrow. So you don't have time to back out."

"Tomorrow. Shit, Max."

Max tapped the crystal, tugged at the band, glanced from the watch to the desk clock to the wall to Aaron Dodge. "Meeting's at three. Call me at one-thirty. Be ready to show your prototypes. And Aaron?" She gestured hopelessly in the fat man's direction. "Wear something? Please?"

He saw the pink Mustang that afternoon in the apartment-house lot and knocked on Kennedy's door. "I'm not usually such a fuckup," he explained. "My lawyer sucker-punched me. I've been pissed off all day. I just forgot. Really."

"Hey, man. No hassle. It can happen. No sweat, okay?"

Kennedy wasn't alone.

And the person she was with—the person who, Aaron Dodge learned, had taken his place in the getaway car—was neglecting to politely de-emphasize his presence. Apparently fond of substituting for Aaron Dodge, now he was shrugging, smiling, and manufacturing stoic clichés on his behalf. "Commitments. Conflicts. Nobody's perfect. Slipups're bound to happen. Glad to help out. Anytime. No biggie, no biggie."

Kennedy introduced him as a friend—a friend she'd met in a reg-istration line at the university. He was Kennedy's age, and wore jogging shoes with three stripes, a golf shirt bearing a reptile emblem, and blue jeans that were not too old, not too new. He looked like he must have a separate barber for each hair. "It's human nature, dude. That's all. Human nature."

The Philosopher LaCoste, Aaron Dodge decided to call him.

With the help of Kennedy's friend, Laura had been installed safely and secretly in a furnished two-bedroom hideout in Peoria, a Phoenix suburb halfway between Kennedy's apartment and Ont Hazel's house in Sun City. They'd agreed to take turns looking in on Laura till she adjusted to exile.

"It'll be tough on her. Hope she's made the right choice. Guess only time will tell." He was the kind of guy who if he'd been a folksinger would've been trying to get the audience to sing along. Aaron Dodge didn't think the color or styling of the car he drove reflected much aesthetic judgment, and the way he backed out of his parking space, accidentally honking the horn twice, testified to a similar aptitude for geometry.

"Where do they come from?" Aaron Dodge asked with a disgusted sigh.

Kennedy smiled. A friend. Sure.

That night they ate at a Denny's. His birthday dinner, though he didn't say so. Afterward Aaron Dodge borrowed a ballpoint from the waitress and challenged Kennedy. On a paper napkin they would list the public events that had shaped their attitudes and compare results. The waitress, who was his age, and the manager, not much older than Kennedy, immediately took sides. On half the docket, Aaron Dodge and the waitress catalogued:

> the initial manned space flights
> a Cuban showdown
> three important assassinations
> integration and civil rights
> their country's only defeat at war
> the first footsteps on the moon

On her side of the ledger, Kennedy, with the help of the Denny's night manager, was able to list one presidential resignation and a measly hostage crisis.

"No wonder you and your friends are such mushbrains," he told her. "Your major social influence was the fine print on your Purgatory lift pass. The only way to learn responsibility is through hardship. I had a paper route by the time I was nine. And I worked my way through college."

"I thought you didn't finish college."

"I worked my way through the year of college I did finish."

"College was cheaper then."

"Wages were lower."

"So you think I should pay for my own education?"

"A story about a woman with no shoes is not complete until that woman confronts a sticker patch."

They all, including the waitress, stared cautiously at the fat man.

"I'll bet you took LSD, didn't you?" the manager asked respectfully.

"Many times."

"There was also Three Mile Island," Kennedy suggested. "For our side."

"An almost only scores in horseshoes."

"Ever see the Beatles play?"

"Not them. Hendrix, though. The Doors."

"Were you at Woodstock?"

"Put that on the list," he told the waitress.

"Vietnam?"

"I don't like to talk about it."

Later, slumped low in the passenger seat of the pink Mustang, Kennedy fiddled with the door handle and stared outside. "Excuse me," he told her. "I forgot. You and your friends weren't raised on confrontation."

"Let's just skip it."

"Fine. We're even."

"What do you mean, 'even'? Where are we going? Take me home."

"You don't have to come if you don't want to."

She mumbled something untranslatable.

"I wouldn't call it a party. Not exactly."

"Drop me off. I'm tired."

"A birthday observance."

That got Kennedy's full attention.

"Just some friends of mine. Nothing spectacular."

She sat up, adjusted the visor over her side of the windshield, and studied the mirror. "I wish you'd told me."

"When you get to be my age . . ." he said, and let her imagine the rest.

"Aaron Dodge. How many candles?"

"Last year a wax museum bought my cake for salvage."

"So. I'll finally get to meet these friends you're always talking about."

He parked two addresses up from an old wood-frame house located on Orangewood Avenue in Sunnyslope. Lulu lived there, along with Wendy Wendy and Buzz, another of Aaron Dodge's friends. Trying to view the property as Kennedy would, Aaron Dodge inspected the unpainted exterior, unlit and unattended premises of a house inhabited by people living, he suddenly realized, in another world. Certainly not in this one. At least not with much enthusiasm. A hedge fronting the lot had encroached on the sidewalk, detouring pedestrians to the strip of unmowed grass between the walk and curb. The yard sloped up from the hedge. Three concrete steps accommodated the rise. Lengths of threaded pipe had been assembled with T's and elbows to make a handrail. Aaron Dodge rattled the screen door and pushed it open, wondering if this other world would ever make any sense to Kennedy St. James.

Not wanting to be the first one there, Aaron Dodge was late to his own birthday. Later than planned. That was the trouble with irresponsible acts. Trying to atone for one, you usually committed a second.

"We were about to give up on you. Hi, I'm Lulu."

"I'm Kennedy. Glad to meet you."

Inside the large room containing the festivities, voices and music competed with a swamp cooler extravagant in size but modest in efficiency. Lulu handled the introductions.

"Everybody, this is Kitty." She created a pause just long enough for her announcement by lifting and then replacing—with the sound of amplified ripping nylon—the stereo tone arm.

"*Kenn*edy," Aaron Dodge said.

His friends raised beer cans or clear plastic party glasses of Chablis and mouthed Hi's. Kennedy smiled and nodded.

"Aaron, there were lots more people here. Before," Lulu said. "And it is a Thursday," she added. Lately any parties planned by Aaron Dodge and his friends tended to be brief and cozy. Have to work tomorrow. Sorry to rush off, but Amber wakes me up at six every day, party or no party. Club soda if you have it, thanks. Can't stay. 'Night, everybody. *Ciao*. Several of his friends had enrolled in courses with names like "Success Management" and "Management Success" and were learning to schedule their time more effectively.

"It's all right. These are the people I wanted Kennedy to meet. No genuine friend of Aaron Dodge's is scared to stay up past ten."

Homemade bookcases verified the temporary alliance of households the mailbox had announced. Multiple copies of *One Flew Over the Cuckoo's Nest* and *Zen and the Art of Motorcycle Maintenance* lined shelves of sagging particle board suspended between cinderblocks. "Suite: Judy Blue Eyes" was playing. The air in the room smelled like vintage bong water. "You hungry?" said Aaron Dodge. "I'm starved."

The broccoli and cauliflower had already been wiped out. Only carrots and celery survived on the vegetable platter. Aaron Dodge picked out a cracker that looked like a steamrolled shredded-wheat biscuit, spread it with chick-pea dip, and offered it to Kennedy. She made a face. He devoured it, plus several others.

"There's beer and wine," said Lulu. "Help yourself."

When he opened the icebox, it took a step toward him; when he shut it, it took a step back. The linoleum crackled underfoot where it had warped and separated from the floor. A smoky gray streak from a recent grease fire in the broiler smudged the oven door.

One good thing about showing up late. No kids. He knew that some of those present were parents. The kind that hauled their sticky-faced menaces with them everyplace. Now, that's not very nice, Prairie. Is that how we talk to our host, Blossom? Brutal disciplinarians. Aaron Dodge, no big fan of children, cultivated a reputation among his marsh-mallow mommy and daddy friends and their hyperactive offspring. The dark. Monsters. Thunder. Ghosts. And "Uncle Aaron."

Kennedy joined him in the kitchen. Buzz followed Kennedy in. He offered Aaron Dodge the butt of a segmented car-radio aerial with a smoking alligator clip soldered to the tip. Aaron Dodge accepted, then offered it to Kennedy, who made a face.

One of the more stable, financially, of the fat man's friends, Buzz was proprietor of Buzzes, a one-room business housed in the attic of a military surplus store in West Phoenix. In a previous era it might have been called a head shop. Besides paraphernalia, you could buy used records and comic books at Buzzes, plus rent explicit video-tapes. Buzz had long, straight chestnut hair parted in the middle and a Fu Manchu mustache complemented by a sparse tussock beneath his lower lip, which he manipulated with his thin fingers as he spoke.

"A little red snapper? Some vitamin V for the birthday boy?" He nodded after Kennedy, who'd asked directions to the phone. "What's the trouble, Dodgers? You're nervous as a Haitian queer in a bathtub full of spit tonight."

"Nothing." He didn't want to talk about it. Not with Buzz.

"How is she?" he asked Kennedy when she returned. She smiled unconvincingly. Aaron Dodge reached for Buzz's smoldering antenna.

Soon he noticed the warmth begin to seep from his extremities. A vein at his temple pulsed with an urgency that forced his left eye partway shut. His heart pattered like a bongo orchestra. He heard a car door slam blocks away. Boot soles double-timing on concrete. *You're-ou're surroun-noun ded-ded, give-ive uv-up.*

"Good shit," he told Buzz, who grinned and twisted his tussock.

After that only a couple of fragments registered.

"Which were you named for?" Buzz is asking.

"I'm sorry?"

"Which of the brothers did your folks name you after?"

"I'm not sure. I don't think they ever mentioned it."

"You were born near the date of one of the assassinations, I take it."

"I believe I was. Yes."

"Which one?"

"I don't know. How many were there?"

"She was a model," Aaron Dodge is saying. "In the same sense that I'm an inventor, that is." He deals Kennedy the color prints one pose at a time. Cody.

He and Kennedy are in one of the bedrooms. Whispering. A child of one of the friends attending his party, a girl, is asleep fully dressed on the room's adult-sized bed. So small she leaves hardly an imprint on the spread.

Cody has the kind of breasts that droop just a little. In all her pictures she's either lying down to flatten them or holding her arms above her head to lift them. Sometimes she's tying up her hair, sometimes waiting seductively in a doorway. Sometimes just raising her arms for no apparent reason, surrendering at gunpoint. A few of the candid poses, now Lulu's property, are tear sheets from men's monthlies Cody sold pictures to.

"It was what she wanted." Aaron Dodge shrugs. "Her dream, I guess. She used to send these out. And get these back." He shows Kennedy a correspondence from a well-known publication. *The enclosed material does not suit our present needs. We are sorry that the volume of submissions precludes a more personal reply. The Editors.*

"The cocksu—"

"—shhh!" says Kennedy.

"It's bad enough having a patent application turned down. But your whole body? Imagine how it must've—"

"—shhh! *Aaron!*"

———

Wrap-up edition of the tv news. Picture, no sound. Bob the Brush pointing out, to Wendy Wendy, a face superimposed near the newscaster's ear. Mary Vanessa Singer.

"It's getting to where you dread seeing a story on anybody under twenty-five," Bob is saying. "When you do, you know to expect desert search parties. Suspicious vehicles in the vicinity of the disappearance."

"I read where religious cults are suspected," Wendy says.

Bob the Brush: "People in her neighborhood have tied yellow ribbons around the trees and cactus in their yards."

Wendy Wendy: "What they need to do is call in a psychic."

Aaron Dodge: "I could never be one of those perverts. I'd eat all my own candy before school let out."

Later, after the party, they sat together in the pink Mustang, parked behind a Jack in the Box on Northern. Aaron Dodge drank coffee from a to-go cup. Watched a toxic beige corona emitted by the Styrofoam seep onto the surface.

"Aaron, studies show that marijuana interferes with short-term memory."

"I know. But all you have to do is wait a week or so. Then whatever you forgot shifts over into long-term memory and it comes right back to you, no problem. Wha'd you think of my friends?"

"They were nice to me. Lulu especially. She kept saying, 'He's usually not like this.' You smoked a lot, Aaron. And on top of the drinking— I guess I didn't know what to think. I didn't know you could be so . . . I didn't know you were . . ."

"I'm a man of appetites," said Aaron Dodge.

6

Kennedy came in while he was wiping a face-size window into the steamy mirror with a towel.

"Whatcha doin'?"

She was an expert at this. Getting in his way by trying to be near him. If he was in the kitchen, cooking a meal, there she'd be, climbing over him to hang a skillet on its nail above the stove. When he entered a room, he couldn't leave it without finding her in the doorway, guarding or trapping him, he didn't know which.

"Shit!" He raised up while brushing his teeth and conked his head on the door of the medicine cabinet, which Kennedy had opened for some reason.

"You bumped your bald spot."

"Bald?" With the tips of his fingers he pressed the chakra at the crown of his skull. Where a bald spot would've been if he'd had one.

"Feel it?"

"That's where my halo used to be." How long had it been since he'd taken the trouble to arrange two mirrors face to face for a review of his haircut? How long had it been, in fact, since his last haircut? In '74 or '5, as soon as it grew long enough, he'd tied it back in a tail. Since then he only undid the rubber band to wash it.

"I've taken shit all my life for having too much hair. Now I'm taking shit for being bald."

"Aaron, there's a party tonight over in Tempe. We're invited. But I don't want you to come. Not unless you really want to."

"Thanks. I'll stay home, then."

"I went to your party. I met your friends."

"Do you want me to go?"

"Do you really want to? You don't, do you? You'd just be doing it to pacify me."

"I'll go."

"You always do this, Aaron. You say you'll do something and then you just go right ahead and do what you planned to do all along. I hate that."

"I can't help it. My short-term memory is decimated."

"Real funny. Dope fiend."

"I'll go. I said I'll go, and I'll go. Is the Philosopher LaCoste coming?"

"Quit calling him that. He invited you specifically, Aaron. He likes you. Don't ask me why."

"That guy's got his head so far up his ass his farts smell like Listerine."

Aaron Dodge stripped the sheets, textured by nightly emissions and oranged by monthly ones, off the Bunkport and borrowed a clean set from Kennedy. She helped him load his invention into the bed of the El Camino. The day was overcast, so they covered it with the green bedspread in case it rained.

"Good luck," said Kennedy.

"Why don't we call Laura. See if she wants to go with us tonight."

"Good idea," Kennedy said. "You call, Aaron. She'll go if you ask. She'll be flattered."

Aaron Dodge shrugged. "I'll think about it."

He stopped at the Kopy Korner to Xerox designs for the Bunkport and JumPropellor in case Max's friends asked for copies. He handed the stack of originals to Wendy Wendy.

"Some party, huh? Say, I like that Kennedy, you know. Where'd you meet her anyway? She's, you know, young."

"I'm not sure it'll work out," said the fat man. "You know how they are at that age. Flighty. How's Bart?"

"I've been reading this like book, you know, Aaron. On relationships and stuff. I can Xerox you a copy or something."

"What's the damage?"

Wendy Wendy rang a zero on the till. Peeped it, actually, since the register was electronic. "Happy birthday. And call me, okay? You never call me."

At ten after three, unassuming in its capacity as a sofa, the Bunkport sat in Max Yoder's office awaiting the arrival of the investors she'd contacted.

"Didn't you agree to dress for the occasion?" Max asked.

"Wardrobe by Oscar De Low Renta," the fat man said, and pivoted on a heel for inspection. He was wearing a charcoal pair of J C Penney twill work pants and one of the "Fuck New York" t-shirts.

"Sometimes I think you purposely sabotage these opportunities, Aaron. Don't you even have a shirt?" Aaron Dodge brought one in from the El Camino and put it on. The mate to his pants. Max snatched the penlight and mechanical pencil from the pocket and flung them on her desk. "They'll think you're the damn custodian," she said.

A few minutes later they arrived.

One was a man named Eelfleet, that Aaron Dodge had never heard of before and that shook hands with just his thumb and fingertips, the way you'd work the mouth of a kid's poodle puppet. But the other two were both surprisingly prominent Phoenicians. Aaron Dodge was impressed already by Max's clout. He recognized the sanitized enunciation of the second man, Dick Banks, whose ads for his own auto dealership were commonplace in the local media. The third of Max's prospects was an influential and respected Phoenix attorney, a Chicano active in the UFW, civil rights, and the sanctuary movement. An advocate of lost causes, the fat man thought. Perfect.

Max unobtrusively but expertly orchestrated the seating arrangements so that when the time came to conduct business two of the three men were sitting on the object central to the negotiations. When Max told them, they quickly stood, glancing behind and beneath them distrustfully. Aaron Dodge assembled. Max described the steps in instructionese.

Minutes later two of the wealthiest men in Arizona had shed their coats and shoes and were arguing over who gets the top bunk, while number three, wearing a t-shirt that slandered a sister state, hopped up and down on one foot at intervals dictated by an appliance designed to beget guacamole.

"I think it went well, Aaron," Max told him once they'd gone.

"Maybe," the fat man said. "But I don't care how rich they are. We are not calling it Mega-Sofa."

On his way out, after loading the El Camino and thanking Max for her assistance, Aaron Dodge asked her receptionist if he could use the phone. An elaborate formula of multiple rings punctuated by hangups and redialings had been devised to insulate Laura from unexpected calls. Aaron Dodge initiated the code, trying to ignore the growing fussiness with which the secretary rearranged the objects within her territory.

"Hi, Laura. Aaron Dodge. What're you up to?"

"Pretty good, Aaron. How are you?"

"Not much. Listen, Kennedy and me are going to this party tonight in Tempe. Why don't you come? Take your mind off your troubles."

"Thanks, Aaron. But I don't think I could. I'd be worried about the kids, and—"

"Ont Hazel would take care of the kids, I bet. Look, I need you to come. Otherwise I'm going to be the only one there without a trust fund."

Laura laughed. "Thanks, Aaron. But really."

"How long's it been since you went to a real party? Not at an officers' club? How long's it been since you smoked a joint?"

She paused. "A while."

"Eight-thirty," said the fat man.

Laura would come along. He would put her in charge of Kennedy, then hitch a ride, leave the party early. Early and without an argument. If he was lucky.

Around seven that night he followed Kennedy next door to hurry her up while she dressed for the party.

"Do I look fat in this?"

"You're asking me that?" Aaron Dodge. More forthcoming than he'd been with anyone, ever, concerning his size.

He hated Kennedy's apartment. Even though its layout was practically identical to his, everything in it was brand-new. Her can opener didn't even have any of that gray-black crud built up on its gears and blade yet.

She put on a turquoise leotard that you could see her nipples through if you looked, and a wraparound Indian print skirt secured by a beaded "New Mexico!" roadside souvenir belt. Also striped kneesocks, and a pair of scruffy black-and-white hightop tennis shoes. She unpigtailed her hair, wetted it, and made it frizz out stylishly with a brush and blow-drier.

"What do you think?"

"You look assembled from an originality kit."

"Are you going like that?"

At Laura's Peoria hideout, Kennedy pressed the bell. Nothing happened. Either too much noise inside or the kids had already wrecked the chimes. Finally somebody opened up.

"A minnow is a baby fish," she said.

"Hi, Sylvie," said Kennedy. "Hi, honey."

"No it's not, stupid." Another small body drove Sylvia's sideways into a Care Bear–pink and Smurf-blue pile of cardboard and plastic on the living-room floor.

"Brett! That wasn't very nice," said Laura. "You help your sister up."

Kennedy and Aaron Dodge transferred toys and pop cans from chairs to the floor and sat. Laura offered some final words—advice, encouragement, sympathy—to Ont Hazel, who in the confusion was never formally introduced to the fat man.

The address the Philosopher LaCoste had provided fixed the party site as Sin City, a Tempe student precinct consisting of two-story motel-size dwellings with apartment-size rents. He parked the pink Mustang on Lemon. Kennedy had brought with her a bottle of 151, Laura had a cantaloupe, and Aaron Dodge cradled a six of Miller Lite.

Packs of young men carrying open containers roamed sidewalks and parking lots, bellowing obscenities at nobody in particular and stopping occasionally to yank a payphone receiver off its cord or vandalize stunted citrus trees. They found the Philosopher LaCoste's complex and located an apartment central to the uproar. In the kitchen sat a twenty-gallon plastic garbage pail, half full when Kennedy dumped in her fifth. Aaron Dodge sliced the cantaloupe with his pocket knife and dropped it in a quarter at a time, skin, seeds and all. He opened one and kept the other five beers under an arm. He'd been to this party before.

It was called a "trash-can bash." Everybody brings a bottle of liquor and a variety of fruit. The host primes the punch bowl with two quarts of Everclear. Guests modify the elixir with miscellaneous contributions as they arrive. Those who dare partake. Laura declined, but Kennedy gaily dipped into the communal potion with one of the plastic vessels provided. She took a sip, grimaced, and offered the cup to Aaron Dodge. He dipped a finger in. It tasted like the El Camino's radiator water when he tested it for antifreeze content.

There are two kinds of bachelors. The kind who at parties you see inside, stiff-arming a doorjamb they've trapped someone against, someone female, who they're filibustering with body language. And the other kind, who at the same parties stay close to the keg, or who you meet out in the yard, inspecting the motorcycles. The fat man saw plenty of the first kind at this party—guys who take their shirts off at volleyball games hours before they start to sweat. He even spotted a few Arizona State football players. The way they pronounced it—"foop-baw"—certified their authenticity. Aaron Dodge finally located members of his own fraternity out by the pool.

The problem drinkers.

The chainsmokers.

The joke tellers.

Later, when he'd finished the six and returned to LaCoste's unit, he found Kennedy and Laura sitting on the floor, sharing an intimate and animated conversation with the Philosopher himself. You couldn't've fitted a six-thousandths feeler gauge between any of the three of them.

The phone was in the kitchen. In use. And several people waiting. He took a butter knife from the silverware drawer and walked outside. The front doors of all the upstairs apartments opened onto a continuous balcony. Aaron Dodge chose one whose front window was dark. He slid the knife blade between the jamb and casing trim and jimmied the lock. Inside, he dialed Wendy Wendy. Busy. He sat on the sloshy waterbed in this stranger's apartment, smoked a number, then dialed again. This time no answer.

Outside, he heard activity down the row, saw an open door, and went in. He found LaCoste there, but neither Kennedy nor Laura was with him. Several couples played the fad trivia game, questions and

answers and hop your token in circles round the board, that was popular then in Phoenix and everyplace else. Aaron Dodge started answering everybody's questions.

What's the plural of RBI?

RBI.

"Stop that, will you, Aaron. Please."

Which of the greenhouse gases originally present in the earth's
atmosphere is today deposited almost entirely in limestone formations?

Carbon dioxide.

"No kidding, Aaron. Cut it out."

The fat man picked up the narrow box that held all the questions,
asked and unasked, and dumped them on the game board.

"Hey!"

"You two want to take it outside?" somebody said. A joke, but Aaron
Dodge responded. LaCoste stood up. Faced him.

"You threatening me?"

"I'm calling you out is what I'm doing, you racquetballing, lap-
swimming son of a bitch."

"Come on, you two. Don't be such babies."

But Aaron Dodge had already started toward the front door, challenging LaCoste with a shoulder as he passed. Downstairs, accompanied by an entourage of onlookers and referees, they crossed pool
deckings, traversed hilly lawns of river rock, and filed between parallel
rows of parked hatchbacks before they reached a suitable location—
tennis courts. Somebody flipped a switch and flooded the courts with
light. The cement was painted green.

LaCoste raised both hands, stiff-palmed, the edges facing the fat
man, and dropped into a bowlegged Tae Kwan Do crouch. Aaron Dodge
clenched his fists and stepped forward.

"Let's go, fucker."

LaCoste struck a blow near Aaron Dodge's sternum with the heel
of his palm that actually hurt quite a bit.

Aaron Dodge knew zip about martial arts, but he was more familiar
with the principle of mechanical advantage than the Philosopher
LaCoste would ever be. He pretended to seize the initiative and threw
a wild right at LaCoste's forehead. LaCoste attempted, as Aaron Dodge
assumed he would, to manipulate the fat man's physical bulk in his

favor. Cooperating instead of resisting, he grabbed Aaron Dodge's up-
per arm and allowed the offensive momentum he'd generated to wheel
them both halfway around. Aaron Dodge was ready. Refusing to resist
his opponent's refusal to resist, he completed their pirouette, waltzed
LaCoste entirely off his feet, hugged him to his chest, and fell on him.
He lost wind when he hit the green pavement.

The fat man stood over him and watched him thrash, his predicament illuminated by the banked lights overhead.

He left LaCoste puking on his knees and walked up the street to
the pink Mustang. He sat behind the wheel for a while. Then, instead
of driving away, he crawled into the back seat and rested on the green
bedspread. He heard LaCoste and his friends pass. A few phrases—
"fat slob . . . I'd like to see him try that . . ."—reached him through
the Mustang's open window.

Berserk. Inexcusable.

Altogether, entirely uncool.

The fat man lit a J and waited for the ugly chemistry in him to
subside.

Females. They always needed somebody, didn't they? And that was
the key word: *some*body. Whatever scene they were part of, they got
caught up in it. Like for a while it had to be the blue-apartment-village
scene, because that was the only scene there was. Then the Laura-
and-her-kids scene came along. Now it would be the college-coed
scene. Jeremy. Justin.

He extinguished the roach with his tongue. Ate it. Settled back on
the green bedspread. Plan. Decide. Think. Mentally, the fat man pulled
on his gray sweats, XXL, and tied the drawstring. Laced his intellect
into shoes with little "N"s on the sides. The dope began to relax him
some.

Her age. Partly you could blame that. People her age never had a
chance. Page through a *Sports Illustrated* sometime. Examine the
liquor ads. Find the naked women hidden in the ice. The sales pitches
directed at her and her friends were so much more sophisticated than
those he and his had been obliged to resist. It's our one big claim to
fame, he told himself. We were imperfectly brainwashed. Lobotomized
with a dull scalpel. Aaron Dodge and his friends. The last generation
of Americans who'd be able to remember what it felt like to be free.

How could he blame people for succumbing? He couldn't. But he did.

Up, he told himself. And mentally he did get up. Climbed out of the car. Ran. Past the tennis courts to Apache Boulevard. Up Mill Avenue to the freeway on-ramp. Back to the West Side. The bale of two-dimensional cardboard boxes still lay unreconstituted in a corner of one of his workrooms. His friends were there. Lulu, Buzz, Bob the Brush, Wendy Wendy. Waiting to help him pack.

When he opened his eyes he still lay in the Mustang's back seat.

"How could he do this? How could he?"

"It's okay. Don't cry."

The passenger-side door opened. He could make out a pair of silhouettes above the curve of a seatback. Kennedy and Laura's voices, muffled by each other as they hugged.

"He doesn't love me! He left!"

"Yes he does. It's all right, hon. We'll find him. Don't worry."

"But why did he do this to me?"

"He loves you, Kennedy. He just doesn't know how to show it is all."

"Why? He left me, Laura. Why?"

"I don't know, babe. I really don't. We'll find out."

Laura drove. Streetlights passed overhead. Aaron Dodge watched them through the Mustang's back window. He listened to sobbed and blurted accusations. To confessions extracted by the brew Kennedy and her friends had concocted.

"It was my fault, wasn't it? I did something. What did I do?"

"No you didn't, hon. Don't say that."

"I love him, Laura. I'm sorry. I'm so, so sorry."

"Shhh. Baby, hush."

And the more he heard, the more difficult it became for the fat man to divulge his hiding place. Kennedy said again: "He abandoned me. Aaron deserted me."

"Don't, Kennedy."

Aaron Dodge knew he could lie still and wait if he wanted to. They'd arrive at the blue apartment village. Laura would help her sister inside. He'd be free to return to his own apartment. To bachelorhood. To home. To his old diet.

No additives, no preservatives, no sugar.

Emotional health food.

"Goddammit son of a bitch fuck." He hauled himself upright, one hand on a shoulder of each front seat, and leaned forward.

"Look! Look, Laura, he's here. It's him. Where have you been, Aaron? Where did you go?"

"Noplace. Not a goddam place. I'm right here."

He sent Laura home by herself in the pink Mustang. All night he watched from a chair as Kennedy slept. Bedside on the floor sat a saucepan part-full of what looked like the same accident the Philosopher LaCoste had been having the last time Aaron Dodge had seen him.

"Don't go," Kennedy said once during the night, never opening her eyes.

During the months that followed, he watched Mary Vanessa Singer's story move to and from the front page, off and back again in an irregular cycle—a fresh installment every day, then every week, then every two, until suddenly a new rumor or a confirmed account would return her to prominence.

In September, on her birthday, the Arizona *Representative* devoted a full page to her. A rehash of everything that had befallen Mary in her absence. It made the fat man furious. Retrospectives and nostalgia always did. He carefully avoided the year-end wrap-up specials the networks aired every January. A recap of the year's major events. Those "On This Day in History" segments of KKGB's irritated him almost as much. Lately commentators and analysts had been provoking the fat man further, attempting to formalize the passage of not just a year or a decade, but of an entire era in American history. Aaron Dodge knew that there could be only one explanation for the sudden interest in the years during which he and his friends had grown up—years that, according to legend, had been full of idealism, happiness, goodwill, peaceful intentions, hope, and love.

They were over.

One day in October he opened a gallon of milk and found a tamperproof foil seal underneath the cap.

It didn't happen overnight. Or in a week or even a month. But eventually Kennedy forgave. He was going to have to spend more time at home, however. Pay her more attention. Stop making fun of her friends. Foreplay somehow entered into the deal. Farting was mentioned.

The fat man knew better than to make rash promises. He stayed home a few nights and yawned in front of the tube. Drove her up to the White Tanks and kicked around dead leaves on a nature trail. Once, after they'd made love, he dug a yellow fluorescent marker out of a pocket of her book bag—the marker she used to highlight important passages in her texts—and indicated areas he said he'd need to come back to later on for review. And then one night on the green bedspread, he told her a story. Ping-Pong balls, fudge ice cream, a pinup calendar, and I-4F. Lowhaefer, Cody, and black cohosh. Avoidance, resistance, evasion, desertion, exile. And fat. That same night, on the Bunkport's bottom bunk, as generations of sturdy females everywhere have done for generations of returning warriors, Kennedy St. James surrendered to Aaron Dodge the ultimate gift. Or what was left of it, anyway.

PART TWO

APPREHENSION AND CONVICTION

7

▼▼▼▼▼▼▼▼▼▼▼▼▼▼▼▼▼▼▼▼▼
▼▼▼▼▼▼▼▼▼▼▼▼▼▼▼▼▼▼▼
▼▼▼▼▼▼▼▼▼▼▼▼▼

That one over there, the shrieker, is Anthony; he's four. The blonde bouncing on a sofa cushion, singing, raising and lowering the front of her swimsuit with both hands, is next oldest: Ginger, five. With the Crayola, on her knees in front of the coffee table—the girl that can't decide whether paper or wood looks better orange, or whether orange looks or tastes better, for that matter—is Sylvia, six. And that's Brett, Brett's the oldest, sitting not a foot away from the set, cross-legged and hunchbacked, hands in his lap, chin outthrust, mouth open—maintaining the classic viewing position of the ten-year-old, except when it's necessary to turn and scream over a shoulder, "Shut up! I'm trying to hear this!" Which leaves only two missing, Heather and Holland. And that's Heather's whine coming from someplace in the apartment, so—

CRASH!—waaaaaaaaaaaaaaaaa! Ah, Holland must've been in the kitchen, climbing on the cabinets again.

The romance and novelty of her situation were beginning to diminish for Laura. You could see it in her face. Aaron Dodge first noticed a renewal of the weary expression—the one she'd worn the day he met her—on an evening when he left the six kids with Kennedy to pick Laura up at the fabric outlet near Christown where she worked part-time.

He parked in front of the warehouse-sized building and went inside.

Floors scuffproof. Lighting fluorescent. Patrons female. Keen-eyed from threading needles, they roamed among bolts of yard goods flung onto countertops or arranged in rows on canted shelves.

Laura wore a smock with magenta stripes and carried a pair of shears. Her job was to stand behind a long table with a yardstick attached face up to the edge nearest her. When anybody brought her a bolt of cloth, Laura would ask how much the customer wanted. Then, like a woman speed-reading ticker tape or the world's longest Chinese fortune, she'd snatch from the bolt in yard-size lengths that amount of cloth and shear it.

"Hi, Aaron. Just about done."

The woman she was waiting on now had piled some fairly intriguing bolts of cloth on Laura's table. "I don't know why I spend what I do on this stuff. Nobody's going to look at it. Supposedly."

See-through synthetics mostly. Beige and black. Plus rolls of skinny fringe, lacy like the ornamented borders of insurance policies. Also spools of elastic, and a group of envelopes with sketches of women in flimsy gowns, panties, and bras printed on the outsides. "Can you believe what they're asking at Goldwater's for this stuff?"

"Make your own underwear, do you?" Aaron Dodge asked.

She quickly gathered the envelopes into a stack and turned the top one face down. "Handkerchiefs," she said.

Laura wrote out a bill and passed it, along with the woman's merchandise, to a cashier. "I'll be ready in a sec, Aaron." The fat man waited by the front door, which he opened for her as the woman with the underwear supplies left the building.

"Thank you," she said. One of the envelopes slid off the top as she adjusted her load. It fell with a slap to the linoleum. The fat man picked it up and returned it. "Dropped your handkerchief, ma'am."

"You look lost in thought," Laura told him as they drove home.

"Can't get lost in a space that size," Aaron Dodge said. "Besides. I was going to say. It's you who looks worried."

"Not really," said Laura. "I do?"

The composure of a person with six children isn't easily disturbed. But Laura had been coping more enthusiastically than Aaron Dodge would've believed possible with the complications a divorce had introduced into her life. And Kennedy. She'd remained a loyal godparent and was now becoming an equally dutiful collegiate, juggling the two responsibilities effortlessly, it seemed. Ont Hazel had emerged from retirement with a grandmotherly zeal. Even Laura's husband, according to her, had accepted with military calmness this estrangement from the life he'd been accustomed to.

Only Aaron Dodge panicked.

The day he realized he was in love again, in love with Kennedy St. James, Aaron Dodge felt like the ex-president must've the morning he woke up and read in the paper that there was a street in Tehran named Death to Carter Avenue. He drove down the street to a Circle K, bought a package of Mint Milanos, and ate them all in the car on the way home. During the next month, in a shameful display of Thanksgiving-style irresponsibility, he gained twenty-five pounds.

His underwater sabbaticals resumed. For hours at a whack, in his own or the tub at Laura's, he'd lay motionless, submerged except for his matterhorn of a nose and the roundish islands of his knees and belly. Those who desired an audience would announce themselves, and Aaron Dodge would assure a degree of modesty appropriate to the consultation by drawing the shower curtain, leaving at one end a breach just wide enough to carry on a conversation through. From here he dispensed advice or replied to criticism.

"Which one are you?" Aaron Dodge would ask. One or another of Laura's six was always needing lunch money. A toy. Hospitalization. Movies cost two, three dollars. Video games ate quarters. Teeth, feet, hair, eyes. Every feature demanded medical attention or clothing. The minute one's vaccination pimpled, scabbed, and scarred, the next developed a chronic earache. They confiscated your pocket change and passed on their colds. They slowly and invisibly drained money, time, and energy like electrical shorts robbing current from a car battery.

"I'm sorry. I've forgotten your name."

"Sylvia. What're you doing in there?"

"Voting."

"No you're not. What really?"

"Resting. Thinking."

"You sure rest a lot."

Aaron Dodge. Dipping his fingers. Flicking bathwater.

"Ma-ahm!"

"Sylvia! Stop pestering Uncle Aaron. You come out of there. This
minute, hear?"

"Mom, Sylvia's bothering Uncle Aaar-on."

"He's splashing me again, Mom. Mom?"

When he wasn't in the tub, he kept a distance between him and
them using a squirt bottle he'd saved—one that had been full of some
sort of cleaner or remover. He'd reloaded it with water and now, if he
was watching a ballgame or reading the paper and didn't want to be
interrupted, he'd discharge his invention at approaching intruders.
Rage, indignation, tears greeted the first few zitzes from the squirt
bottle. But quickly they learned, and soon the most he had to do was
pick it up and aim it in order to guarantee his privacy.

"So what's the trouble?" Aaron Dodge asked Laura. He extended
the distance to her apartment by turning onto Black Canyon and driving south.

"I feel a little overwhelmed," Laura said. "I'm just beginning to
realize all the responsibilities. Here I am, rid of the one big one. And
now I've got a million of the little and middle-size kind."

"Six I can think of right offhand."

"I'm scared, Aaron. This is supposed to be his first weekend with
them."

Aaron Dodge knew about the arrangements. Lawyers had conferred.
Judges had ruled. Temporary rights had been granted and temporary
compensation awarded. "I'm an expert on custody proceedings. Everybody I know's been divorced at least once. Try me."

"It's terrible. He hasn't even sent a check yet."

"Perfect excuse. If you're worried, then don't let him see the kids."

"That'd be ugly of me, don't you think? Maybe if I'm fair he'll be
fair."

"I see what you mean. I doubt if you're right, but I see what you
mean. Look, I've got an idea, Laura. All you have to do is this one
thing. Tell him we'll deliver the kids. We'll drive to Tucson. He won't
have to come pick them up."

"Aaron, I believe I'm doing what's best. Don't you? I'm sure I'll see
that better once all this is settled."

"You might, you might not. Just because you do the right thing's
no sign you won't feel like shit afterward."

———

On Saturday morning, the morning they were to take the children to Tucson, the caravan rendezvoused at Ont Hazel's house in Sun City.

Aaron Dodge always enjoyed seeing Hazel, a compact, dynamic, and cheerful woman whose hairdo, reminiscent of spun aluminum, looked like one of the technological breakthroughs they're always crediting to NASA research. Her house was decorated with family photos shot against studio backdrops—groupings in which everybody's smile looked held on by clothespins that had been air-brushed out of the picture later. Several of the shots included Hazel's late husband, Kennedy and Laura's uncle, who'd died of a heart attack after failing to notice the "microwave in use" warning on the door of a restaurant where he was about to have lunch. Ont Hazel possessed a wry dignity often encountered in those who've watched the something or the someone they most cherished expire ridiculously.

When they arrived, Ont Hazel had coffee ready and some iced breakfast rolls. They were late, the way people with children always are. They found their unofficial escorts—four volunteers enlisted by the fat man—alone with Ont Hazel in her living room. One of them ran a South Phoenix tattoo parlor. Another worked as a hidesmith and specialized in bikers' leathers. The third was a Teamster who hauled truckloads of papers to substations throughout the city of Phoenix for the Arizona *Representative*. Buzz was the fourth. Seated on Ont Hazel's practical furniture, massive, stringy-haired, and dressed in inky, greasy boots and denim, they looked and smelled like they'd been sent to announce the official demands following a prison takeover.

"Kennedy, Laura, meet Rat Lips, Sausage, and Jowls. Kennedy, you remember Buzz?"

"Hi, Buzz."

"Laura, this is Buzz."

"Pleased to know you."

Sausage was holding his coffee mug by the side opposite the handle because none of his fingers would've fit through.

"These are them. The kids I told you about. Laura's."

Either they'd all elected to crowd in back of Laura, or Laura was purposely keeping herself between them and Uncle Rat Lips, Uncle Jowls, Uncle Buzz, and Uncle Sausage. Aaron Dodge thought he should explain. "I figured it would be a good idea to have several adults along."

The fat man would bring the weight. Buzz would add the height. Rat Lips, Jowls, and Sausage would supply the ugliness, strength, and air of businesslike cruelty so indispensable to a persuasive eviction squad. Laura's husband would be given a choice. Cooperate, pay up, and see the kids as planned. Don't cooperate, don't pay up, and meet Aaron Dodge's friends.

Ont Hazel volunteered her LTD to make the trip more comfortable. They left the two cars they'd come in, the El Camino and Mustang, in Ont Hazel's drive. Laura's husband was living at a new address, and Aaron Dodge could offer Rat Lips and the others only vague directions. They would follow the LTD in a traveler's-check-purple station wagon that belonged to Jowls.

They found Laura's husband living in bachelor squalor in a mostly deserted trailer court so near the air base that the concussions of takeoffs and landings occurred as regularly as traffic noise. They didn't need to search for his trailer space. They were led directly to it by loud and unmistakable evidence.

"The son of a bitch is shooting off a pistol in there," said Sausage. Another blast accompanied the statement. They'd driven past the row of trailers and parked in front of a building made official-looking by a gravel lot, Coke machine, and public phone.

"Let's waste the motherfucker," said Rat Lips. "I'm ready." A jet roared over. The children stared from behind the windows of the LTD.

Aaron Dodge went in alone. No manager's office in the building, just a long, narrow room—washers on one side, driers on the other, tables in the middle. An underfed man with stubbly gray sideburns sat on one of the tables. He wore a bathrobe and shoes with no socks. A suitcase lay open beside him. Clothes circulated in a drier behind.

"You hear that?" said the fat man.

The man looked up from the paper he was reading. "Ain't deaf."

"Hasn't anybody called the cops?"

"I ain't."

To the rear of the building, Aaron Dodge found a swimming pool with no water in it, protected by a ravaged fence with flexible slats latticed into the chain link and a sign listing hours and rules lying at the bottom. He returned to the lot. Both cars were there, but not his four friends.

Laura pointed in the direction of the trailers. "Don't go after them," Kennedy said from the back seat. "Aaron," Ont Hazel said. "Don't." They were being careful to seem calm for the kids' sake, but some of the younger ones had already started to whimper. Obviously Laura hadn't anticipated a situation anywhere near this hazardous, or she'd've left the children in Phoenix.

When he caught up, his friends were crouched behind a car parked in the driveway parallel to the trailer. Rat Lips had brought a pistol along, which he was preparing to use. A couple of metal garbage cans sat beside a redwood set of stair steps that made up the difference between ground level and the trailer's doorsill. Rat Lips fired. The one he hit must've been packed full of trash, because the impact resulted in a solid-sounding shrapnel *ka-choonk* that caused the can to rock back and forth. The second can produced an echoey clang and fell over with a rattle and crash that evidently satisfied Rat Lips. He fired twice more. The racket earned the attention of the trailer's occupant.

Following a brief siege consisting of shouted offers and counteroffers, the door swung open. Presently a hand deposited a revolver at the threshold and withdrew.

The posse advanced.

He was wearing a t-shirt and a pair of drawstring hospital greens. He stood aside. One at a time they stepped indoors, over the surrendered handgun.

A breakfast bar separated the kitchen and living room. Milk containers, beer and tunafish cans cluttered countertops. The tv was on but without the audio. At one end of the living room sat a pile of cartons, a few of them open, exposing packed belongings. To the sides of the boxes numerous beige-and-black two-hundred-foot benchrest targets had been pinned—none perforated by fewer than a dozen rounds. Another jet rumbled over.

"Taking a little target practice?" Sausage asked.

"What do you want? Where are my kids?"

"Didn't bring them," said Buzz.

"Where's Laura?"

"No child support, no children," said Jowls.

"That bitch won't see a cent of my money."

With a two-handed shove, Jowls seated him on the couch.

Sausage crowded in at his left, Rat Lips at his right.

The negotiations began.

Later, when they returned to the vehicles, they brought with them several large cartons that he'd confessed were full of Laura's and the children's things. They'd left others behind but decided not to return for them this trip. A man with a gun seldom owns just one.

"Here," Aaron Dodge said to Laura. "All the cash he had on him."

They loaded cartons into the lavender station wagon, whose finish still displayed the faint outlines of peace and flower decals that had peeled off at the end of an ancient era, and drove back to Phoenix.

The boxed belongings he'd helped free from the mobile manor in Tucson settled over the three apartments—Laura's, Kennedy's, his— like fallout from a population explosion. Sweaters the size of gloves. Shoes no bigger than Snickers bars. Little plastic soldiers painful to step on. Skinny picture books filled with gentle youngsters and patient adults, their pages savagely vandalized and sealed with snot and sugar. The six, in clusters of two, three, or more, circulated as freely as their miniature and nationally advertised possessions, threatening to erase the boundaries between separate dwellings. Not even Ont Hazel's house in Sun City escaped the invasion.

A schedule had been instituted designed to sacrifice the privacy but preserve the sanity of each of the children's coguardians—Laura with her part-time job, Kennedy with her university classes, and Ont Hazel with her obligations to church, lapidary, and lawn bowling. It was a routine whose pattern, if it had one, Aaron Dodge had yet to decipher, but didn't care to ask about either, for fear he'd be told the timetable included him.

The fat man successfully avoided opportunities to discuss the situation until he and Kennedy found themselves unexpectedly alone in his apartment one afternoon in mid-October, when somehow the six had all ended up with Laura and Ont Hazel. Either that or they'd murdered each other in a room whose location their decaying bodies had yet to divulge.

"I don't begrudge anybody a little Christian charity. Agnostic charity.

Whatever," the fat man said. "Rides, okay. Babysitting, within reasonable limits. But look at this." He pointed to the tv, the one he'd owned for nearly two decades. Its screen now blank. All the knobs yanked off, lost. Permanently tuned, the last time he'd checked, to a Spanish-speaking UHF station.

"It's temporary, Aaron."

"A week. That's temporary. Temporary is a month. This is not temporary."

"You're the one who's always talking about responsibility. I'm being responsible."

"They're not your children."

"Don't forget I am godmother to half of them."

"Doesn't that only go into effect if Laura dies or something?"

"You don't have to help if you don't want to."

"I'll contribute," said the fat man. "In my own way."

"And how's that?"

"By keeping myself fresh in case reinforcements are needed."

"You know, Aaron. I've been thinking. I just want you to consider this is all. But see if you don't think it's a terrific idea. Good for us and good for Laura too. We already spend so much of our time with each other. What if you were to move in? We could live together."

"Aren't there government agencies that assist in cases like this?"

"I wouldn't have to tell Olivia. And I could let Laura have half the rent money she's sending me." Olivia's was a name that seldom came up when he and Kennedy talked. Their age difference made the subject of parents an uncomfortable one for the fat man.

"Why can't you just ask Olivia for money straight out? Are you afraid of your own mother? And don't forget the eviction squad. More visits could always be arranged."

"Aaron, if you'd spend half as much time helping Laura as you do lining up other people to help her, pretty soon she wouldn't need any more help."

"Thanks. You're really bending me over backwards to accommodate your sister."

"You'd be helping out a lot, Aaron."

"What about Ont Hazel?"

"She's retired. She's already raised a family. Ont Hazel's doing more

than her share already. This wouldn't cost you a penny, Aaron. In fact
you'd be showing a profit every month."

"You've never lived with anybody before. It's more complicated than
this."

"Complicated how?"

"I don't know. Too complicated to explain. Trust me. I've been
through it, you haven't."

"With who? Cody? I thought you never lived with Cody. That's what
you said."

"I don't want to discuss Cody."

"You brought her up, not me."

"I'd practically moved in with her. I already told you that. She'd
asked me. Then all of a sudden—"

"—the car wreck. And you were with her?"

"This black Karmann-Ghia I used to have. She drove it to California.
She was there when she died."

"So you felt responsible?"

"I got a letter. From her mother, I think. No note, no return address.
With a newspaper clipping inside. A Xerox. You know. One-vehicle
accident, services pending. Except the date pending was about a
month past already."

Kennedy sighed. "You have an excuse for every occasion, don't you?"

"All I'm saying is, quit trying to rush me."

"Will you think about it, Aaron?"

"Let's not panic. We still have plenty of options left before people
start moving in with each other."

"But will you?"

"Consider it? Of course. Sure."

"I love you, Aaron Dodge."

"You what?"

"I said I love you."

"Your tough luck," said the fat man.

That night, as they unpacked more of the assassinated cartons in
Laura's apartment, separating the books from the bullets, Laura began
to cry.

"That man should be hung," said Kennedy.

"Do insurance companies pay claims to victims of capital punish-
ment?" Aaron Dodge wondered.

"Don't worry," Kennedy told her sister. "We'll figure something out."

The next day Aaron Dodge withdrew the contents of his account at the Camel-Op Credit Union and deposited the money in Laura's checking.

"I can't accept this," Laura said when he handed her the bank receipt. "I'll pay you back, Aaron. I promise."

"I'll help too," said Kennedy. "Maybe I should take out a Guaranteed Student Loan."

"And maybe," said the fat man. "I'm just suggesting this is all. But maybe you could consider asking *Olivia* for some help?"

"So what's new, Aaron Dodge? I hear you're moving in with your new friend."

"Where'd you hear that?" he asked Lulu.

"Well? Is it true?"

"We're discussing it."

"Don't do it," said Bob the Brush.

"I haven't decided yet. I mean she's so fucking perky and cute. Nobody that happy really understands life."

"What's wrong with living next door?" Bob said to the fat man. "Next door is plenty close."

"Financial considerations," said Lulu. "Kennedy's sister is divorcing and the husband won't pay child support. Which is so typically male."

"How'd you—"

"Buzz was in earlier. May that man of hers be struck down by a lightning bolt, is all I can say."

"God doesn't do that any more," said the fat man. "Nowadays people get targeted by the Moral Majority."

"What did you say she's studying in school?" Lulu asked.

"Hospital management. She switched over from the humanities. After she met me."

"Christ," said Bob the Brush.

"What a future," Lulu said. "For both of you. You could father children far into your fifties. Her biological clock has barely started ticking."

"It's still in the box."

"If money's the problem . . ." Bob said.

"*A* problem," said Aaron Dodge.

"If it's money you're worried about, why don't you—"

"She's got rich parents," Lulu said. "Doesn't she?"

"One," said Aaron Dodge. "Olivia."

"Can't they ask Olivia for money?"

"They don't seem to want to," said Aaron Dodge. "Don't ask me why. Pride, I suppose."

"What about the old man?" said Bob the Brush.

"Heart attack."

Bob and Lulu watched him. Silently. They didn't need to say again what they'd said too many times already.

"Stress," the fat man said quickly. "The guy's job nailed him. It had nothing to do with his weight."

Long past midnight, once he was certain Kennedy would be asleep in her own unit, he returned to the blue apartment village.

He filled the tub.

Climbed in.

Invisible grit coated the bottom and sides where Kennedy or Laura had scrubbed with cleanser. A considerate gesture? A bribe? From underwater, the fat man stared up, deciphering flecks of toothpaste on the bathroom mirror. His mirror. His toothpaste. His bathroom. Would she insist on installing skidproof rubber asterisks on the floor of his tub so Laura's six wouldn't break their necks while showering? Right now he didn't want to talk about it.

Her father was a pushy Mick from Chicago. Nothing against the Irish, nothing against Chicago, but when Franklin St. James shouldered open the bathroom door without knocking and dragged his suitcases in, he eliminated, as far as the fat man was concerned, any possibility of friendship or even civil relations. He looked like a man with nothing smaller than a fifty in his wallet and carried articles of luggage whose sizes and shapes indicated a determination to dispatch this crisis without delay and possibly work in a match or two of some racquet sport before flying home.

Until tonight's intrusion, Aaron Dodge had considered her father one of the pluses in this relationship. Like his own, Kennedy's was dead. And reminders of Franklin St. James seemed to bring out some of his daughter's most attractive qualities. Spunk, wit, a tender perversity. They told each other dead-father jokes.

"What're you getting yours this year?"

"Room deodorizer. You?"

"Nail clippers."

"I was thinking a worm farm."

"A skylight maybe?"

"A field guide to molds."

"I'm ordering mine a video cassette. *Pink Flamingos.*"

"I don't get it."

"An underground classic."

Franklin St. James set down his bags, one of which he straddled and used for a chair.

So.

You're the boyfriend.

All right. Okay. Didn't expect anybody quite so . . .

Flamboyant. But . . .

He rubbed his palms together. Placed them on his knees. Stood up. Paced. He opened the medicine cabinet and explored with a finger, moving aside pill bottles, probing behind Band-Aid boxes.

Know what I was doing when I was your age?

Aaron Dodge answered from the deepest part of the tub. Porcelain and water translated the remark into bubbles and a noisy *Quorrrrrk!*

Franklin St. James colored briefly, but continued.

What're you? Thirty? Thirty-five? Boyfriend, you better take a look at yourself. That car out there dropped off the blue book ten years ago. And still living in apartments? No equity? Tell me, where would a person like yourself get credit? Dickey's Quick-Loan maybe. Not at any bank I know about. Even assuming you had the cash to get started, you realize what life insurance would cost you a month? At your age?

All I see here is a couple of rooms full of gadgets. I doubt half that stuff even operates. I know. An inventor. Creative. Aaron's Enterprises, right? But what have you *done,* boyfriend? Because that's all anybody is, see? You are what you do, not what you say you'll do. Or wish you could do or thought you'd do or might do. And boyfriend, you aren't what your buddies do, either. Or what some group you belong to or some charity you give to does. I'm what I do. You're what you do. Understand me, boyfriend?

He returned to the medicine cabinet.

Stared inside.

The fat man expected some comment like: Where's the roll-on? The mouthwash? The name brands? But instead Franklin St. James reached carefully inside and withdrew a tube of contraceptive gel. He turned it lengthwise and regarded the side on which ingredients and instructions were printed. He slapped it once across his open palm like a blackjack. Without turning to face him, he spoke to Aaron Dodge.

Better not let Olivia see this, boyfriend.

Not unless she sees a diamond along with it.

Olivia? Did he think Aaron Dodge was afraid of her? And a diamond. Even more ridiculous. A commitment, emotionally and financially, far beyond the fat man's means. Still, the essentials of Franklin St. James' lecture had penetrated. Time to nuke or shut the microwave, boyfriend. That fatherly advice, along with Kennedy's shy proposal, constituted a persuasive argument. But Aaron Dodge, a bachelor, naturally required reasons of his own before he'd consider disrupting his routine. In addition to the usual romantic justifications, these included the collection agency his landlords had sicced on him the previous summer. Their requests for remittance had long ago escalated past friendly reminders and gentlemanly protests to direct insults and threats. One lunchtime not long after the arrival of the most recent notice, he opened his door and found the woman from apartment number one on the other side, her finger aimed at his stomach.

"That's him," she said to a man accompanying her, who shrugged and with a nod redirected Aaron Dodge's attention to the woman from number one. "My wife. Every day she's here waiting for you. 'He's never home,' she tells me. So I say to her, 'This guy's never home. What're you doing waiting for him to get back? A guy that's never home, you catch him on his way out.' "

Aaron Dodge assured the couple from apartment one that he intended to remit. "I'm moving," he said. "My plans are the same."

The fat man remitted on a Saturday in late October. A quarterly installment of his self-employment tax was overdue, and he couldn't afford it and November rent both. A yes to Kennedy would belatedly honor the thirty days' notice he'd given his landlords four—or was it five?—months before. The move, when it finally came, covered a distance of fifteen feet, from one side of the wall separating their units to the other. But not, as it turned out, from his side to hers. The fat man, as he had so often in his life up to now, managed to reproduce an amazing effect. He elicited the aid of an old, trusted, and loyal friend. Not movement, but the illusion of movement.

The fat man was an inventor. You know. Imaginative. Occasionally bold, frequently observant. He'd noticed before, and his visitors and friends agreed, that at the blue apartment village, as in most other giant complexes, numbers seemed to have been painted on doors by an author of mathematics inference test questions who'd lost his job because his were too hard. A skier buried by an avalanche would've had better luck telling up from down, east from west, 3A from 4A, than Aaron Dodge and his neighbors. Because moving into Kennedy's apartment would've meant relocating his bedroom workshops, picking up and putting down unfinished projects representing half a decade of rejection and frustration—a prospect too gruesome for the fat man to entertain—he decided instead to add further to the numeric confusion surrounding him.

He unhinged their two blue doors and exchanged the one with his address on it for Kennedy's. They emptied her apartment. Cleaned the oven and tub. Aaron Dodge notified the couple in number one that he'd vacated. In a characteristic Aaron Dodge manuever, the fat man succeeded in evading his previous obligations as a tenant, transferring subsequent responsibility to Kennedy, and abandoning a location he'd never occupied—all without ever actually going anyplace.

"You took her address," Lulu said to him the following week at Camel-Op. "How romantic. It's almost like agreeing to take her name or something, isn't it?"

"Maybe I'll keep both addresses and add a hyphen in the middle."

Before he finished breakfast, a store worker beckoned him to the phone in the stockroom. Kennedy calling. "Did Laura give you money?" she asked.

"She paid me back. Out of what Olivia sent you this month for rent."

"Do me a favor, Aaron? Tear up that check? She wouldn't say so, but Laura really does need it."

"I already cashed it." Actually the check was still in his pocket. He'd planned to deposit it as soon as the credit union opened.

Kennedy was silent for some time before she said, "Do what you think's best, Aaron," and hung up.

Disenchanted, he returned to his breakfast. But before he could take another bite, a second call interrupted. Tulane Wiggins. First Friday of the month. Tonight at Ernesto's. Again he climbed back on the corner stool. For the third time Lulu served the breakfast he'd ordered. She'd been attempting to preserve it under one of the phenol-free heat lamps that illuminated a stainless-steel sill in the window separating her from the cook. The fat man, considering his spongy eggs, his solidified waffles, quickly lost his appetite.

At lunch he managed to evade the subject of the check, still in his shirt pocket. Kennedy wouldn't mention it in front of Laura. But obviously the financial dismemberment they'd all three been undergoing occupied their minds. That night at the supper table the tension began to show.

"What is this?" Brett asked.

"I don't like it," Sylvia said, and pointed with her fork.

"Me either."

"Eat it," the fat man said, and pointed with his.

It had been his idea that Laura become a Camel-Op member. The monthly food budget for her and her six required no statistical enhancement. It was enough to feed a family of seven for a month. In exchange for a couple of hours a week of carrot sacking and cheese chopping, Laura could buy groceries at ten percent off. The discount helped. And mimeographed recipes were available free at the checkout stand. But you could get away with calling millet and buckwheat groats Rice a Roni just so often.

"Falafel," Kennedy said. "It's good—" *For you,* she seemed about to say, but censored herself.

"Will it make us grow up big and strong?" Sylvia asked.

"Like Uncle Aaron?" Brett asked. "I don't want to be that big."

Everybody giggled. Brett and Sylvia, the two oldest, the two with the most practice, often teamed up this way to increase their mother's—and uncle's—miseries.

"Just try one bite," said Laura. "You'll like it I bet."

"No I won't. It's squash."

"Eat it," said Aaron Dodge.

"It is not squash. It isn't even the same color. Look, Aunt Kennedy likes it."

"Yum," said Kennedy.

"No dessert unless you take at least three bites."

"What's dessert? Grass?"

"No," Sylvia said. "Dirt."

"Eat it," said Aaron Dodge.

"I don't have to. You're not my—"

"Hush! You're to mind your Uncle Aaron, you hear me?" Laura grabbed his arm and twisted. "I don't *ever* want to hear you talk that way again!" She yanked him off his chair, shaking him with one hand, swatting at his backside with the other. Tugging so violently that she whiffed on two of three tries. Finally she returned him, blushing and disoriented, to his chair, and the meal continued in silence.

They'd drive you absolutely batshit if you let them. But that was only seventy, eighty percent of the time. Some days, when they welcomed him home, the fat man would crouch at the front door. Boost one of the smaller girls, Heather or Holland, onto his back. Stand and shrug her, giggling, over a shoulder. Pass her behind him. Hoist her into the air two-handed, catch her, and lift her piggyback astride his giant neck. While the others tugged at his arms and pant legs, begging turns.

He was so much bigger.

But there were so many more of them.

At just before seven o'clock, the fat man scooted his chair away from the table, and with his half-finished supper escaped to the living room. He plugged the set in, then proceeded to the bathroom, scraped his plate, and flushed.

La Low-tay-REE-yah! Low-tay-REE-yah! Low-tay-REEEE-yah!

Short and round, with a clipped graying mustache and wavy black hair, Jackpot Jack wore tasseled loafers. A two-tone Western-style shirt with pearl snaps. A bolo tie secured by a silver dollar-sign inlaid with turquoise.

Moo-cho dee-naaaaaaaaay-ro!

He spoke as if attached intravenously to a keg of adrenaline stored off-camera, pausing at frequent and clearly unbiased intervals—mid-paragraph, mid-sentence, mid-word—to translate English to Spanish or vice versa.

Gar-GAHN-chew-wahn!

This week the fat man had bet the ISBN number of a paperback that kept accosting him at the supermarket checkout stand. You know. One of the ones whose covers identify the author in letters twice the size of the title. But it had evidently exhausted all its luck on its way up the best-seller list. Aaron Dodge unplugged the set, yelled, "Bye, everybody!" and left the apartment, pocketing his receipt. Jackpot Jack's latest enticement guaranteed a free chance for every five losing chances you collected.

What he'd seen so far of November seemed a copy of the previous May. Relentlessly scorching and oppressive. Doubly, since spring and fall were seasons when, even in the desert, you anticipated periods of relief. During the drive to South Phoenix, KKGB announced the temperature following every record. Still above a hundred. Even higher inside the El Camino. He found the lot behind Ernesto's empty. At this hour? On a Friday? The front door, propped open, offered a depressing explanation. Hot enough to bake brownies in there.

"Hey, buddy! Hey, you! Hold it. Hold on. Be fixed any minute. Got somebody working on it now." The bartender pointed with an empty beer glass to ductwork mounted on the ceiling. "Sixteen-seventy-five an hour. Better be any minute." He filled the glass. Set it on the bar. "Complimentary, my friend."

At half past eight Tulane still hadn't arrived, but at least the refrigeration seemed to be operating. Vents overhead rattled and sighed. The man responsible sat to Aaron Dodge's left, a stool away. An Olympia. A Merit. A haircut so short you could count the moles on his temple through it.

"Freon?" Aaron Dodge asked him. "Compressor?"

This guy was almost as fat as him. He wore a striped uniform shirt with a navy blue "Carrier" logo sewn on the back. He pulled a wadded handkerchief out of his hip pocket and toweled his neck with it.

"Thermostat? V-belt?"

"Bearings. 'Bout like so." Without looking at Aaron Dodge, he indicated their size, pressing a thumbnail into the tip of his pinkie.

By ten Ernesto's was comfortable inside. And full. They'd shoved aside the empty stool between them, the two fat men, and were starting to tell each other things. Funny things. Sad things. Exactly the kinds of things Aaron Dodge needed to hear and say tonight. Olivia came up. So did Mary Vanessa Singer. And the check still folded in Aaron

Dodge's pocket. When Tulane finally interrupted, Aaron Dodge had almost forgotten he was overdue.

Equally drunk, they each had a lecture ready, he and Tulane—more irritated, probably, with the legalities enforcing this partnership than with each other. "Man, you post to be the responsible one. Why I half a be huntin' you ass down all a time? What you try a do, put me back to jail?"

"Hey, it's ten o'fuckin' clock. If you were still delivering papers for me, you'd've been fired two hours ago."

The previous month's meeting had taken place at the apartment Tulane, his wife, and their two kids shared with his mother-in-law. The number of times the phone rang during the visit, and the number of rings he counted the times Tulane chose not to answer, had given Aaron Dodge more of an indication than he wanted of the nature of Tulane's then current profession. Hustling a buck that way might've been okay in 1970 for Aaron Dodge and his friends, but Tulane, at his age, in these times, with his record, ought to have been behaving more discreetly. So he was happy to hear that the present month had produced for Tulane Wiggins a situation he hadn't enjoyed since he'd quit the *Representative* in '75. Employment.

"I'm chauffeurin' watchdogs," he told the fat man.

"Great. Sounds good."

"It eats dick, man. Five in the damn morning. Drivin' this like dog-pound truck all over town. Gettin' bit by them Doberman Pinchers. Man, I post to be carryin' a gun, even. Only they won't let me, 'cause a my arrest."

"If you pick the dogs up, somebody must deliver. Pretty soon, you do a good job, maybe you'll be working afternoons."

"Shit no. Boss, he drops 'em off hisself. All I do's get bit and shovel turds. Man, I thought you was movin'. What you still doin' here?"

The fat man shrugged. "I met somebody. You know. A woman."

Tulane laughed. "Man, you 'bout as dumb as me, ain't you? Listen. I got to ax you a favor. Temporary I need like a cash loan off you, man. What you say? My old lady, you know? Her mama sick."

"Tulane, you probably won't believe this, but right now—"

"Now, don't you be like that. I know you got to have *somethin'* to lent her, man."

"Not just now. I don't, Tulane."

"You some kind a inventor, ain't you?"

Aaron Dodge shrugged.

"Man, you ever invent anything I might a seen?"

"I don't know. Probably not. I invented this kind of automatic stop that keeps typewriters from typing off the end of the page."

"A which?"

"A line-feed counter attachment."

"No shit. What they give you on a idea like that?"

"I'll collect royalties. If they decide to manufacture it."

"You old lady got a mama too, don't she?"

The fat man smiled. "Sorry. Can't, Tulane."

"That's okay, man. I get the money myself. I know where I get it."

"Be careful, now."

"Man, you ain't leavin' me no choice."

"What's wrong with her? Your mother-in-law?"

"Sugar die-beat-us? I don't know. I think somethin' like that. She old, man."

"I don't think I met her last month, did I? When I visited your place?"

"Man, great idea! You come on meet her. I interduce you."

"Maybe another night."

"You got to a lease do that. Man, I ain't axin' you for no million bucks."

Aaron Dodge picked up a dead Olympia with his left hand, invested as much of his current state of mind as the can would hold, and crushed it. He looked around. Sometime during the past hour, the fat man he'd spent the evening with had left without him.

They loaded Tulane's bicycle in the bed of the El Camino and drove to his South Phoenix neighborhood. Fire escapes, barred windows, lawns of packed earth, garbage cans bashed in and overturned in the street. Tulane introduced him to the old woman, whose print dress reminded him of the walls of rooms he'd grown up in. She was heavy, silent, gray-headed, and wore rimless glasses that she frequently nudged back onto her nose with a finger as she rocked, the attention of her eyes and hands divided between the television and the sewing on her lap.

Tulane and his wife invited the fat man to their kitchen. "She looks okay to me," he told them. "I mean for her age. How old is she?"

"She forgets stuff," Tulane's wife said. "She'll like be talking to you and say the same thing she just said about five times in a row or something."

"What's she taking? Any medications?"

Tulane opened a cupboard. On one of the shelves the fat man saw a cluster of prescription bottles. Half a dozen at least. None of his friends were doctors, but he gathered up the amber pill bottles and took them to the phone. He woke Ont Hazel and read her the labels. A heart decongestant, a blood-pressure stabilizer. Antidepressants, mood stimulators.

He asked Tulane and his wife if either of them supervised the old woman. Was she taking the right pills the right number of times per day? Could she be forgetting the heart and taking four blood pressures instead? Mixing up bottles, mismatching colors? Didn't they realize that indifferent physicians could well be prescribing new pills based on symptoms produced by incorrect dosages and dangerous combinations of other pills and charging their mistakes to Medicaid?

Tulane and his wife looked at each other.

Neither of them spoke.

Then the fat man remembered. Practically children. Not even twenty yet. As young as Kennedy. A few aging illusions—mothers, doctors, probation supervisors—still stood between them and permanent disenchantment.

They were both staring at the fat man.

"He can't," Tulane told his wife finally. "He ain't got no money to lent us."

Nearly a week passed before Kennedy finally coerced an explanation from Aaron Dodge.

"Aaron, what finally happened to that check? Laura said it cleared. Is that true? You kept it? After what I said?"

"I spent it," said the fat man.

"On what?"

He shrugged. "Look, I don't have to account to you for every cent I spend. It was mine."

Aaron Dodge avoided the argument by leaving before it began. But he didn't find any sympathy at Camel-Op either. "You stupid shit," Bob the Brush told him. "I've heard of knee-jerk liberals, but you're twitching like a dissected frog hitched to electrodes."

"It was a loan."

Bob laughed. "He'll spend it all on weed and crack. You know that, don't you?"

"Fuck you."

When he got home from Camel-Op, late, he found Laura waiting up for him. Smoking a cigarette, watching tv.

"I spent it," he told her. "I spent the goddam money. All right?"

"Ont Hazel told us about your phone call."

The fat man stared at the screen. Facial tints fluctuated infra- to ultra-fleshtone, modulating eventually to the sickly greenish shade of the stripe on an unsold white sidewall. He whacked the chassis with his open palm. Pounded with a fist. "She was a nice old lady. She needed it more than me."

"Or me."

"Maybe. What are you going to do now?"

"I don't know."

Olivia arrived on a cloudless Tuesday. Flew in aboard a jumbo that seated forty across. That left Chicago after dark and reached Phoenix in the daylight, landing at Sky Harbor an hour and a half before it took off from O'Hare.

She misaimed a kiss at the cheek of each of her daughters, then bent to crush the children's faces to her abdomen. They'd had room to bring only two. Heather. Anthony. She handed the girl a stuffed animal that looked like it had been purchased on the premises.

"Total," Heather said. It was a turtle.

In a concourse lounge, Olivia paid for soft drinks and cocktails, revealing, when she opened her pocketbook, enough plastic to shingle a roof. She was tall. Plump. Expensively dressed. Her complexion looked like it had been finished with a belt sander and primed with a coat of beige spraypaint. As they drove home from the airport, Aaron Dodge glanced in the rearview mirror and realized, alerted by Olivia's expression, that they'd forgotten to remove the green bedspread from the back seat.

The fat man hadn't been polite to anybody in years. By the third day of her visit, he was exhausted. He spent most of his time—even more of his time than usual—underwater or at bars and diners in order to elude her.

"Her sunglasses are worth more than my car," he told the pretty countergirl, probably not out of high school yet, if junior high, at the Winchell's on West McDowell. Her bodice labeled her "Ashli." A headful of gum. A machine-gun giggle she interrupted herself with every few seconds.

"She goes for those restaurants where the waiters wear cummerbunds and the check arrives in a little notebook."

Ashli giggled.

Though he supposed Olivia was a harmless and pretty much average American mother, she and her tiresome ostentatiousness left the fat man with a sudden urge to talk to his own mom, and he asked Ashli for change to make the call. He'd expected Olivia to be more like Esther Dodge, who was generous even if she'd seldom enjoyed the means to fully implement her good intentions. In fact she probably didn't enjoy those means precisely *because* she was so generous. He dialed the house on Encantero Drive from the Winchell's public phone. When a man answered—husband number seven—Aaron Dodge realized that he'd failed to remind himself that his mom had been working third shift at one of the semiconductor plants on the East Side. He hung up without speaking and returned to his coffee.

Only one sitdown customer—the fat man. So Ashli passed the time by filling up cute Hallmarks with a kelly-green fountain pen of impractical diameter. She held it as if she rarely used one, rigidly upright between a thumb and knuckle.

"Snazzy ink."

She giggled.

The Muzak tape played "The Age of Aquarius."

Around midnight, the donut chef pushed through a swinging door that led to the kitchen, wiping his hands on the skirt of his apron—white like the rest of his uniform and splotched with yellowish circlets of grease. He scooted onto the counter. Lit a Marlboro.

"How you are doing, my friend? Again out late after dark, I see. Welcome." His name was Dibadj. Iranian. But careful to call himself "Persian" since Khomeini.

"How is my Lulu?"

Dibadj was an acquaintance of Lulu's. A little more than that, actually. He was her husband. Sort of. They didn't live together; in fact, they didn't communicate at all except through Aaron Dodge. A couple of years ago Lulu had needed five hundred bucks. Dibadj required a green card. The fat man had arranged the marriage for his two friends.

"She says hello."

"Good. I too. And if she wants to know am I doing well, tell her please yes."

The fat man nodded.

Ordered another long john from Ashli.

Dibadj picked up a newspaper from the countertop.

In Phoenix, if you were looking for a cop this time of night, the all-hours donut shops tended to be a better bet than 911. Two came in and sat at a booth after ordering chop sueys and hot chocolate.

"Officers," Dibadj called to them. "Welcome, my friends." He frowned, redirecting his attention to the paper he held open before him.

"Please what is a mud race?" he asked without looking up.

Aaron Dodge saw the two cops glance at him.

"A bunch of drunk cowboys drive their four-by-fours and bigfoots full-speed at a mudhole. Make it through, you win. Get stuck, you lose. Most people get stuck."

Dibadj nodded.

Ashli giggled.

Aaron Dodge had seen the article that seemed to be confusing Dibadj. That weekend a group of mud racers had transported their trucks and kegs to a wash on the Agua Fria—a crossing where water pooled after flash floods. For most of a day they drank and attacked the saturated ground. Then, near sunset, while his friends winched out an unsuccessful competitor, somebody noticed among the ruts and wallows an object churned up by the wheels of their machines. A tennis shoe. A child's shoe. With a Velcro strap instead of laces. The police searched up and down the Agua Fria all the next day. No further evidence.

When the two cops' breaktime ended, they ordered coffees to go. As they left, the fat man climbed off his stool. Paying his bill, he paused at the register. Volunteers had distributed homemade collection containers at some of his favorite diners, usually at the checkstand, near the toothpick dispenser and the display of unbreakable combs. This one was a coffee can, a slot cut in its plastic lid, a mailer bearing a photo of Mary Vanessa Singer and a solicitation taped to the front. The fat man stuffed in a donation, though the amount, the few dollars, would likely be missed at home.

"Aaron," Dibadj said. He accented the second syllable. "Tell her please this for me. Tell I am saving. Tell I am an honest man."

"Sure," the fat man said. "I will." Dibadj meant saving for their divorce—part two of his arrangement with Lulu.

He returned to the blue apartment village at what he assumed would be a safe hour. Olivia was supposed to be sleeping at Ont Hazel's in Sun City. He didn't disturb Kennedy. He found her curled up, wearing a bathrobe of his, in a chair near the television, its screen covered with electronic snow the color of sifted glitter. By its light he undressed and hung his pants and shirt on a bedpost of the Bunkport, which somebody had taken the trouble to assemble for him, then unplugged the set.

As he climbed into the bottom bunk, he encountered an obstacle.

The warmish, solid mound heaved up once. Snorted. Groaned. Thrashed. The fat man stumbled backward, bumped the coffee table, lost his balance, fell.

Furniture crashing into furniture.

A papery cascade.

Toppled objects thudding to the carpet.

"Aaron!"

Kennedy grabbed him from behind and pressed her face close to his ear. *"What are you doing?"*

"What the hell's going on?" He pointed to his bed.

"It's Mother. She decided to stay over. She wasn't feeling well."

Olivia had evidently slept through the disturbance. They watched her together. Her bulk had resettled except for an arm and hand that extended from underneath the bedclothes, beyond the boundary of the mattress. They listened. She smacked her lips loudly, persistently, as if trying to dislodge molasses from the roof of her mouth. Then she was silent.

Kennedy laughed quietly against his neck. "I wish I'd been awake to see it."

"We didn't need an audience, we needed a referee."

"Sinus. She says she gets sinus. She says it's all the transplanted vegetation around here. Pollen or whatever. She says they should've never brought any of that stuff to the desert. She says when she used to come here with Daddy—"

He looked past his shoulder at her. Smiled. Touched her cheek. She smiled back, and her hands wandered downward, across his chest. He lifted an arm, she ducked underneath, he brought her closer and kissed her. He saw her glance once at the Bunkport as he rolled onto his back and pulled her on top of him. She laughed, resisted for a moment, then pressed against him. She unbelted the robe and spread it open to cover them both.

"*Shhh,*" she said. "Be careful, Aaron. Be quiet."

The next morning Olivia and Laura needed the Mustang for sight-seeing, so Aaron Dodge drove Kennedy to ASU. On the way she admitted that she and her mom had talked. About him.

"Wha'd she say?"

Kennedy sat on a wire milk crate, her book bag on her lap. The El Camino's passenger seat was still junkbound someplace in his bedroom workshop back at the blue apartment village. "You can probably guess," she said.

"Twice your age. Three times your size. Shitcan the fucker. And you said?"

"How much you'd helped Laura and the kids. How you were patient. Gentle. Resourceful. And I guess, in your own way, mature."

"And she said, Shitcan the gentle, mature, *resourceful* fucker. Right?"

"She was diabolical, Aaron. She started telling me what all my high school friends were doing. That I should apply at Champaign-Urbana. She wants to fly me home for Christmas."

"And?"

"I told her to send me the price of a ticket."

The El Camino swerved. Aaron Dodge glanced at Kennedy. She was smiling. "The *price* of a ticket, Aaron. The money." She reached across and placed her hand over his on the steering wheel.

As usual, he wondered who she was seeing when she looked at him this way. Kennedy had this peculiar ability, it seemed. To respond as strongly to potential as to fact. Sort of like an experienced contractor who walks into a building and, squinting, holds up his clipboard to mask what isn't up to code, mentally completing a total renovation to replace the dump you currently live in.

Her misgivings concerning the fat man didn't shorten Olivia's stay any. But it looked like putting up with her would prove worth it. At the airport, a week from the day she'd arrived, in one of the concourse lounges, she signed a check, using a tiny gold pen she slid from a leather sheath beside her pocketbook calculator. She ripped it out, folded it, and handed it to her daughter with a businesslike smile that seemed to say: Laura dear. Only one sin is more deserving of scorn than screwing up your marriage, and that is screwing up your divorce. Only one weakness outranks needing help, and that, love, is asking for it.

On their way out of the terminal, aboard a moving sidewalk which carried them in that direction, Kennedy kept asking her big sister: How much? How much? Finally Laura reached into her purse and unfolded the check. What she saw halted her in her tracks on the treadmill.

Kennedy turned and hurried upstream to where she stood. Took the check from her. Examined it. Handed it to Aaron Dodge with a panicked expression.

That night, with Laura and Kennedy nearby exchanging worried looks, he called Max Yoder's home number. For legal not personal advice, but Max offered some of both.

"Obviously she disapproves of you, Aaron. Clearly she's punishing you and Kennedy by punishing Laura. Plus she probably believes that by withholding support she'll force Laura to return to her husband. That's my personal opinion. Don't you tend to agree? Aaron? Are you there? Okay, sorry. I'm butting in, aren't I? As I was about to say, legally, financially, her situation might be more defensible. Olivia may not have all that much money to offer. Unsound judgment, poor investments, irresponsible estate planning. These things happen all the time nowadays."

"So do cruelty, intolerance, and greed, Max."

"Kennedy's father is deceased. Am I right?"

"When did I tell you that?"

"And some years before his death he divorced Olivia. Correct?"

"She divorced him. Did somebody talk to you about this already?"

"I've seen it all before, Aaron. Imagine the scenario. Mr. and Mrs. Gray divorce. Mr. Gray agrees to alimony and child-support payments. Fine. Temporarily. But eventually he remarries, thus increasing, perhaps doubling, the number of his heirs. So, when he dies, what happens to his money? If the children get their inheritance at this point, fine again. But what if Mr. Gray leaves everything to his second wife, the new Mrs. Gray? And what if the new Mrs. Gray then remarries? Becomes Mrs. White? Naturally Mrs. White's loyalties reside with her own children—the late Mr. Gray's stepchildren. And Mr. White, her new husband, also has one, maybe two sets of heirs to consider. He's probably never even *met* Mr. Gray's children. Will the White estate include provisions for the Gray children? Likely not.

"Meanwhile the original Mrs. Gray has also remarried. She's now Mrs. Black. If the Gray children are fortunate, Mr. Black is responsible. Has assets of his own. But if he isn't, if he's a spendthrift or scoundrel— well, I think you see what can happen, Aaron. The Black estate may not benefit the Gray children any more than the White estate did. The predicament even has a name," Max told him.

"Birthright dilution," Aaron Dodge announced as he hung up. Another contemporary phenomenon that had become commonplace before the fat man knew it existed.

About the time winter should've been approaching, fall arrived. The fashionable Scottsdale stores imported leaves that had fallen elsewhere for the mannequins on Fifth Avenue to walk on. Laura, Kennedy, and the fat man waited. Frugally, whenever possible. The November check didn't show. Not by the fifteenth. Or by the twentieth. Finally the husband unfisted. The amount didn't correspond to the court-determined figure, but Laura would've accepted it. The eviction squad, though, vetoed her objections and reassembled for a second trip to Tucson. Her husband seemed to have run out of either spunk or ammo. He fired only once from inside as they approached the trailer. Inaccurately. (Due, the fat man speculated, to the broken finger on his shooting hand which probably hadn't healed yet.) They brought another inadequate check, signed illegibly and with the left hand, back to Laura and her six. Her husband, the fat man warned Laura, had sunk into a mudbank of detachment and isolation from which neither insult, harassment, nor outright assault would budge him.

The Sunday after Thanksgiving, Aaron Dodge visited the trailer court alone. By this time disenchantment had claimed the premises irretrievably. He'd hauled away the trash, mopped the floors, stacked the magazines, and installed a weight machine in the corner that the bulky possessions of a household of eight had once occupied. The fat man found him lying on a bench upholstered in candy-apple vinyl, pressing 240 pounds, making the noise of hydraulic brakes as he breathed in and out. The showdown was brief.

"They're your children," Aaron Dodge reminded him. "Sylvia, Heather, Holland, Brent."

"Brett," Laura's husband grunted. "No they're not. Not any more."

"You can't say that."

"It was her decision. She left. Took the kids. They're her responsibility now."

A thunderous sonic boom rattled the trailer windows.

"Don't you want to see them?"

He opened a closet door with a mirror attached to the inside and inspected himself. "Sure, I'll see them. Tell her to bring them around. But I don't owe her anything. Not a nickel."

After the drive home he reported to Laura and Kennedy. "Stay away from him," he told Laura. "I saw it. He has that look in his eye. 'I'm going to court anyway. Divorce, manslaughter—makes no difference to me.'"

"But I thought you said he has the place all cleaned up," said Kennedy.

"That's what I mean. Living contentedly in tiny, immaculate quarters? Clocks wound, rugs flat, four hubcaps on his car? A bachelor? Believe me, I was scared."

"That's normal for him," Laura said. "He's always been that way. Fussy, impeccable, compulsive."

"I guess you'd know. But still . . ."

A postcard arrived at the beginning of December. Laura's husband evidently had decided to neaten up financial arrangements along with closets and countertops. The house he and Laura owned, vacant since summertime, could be rented to winter visitors if she approved. But first they'd need to divide and remove any belongings that remained inside.

"Don't," Aaron Dodge advised. But they both knew Laura needed the money the rental would assure.

Immediately he phoned Buzz. His friend spoke for the rest of the eviction squad as well when he said, "The fifteenth? Of December? Sorry, man. You know we take the bikes down to Mexico every year this time. Pie de la Cuesta by Christmas, man."

Laura agreed to meet her husband in two weeks, on a Sunday, at their unoccupied home in the suburbs of Tucson.

8

Living with somebody.

Wow.

Your toilet-paper consumption doubled immediately. You returned from grocery shopping with fifty bucks' worth of gum and shampoo and nothing to cook for supper. There was never gas in your car. Diet-soda cans rolled from under the seat at every red light. The first day, you both forgot how to look for anything you'd misplaced and instead constantly demanded of each other, "Okay, where'd you put it?"

Cohabitation did have its moments, though. From the beginning, Laura's six, when they stayed over, regularly brought to the fat man science and arithmetic questions they'd saved from school—plus other, tougher questions. Uncle Aaron, what makes the wind blow? Is a scorpion a baby lobster? Why do paralyzed people wear coats? Do you believe in God, Uncle Aaron? And you had to think. You were supposed to know. Forget answers like *Well, sweetheart, I do believe in like a positive force that resides within each of us and sort of unites mankind in a, you know, spiritual way.* Save that kind of trash for adults. And Kennedy? Her presence also called on talents he hadn't exercised in a while. One night she bashfully followed the kids with a question of her own, a problem from statistics. He remembered an applicable formula out of an engineering text he'd read. In the middle of writing it for her, he looked up. They smiled at each other. "Too much," he said. "I'm helping her with her homework."

Privacy, though, became a precious commodity. A vague assurance that crisis awaited every time he returned to the blue apartment village made absences from home doubly alluring. "Tell her you need space," Lulu advised him. Wendy Wendy said he should call from payphones several times daily and leave self-affirming messages on his answering machine. Instead, one afternoon when Kennedy returned from classes, he said to her: "I think maybe I'll, oh, I don't know, maybe check into a motel tonight or something."

"Fine," Kennedy said, and began to cry.

"It's the kids. They're really bugging me."

"Fine. You don't have to explain."

"It isn't you. Honestly."

"I know. I don't mind."

"Thanks. I appreciate this. Just one night, it's not a big deal." He opened the closet and brought out a small plaid satchel.

"What did I do, Aaron?"

"Nothing. I told you it was the kids."

"I'm sorry."

He packed a t-shirt, a bathrobe. His toothbrush and razor.

"At least leave me the address where you'll be."

"You promise you won't—"

"I'll stay away. I won't call."

He tore a corner off one of the nihilistic crayon drawings taped to the icebox door.

"Only if there's an emergency."

They compromised. While Kennedy watched, he looked up the phone number of a motor court in Glendale, thumbing first to several decoy locations in the book so as not to betray the alphabetical position of the motel's name. He left Kennedy clutching the scrap of art on which he'd written the number.

"Goodbye, Aaron. I love you."

He had fun anyway. He watched a tv that worked. Called out for pizza. Sampled one of each flavor from the soft-drink machine in the motel breezeway. He ignored the phone the first time Kennedy called. And the second through sixth times too. He napped on the double bed.

Sometime between midnight and dawn, he filled the bathtub. Climbed in. He slid under, as far as the narrow, shallow tub permitted, feeling like the most prominent topographical feature of a lake bed exposed by drought. Soon, and not unexpectedly, a visitor opened the door and walked in.

Cody wore a sweatshirt and a pair of those Lycra Spandex jogging tights that could make you follow a woman ten blocks in the direction opposite where you thought you wanted to go. She said hi. Turned to inspect herself in the mirror. Borrowed his pocket comb from the pants that hung on the back of the door and began to work it through her hair.

I like this new friend of yours. Very much, I have to say. For one thing, Aaron Dodge, she's intelligent.

She tore a bristly knot of tangled blonde from the teeth of the comb, frisked it between her fingers, and let it glide to the bathroom floor.

Which is good. I guess. As long as you've discussed her plans. Three more years in Phoenix while she finishes college? Graduate school? All I worry about is her group of friends. Will you fit in, Aaron Dodge? You with your one semester at Glendale Community? Then she graduates and it's—what?—fifty thou a year? How will it feel when all the mail arrives addressed to her? When your friends start to refer to you as "Kennedy and Aaron" instead of vice versa? So many adjustments, Aaron Dodge. But it'll be worth it. Don't you think?

She picked up a miniature soap from beside the sink and smelled it through its wrapper. Lifted the lid and broke the sanitized band sealing the commode.

She's so beautiful, Aaron Dodge. Such a lovely young woman. But with the AIDS scare and all, I'm sure you won't have to worry about affairs.

This is going to be good for you. I approve. Definitely. Even if it doesn't last. Aaron Dodge, the woman you finally decide to settle down with will reap the ultimate benefits of this fiery little fling. You realize that, don't you? Because listen. You'll learn to stay home more. Less caffeine. Moderate hours.

She switched on the high-intensity lamp recessed in the ceiling.

Did you say she's entering the health-care field? Good. She'll have you on a diet in no time. You know. Never eat standing up. Keep your television at least two rooms from the room in which you eat your meals. Cover all leftovers with opaque wrapping materials and store in the freezer. You'll spend the rest of your life squeezing lemon wedges over three-ounce salads. Sounds nummy, huh? But really. I hope it works out, Aaron Dodge. Congratulations.

Cody gently pulled the bathroom door closed behind her as she left. He heard her slam the outer door shut with conviction on her way from the motel room. Underwater, the fat man smiled. Her visit expanded a view of feminine nature Aaron Dodge had secretly held since his first argument with a member of the opposite sex. Now he knew. Not even the grave could confine a woman's jealousy.

At checkout time he returned with his plaid satchel to the apartment, refreshed, an inventor again, happy in spite of all the reasons he shouldn't've been. He drew an installment of "Aaron's Inventory."

Always finding chewed-up bits of wood in your salsas and daiquiris? Next time you use the blender, don't mangle another spoon. Open a package of choppable, whippable, pureeable, edible—yet flavorless—"SpinStirs," the culinary concept of Finley Sykes, Glover, VT.

Then he found, wedged upright between the salt and pepper shakers on the kitchen table, a note from Kennedy. Those half-dozen calls the previous night. They hadn't been hers. They'd been calls from the faceless, educated spokesman that represented Tulane Wiggins in the mail and over the phone. He heard the voice again when he played back the messages on his answering machine. "Mr. Lewis Dodge? Please meet with Mr. Tulane Wiggins at . . ." and an address and time followed.

But the address wasn't the address of Ernesto's.

And somebody besides Tulane Wiggins waited for him there.

He didn't have the high-pitched, quacking nasal voice, abbreviated, pudgy limbs, or largish head that the fat man had always associated with midgets. He was proportioned like an ordinary boy of twelve or thirteen. He said his name was Magdalena. With him was a man named Phil Dixon, who wore a Tom Landry hat and whose receded gums made his teeth look at least an inch long apiece. His business card identified him as a private investigator. Their meeting place was a bar called the Boa Constrictor on East Garfield.

"You know a black dude?" Dixon asked. "Name Tulane Wiggins?"

"Depends. What did he do?"

"Tulane speaks quite highly of you," said Magdalena.

"I bet."

"No. Really. And Tulane's not all that free with his compliments," said Dixon.

Dixon smoked. And Magdalena had till recently, the fat man suspected. The urgency with which he chewed his gum suggested it meant far more to him than a mild sucrose fix.

"How do you two happen to know Tulane?"

"Jamaal Stokes. That name mean anything to you? Tulane's probation officer."

"Ah. I think I know who you mean. I believe I've talked to the man by phone."

"Good," said Magdalena. "We know Jamaal. Jamaal knows Tulane. Tulane knows you."

"We're trying to be as up front about this as possible," Dixon said.

"Try harder."

"We're seeking an honest individual, Mr. Dodge," Magdalena said. "Honest, but not fanatical. You know."

"I think I need to be someplace," said the fat man.

"Just listen. Okay? Everybody knows you do, like inventions. Right? You're in the paper."

"And?"

"Perhaps, being represented in the paper every day as you are, you've read about—" Magdalena paused as the barmaid approached.

Phil Dixon and the fat man ordered beers.

Magdalena wanted a Scotch.

"Don't shit me," said the barmaid.

"Oh," said Dixon. "He's of age. Don't worry."

"You think I'm blind?" the barmaid asked.

"Here," Magdalena said, and brought out his wallet. The fat man glimpsed something shiny, metallic inside as he reached for his license and flipped it onto the table.

The barmaid inspected it. Shrugged. Walked away.

"May I?" The fat man picked up the ID. Height, four feet two. Weight, ninety pounds. Age, thirty-five.

The barmaid distributed drinks and picked up the bills Dixon had left her. Nobody spoke. She moved to a nearby table and began to wipe it with a bar rag.

"Wait," Dixon said. He stood. Walked to the jukebox. Inserted change and returned to the table. When the racket began he said, "Maybe you've read about this unfortunate incident that's happened here in town. Concerning the little girl. Mary Vanessa Singer?"

"You're familiar with the story?" Magdalena asked.

"I drink milk," said the fat man.

"What's your opinion? What do you think happened to her?"

"I think she's dead."

"How come?"

The fat man shrugged. "A feeling."

Magdalena and Dixon consulted each other. Steadily. Silently.

"What if we could prove to you," said Dixon, "or at least convince you a strong possibility exists, that Mary Vanessa Singer is alive? Would you be willing to help us find her?"

Emotion spread through Aaron Dodge's body like the effects of a double bourbon. He answered immediately, enthusiastically. "You bet. Sure I would. I mean probably. Maybe. I don't see how I could do anything, though."

" 'Maybe probably' won't get it," Magdalena said. "We have to have a definite yes, Mr. Dodge. Or else we can't share our information."

"You have a definite no in that case."

"Wait," said Dixon. "Okay? Just wait. Listen. I can tell you this much. I'm employed by the little girl's family. Officer Magdalena is a police officer."

"Off-duty," Magdalena added. "Or else I wouldn't be here."

"I don't believe we have to spell it out for you, Mr. Dodge," Dixon told him.

"Spell it out for me," said Aaron Dodge.

"Look at me," said Magdalena. "I'm sure you can see how valuable a man of my stature could be in certain types of police work."

"You trap weirdos," he said to Magdalena. "Child molesters. Okay, I get it."

"Then can we have a decision, Mr. Dodge? Otherwise we'll be going."

The fat man thought of Mary Vanessa Singer. At least of her photo. In the paper or on posters you were always seeing the same one, like a trademark or logo—obviously a school portrait. Outfit, dark plaid with a blunt white collar. Hair, medium in length, medium in color, parted in the middle, and held behind the ears with plastic barrettes shaped like bows. And her smile—straighter teeth would've only detracted from it. A kid who'd smile like that at some free-lance photographer's cornball joke you could imagine going after just about any bait.

"Could I think about it? No, never mind. I mean yes. I'll help. If I can."

"Good," said Dixon. "Your friends weren't wrong about you."

"About a week ago," said Magdalena, "somebody found a lottery ticket on the sidewalk. Here in Phoenix. Besides the usual printed information—the six numbers and all the computerized crap—somebody had written on it: 'Still alive. Mary Vanessa Singer.' The experts say it's her handwriting."

"Nobody knows about this," Dixon said. "No media people, I mean."

"Before the public could be informed, something else turned up," Magdalena said. "Currency. A bill. Understand that nobody, nobody, Mr. Dodge, knew about that lottery ticket."

"Same handwriting," Dixon said. "Same six numbers scribbled on it. Same message."

"We believe that if a certain individual plays those six numbers on a regular basis, and if we can locate this individual, we'll have found the person responsible for Mary Vanessa Singer's disappearance. Or at least someone who knows a lot more than us."

"I still don't get what you're after from me."

"The Lottery Commission won't cooperate," said Dixon.

"They say they couldn't deliver the six numbers even if they wanted to," Magdalena said. "And certainly not on a long shot like this one. You know. Watergate. That Iran-hostage-rescue flub-up. People get conservative. They insist their game isn't for sale. Can't be fixed. No matter how desirable an outcome might be anticipated."

"But," said Dixon, "the right person, an inventive person, might be able to . . ."

"Hold it. So you're saying—"

"We'd appreciate your assistance, yes."

"So what you're asking is—"

"We'll pay you, of course."

"So what you want is for me to—"

"I think we've revealed all we can, Mr. Dodge."

"You want me to reinvent the wheel of fortune?"

The two men looked in opposite directions. Throats were cleared. Hands thrust into pockets. Feet repositioned beneath the table. Glances exchanged. Officer Magdalena spoke for the team.

"That's affirmative, Mr. Dodge."

The fat man, driving home, did something he hadn't done since meeting Kennedy. He parked on a street that dead-ended at a black-and-yellow barricade, on the other side of which lay broken and upheaved sections of what had once been a sidewalk. He found a more or less level slab and sat dangling his feet over a low precipice, below him the bed of the Salt River, above him the moonless desert sky, its stars not quite defeated by the city's orangish, upreaching glow. In the springtime, rains and runoff would cause water to be released from spillways to the north, and a dirty, foamy, coffee-colored stream would float sticks, Burger King cups, and rock-concert programs through the Valley. But mostly the riverbed lay dry and empty, as it did tonight, detained in its serene and occasional rush to the sea. The fat man considered it a perfect location from which to meditate on his problems and possibilities. Here Aaron Dodge had recognized the necessity for many a tough decision, and put off the making of it. Planned many a dramatic action that could've altered the course of his life, and talked himself out of it. Rationalized one courageous evasion after another, inspired by his surroundings.

Postpone, Big River, postpone.

Perched again on the familiar sandy bluff, he considered and reconsidered his newest opportunity. This time he'd accept. At least he was pretty sure. He'd almost decided. Irrevocably, just about. Here, he knew, was a chance to devote himself wholly to an undertaking he truly believed in, truly understood. Not six ill-natured and undisciplined personalities, but straightforward mechanical-engineering principles. He knew Laura would've approved if he'd been able to tell her. Which he couldn't, of course. Not her or Kennedy or any of his friends. He knew already that to them what he was about to do, since it would have to be done without them, would reflect unnatural priorities. A lack of values and principles. But the fat man didn't worry. He also knew that this was the way the average adult American male lived most of his life—in pursuit of a mysterious and secret goal that routinely and ruthlessly excluded every other human being, and made him seem to his family and friends entirely incapable of the simplest everyday act of courtesy or affection.

The fat man returned, astounded, to the blue apartment village, determined to donate every twitch of energy, every second of his time to helping bring Mary Vanessa Singer home. He began immediately. He told Kennedy he had work to do and locked himself in his bedroom workshop with a pot of coffee.

An hour later the pot was empty. He could hear the television through the wall. Kids laughing and shrieking. Kennedy pleading. Laura's marital problems barged in. Plus the recent financial difficulties. He couldn't concentrate. He stared at his drafting table, at the hunks of machinery lying around. Blueprints, catalogues, invoices. What was wrong? This was supposed to be it. For years he'd been keeping himself mentally ready for exactly this opportunity. Hadn't he?

After the 10:00 P.M. news, with everybody else asleep, he filled the bathtub. Climbed in. Waited underwater. For once nobody intruded with advice or assistance. He climbed out, dried himself, dressed.

Friends wouldn't visit him?

Then he'd visit a friend.

Bob the Brush lived in a trailer court in Glendale. Whoever owned it took the word "yard" literally when they doled out the grass. On the scrap of lawn beside his trailer sat a giant white satellite dish, a screeching eagle clutching a quiver of arrows painted in its center. Aaron Dodge parked behind his friend's pickup and honked twice to announce his arrival—as formal a request for an invitation as Bob the Brush required.

Inside, he found Bob watching. Educational channel. Science program. He extended the six-pack he'd brought. Bob shook his head.

Showed his unfinished can. The fat man, after detaching one, slid the other five into the icebox.

"Want to see something on the fuck channel?"

"Sure. Or this is fine too." He indicated the screen with a nod. "What's it about?"

"I don't know. The climate on Mars."

Bob's place smelled of scorched sawdust and 3-in-1 oil. As with Aaron Dodge's, you couldn't've really called it "furnished." "Equipped" would've been more accurate. Every room other than this one and the bath—and that included what had once been the kitchen, separated from them by a short breakfast bar—contained machinery of some sort. Radial arm, table, and band saws. A router, a jointer, a lathe. Bob the Brush was a hardware man. But his real skill—a skill not much in demand nowadays—was pattern-making. Somebody wanted one or a limited quantity of a prototype or discontinued part. A car or gun collector, maybe. An inventor like Aaron Dodge. They'd come to Bob the Brush, who'd cut and assemble a wooden pattern, exact to five-thousandths of an inch, which they'd then take to a foundry to be translated into metal. Bob also did another type of woodworking. On the wall of a room down the hall from where they sat, along with his carpenter's squares, protractors, and calipers, hung Bob's gallery of human hands. Tracings. Large, small, left, right. With missing fingers, some of them. They'd been mailed to Bob's P.O. box from addresses all over the country—responses to ads he ran in the back pages of gun magazines.

CUSTOM PISTOL GRIPS
HAND CARVED

"What're you doing this weekend?" the fat man asked.

"Nothing, I guess. I'm supposed to have the kids. Why?"

He told Bob about Laura's husband and Tucson. How the eviction squad would be out of town.

"If you can't get anybody else, call me. Maybe I'll bring the boys along."

"That's okay. Don't worry about it. So how old are they now?"

"The stepfather is a jeweler. Works in a jewelry store. Diamond pendants and promise rings. He pierces ears. I try to have an influence. But you know."

"Bringing kids along wouldn't be a very good idea, I don't think."

"Eight and ten," said Bob. "They're eight and ten." Aaron Dodge glimpsed a distant conversational possibility. Deflect Bob's attention from sons to daughters, from there to Mary Vanessa Singer.

Instead he said: "There is another favor—a big one—you could do me. You wouldn't happen to have a . . ." He aimed an index finger at the tv screen. Pulled the trigger. "Like an extra that I could borrow?"

Bob smiled. "You bet I do. Fact, I was thinking of offering. I heard from Lulu about your old lady's troubles. Her sister's, I mean." He left the room and returned promptly with a handgun. Beautiful weapon. Except that the original set of grips had been removed and no new ones fitted to replace them. Nothing to cover the ugly metal skeleton underneath. "I never did give you anything, did I, this year? So here you go. Happy birthday."

Aaron Dodge hesitated.

"Take it, pucker-butt. It's a goddam gift. You want to offend me?" Bob left it on the coffee table and after rummaging in a drawer beyond the breakfast nook brought over paper and a pencil. "Let me see your hand."

The fat man didn't.

"Here. Reach out your fuckin' hand. All I want to do is stick it down my pants, you fag."

Bob sat on the sofa beside him, moved away the beer cans and ashtrays, and slid the sheet of paper onto the tabletop. He took hold of Aaron Dodge's wrist. Maneuvered his hand palm down onto the piece of paper. Centered it.

He began at the base of the thumb, talking as he worked. "I don't got no others that'd suit your needs right now. Caliber and so forth. I can give you a pair of grips temporary. Or you can just wrap that jesse in tape. It'll do you."

Aaron Dodge watched the pencil describe the shape of his hand, briefly alerting nerves along its path. Tickling lightly. Descending the valleys between fingers. Hugging the curves. Bob steered carefully, slowly, kneeling between the table and sofa to examine his progress.

When he was done, he turned Aaron Dodge's hand palm up. "I know

guys like him. That's why I'm telling you. You're doing the right thing."
He placed the pistol without handles in the fat man's palm and closed
his fingers around it.

He told Kennedy he had work to do and asked for Saturday. She agreed
to spend the morning at Hayden Library and the afternoon helping
Laura with the children. The fat man watched the pink Mustang drive
away, closed the front door, and headed for his bedroom workshop.

On the way he decided to fix breakfast.

They were out of eggs, so he drove to a Circle K and bought a dozen.
He cooked a large meal, telling himself if it lasted him through lunch
he'd have that much more uninterrupted work time. While the bacon
fried, he taped the news photo of Mary Vanessa Singer, her school
portrait, on the wall above his workbench. After he ate, there were
dishes to do—he didn't want to leave Kennedy that chore—and while
he rinsed and dried he noticed a dripping faucet. A friend from the
complex across the street had borrowed his tools, so he walked over
to borrow back his allen heads and pipe wrench. He found his friend
in the lot with the hood of his car up, a thick Chilton's manual spread
open on the fender. The fat man offered to get him started on his
tune-up.

Kennedy returned around five o'clock, while the fat man was de-
greasing at the kitchen sink. He didn't speak to her but proceeded
directly to the bedroom and closed the door after him. Less than an
hour later, irritated, he returned to the kitchen. She wasn't there. Or
in the living room or bath. He called her name. He finally found her
sitting alone in the complex's brightly lit communal laundry facility.

"I can't work with you around. You're always interrupting me."

She looked up from the book she was reading. "What?"

"I said I'm going out," he told her.

The fat man made a phone call or two before he left, still feeling
edgy, preoccupied. Tomorrow they'd be driving to Tucson, he and
Laura and Kennedy. Since discovering that the eviction squad wouldn't
be accompanying them, he'd made calls, soliciting replacements. Besides Bob the Brush, he'd asked Dibadj, the donut chef at Winchell's,
who'd introduced the fat man to a friend of his named Fuad—a short,
aggressive Palestinian with a full black mustache under siege from all

directions by several days' worth of bristly five o'clock shadow. This Fuad had bragged the whole time Aaron Dodge talked to him about bomb threats he'd phoned in to the Valley Bank central office, American Express headquarters, and other local strongholds of the stinking imperialist hyenas. Aaron Dodge's conversation with Fuad and his efforts since to enlist allies had persuaded him that a sensibility poised anyplace between unthinkable viciousness and unthinking restraint would not be simple or safe to locate in times like these. A theory attested to by tonight's series of phone conversations. So he decided to do something he'd tried only occasionally in his life up to now. He prepared to confront potential complications single-handedly.

He found the El Camino's passenger seat, shrouded by a plastic garbage liner, in a corner of his bedroom workshop, carried it outdoors, and heaved it into the bed of the El Camino. He wound the butt of the pistol Bob the Brush had given him in tape and loaded it. He shoved the gun into the console hutch behind the gearshift—the narrow space that would've been between the seats if there'd been more than one—and drove far up into the foothills north of the city.

There he parked, dropped the tailgate, and dragged the seat to a flat spot near the base of a rockslide, where he propped it upright. He returned to the El Camino, climbed into the driver's seat, and flipped on the high beams. Bringing the pistol with him, he climbed out and stood near the front fender. He aimed, selecting an area on the seat's backrest above and to the left of center. He fired—once, twice. The seat fell over on its side. He fired again—three, four, five, six, click click click—into the fire-retardant straw batting on the seat's underside. He emptied the hot brass casings onto the ground and reloaded. He crouched and fired. Pirouetted and fired. He shot from the hip, feeling a lightness in his bones, stirrings in his stomach. He squandered a fresh six, thinking of Laura's husband, but also—he couldn't help it—of Laura and the children. Of Kennedy. Dixon and his midget friend, Magdalena. Even Mary Vanessa Singer.

He put down the gun. He walked to where the seat lay, lifted it above his head, and carried it to the right side of the El Camino. He set it on the ground and opened the door. The dome light responded. With its help he fitted the seat to a pair of steel runners welded to the floorboard and locked it in place with the adjustment lever. He reattached and lubricated the two powerful black springs that propelled the seat up and back, up and back, to assure the comfort of a passenger.

The fat man covered the holes he'd blasted with a fresh garbage liner, and Laura sat there the next morning on the way to Tucson.

They left her six and the pink Mustang with Ont Hazel, and Aaron Dodge drove south, Kennedy beside him, riding in the middle on the green bedspread, which they'd stuffed between the seats to pad the console hutch. On the way Aaron Dodge warned Laura.

"Don't let him get you alone. Stay close. Kennedy, you too. The three of us can't lose sight of each other. Understand?" But the precautions seemed to make Kennedy and Laura more instead of less nervous. And besides, the El Camino made so much racket at sixty that they had to yell to hear each other. So finally the fat man shut up and watched the road.

They arrived early afternoon and found the white Lynx that belonged to Laura's husband parked in front of the house. The little hatchback bothered Aaron Dodge immediately. Anybody seriously contemplating a move usually managed to borrow a truck or van. As Kennedy and Laura climbed out the passenger side, Aaron Dodge reached beneath the green bedspread for the pistol, hidden among maps and spare fuses in the console hutch.

Laura and Kennedy stood in the driveway between the car and the house, glancing uncertainly from one to the other. "Wait," he called to them.

He'd rehearsed holstering techniques the night before and had discovered that only in Westerns did anybody, or at least anybody his size, carry a revolver in his belt or waistband. Every time the fat man tried it, the gun immediately slid down his pants, funneled through a leg and out a cuff, and went spinning across the kitchen floor, caroming off appliances and baseboards. He finally invented a less romantic but more effective method of concealment. He put on a pair of cutoffs backward underneath his pants and used a hip pocket for a holster. He remembered standing in front of Kennedy's full-length mirror, his trousers around his ankles, zipping himself into the cutoff jeans. It was the first time in ten years he'd cared to observe more than his face, and the image he saw reflected belonged to a man advancing from the waist up and retreating from the waist down. Though horrified at how he filled the mirror, he couldn't help smiling at the same time, and again now as he fitted the pistol into its hiding place.

He preceded Kennedy and Laura up the driveway to the porch. Laura's husband opened the door before the fat man rang the bell.

"Hello, Brett. How are you?" Laura said.

"Hi," said Kennedy.

He didn't respond except to turn and walk away from the open door.

Aaron Dodge watched him carefully as he led them through the house, indicating the few items he preferred. Almost everything either he or Laura wanted had already been removed. The furniture and other belongings that remained would be hauled to the Salvation Army. They began to gather items and carry them outside, or pack them into boxes. The fat man had brought along a staple gun, pliers, and the collapsed cardboard he'd collected for his adventurous move back in May.

"Let's remember to ask for receipts," said Aaron Dodge. "You can take donations off your taxes, you know."

Wearing the shorts was uncomfortable enough, but every time the fat man bent over, the pistol barrel stabbed his thigh. Its butt had already chafed a spot raw. Even so, he couldn't stop himself. The minute he saw the dust-covered bedsteads and bike frames in the garage rafters, the out-of-fashion wardrobes hanging in every closet, ideas arrived without an invitation. "Listen," he said. "I know this isn't the happiest of occasions. And you guys don't have to do this if you don't want. But maybe it would be just as easy, and we could turn a little profit at the same time, if we . . ." He hesitated. A frivolous idea?

"What?" Laura said.

"Nah. Skip it. It's stupid." It was an idea anybody might've thought of. But due to the strained relations between Laura and Brett, it seemed a little unorthodox.

"What?" said Kennedy.

"Three of us, see, could take the cars. Haul stuff away. And meanwhile the other one could stay here and . . . But we'd have to move everything out onto the lawn. That would take extra time. I forgot about that."

"What?" Laura's husband said.

"I bet it wouldn't take that long, though. And it might even save us time in the end. A yard—"

"—sale!" said Kennedy.

A perfect way around a confrontation. Laura would stay behind, tending her tv-tray checkout stand, her jewelry-chest cashbox, while he and Kennedy and Laura's husband drove carfuls of discards to the charity agencies.

Laura's husband shrugged. "Shit, I don't care. But whatever we're doing, let's do it."

It took them two hours to drag everything onto the treacherously landscaped rock lawn in front of the house. Then they loaded the two vehicles with the items least likely to sell. On the first shuttle to the thrift store, Aaron Dodge stopped at every intersection between the house and the suburb's main thoroughfare to post a hand-lettered announcement. By the time they returned, bringing back singles and change for Laura's till, the yard was full of shoppers. Strangers pursuing a bargain. Neighbors competing for the prize specimen from this typical but sad exhibition of middle-class overconsumption. A piece of Laura and her husband's misfortune to take home with them.

Two more trips downtown and back and the sale was over. They'd drop off the last of the unsold belongings on their way out of town. Laura sat on the living-room floor, counting bills, stacking quarters. After she'd divided the take, she stood and offered Brett his share.

"Split it?"

"You keep it," he said.

At that moment the fat man was certain. They'd drive back to Phoenix and Laura wouldn't see the guy again until they faced each other in a courtroom, plenty of lawmen present to chaperone. He'd relaxed so completely that he left Kennedy and Laura alone with Brett, and in the kitchen opened the icebox to investigate. Two beers. A diet 7-Up.

"Anybody thirsty?"

As he walked into the living room, offering the three cans, he saw the gun. Brett's gun.

Either his instincts or his reflexes failed him. He should've reached for the pistol Bob had supplied. But he didn't. Couldn't. Not that it would've made a difference. Her husband had already leveled his military automatic at Laura.

"Brett. Please." She lifted a hand. Took an uncertain step toward Kennedy.

Brett's eyes didn't register the movement. Nor did his gun hand. Instead of keeping the pistol trained on her, he slowly raised it. He fitted the barrel against his chin.

Kennedy must've recognized then what was about to happen. "Don't," she whispered. "Brett?" Before the fat man could reach out to stop him, or even fully understand his intentions, Brett pulled the trigger. He shot himself. Himself instead of Laura.

Aaron Dodge felt the concussion through his entire body. Brett seemed to have been yanked off his feet by strings. The dome of his skull disintegrated. Erupted. Fragments of bone and flesh and hair flew at the walls and carpet, and at Aaron Dodge, who felt them, warm and wet, on his clothes and against his skin. The man and the heavy pistol made separate, distinct sounds as they struck the floor.

The fat man's ears hadn't quit ringing, and the smell of gunpowder was still strong, when the police and ambulance arrived. A detective squatted beside the body as attendants rushed a stretcher in, and outlined Laura's husband in chalk.

9

All the saddest people in the world showed up at Camel-Op on Christmas morning every year. Lulu opened for the sake of her regulars—the agnostics, atheists, and followers of nontraditional faiths. The divorced, the unmarried, the jilted, and the gay. Those excluded, without, or far away from families. But strangers also appeared on Christmas—more of them than on any other day of the year. Nobody could go to work. Or shoot pool or watch ESPN at a bar. Auto-parts houses closed. And video arcades and malls. So people came to Camel-Op instead. And if you looked, you could see more enchantment in these strangers' faces than in any child's on Christmas morning. All you had to do was watch as they parked and approached the front window, then peered between cupped hands through the glare on the plate glass and found that when they pressed against it the door yielded.

Out of habit the fat man stopped by.

Had coffee.

Lingered in the company of this, his family.

He spent the rest of the day at Ont Hazel's in Sun City, drinking beer and working on her car while Laura's six played with their toys. They hadn't, according to Laura, received anywhere near the usual haul, but they didn't seem to notice, or at least they weren't complaining. Since the Sunday in Tucson, everybody had been extra considerate, the fat man included. He was now willing to concede, temporarily at least, that he couldn't let Laura face her difficulties alone. Laura seemed to understand that his more frequent presence represented a tentative commitment, and she and Kennedy showed their appreciation in subtle ways, as if they sensed they were keeping the fat man from something important. Nights when he could, he sat in his bedroom workshop, staring at her photo, trying to figure out what about Mary Vanessa Singer and her story touched him past all the layers enclosing his small, overworked heart. If her misfortune mattered, then shouldn't Laura's matter even more? The question bothered him all through the holiday season. One day while he wandered in a shopping plaza, among crowds of people exchanging and returning gifts, he encountered a long table stacked with baked goods. HELP FIND MARY VANESSA SINGER. He bought a pie and ate it sitting in the El Camino, without ever leaving the lot.

Laura's husband wasn't dead. This was the fact that made even a modestly optimistic holiday mood impossible. He lay in a Tucson hospital, kept alive by machines. He'd hit what he was aiming for. No worry would ever enter that mind again. But, passing through, the bullet had missed whichever brain center fed a last, weakest connection to life. The slug, if the cops hadn't rescued it in their investigation, was probably still in the attic crawlspace near the hole it had opened in the ceiling. Maybe someday a child rummaging up there would find it, suspended among pink layers of insulation.

He lived past New Year's. Laura signed papers. The machines could be disconnected. Possibly. Eventually. But what about now? The fat man tried to help Laura find out.

"What do you want, Aaron? You called me right in the middle of Garrison Keillor's monologue."

"One quick question, Max. Is it true that when somebody offs himself his beneficiaries can't collect on the life insurance?"

"Aaron? What are you considering?"

"Not me, Max. Laura's husband. You know. Kennedy's sister, Laura. Her husband tried to snuff himself. What I want to find out is, if he dies, does Laura collect?"

"That's tragic, Aaron."

"It is."

"I'm so sorry."

"I know."

The two friends paused briefly. Embarrassed because neither of them seemed able to feel the appropriate emotion. Either that or waiting in case one of them suddenly remembered how.

"You were asking about the policy," Max said finally. "Precedents indicate that a claimant doesn't necessarily forfeit any rights by taking his own life. The actuarial tables can't support a statistically significant likelihood that suicide will occur with any more frequency than, say, a traffic accident or heart attack. Except, of course, in the initial months of coverage."

"Really?"

"Of course really. What's his current condition?"

"In the hospital. They're keeping him alive with machines."

"Life-support systems. They're a tricky legal issue, Aaron."

"He has the insurance. And a pension. Laura would be in good shape. But first . . ."

"I see what you mean. It must be very difficult for Laura."

"Even if he hurries up and . . . you know, things still might be complicated. They were in the middle of a divorce."

"They could base a bar exam on this poor woman," said Max. "What do you suppose you'll do?"

"I don't know," said Aaron Dodge. "Become a capitalist, I guess."

Kennedy offered to quit school and do something instead. The fat man told her no. Not yet anyway. Laura's husband might come through for them anytime, maybe even before her first tuition installment was due this semester. Meantime Aaron Dodge accelerated his own efforts. The potential investors Max had lined up for the Bunkport were "foot-dragging," as she put it. Investors in Aaron Dodge's projects always seemed to have particularly heavy feet. But he had more of the New York t-shirts silk-screened and placed on consignment in shops near the universities in Tempe, Tucson, and Flagstaff, along with a second design. On the new shirt he'd reproduced a drawing of snowflakes, magnified and falling against a square of black sky, each crystal accompanied by a tiny circled "C" or "R," or a tiny "T.M.," or a "Reg. U.S. Pat. Off." Underneath, a caption read: "Every Snowflake Is Different." He also managed to sell, to a mail-order distributor of erotic gadgets, garments, guides, lotions, potions, and confections, the idea for a flavored, edible suppository whose package promised women increased frequency and men enhanced enjoyment of oral sex. Kennedy, inspired by a particularly successful test session, came up with a name for the new product: Choc-Clits.

But there seemed to be no limit to the needs of Laura and her six. No sense that they would ever understand or care how much they required. Availability evidently didn't enter into their calculations. Whenever the fat man thought Laura might be catching up, she revealed a new line of credit she'd overextended. She probably had debts saved up in Swiss accounts just in case prosperity threatened. And though it was true that in other areas, most notably affection, she and her six could give as extravagantly as they took, still Aaron Dodge's every instinct told him to disjoin, pull out of this bankrupt operation. Which he knew he wouldn't do. He did have values, goddammit, even if he had spent his entire life eluding situations in which he might be called upon to apply them.

His well-advertised and lifelong fidelity to bachelorhood left Aaron Dodge in the awkward position of having to invent excuses for what, coming from anybody else, would've been considered improved conduct.

They were staying in Peoria most of the time, he reassured his friends. At Laura's apartment. I try to have as little contact as possible. But what am I supposed to do, let them go without designer jeans? Run wild in the malls? Wreck their chances for competitive SAT scores?

He didn't mention Kennedy. He didn't mention Mary Vanessa Singer. He didn't admit that because of them he'd begun to suspect that what he'd once believed about love might not be true after all. Love wasn't just for convenient occasions or for preferred recipients. Your capacities and people's needs couldn't always be stored separately, like the tube of resin and the tube of catalyst in an epoxy kit, and only allowed to come together under carefully controlled conditions. What you were trying to avoid had a way of contaminating what you were trying to accomplish. Every uncomfortable day he spent in the vicinity of Laura's six convinced him more thoroughly of that.

One of the most uncomfortable occurred not long after their holiday recess ended. Brett and Sylvia, the oldest two, stepped off the school bus with fingers grimier than usual, that left faint gray smudges on the pamphlets they'd been given to bring home to Laura. *What Every Child Should Know*. Brett and Sylvia attended in the same district Mary Vanessa Singer had. They and their classmates had been printed that day by the Phoenix police to make identification possible in case of an abduction.

The kids didn't seem particularly troubled. School hadn't been canceled, nor programming interrupted. How serious a crisis could it be? But clearly the pamphlets called for immediate attention. Which Laura would've provided. Which Laura was perfectly capable of providing. Which Laura, judging from the way she objected when Kennedy and then the fat man offered to help, didn't in fact trust anyone else to provide. But finally she agreed to share the responsibility. She'd talk to the two oldest, Brett and Sylvia. Kennedy would talk to the middle two, Ginger and Anthony. Aaron Dodge would be allowed to assist where he was least likely to cause any irreversible harm, by talking to Heather and Holland, the two youngest.

There were closer parks, but he chose Encanto, an oasis of shade, flower beds, transplanted palms, and man-made lagoons located near the section of downtown where the numbered West Side avenues and the parallel, identically numbered East Side streets passed each other at Central, Phoenix's version of Main. They left the car in the gravel lot. Walked to a grassy bank and sat on benches. They'd stopped for lunch on the way, and now Heather and Holland broke greasy leftovers into pieces and tossed them. Targets spread where mouths touched the surface for crumbs. Noisy ducks, each trailing a V-shaped wake, wedged in to compete, splashing the ringlets apart. The girls took occasional bites from their cold sandwiches as they watched.

Aaron Dodge went over the information, what every child should know, point by point. No rides from strangers. Stay in public areas, especially with unfamiliar people present. Don't be afraid to say "no." To call for help if something someone does frightens you. Know the proper and improper ways of showing physical affection. Heather and Holland listened. Asked questions. But at their ages a significant barrier existed to effective education. They didn't know what sex was. And how do you explain drowning to somebody who hasn't learned about water yet?

With the arrival of the pamphlets, Aaron Dodge began to notice a change in the kids. "Preoccupation with death" didn't seem too melodramatic a way of putting it. School-days portrait packets had been distributed, and one January morning he found Brett and Sylvia—"the two oldest," that's how he'd learned to remember them—watching Saturday cartoons and taping their own faces over the missing-children photos on the back panel of an empty milk carton. Soon after that he watched Heather and Holland, "the two youngest," deeply engrossed in a disturbing game. Unless he was misreading the evidence, they'd placed one of their dolls in intensive care. An old transistor radio attached by the earplug monitored its heart. Oxygen reached it through a length of spare phone cable from the fat man's workshop, connected at one end to a soft-drink bottle and at the other to a mask made from half a walnut shell and a rubber band. That was his first hint that the children's main source of worry might not be the pamphlets, and the potential threat they implied, but a much more private and already substantiated tragedy.

On Super Bowl Sunday, while Laura and Kennedy pulled for Chicago in front of his set, the fat man broiled burgers for the six kids. Something seemed to be bothering Anthony—one of "the middle two" along with Ginger. While the others ate, Anthony led him outside. In the apartment-house lot he'd discovered a jackrabbit. Road kill. Guts glistening like an unspooled cassette cartridge. "Is my daddy killed?" Anthony asked.

The fat man knelt beside the fresh remains and poked them with a run-over drinking straw he'd peeled from the pavement. "Not this killed," he said. Aaron Dodge had read, in one of the advice columns that appeared near his in the paper, about ways to help children express their grief. "Shall we give it a funeral?" he asked.

"Why?" said Anthony.

"Come on. Let's."

Anthony shrugged. The fat man looked around for a suitable coffin. Had to settle for a fried-chicken takeout carton, mashed flat like everything else that lay in the lot for more than ten minutes. "What now?" he asked, and scooped up the limp corpse.

Anthony pointed. Aaron Dodge followed, bearing the deceased on its cardboard bier. Anthony stopped beside the dumpster. Lifted, with

Aaron Dodge's help, the heavy bar latching its porthole. When it opened, eggshells tumbled out. A tuna can full of coffee grounds. With his free hand Aaron Dodge compacted trash to make room inside, then passed the responsibility for final disposal to Anthony. Anthony held the flimsy shingle, sagging from the weight of the carcass, unsteadily above his head, tilted it, and let the body roll off. He shoved the cardboard in after it and the fat man shut the hatch.

"Should we say something?" Aaron Dodge asked. "A few words?"

Anthony had started to cry.

Laura's husband wasn't dead, of course. But in view of his current condition it would've seemed hypocritical, misleading, not to let Anthony assume the worst. The inevitable. "You know," said Aaron Dodge, "my dad died too. When I was about your same age."

"Really?"

"Yep. I was scared. Scared my mom would die too. My friends would die. Everybody would die and I'd be by myself."

"Really?"

"Really."

"My mom's not going to die."

"You bet she's not."

"And you're not."

"Nope. You're right about that."

"And Aunt Kennedy either. And Mrs. Moreno's not." A worker at Anthony's day care.

The fat man took Anthony's hand and led him back inside, helping him list as many names as they could think of on the way.

Brett, Jr., and Sylvia.

Ginger. Heather and Holland.

And Mary Vanessa Singer. Maybe.

On January 28 the list shortened abruptly when the *Challenger* disintegrated over the waters off southern Florida, with children all over America on board via classroom tv's. Brett and Sylvia—the two oldest—came home early, stepping off the bus with purple fingers this time, and freshly mimeographed advice for Laura—more of What Every Child Should Know.

Thirty-five thousand posters had been distributed nationwide to service clubs, state, county, and municipal police departments. Appeals had been placed in bowling centers, banks, and post offices. Inside photo-finishing packets. On tollway tickets, on grocery bags.

Locally, chocolate drives, car washes, and flea markets had been organized. A malamute puppy had been auctioned off forty-some times.

The Hell's Angels had been implicated. The Way, International. Moonies, Krishnas, crackheads. Islamic Jihad.

The fat man wondered why Dixon or Magdalena hadn't called. No pressure, no advice, no instructions. Maybe they realized what they'd asked him to do would be difficult and would take time. He doubted it, though. Nobody ever had any respect for anybody else's profession. Especially not Aaron Dodge's. They always expected you to turn out ideas the way Taiwan turns out piggybanks and key chains. Or maybe Dixon and Magdalena had received other information since their meeting with the fat man. Captive or runaway? Alive or dead? Maybe the risks involved in doctoring the lottery didn't seem worth taking any longer. Concerned that he might've squandered his opportunity, Aaron Dodge—without directly identifying himself, in case the precinct monitored its phones—called Officer Magdalena and arranged a meeting for that night at the Boa Constrictor.

Magdalena and Dixon explained why they hadn't contacted him. "There's been some question concerning your involvement in a matter currently under investigation by the Tucson department," said Magdalena. "And some other irregularities have also come to our attention."

"We did some background checking," said Phil Dixon. "Can you tell us about your former military status, Mr. Dodge?"

"Medical deferment," said the fat man.

"I see," said Magdalena. "And then there's this young woman. Your companion, I believe."

"Kennedy? What about her?"

"Cohabitation, Mr. Dodge?" said Dixon.

"Understand, we're not presuming to offer moral judgments," said Magdalena. "Just being careful is all."

"It's 1986, Magdalena. Come on."

"Well, if you're still interested, and you think you can keep your name off the six o'clock news . . . ?"

"I'm interested."

"Any progress to report?" asked Dixon.

"Not much so far. You know, with my friend and her sister. Their problems. It's kept me kind of busy."

"Right."

"Look, I want to do this. But I need . . . Hell, I don't know."

Dixon and Magdalena traded empty expressions. "I know some people," Magdalena said. "I might be able to introduce you. If that'll help. Tomorrow?" he asked, and the fat man nodded. "Tomorrow's good. Sure."

Intervention.

Teen counseling.

Independent-living skills.

From Seventh Avenue the Florence Crittenton Center looked like a real-estate office. Quiet. Clean. Two women behind a motel-style check-in responded to Officer Magdalena's questions, directing most of their answers to Aaron Dodge. They reserved two beds for runaways here. The rest went to pregnant girls or girls destined for foster homes. Nobody had to tell the fat man that a Mary Vanessa Singer would be unlikely to turn up at Crittenton. The girls here had been through a process. They'd been in trouble, real trouble, bad trouble, but their trouble had been passed around. Addressed by agencies and professionals. They came here for healing, not for stitching up.

Magdalena had met the fat man at the blue apartment village after lunch, promising him the information he'd asked for. Something beyond what he could read in the paper. Crittenton was the first stop. Now they headed via Osborn toward the center of town. Magdalena drove.

"You ever get stopped? You know. For looking underage?"

Magdalena didn't answer, so Aaron Dodge turned his attention to the radio. Municipal property, Magdalena's tan Escort hadn't been equipped with factory anything, but he'd brought along a powerful-looking portable—the kind that picked up both official and public transmissions. As they turned onto West Willetta, the fat man balanced it on his knees and spun the selector.

At every stoplight, Magdalena had to slide forward in his seat and fish for the brake pedal with his foot. "Technically, you'd be called what? A dwarf? A midget?"

"I'm a shrimp, Mr. Dodge. All right? A little bitty short fella. A runt."

"Yeah. Well, all right."

Tumbleweed came closer to fulfilling Aaron Dodge's expectations. Plain stucco house. Very middle-class neighborhood. Bianca, the woman on duty, wore Birkenstocks. A white sweatshirt underneath faded farmer-alls. She showed them around. In the bedrooms, mattresses lay directly on floors. A chair. A bureau. Everything had that donated look. Bianca called them "crisis kids." Crisis girls. Crisis boys. They were told three to five days, but Tumbleweed kept them up to thirty. DOC referrals, mostly—Department of Corrections. The fat man had visited halfway houses before. Friends coming off drugs. This place felt the same. Real tired people. People holding on. Grateful for a rest.

In the kitchen, a slim teenager, Mandy, fried burgers at a gas range. Barefoot. Hard Rock Cafe t-shirt. Red bandanna tied into a belt loop of her cords. Gum. When Aaron Dodge said hello, she looked away, her long hair slipping off a shoulder to partly conceal her smile. Magdalena showed her the photo of Mary Vanessa Singer. Mandy glanced at it, then at him, and shook her head.

It got worse after Tumbleweed. It got like Mesa Rehab. Like Maricopa County Juvenile Court Center, on Durango, west of the freeway. They saw a boy—short, cowlicked hair, unbuttoned plaid flannel shirt for a jacket—exiting the round, sterile court building in the custody of an older woman. His mother, or else she hadn't earned the expression on her face. In a restroom inside, Aaron Dodge found an electric hand-drier. Faucets that turned themselves off. A polished metal rectangle instead of a mirror. The walls, too, had been built vandalproof, but above the urinal, squeezed into the eighth-inch of grout between tiles, tiny, carefully lettered graffiti survived. *Young, dumb, and full of cum*, somebody had written. In the vast, nearly empty parking lot he spotted a desert-colored Mercedes with vanity tags.

NI 4NI

"You're an inventor, Mr. Dodge. What do you think could be done?" They were driving through South Phoenix now. South of the interstate, south of the tracks and the dry bed of the Salt River. "Say I was working for the newspaper. How would I protect my carriers?"

Aaron Dodge had already given this question his professional attention. A variety of electronic gadgets and equally complicated tactical maneuvers had occurred to him before the natural, simple, correct—but also unworkable—solution finally surfaced. "The best thing—this would only work for paperboys, not all types of kids. But the best thing—and I'm not suggesting they should do this; it's inhumane, I admit that. The best thing really would be just to chain them to their bikes or wagons or something big and bulky like that. I'd like to see anybody try to drag a kid tied to a goddam red toy wagon into his car. It's partly a philosophical thing, though. Like a moral thing. Who's the criminal? Who deserves the handcuffs? How much of a kid's childhood are you willing to take away to protect him? You can't make him swallow a radio transmitter or anything. It's not his fault he's vulnerable. Or hers."

At five, when the government shut down, their tour turned informal. They drove past the Phoenix Club, a bathhouse. Zorba's on Scottsdale Road. Papago Park. Hot Bods. Trax, a leather bar on East McDowell. Magdalena didn't talk. He let Aaron Dodge view what was out there to be viewed. Boys, mostly. Slender. Wearing tall clogs. Tapered jeans. With upturned collars, faint mustaches, cigarettes.

"Is this what you had in mind at all?" Magdalena asked. They cruised out of the district. "I don't know how inventors get their ideas."

"I really didn't have anything in mind. That's been the trouble. Sure, this is helping. If that's the word."

"I can only show you what I see, night in and night out. In my job."

"I appreciate it."

By then he'd given up on the radio and shoved it under his seat. He thought Magdalena might be about the right age, though, so he asked. "There used to be this one station. While I was growing up. Ever listen to it? KDKB?"

Magdalena shrugged. Shook his head.

"I think I had all six pushbuttons to my car radio homed in on it."

"Doper station?"

"Not really. At first maybe. It got to be big time, though, later on. They sold it for a million bucks. Now it's nothing. Same call letters, but standard Top 40 crap. I called up one time to ask about some of the people that used to work there. Talked to the station manager. Bitch was really defensive."

"Me, about all I ever listened to was KJ, I think. It and the other 'kicker stations."

"I was just thinking of what I must've been doing when I was their age." The fat man nodded at his window. Only a few shoppers and street people out there now. But he knew Magdalena understood what he meant. "And that station was the first thing I remembered. 'Progressive,' they used to call it."

"I remember Spero's Basherooney," Magdalena said. "Frank Kush. Bobby Winkles. Wallace and Ladmo."

"The Normal Brothers," said Aaron Dodge. "Hans Olsen. William Edward Compton."

"You ever call cops 'pigs'?"

"Never. With me it was always 'Officer, Sir.' Same as your friends always called every freak 'Young Man.' 'Young Lady.' 'Miss.' "

Aaron Dodge thought of Cody. Brad Moe. His friends. Looking at Magdalena, he realized that he'd probably never had much of a social life. "I guess I listened to a lot of radio," he said, and tugged at the waistband of his trousers. "Because you know, my physique, it held me back a little with the girls at times." He told Magdalena how he'd gained weight, and why.

"You were lucky. Me, I wanted to go. ROTC. Army. Indochina. More than anything. Maybe it was just because I knew they wouldn't take me. But still."

They parked the tan Escort as local neon started to assert itself against a clear, cold desert sky. The moon was up too, bright as a drive-in movie screen. Adult bookstores. Arcades. Bars with choppers and hogs lined up out front. Kitchenettes and trailer courts. Pawnshops and gun shops. Package liquor. Used cars. Occasionally one from a tight group of Chicanos or blacks would sling a look over his shoulder as they passed.

People spoke rapid Spanish. Glass crunched underfoot. They walked past the tattoo parlor where Rat Lips worked. Steel mesh drawn across the door and windows. Padlocked. They walked with their hands stuffed in their jacket pockets. Into the rhythm of city walking. Look straight ahead. Watch where you're going. Watch who's coming. Stay in your lane but do not yield. Eyeball nobody but if they eyeball you eyeball them right back. They arrived at Ernesto's and found a table in the smoke and noise.

"What happens is this," Magdalena said. "A runaway, she'll usually end up down this part of town. These tattoo parlors and biker bars, they're the worst places. They'll offer a kid a free meal. That's the way it starts a lot of times."

"So you think she ran away?"

"Me personally? No. I don't think that at all. It's a possibility. It happens. So I don't ignore it."

"What do you think happened?"

"I just told you I don't think anything. All's I know is what *can* happen. What can happen is like what I just told you. That's one thing. Another thing that can happen is, there's guys. We apprehend one of these individuals, he'll invariably have himself a collection. Many, many photos. I seen this one guy's collection, it had in it young children's underclothing and this type of thing. They trade. Run ads in the paper. Send out newsletters, practically. You wouldn't believe. A lot of these individuals will have a certain type job. They'll be a schoolteacher, a club leader. Sometimes church, even. These video arcades they have all over now, these are places they'll work. What I'm saying to you is, we might be entirely in the wrong section of town tonight, Mr. Dodge. Any more you never know."

They returned to the tan Escort, and then to their own section of town. Once during the ride, almost as if he were the boy he was paid to be, Magdalena looked up at the fat man and asked: "Mr. Dodge. Tell me. I mean, not that I don't appreciate it, but how come you agreed to be doing this?"

The fat man shrugged.

"Any kids of your own?"

"Didn't that show in the background check?"

Magdalena laughed. "You could be divorced or something."

"No kids," said Aaron Dodge.

"Then why?"

"I don't know. It's one of the little endearing things about life, isn't it? How it'll walk up to you one day and offer you a shiny new bike, and then the next day drag you off in the woods someplace and bung you till your guts fall out."

The fat man found Laura and her six to be only slightly more cooperative recipients of his benevolence than Mary Vanessa Singer. At home, the accoutrements of middle-class splendor that Aaron Dodge had avoided accumulating all his life now confronted him everyplace he looked. Board games, radar ovens; electric carving knives, can openers, and coffee grinders; lawn-care implements; throw pillows and paintings of wild geese soaring free over misty fall landscapes. Things nobody would buy but that Laura had paid too much for to give away. Laura had brought home all she and her husband had exempted from the yard sale in Tucson the Sunday he'd shot himself, but because her apartment wouldn't hold it all Aaron Dodge had been persuaded to consolidate his two bedrooms full of apparatus, plans, and ideas into one and offer the second bedroom as a warehouse. Temporarily, of course.

Meantime her husband's brain, preserved in its leaky shell, looking like it had had done to it one of the operations printed above the buttons of blenders, continued to transmit its waves. When Aaron Dodge visited the hospital with Laura, he watched them. Neutral, elapsed messages to the universe. The direction of the waves never deviated. Their magnitude never varied. They enjoyed the protection of the legal and medical professions. They couldn't be tampered with. Hindered in any way. All the fat man wanted for the brain from which they flowed was the last thing it had wanted for itself.

Laura took on more hours at the fabric outlet.

Aaron Dodge sold one, two, three of the extra cars parked behind the blue apartment village.

Then, in February, a fortunate opportunity came the fat man's way. At least it seemed fortunate at first glance. The quarterly newsletter *Camel-Options* arrived in his and Kennedy's mail at the beginning of the month, and Aaron Dodge learned that a bug infestation had struck the community grain supply. He felt an odd sort of relief as he read about the disaster. Tiny brown moths were hatching from invisible eggs their parents had laid in the cornmeal and wheat berries. They'd been seen fluttering up into startled faces as members uncovered the leaky miniature silos in which bulk items were displayed. The article, which included a plea for volunteers, announced that new, bugproof bins would be built. Aaron Dodge smiled. He knew who'd be invited to supervise construction. Using the building project as an excuse, he'd be able to claim time to study the jackpot machine. Plus he could earn money to give to Laura while escaping her household and its daily quota of chaos, whose residue clung to him like soap slime after a bath in soft water. Later that day the phone call came.

The following Monday, Aaron Dodge waited at Camel-Op for his work crew to assemble. He ordered toasted rice cakes and oatmeal sweetened with apple juice and mapped out his strategy on a paper napkin for Lulu.

A public-radio morning news program played through the store's speaker system. Sunlight penetrated a south-facing window that over-looked the street. Seated behind his coffee cup at Lulu's counter, Aaron Dodge watched them straggle in one by one and stare sleepily at a sign-up sheet thumbtacked to the bulletin board. Clearly his detail would be composed of the usual rangy contingent of unemployed freaks, plus students, housewives, and members who, like Aaron Dodge, worked part-time or free-lance.

"How long you figure it'll take you?" Lulu asked.

"Alone, two weeks. With help, a month."

Finally Aaron Dodge walked over to the volunteers and introduced himself. They were a miscellaneous group, individually and collec-tively. As he explained their mission, a tense, thin woman wearing hiking boots and a teal beret repeatedly extended a tape measure to arm's length, then clicked off the safety and let its springy yellow ribbon retract with a slithering snap. The fat man could see that he'd been presented with a challenging group to lead.

He'd participated in Camel-Op service projects before, and was able immediately to divide his unit roughly in two. Half were gentle ide-alists. Mild, vacant, serene. When you spoke to them, they never heard you the first time, and when you assigned them a duty, they responded with half an hour of meditation. Their answer to every attempt at communication was: Tell me about it, Righteous, Check it out, or I hear you. The others, led by the woman in the teal beret, comprised a platoon of militant drudges who defined their progress in life by cataloguing all the things they'd stopped doing. No tobacco. No red meat, caffeine, or sugar. No tv. Aaron Dodge eventually isolated a giraffish, snaggle-toothed, and stoned-looking Sikh, turbanned and reeking of garlic, who said he'd given up construction work to join a local ashram. His name was Deli Elope, and Aaron Dodge appointed him foreman.

The two of them spent most of that first day attempting to discourage as many assistants as they could. Deli Elope satisfied the mystical volunteers with simple tasks which they could spend the morning grasping the cosmic overtones of. The others Aaron Dodge assigned impossibly complex duties, employing a vocabulary punctuated with carpentry and engineering slang. And since they'd been everywhere, seen everything, done everything, they refused to admit that they didn't know what he was talking about, flubbed their responsibilities, and didn't return after lunch. Deli Elope finally drove off the woman in the teal beret by suggesting, as they were positioning some two-by-fours, that she move one "just a cunt hair to your left."

At quitting time, Aaron Dodge congratulated the survivors and bought a round of ciders from Lulu. They'd reassemble tomorrow morning to continue their work.

He called Max Yoder from the phone in the stockroom.

"Where have you been, Aaron? You're just impossible to reach." An electronic *twink* at her end of the line told him it was four o'clock.

When Max's watch twinked five, they were sitting at a table in La Cuchara Grasosa, sipping Sun Belts. A novelty drink concocted by El Holmes, the head bartender, a Sun Belt consisted of a shot of golden Galliano floated between a shot of white crème de menthe and a shot of tequila in an aperitif glass. The fat man had invited Deli Elope along, and Lulu, who was at the bar swapping owlshit with El Holmes, also a degree holder of some sort.

"Have you heard anything?" he asked Max.

"They say they're still interested. Reluctant, though, to make a firm offer."

"But you expect they'll come through?"

"I couldn't speculate, Aaron. Tell me, have you been working on any new ideas?"

"How does this sound? Electronic phones for naturalists. Instead of that standard warbling sound, these would do actual bird calls. The cardinal. The nighthawk."

"I see. Anything else?"

"A guitar. For music teachers. It's equipped with a transparent Fiberglas fingerboard and comes with a set of removable cardboard charts. You insert one into a slot that runs the length of the neck. The charts have little red spots at the finger positions associated with each musical key."

"So you're working. That's good, Aaron. That's important."

La Shorty joined them. He was wearing an elastic leash on his sunglasses, the kind that had once been identified with librarians and telephone operators but was now apparently a chic fashion item. "Aaron Dodge! Where have you been? We've had to throw out food every night for months." La Shorty brought more Sun Belts. They raised their glasses and waited for somebody to think of a toast.

"Reality is fluid," Max said finally, and they drank.

Her wristwatch twinked.

It must've been a full moon or something. Bob the Brush showed up. So did Wendy Wendy. And another round of Sun Belts for Aaron Dodge and his friends. La Shorty introduced the new arrivals to Max and Deli Elope, competing with the tv, the jukebox, and a dozen other conversations that faced the same opposition.

Monday Night Football was playing on the tv in back of the bar. Either pregame or halftime. Or maybe postgame. Aaron Dodge realized he probably ought to ask somebody which. Wendy Wendy wet a fingertip, pressed it to the crumb-size tortilla fragments at the bottom of a serving basket, and licked it. Then she drew the finger lightly across Aaron Dodge's forearm and smiled.

Twink.

Somebody bellowed his name. When Aaron Dodge looked up, El Holmes was holding the payphone receiver in one hand and pointing to it with the other. Kennedy. Wanting to know when he'd be home.

"What time's it getting to be?" he said.

"No shit?" he said.

"Pretty soon," he said.

"No, really," he said.

Twink, the bar lights were up. Twink, the waitresses were smoking cigarettes, emptying their change aprons onto the bar. Then he was in the parking lot and Max was inviting everybody to her house in Paradise Valley for an after-hours party.

Men of Aaron Dodge's physical stature could be counted on to undress only in emergencies. And then only in private. And then only in the dark. The cascading slabs and unpigmented expanses of this torso were secrets better left unrevealed. That's how Aaron Dodge felt about it. So nobody was more astounded than him by what he did at Max's.

As soon as they arrived, Max started drawing draperies, flipping switches, and twisting rheostats. Her efforts revealed a floodlit patio and fenced yard, which Aaron Dodge was about to investigate when Max's husband emerged from a hallway, tying the sash of his bathrobe and squinting. Aaron Dodge had met him before. He was one of those husbands with a separate career, bedroom, and last name—a man in whose case all work and no play had lived up to their reputations. He was a Republican and a tennis player. Last person in the world the fat man would've expected to agree with on any subject. Yet he found himself drunkenly apologizing for this invasion of privacy as Deli Elope, La Shorty, Wendy Wendy, and the others deposited their twelve-packs and gallons of Chablis in his refrigerator and began to shed their clothes on the man's kitchen floor.

He didn't respond. He ignored Aaron Dodge and the rest of the strangers who were making it impossible for him to sleep, exchanged a few threats and insults with the woman he loved, and went back to bed—all options the fat man suddenly wished he could pursue. But he'd left the El Camino in the parking lot at La Cuchara Grasosa and accepted a ride from somebody who'd claimed to be sober.

So Max had a sweatbox. So what? Wedging naked onto slatted ledges beside a corral of ticking stones didn't interest Aaron Dodge. So everybody else was skinnydipping. Big deal. Max's heated pool and its one blue headlight were no temptation to him. He stood by with a Michelob in one hand, counting his pocket change by feel with the other, as the sleek dolphin bodies of his friends, moist with sauna sweat or pool water, bobbled and flounced past.

No thanks. Maybe in a little while I will.

You go ahead. I'll keep an eye on your stuff for you.

Then he saw it. Aaron Dodge didn't know they manufactured them on such a scale. The diameter of a moon crater, this one pulsed and surged at its center. Glowed with an eerie phosphorescence like the morning-glory pools he'd seen in Yellowstone publicity. The Jacuzzi, he heard somebody call it. Aaron Dodge shrugged out of his parachute sportshirt and dropped his bigtop trousers. His friends whistled and cheered.

Gooseflesh climbed his ankles, spread past his knees, his butt, his belly as he lowered himself in. He didn't stop till the level reached his chin, lapped against his closed mouth, and erupted toward his nose.

Aaron Dodge shut his eyes.

Occasionally an anonymous shoulder pressed against his, or a shaved feminine calf chafed one of his own. He was aware of nothing else. Which tonight was exactly the way the fat man wanted it.

One of the differences between a bachelor and a man foolish enough to risk forfeiting that status is that the first tries to upchuck accurately while the other concentrates on a quiet delivery. So Aaron Dodge observed as he knelt in his bathroom—his and Kennedy's bathroom—soon after Max's party ended. Either his own hunger for self-preservation or the protective instincts of his friends had operated efficiently enough to return him to his doorstep at an hour when the mere presence of a vehicle without official identification on its doors could attract suspicion.

"Aaron?"

The overhead light blazed on.

He leaned against the bathtub, shielding his eyes from the fluorescence with an arm. "I just had a great idea for a bumper sticker," he said. " 'Have You Hugged Your Toilet Today?' "

"Are you all right?"

Aaron Dodge knew enough about women to be sure that if he admitted he was he'd never get to sleep tonight. "What does it mean when you have a sort of tightness across here, that extends down into your left arm, and—?"

"Aaron. You better not be serious."

"I'll recover. Go back to bed if you want. I need to get something in my stomach first."

"I'll fix you some eggs."

"No need to fuss. Get some sleep."

"You sure?"

"Positive." The fat man stood up and prowled in the direction of the kitchen. Kennedy followed.

He began fixing himself a sandwich.

"You worried me."

"I was with some friends is all."

"You could've called."

"I didn't think to."

"You said you'd be home soon."

"I did?"

"When I phoned the bar. You said."

"If I did I forgot."

"You did. Look, your hair's all wet." She touched him.

"We went swimming."

"Where at?"

"A friend of mine's. Max's."

"You aren't the only one who likes to swim, you know. I like to swim."

"Let's go to bed. Aren't you tired?"

"No." She followed him to the Bunkport. He undressed and switched off the lamp.

"Okay," said Aaron Dodge. "Maybe I fucked up."

He stroked the bulge in the mattress above. Kennedy rolled away from the insulated caress.

"I fucked up, didn't I?"

"I admit it. I fffff . . ." He paused, but Kennedy wasn't finishing any sentences for him tonight. Today. This morning.

Twink.

"What was that?"

"What?"

"That noise. That beep." Kennedy switched on the lamp.

"I don't know."

"It sounded like it came from . . . here."

His pants were hanging on a bedpost. Aaron Dodge could see the tiny buckle and part of a leather band protruding from the watch pocket. He remembered. Max had given it to him for safekeeping just before she jumped into the pool. Now Kennedy saw it too.

"This is a woman's watch. Where'd you get this?"

Shameless impropriety?

Sleazy nooners at the Erotica Motel?

Or just the same competition Kennedy had faced all along?

Briefly, a fourth female entered Aaron Dodge's life, further threatening his already unsteady commitments to Kennedy, Laura, and Mary Vanessa Singer. The rival Kennedy's accusations helped assemble kept unreasonable hours, or must've, because it was late at night that Kennedy objected most fiercely to the fat man's absences. He met her at bars and diners with names like the Ostrich Feather, the Cufflink, the Loophole Café and Fine Print Lounge, publicly flaunting the affair to add to Kennedy's humiliation. She smoked, because that's how the fat man smelled when he returned from their assignations.

At Camel-Op, with friends, he made the entire incident sound like a joke. He griped to his newest acquaintance, Deli Elope, while they worked together on the bins. He'd suffered through this with women before, he told his friend. Though it was clear he hadn't committed the misdeed he was being punished for, he'd nevertheless failed simply by permitting the appearance of misconduct, and now he'd have to pay. And pay. He'd have to accept responsibility for the manufactured indiscretion, plus all the retroactive blame he'd been accumulating since the first time he'd ever answered "Great" without bothering to look when Kennedy asked how a color combination worked on her. It was like when a state trooper pulled you over, he told Deli Elope. He knows he's got you on a chickenshit taillight violation, so now he can start scrounging for the real dirt—the expired license, the lapsed registration, the heroin behind your door panels.

Easy to laugh from among the shelves at Camel-Op, where blood was ketchup, but at home the intrusion of "the other woman"—though Kennedy could maintain the illusion of her presence only for a week or so—provided a new source of tension in their extended household. Made the lack of privacy, the overcrowding that much more oppressive. Laura, to her credit, reacted diplomatically, even good-naturedly to their quarrels. Obviously she didn't want to confirm Kennedy's suspicions by implying that another woman was a possibility, but neither did she want to insult the fat man by laughing out loud.

It took the suggestion of an infidelity to make him notice what Kennedy had apparently sensed for months. Like so many men he knew, he'd migrated listlessly from the emotional desert of bachelorhood to the emotional quagmire of sustained involvement without pausing for so much as a snapshot of the spectacular scenery between.

Though he knew he loved Kennedy, too often he got up in the morning without talking to her, spent the day without thinking of her, and went to sleep at night without touching her. And while this arrangement seemed pretty typical to him, and tolerable to the majority of couples he'd observed, still he couldn't blame Kennedy for feeling gypped. Clearly he was either going to have to reveal the actual cause of his preoccupation—Mary Vanessa Singer—or accept the consequences. Kennedy's mistrust. The assumption that there was something wrong between them.

He'd try staying home more, he decided. But that turned out to be the extent of his compromise. As close as he came to any kind of confession or revelation. Holed up in his bedroom shop, working, or with friends at Camel-Op, Aaron Dodge began to see that he really did have a mistress. And always had. He was crazy about her. He'd do just about anything to be with her. Invent excuses, lie, offer partial or misleading explanations of his sudden departures or tardy returns, then ask friends to cover for him. He bought her presents. Never told her no. Lapsed into rapturous thoughts of her in the middle of conversations, in the middle of arguments, in the middle of lovemaking. He met her every time she called, wherever she asked him to, in spite of the risks and fuck the consequences, and when she didn't call he went looking for her. Every bar and diner he could think of. Then the desert, the mountains. Searching far into the night. No way would Kennedy ever catch them together, because the minute Kennedy walked into the same room she disappeared. She was someone, the fat man admitted sadly to himself, that he didn't intend to stop seeing.

He found himself enjoying the Camel-Op project less and less. The scene at home when he left, the guilt during the time he spent away, the coolness when he returned. He began entrusting the work crew to Deli Elope's supervision more days than not. Alone in his bedroom, watched by the photo of Mary Vanessa Singer, he slowly accepted the prospect of addressing the work assigned him by Dixon and Magdalena. Kennedy seemed pleased.

Until, on one of those days in early March when nobody could believe it was this hot already, she came home from classes and, believing she was alone, tuned in a soap and began to undress in front of the tv. Just before or just after she unhooked her brassiere, depending on whose report of the incident Aaron Dodge chose to accept, Bob the Brush walked in.

"He has a key," the fat man explained to Kennedy later. "Sorry. I thought I told you."

"You have no right to indiscriminately hand out keys to this apartment."

"Bob has a key to my apartment, I have a key to his. We're friends. We borrow each other's tools."

"How many keys are there? Who else can I expect to barge in?"

"Look, I'll tell him to make noise next time. Or put a note on the door or something. He feels bad about it. He's embarrassed too."

"There isn't going to be any next time. I want that key." Kennedy pointed emphatically into her open palm.

"Hey. Don't tell me how to treat my friends. I've known Bob a hell of a lot longer than I've known you."

"Maybe you should move in with *him,* then."

"Besides, what's the difference? We keep a goddam key in the mailbox. Because somebody who lives in this house never knows where hers is. Any goddam pervert off the street could walk right in."

"What do you care? It wouldn't be you who'd get raped and strangled. You're never here. It'd be me. And you'd never even know it unless one of your stupid friends read about it in the paper. You don't care about me."

"Maybe you'd understand if you owned anything worth stealing. You've either lost or broken everything valuable you've ever owned."

"What's so special about this *crap?*"

"Any 'crap' you see around here belongs to you and your sister. Everything of *mine* worked perfectly until you moved in. You and your sister and her goddam pygmies."

"You can't wait to dump me, can you? You've got one foot in the street already. You hate me."

"Laura has a key."

"I don't care. I don't want other people owning keys to this apartment. I don't trust that Bob. Or any of the rest of your friends. They're weird."

"Just because they don't have daddies bankrolling their holidays in Arizona like your friends."

"They make me feel stupid."

"All your friends ever do is talk about their haircuts and compare tans. Why don't they tattoo labels right onto their foreheads and get it over with? The biggest decision any of them ever had to make was whether to get one or both ears pierced."

"You better shut up about my friends."

"Forget it. I'm going out."

"There. See? I can't believe it. You're leaving again."

"Why shouldn't I? You're impossible to have a conversation with."

"Okay then. Go. I don't care. Go get a thousand keys made up. Hand them out on the street. Say, 'Here. Go ogle my girlfriend. She's probably getting ready to take her clothes off right this minute.' "

"I'm splitting."

"Good. Get out of here. Go. Now."

The fat man yanked open the front door.

"Where are you going? Wait. Come back here. Don't go."

Later he watched as Kennedy, dressed in just an old white shirt of his, opened the refrigerator and stared inside. The interior bulb projected her shadow across the dark kitchen. From his seat at the table he appreciated the silhouette of her hips, the profile of a breast as she bent to pull out the vegetable crisper. People of size like to eat without lights on, and the two of them snacked in silence, occasionally touching across the whole wheat, the carrot sticks and cheeses, the bowls of ice cream and cereal that separated them.

"I've gained," Kennedy said. She pinched her stomach and frowned.

Celery crunched. A spoon fell to the floor.

"If you put on more than ten pounds, you should have your diaphragm refitted."

"Really?"

Chair legs scooted. The refrigerator murmured.

"Do I look like I've put on ten pounds?"

"You look great."

"Can you eat the rest of this?"

"You don't want it? I was just saying that, if you ever do, sometime in the far distant future . . ."

"But you'd tell me, wouldn't you?"

He opened a beer.

Kennedy smiled at him. Propped an elbow on the table and rested her chin on her hand. "Am I a good lover?"

"You fuck like they were paying you by the hour for it."

She propped her chin up with the other hand. "What's your favorite part of my body?"

"I don't know. I can hardly remember what they all look like. You might have to refresh my memory."

He envied Kennedy. She evidently thought this had been a serious falling out. Plus she probably assumed it was over. That they'd ended it in the Bunkport. Intimacy as apology. Romance as compromise. Sex as diplomacy. It was like thinking an Olympics could resolve the arms race. She had no right to be so happy based on such a blatant misconception. Still, he wished he could share that misconception. Sleep. Sex. His favorites were the problems you could solve in bed. He knew everything would be fine, or at least a lot better, if he'd only get to work. He'd virtually stopped reading the paper. Every time he saw Mary Vanessa Singer's photo, he turned the page. Lately he'd been considering an option that might allow him more time alone to catch up. He mentioned it now to Kennedy.

"Laura's pretty crowded at her place, isn't she?"

"More than pretty."

"And we're definitely crowded here. I think I know what we can do with some of the stuff."

"What?"

"You'll see."

Pack Rat Mini-Storage's six parallel rows of unpainted cinderblock cubicles sat like identical sidetracked freights in a stranded lot off Baseline Road west of 38th Avenue.

The fat man parked his yellow El Camino beside unit A. Plate glass had been substituted for its aluminum garage door. Above the entrance swung a narrow shingle. OFFICE. Inside, pressed-wood paneling covered the windowless walls. A grid supporting foam tiles and a bank of fluorescent lights sagged to within inches of his head. Trailing across the concrete floor toward a desk, an extension cord fed a floor fan and telephone-answering machine. A woman, circles the color of cooked rhubarb under her eyes, sat reading *Interview* and drinking a Tab.

"I'm interested in one of your storage spaces," Aaron Dodge told her. She handed him a broadside photocopied on gold paper. He asked about lighting, patrols, liability, price. For fifty per month and a fifty-dollar deposit he could secure a deluxe ten-by-twenty-footer. He signed the rental agreement and on the way home bought a hefty padlock and added the key to his ring.

The fat man had the afternoon coming to him. He'd left Deli Elope in charge of the work crew, and Laura was also at Camel-Op, logging an extra shift to increase the family's working-member discount. Kennedy had hauled the kids to Ont Hazel's in Sun City.

He worked alone. Toys, kitchenware, books, bedding—anything he thought Laura and the kids could do without temporarily. He'd hoisted half a truckload aboard the El Camino's scarred tailgate before he recognized the opportunity he was missing. He'd been moving the wrong person. He manhandled everything back inside. Beginning again, he stripped the bedroom walls. Designs, sketches, notations for future "Aaron's Inventories." He collapsed his drafting table. Unplugged the Commodore 64. He sleeved the floppy disks on which he'd stored ideas so far untranslated from words to reality. He lugged away inventions he'd forgotten he'd invented. His Pic-Chairs, a collaboration with a painter friend, were space-saving fold-up chairs with original landscapes and still lifes painted on the rear of the backrests and the undersides of the seats. Folding brought the two halves of the painting together and allowed the chair to be stored on a wall like art. His Mason-jar lamp—an electric candlestick that instead of a glass chimney utilized grandma's antique canning jar as a globe. Available in clear, amber, or blue. You learned after a while not to invent things you might end up caring deeply about. Everything was a fad anyway. He'd watched too many friends taken in by ideals and dreams. You could spend your life on a project like that.

Three hours after he'd unloaded the first, all but one of Aaron Dodge's inventions sat inside the cold, cramped, dark cubicle at Pack Rat Mini-Storage. He lowered and padlocked the door. Consulted his watch. Estimated the chances of encountering Kennedy if he returned to the apartment. At some point during the afternoon he'd realized that this moment would arrive. He'd have to decide. Would the move include only items essential to his profession? Or expand to include private possessions? Was this move the one he'd started planning last May?

She wasn't home yet when he arrived. He heaved both cushions into the cab of the El Camino, then stood the Bunkport's heavy, six-foot frame on end in the living room. He studied it briefly. Crouched. Inhaled. Then consented to its substantial weight.

The fat man grunted and staggered. Lurched backward and sideways trying to distribute the load. Shifting from one foot to the other, he gradually repositioned himself to face the doorway. One step in that direction would mean unstoppable momentum. But before he could take that one step, the phone rang.

Aaron Dodge was an inventor. A free-lancer. Nature compelled him. Bent double under his burden, he grabbed for the wall phone. As he lifted the receiver, his center of gravity shifted. The fat man struggled. Stumbled. Lunged.

Collapsed.

The Bunkport buried him. Pinned to the floor beneath it, he dragged the receiver toward him by the cord and spoke in its direction. "Hello?"

"What are you *doing*, Aaron Dodge?"

"Nothing. I tripped. But I'm okay."

"You better dash right over," said Lulu.

"What's wrong?"

"Quick," she told him. "Now."

He rolled the Bunkport off him and lay beside it, breathing hard, staring up at the ceiling.

At Camel-Op he found Deli Elope and Kennedy sitting dejectedly at Lulu's counter.

"What happened?"

"You tell," said Kennedy.

"I'm sorry, Aaron," said Deli Elope. "It was my fault."

"It was nobody's fault," said Lulu. "Just crummy luck is all. More crummy luck. Poor Laura."

Deli Elope reconstructed for Aaron Dodge the moment of disaster. The sound of splitting wood and a scream had caused him to look up from the work he was doing on the bins. He saw Laura, a banner she'd been about to hang trailing her like a tangled parachute, crash-land spectacularly at the base of the ladder, inches from some burlap bags of exotic coffee beans that could've changed Aaron Dodge's life. Deli Elope commandeered a filleting knife from Housewares and split the inseam of Laura's jeans. The leg had already begun to color and swell. When the ambulance arrived, an attendant sedated her and placed the leg in an immobilizer.

"Sorry," said Deli Elope.

The fat man shrugged.

It was past dark when he and Kennedy returned from the hospital. The Bunkport still lay capsized on the living-room floor.

"Where is everything?" Kennedy asked. "Where's the tv?"

"I moved it," said Aaron Dodge. "Instead of Laura's stuff. I rented a storage space."

"What on earth for, Aaron?"

"I don't know. I guess I was thinking it could be my, you know, my workshop or something from now on."

"You moved out. You were leaving me. Us."

The fat man shrugged. "Not really. I was just . . ."

Kennedy started to cry. Aaron Dodge moved next to her. Held her. She tried to push him away but he forced her to be held. He held her with his physical strength, the amount of him.

"I won't go," he told her.

The hospital released Laura the next day. The minute she put her crutches down, the kids, all six, insisted on autographing the cast. But since most of them couldn't write yet, their attempts, painstakingly aimed at reproducing their elders' illegible signatures, came out doubly indecipherable, and in their intricate meaninglessness seemed to verify, authorize, acknowledge, endorse—in a mysterious but powerful way—everything that would happen next.

PART THREE

SAFE RETURN

10

His first concession was a part-time job at a place called Pizza on Wheels. The rims of the delivery truck he drove were painted cheesy yellow with pepperoni polka-dots. He wore a loose, checkered uniform which his new bosses suggested he purchase, since none of the ones they provided would fit him. The first time he put it on, the fat man reminded himself that integrity was like virginity. Nobody expected you to keep it forever. If you were judged at all, you were judged on the basis of how long you held out.

Laszlo and Tony offered carry-out only. No booths or tables, just a counter with a work area behind—more like the setup inside a dry cleaner's than a restaurant. Which added a savage territorial aspect to the work accomplished there. In a grocery or department store, the help, if they're lucky, can retreat once an hour to a row of vending machines or a lounge for coffee and a smoke. The rest of the time they're out front with the merchandise and shoppers. But at Pizza on Wheels, employees controlled the territory, all except a narrow aisle facing the register. As a result, customers encountered a unique work ethic there. A patron walked through Laszlo and Tony's door and immediately he was outnumbered. Everybody knew the rules but him.

What'll it be, mister?

Uh, let's see. How big's a medium?

Laszlo would roll his eyes. Aim his ballpoint at three round aluminum pans, each with a price printed in its center, mounted on the wall behind him. And this was only the beginning of the humiliation.

No wonder call-in orders predominated at Pizza on Wheels. That way it was *you* invading *their* territory. You find the address and somebody'll be having a party or watching a Suns game on cable. A lot of times they've already asked on the phone how much including tax they'll owe. A hand shoves money into yours, dropping pennies all over, and shuts the door in your face. Or else they'll give you six cents and call it a tip. They'll try to underpay, or they'll make you hold the box while they open the lid and inspect. Is it cold? Is it the right ingredients? Has all the cheese slid off and glued itself to the cardboard because you didn't hold it perfectly level while you climbed the stairs, stepped over the basketballs and skateboards, avoided the dog? Your windshield's always fogged, every porchlight in the world's burnt out, the house numbers are amoebas, and all the streetsigns read like Arabic. You walk through the back door at some ungodly hour, weatherbeaten, insulted, sleepless, and short-changed, and Laszlo and Tony look at you like you're spying on their conversation, even though you don't speak a word of the language. You're an intruder to the people you deliver to and an intruder to the people you deliver for. Your one refuge is the cab of the delivery truck. A radio, a heater, a street map, a lighter, a matchbox full of reefer zipped into the change pouch.

At 5:00 A.M., when his shift ended, the fat man usually drove to Camel-Op for coffee. For the smell of something else baking. Maybe a fresh honey-glazed cinnamon-raisin nut roll the size of a manhole cover. His arrival coincided with the morning paper's. He'd buy a *Representative* from the machine near the bus stop across the street, using change from his tips, and search the front page and "Metro" section while Lulu leaned across the counter and helped.

Mary Vanessa Singer was dead.

They'd never find her.

Years of cynicism paid off for the fat man at times like this. Among friends, he was able to disguise his interest in the disappearance with the kinds of comments they'd come to expect from him.

"More stolen cars and stray dogs are recovered every year than missing children," he told Lulu one dreary morning in March.

"You haven't seen the reward they're offering," she insisted, and quoted a news account from that day's edition. The reward, pledged by the newspaper, local banks, car dealerships, welding shops, law offices, bakeries, and landscaping firms, had been split into three unequal shares. A large amount "for information leading to the whereabouts." A larger sum "for the safe return of." A third, middle-sized bounty "for information leading to the apprehension and conviction of the person or persons responsible." Together the three figures amounted to something close to what a respectable lottery payoff might've. And it looked like the totals would continue to inflate. Agent Orange, the fat man's friend from his own days as a carrier, was organizing a rock benefit. Nationally known millionaire musicians would perform.

"When millionaires get together," the fat man said, "there's only one ultimate beneficiary. Millionaires."

Somebody else was planning a hundred-dollar-a-plate dinner with proceeds going to the search fund.

"Not even I could get my money's worth at that price," Aaron Dodge said.

" 'While the community slept,' it says here. I like that," said Lulu. "She disappeared 'while the community slept.' It's so accurate. On so many levels."

"She's dead meat."

"You don't know that."

"Dead and probably better off that way."

"Hush, Aaron Dodge."

"Better dead than in the back of some shag-carpeted van getting buggered and face-fucked by a half-retarded drooler."

Finally a stranger, a young man with a sparse, wiry beard and compassionate maple eyes, protested from the far end of the counter. "You're a real pessimist, aren't you, friend?"

"I used to be," the fat man said. "The world caught up with me."

Aaron Dodge, while he faked disinterest and misled his friends, had moved the last of his equipment to the mini–storage unit in order to assure his privacy. But an important element remained unprovided for—something he couldn't work at the laboratory without. One morning in late March he postponed his daily stop at Lulu's. Still dressed in his sauce-splattered uniform, he continued west on Grand Avenue, past the underpass, through the light at 83rd and Peoria, toward Sun City.

He slowed in front of Ont Hazel's house, observed a light in the kitchen, and backed the El Camino into her driveway. He shut off the engine and headlights and saw Hazel's porch bulb come on.

"Aaron! Is that you?" She'd opened the door only as far as the lock chain allowed.

"Decided to take you up on your offer," Aaron Dodge said, and nodded in the direction of Ont Hazel's carport. "Sorry if I surprised you."

Wearing an ASU sweatsuit, a gift from Kennedy, and slippers, she joined him in the driveway. "I'm pleased you did." She stooped for the morning newspaper, then pointed with it in the direction he'd indicated. "Guess I should've sold the thing. But I kept wondering if I might . . . oh, I don't know."

"Take up the sport yourself someday," said Aaron Dodge. "Sure." The electric golf cart, a three-wheeler with a surrey top, had belonged to her late husband.

"Aren't you chilly in that?" Hazel stared at his flimsy delivery smock as he climbed from the El Camino.

"Insulation," the fat man said, and grabbed a handful.

He'd brought along planks, three eight-footers, which he dragged from the truck bed. He positioned each with an end propped on the tailgate, the other resting on the driveway cement.

"Aaron, I have to say. I just think it's a wonder. Your providing for Laura and the children. So generous and kind." The fat man shrugged. He'd been loaning his paychecks from Pizza on Wheels. Loaning in the same sense that you loan piss to a urinal.

"I'll fetch you the key," Ont Hazel said.

Aaron Dodge unplugged the cart from its battery charger and climbed aboard. Ont Hazel returned with the key. The solenoid clucked, the electric motor whirred as the fat man maneuvered it from its parking spot beside Ont Hazel's salt-lick-yellow LTD and aimed it at the ramp he'd constructed.

"Be careful, Aaron."

He floored the footfeed.

The lumber underneath chattered and heaved as the cart struggled against the incline. A pulley-belt shrieked. He smelled hot rubber, arcing electricity. He felt a bump and surge as the cart dove into the truck bed, and yanked the handbrake on. One of the boards clattered to the pavement.

"Gracious," was all Ont Hazel could say.

Later he unloaded at Pack Rat and drove the cart inside. He shut the door and aimed flashlights from several angles. Their crisscrossing beams illuminated his work. He lifted the seat cushions, exposing the six auto batteries that powered the cart. He loosened the harness that fed the motor, reconnected it to an adapter he'd rigged, and wound the splices with friction tape. Earlier in the week he'd mounted floods, one in each corner, wired to a single switch.

He flipped it on.

The storage unit filled with dim light.

"What size shoes you wear?" Dixon asked.

Aaron Dodge shrugged. "Twelves. Eleven-and-a-halfs. Why?"

"I knew they'd have to be big for you to step in this much shit."

The fat man had just finished describing the accident. Detailing for Phil Dixon his obligations to Laura and her six. Not that Dixon was his idea of the perfect person to confide in. In fact, talking to Dixon was a lot like picking up a tennis ball after a dog's been chewing on it. But since he wasn't supposed to discuss Mary Vanessa Singer with his real friends, his only other choice was to try and make real friends of the two people he could discuss Mary Vanessa Singer with.

When he'd offered to buy a few days earlier, the fat man had envisioned the type of conversation a couple of guys might have over lunch hour in an orange booth someplace. Sucking on toothpicks. Tasting onions. Propping elbows behind them on vinyl backrests and feeling faint static charges tug at the hair on their forearms.

That's fucked, man. You don't get to screw the bitch. You ain't allowed to hit her kids. All's you get to do is pay out the ass.

It's an unnatural situation.

You don't need it.

But what can I do?

That's just it. What can you do?

I've got to live with myself.

You have to live with yourself. All this women's-lib shit, this Affirmative Action crap, but in the final analysis who pays the rent?

There you go.

Let the Supreme Court chew on that a while.

A little bullshit and pity. That's all the fat man wanted. But instead the place turned out to be Scottsdale. The booths turned out to be refinished wooden pews, all occupied when he and Dixon arrived. They ended up at a table. Seated in the kind of chairs a fat man dreaded. Deck chairs. He'd placed himself at one's mercy and hadn't moved since, fearing that any gesture might buckle its chrome frame, any fidget accelerate him through its taut canvas bottom like a watermelon through a Kleenex. It was one of those places where the waitress circled your order on her preprinted pad instead of writing it. Where you asked for coffee and had to select a blend, which arrived defaced by a drift of whipped cream. And Dixon was at least as disappointing as the burger—served disassembled and featuring a bun that left tiny seeds impacted in your teeth.

"Does this mean you want to weasel out of our arrangement?"

"Not at all," said Aaron Dodge. "I'm just trying to explain why I'm taking so long."

"You don't have to explain anything to me, Mr. Dodge. Me and Magdalena, all we're interested in is progress. Progress, Mr. Dodge?"

The fat man shook his head.

Dixon wore a madras sportcoat and a yellow Ban-Lon polo shirt. He held his cigarette between his first two fingers and flicked at its tip with his third, spraying the vicinity of an ashtray in the center of the table.

"Can you aim that thing in another direction?" the fat man said.

"Hey, this is the smoking section."

"Yeah, and they got a bathroom here too, but that doesn't mean I can piss on you."

Dixon spoke casually for the most part. Seldom directly, never sympathetically, but always casually. If there was something he preferred not to say, he wrote on his napkin with a Bic he'd borrowed from the waitress, pushed it across the table to Aaron Dodge, then scratched out his message and the reply when the fat man passed it back.

"Too many winners lately," one of his notes said. "No big hurry fr. yr. end."

"Bidding up the pot?" the fat man's answer read.

"Min. $5 mil.," said the note Dixon returned.

Evidently he and Magdalena worried that a smaller jackpot would fail to interest their pervert. Lottery Commission stats pointed to a noticeable increase in activity when a payoff reached the figure Dixon had indicated. The fat man could understand why. Five million sounded like a sum large enough to overcome anybody's caution.

Aaron Dodge tried again. Dixon couldn't be as unbefriendable as he acted. Did he have a wife? Kids? Dixon uncapped the pen they'd been exchanging information with and investigated an ear with the sharp little appendage that fastens to your shirt pocket. He said divorced. Said the kids were with her. East Coast, he said.

Beyond disenchantment, the fat man thought then. Completely unreachable, like so many men he knew. Men who'd dissolved marriages, checked parents into nursing homes, conceded custody of children, then settled into lives they at last understood. Could be he was looking across the table at his own future.

Dixon glanced at his wristwatch. "Look, I've got to run. My akita. She has to have this special food, vet's orders, which I ran out of it two days ago. So . . ." He stood and shook hands with the fat man. "Stay in touch, okay? And keep an eye on that jackpot."

Lunch with Phil Dixon cured his hunger for understanding. What can you do? You accept full responsibility. Double responsibility. But to everybody concerned you look like you're only half trying. Like you're shirking your duty. Reveal all your facts, you're a traitor. Reveal all your feelings, you're a whiner. Alone mornings inside the mini–storage unit, wearing his idiotic Pizza on Wheels outfit, the fat man slowly got used to the facts. And the feelings.

At that point, early April, the lottery jackpot stood at around four hundred thousand dollars.

If Kennedy's notorious other woman really did exist, if mentally and emotionally the fat man's machines and ideas amounted to a mistress, then the mini–storage unit corresponded to the couple's love nest. When he could avoid staying home and babysitting, or when he managed to evade his extra job, he took advantage of the quiet and solitude waiting in the diluted light at Pack Rat. But with spring close he wasn't sure how much longer the clandestine arrangement would last. Daily the heat inside his stall was building. At dawn, when he lifted the door, a fierce exhalation greeted him—the smell of metal and concrete irradiated by desert temperatures. Cooked, disenchanted air that took all the pleasure out of breathing. But he stayed and worked. Shirtless, sweating.

Early, following his shift at Pizza on Wheels, he'd arrive and unlock the cubicle. He'd remove a battery from the yoke of six in Ont Hazel's golf cart, install it in the El Camino for a boost, and replace it with the one he'd removed and charged the previous day. But even with frequent rotations the cart batteries wouldn't power much other than his lighting system, so some mornings the fat man would say fuck it, tap into the line that supplied the Pack Rat office module, and feed the additional wiring through a hole he'd drilled in the mortar crevice between two cinderblocks in the back wall of his unit. One April morning he confiscated enough juice to watch tv. With the help of a VCR that belonged to Wendy Wendy, he examined a tape of *Jackpot Jack* reruns. He'd been recording the show on Wendy's machine every Friday since he'd borrowed it (supposedly to entertain Laura while she was housebound in her cast). He'd punch the freeze button, halting numbered balls in mid-ricochet, and study individual frames. In this way he identified the machine's most obvious design characteristics. He made detailed drawings from a variety of angles.

Inside his cubicle, as he attempted to reconstruct the jackpot machine from incomplete information and unreliable clues, he often wondered out loud if his efforts would ever be recognized. More than once he'd told himself that Dixon and Magdalena could be anybody. A couple of crooks. One crook says to the other crook: This guy, this inventor, he's in the newspaper every day. Know who I'm talking about? Fat guy? I say we convince this chump to rig the lottery for us. We let him do all the work. We stay clear of it. That way: He succeeds? Super. He doesn't? He gets himself busted? We never heard of him. And I know exactly how we set this Dodge guy up. You see this article on the front page? This papergirl item . . . ?

Even conceding the authenticity of Dixon and Magdalena's original story, it didn't seem likely to the fat man that the same person would play the same six numbers for this long. But Phil Dixon had assured him during their lunch in Scottsdale that evidence existed. Evidence equal to any they'd uncovered prior to soliciting his aid. Like what evidence? Dixon, condescending as usual, had insisted the fat man didn't understand the type of personality they were dealing with. He'd mentioned painstakingly detailed computer files maintained by collectors of child porn. Alphabetized, categorized, subclassified, and cross-referenced. Backed up by handwritten diaries describing contacts with children. Illustrated by snapshots mounted in albums and sentimentally captioned. Supplemented by soiled underpants sealed in plastic and labeled with school photos like the one of Mary Vanessa Singer that was always appearing in the newspaper. For somebody who might concurrently be packaging fingernail clippings and freezing bags of feces, the selection of identical lottery chances for a dozen or even a hundred weeks running didn't represent, in Dixon's opinion, even mildly compulsive behavior. Dixon seemed to enjoy cataloguing the graphic insinuations. But they didn't sway Aaron Dodge. He told Dixon to arrange a talk with Officer Magdalena.

Magdalena refused to meet with him in public. In order to set up a meeting, the fat man had to surrender an important piece of information. The location of his hideout. Magdalena met him at Pack Rat on a Sunday morning.

"Jesus, it's a fucking sweat lodge in here. How can you stand it?"

The fat man shrugged. "You should see what's going on at my apartment if you want to talk about merciless torture."

"Secrecy-wise, though, I have to admire your standards." With an approving nod Magdalena observed the contents of the cubicle. The soles of his little shoes scraped the concrete floor like sandpaper as he pivoted from foot to foot to take in every detail.

"Surely he's left Phoenix with her," Aaron Dodge said, once he'd brought up the subject of his doubts. "I mean, how could he not have by now? Anybody would."

"Once again you're employing an average, man-on-the-street line of mentality, Mr. Dodge," Magdalena told him, indicating by a sawing motion of his hand a consistent forward progression. "Publicity, media interest, photos. He's probably filling scrapbooks. The pictures of this little girl, right there beside the Colonel Qaddafi bombing raids and the Space *Challenger* shuttle exploding? Consider from his perspective, Mr. Dodge, how all this would increase the excitement."

When the fat man needed further encouragement, Magdalena reluctantly told him more. In a Phoenix bank, at a kiosk where patrons stopped to fill out checks and forms, in a cubbyhole along with other, blank transaction slips, one had been discovered bearing a familiar message.

Still alive, Mary Vanessa Singer.

And alongside her signature, the six numbers, listed like deposits.

"This is an intelligent youngster. Opportunistic," Magdalena said. "Yet they feel guilt, Mr. Dodge, these children. Most won't betray the individual exploiting them. Inside, they know right and wrong. Yet this adult. This, to them, symbol of authority. He's saying what's wrong is okay. Mixing them up. They morally don't know what to believe any more. What I'm saying is, these numbers, they're a unique, once-upon-a-blue-moon type of opportunity. She can implicate this individual, and yet say to herself: These are numbers. This is not really him. The man. His street address. His name. His face. You should trust us, Mr. Dodge. You should help out this little girl."

By the day of Magdalena's visit, the jackpot payoff had already risen past a million dollars.

The following Tuesday morning, after working in the mini–storage unit since dawn, the fat man locked up and phoned Max Yoder from a booth at a Circle K on Baseline Road.

He had to time his calls to Max carefully. Mondays before noon or Fridays after, you could forget. Anytime between ten and two the other days, she'd be at lunch. From just past nine to ten and from two to five she was either With a Client, On the Other Line, or Away from Her Desk Right Now. That left a fleeting opportunity at the beginning of the workday. Reach her before the receptionist arrived. Early, while she watched the swirling beige foam disappear from the surface of her first cup of instant. While she stared about in bewilderment, inhaling the stale, air-conditioned gases, her sinuses slamming shut for the day. Your one chance to get through. At that moment she'd talk to anyone.

"Max, I need a favor."

Silence from Max's end.

"Max? Listen, okay? Can I ask a favor?"

"Oh. Aaron. Good morning. How've you been?"

"Fine. Can you get me a copy of a design, Max?"

"What can I do for you, Aaron? Just a sec, all right? Can I put you on hold?"

"Listen, Max. All I need is to see this one patent application. You still there?"

It was possible to obtain designs for any product patented in the U.S. from the National Patent Office in Crystal City, Virginia, and from patent depository libraries in a number of large cities, Phoenix included. But you needed the patent number or you were in for a long search.

"Can you help me out, Max?"

"I just flew back from Washington yesterday, Aaron. I wish you'd called me about this last week. What did you say the name of the product was?"

"Thanks, Max. You know that machine that scrambles up the numbers when they pick for the lottery jackpot every Friday? I need to know how it works."

"What do you want with those plans, Aaron?" Max sounded awake now.

"I just need them is all. I want to design my own machine. Sell the idea to the lottery people. I know I could do better—"

"That's absurd, Aaron. What an absolutely transparent lie."

"I can get the plans myself if you won't."

"Do you know the patent number?"

No answer from Aaron Dodge. Without the number he'd have to either fly to Virginia himself or search for days in the *Gazette*s at the patent depository of the ASU library.

"That's what I thought," Max said.

"When can we get together? We need to talk about this."

"I don't know. Lunch? Friday?"

"Before then."

"I do this for a living, Aaron. You're not my only client."

"Okay. Friday, then. I'll pick you up."

Max made him eat lunch with her at one of those places downtown. Striped awnings. Colorful umbrellas advertising famous sparkling waters, expensive vermouths. His presence created an immediate bottleneck on the veranda. Waitresses holding aloft full serving trays

searched desperately in every direction, their customary delivery routes
sealed off in the vicinity of the fat man's table. Arriving diners met
departing diners head-on. Busboys dressed in starched jackets and
carrying full water pitchers collided, cursing each other in Spanish.

"So, Aaron. How's your woman friend?"

The fat man shook his head helplessly. "You're married, Max. Tell
me. How do you know if you're happy with somebody?"

"Oh, I don't know. It's hard, Aaron. Joy is subtle."

"Are you happy?"

"Me? Oh yes. Lately, very."

"How can you tell?"

"Let me see. Well, now, when Curran and I fight, divorce is, I don't
know, probably third or fourth on the list of alternatives I consider."

"She loses everything, Max. Not one ballpoint in our house has a
cap on it. I have no idea where my pica stick went. She inserts cassettes
into the player with bread dough on her hands. Max, I used to own
three windbreakers. My own are bad enough. To think I could be
responsible for the rest of my life for somebody else's mistakes too—
it terrifies me."

"Umm. I know. In terms of tax liability alone the implications are
overwhelming. But we all have our quirks, Aaron. I'm certain Kennedy
dislikes habits of yours."

"She finishes my sentences."

"That's one of the things marriage is good for. I think. It makes you
more tolerant. Less selfish."

"She's generous all right. Did I tell you I used to have three
windbreakers?"

By the time their food came, traffic had adjusted and Aaron Dodge
felt less conspicuous. "Max. Listen. No kidding, what about the jackpot
machine? Those designs?"

"Impossible."

"But I've got this great idea."

"Convince me."

"Really. It'll work. But I'd rather not talk till I'm further along. Bad
luck."

"Sorry, Aaron."

Magdalena and Dixon had of course described in detail what would happen to him if he repeated any of the story they'd shared with him. He didn't know the six winning numbers yet, but what he did know would surely queer the whole setup if he didn't keep it to himself. Nobody suspected yet what he really did every morning. Where he went. His friends must've assumed he'd been spending more of his time at home with Kennedy. Kennedy and Laura believed he was off drinking coffee someplace, wasting time with friends. He'd been able to satisfy Dixon and Magdalena's requirements up to now. But Aaron Dodge's behavior as well as his physique had been shaped inside dine-rites and at lunch counters. He wasn't a man who by nature hesitated if his information would buy some of yours.

"Okay then," the fat man said. "Max, doggie-bag that mess. Let's get out of here and I'll tell you a real story. Get ready to be convinced."

The fat man drove to Encanto Park, and he and Max sat on a bench beside the lagoon, Max tossing bits of her three-dollar croissant to ducks huddled onshore. There he told her the truth, as much of it as Magdalena and Dixon had entrusted to him, and waited for Max's response.

She stared at the water, her hands thrust into her sweater, as some of the flock's bolder members waddled close to the bench, quacking unenthusiastically. Max. He couldn't imagine her with a child on her lap. Or drinking beer straight from the bottle. Or sitting in the bathroom with her pants around her ankles, reading the funnies. She knew the emotion appropriate to a situation and always showed the proper one at the proper time, reacting as if she were catching tricks in a game of spades. But she wasn't like the rest of his friends. While they'd contracted mono and hepatitis, she'd been scoring in the ninety-ninth percentile on those nationally regulated exams with three initials. While Aaron Dodge lay on his back in an alley behind some theater, stealing transmissions from the cars of couples watching *Funny Girl* inside, Max had been in Chicago, a delegate to the Democratic convention. While he ate himself into his present condition, she'd been in law school at Duke. Max had spent her life doing smart things. The fat man examined her profile, realizing he had absolutely no idea what she'd say to his request. Whether she'd believe his story. Whether he did.

When Max finally looked at him, she was crying. "I can't, Aaron. I can't get involved in something like this. And you shouldn't either. I won't help you. I'm sorry."

"But think about it, Max. A chance to do something with your . . . your power, your position, your degree. Didn't you tell yourself that's what they were for the whole time you were working toward them?"

"But this is just crazy, Aaron. This isn't the right opportunity. Look what I'd be throwing away. All I'd be risking."

"Right. Not like me. Easy for me to talk."

"I didn't mean—"

"Look. Do me at least one favor. Don't mention this to anybody."

"Of course I won't, Aaron. You know me better than that."

"I thought I did," said the fat man.

He didn't much begrudge Max her doubts. In fact, the strength of his own commitment might've been influenced by her judgment if it hadn't been for an article that appeared in the *Representative* that weekend. As it often did, the Sunday paper contained several references to incidents more or less convincingly linked to Mary Vanessa Singer's disappearance. A composite drawing had been released. The subject: Male. Dark. Balding. Heavy. Now the sketch always accompanied the photo. Whenever they appeared together in a new area of the country, fresh sightings would be reported. Mary Vanessa Singer eating at a turnpike oasis accompanied by the man in the police sketch. Mary Vanessa Singer sledding in a New England suburb, supervised by men in look-alike ski masks, one at the top of the hill, the other at the bottom. The final news item the fat man came across reported that her parents had literally copyrighted Mary Vanessa Singer's name. It, along with the growing volume of abduction-awareness literature that now existed thanks to the rallies, forums, workshops, public appeals, and ad campaigns they'd initiated in order to bring about their daughter's safe return.

Copyright.

As in legal.

As in lawyer.

The fat man completed the connection instantly, but read further to confirm his suspicion. It was true. The Singers had engaged Max as their attorney.

Bob the Brush knew this one guy, a regular at the Denny's on East
Van Buren, who worked as a landscaper but who'd gotten into some
financial difficulties because he also raised bull terriers in his back
yard and hadn't reported any of the extra income since probably about
1973. He happened to tell Bob and the fat man over coffee one night
how he'd worked out a trade—two terrier pups for the free-lance services of an H & R Block representative from Goodyear. In fact, it turned
out that the reason he was here tonight was to meet with the guy and
discuss his tax situation. The bookkeeper showed up around eight.
The four of them moved to a booth. Come to find out, this H & R
Block man, while negotiating in the landscaper's behalf, had become
halfway-good friends with an IRS auditor who happened to be in the
same fitness club with a certain CPA whose firm the state commission
had hired to safeguard one of two combinations that together opened
a vault at the tv studio downtown where the commission stored the
lottery jackpot machine between weekly episodes of the payoff.

"No shit?" said the fat man. "Now, there's something I wouldn't
mind seeing sometime. How about you guys?"

On Friday the six of them—Bob, Bob's friend the landscaper, his
friend from H & R Block, his friend the IRS auditor, his racquetball
partner the CPA, and Aaron Dodge—observed as a security officer
approached the vault door, keyed in his combination, and stepped
aside. A couple of other people had also come along for the tour. A
girlfriend of Bob's. The bookkeeper's wife and kids. Laura. Her six.
Kennedy and Ont Hazel. They watched the CPA come forward with
the second combination. The security man jacked a heavy chrome
lever, swung the door open, and entered the vault.

An usherette in a KPHX blazer explained that a log maintained by
lottery security acknowledged all "accesses." She peeled away and
displayed to her audience half of a cellophane seal, bearing a dense
block of copy and pretentious insignia, that the vault door had ruptured
as it opened. She knelt and stuck it playfully to Heather's forehead—
a souvenir.

The fat man had been hoping that the jackpot machine would be
cared for in the manner characteristic of most state-funded activities.
One person works, three others stand and watch, and everybody quits
in the middle for lunch, distributing a few orange cones so they'll

recognize the spot when they return in a couple of weeks. But somebody other than the surly administrators in charge of license renewals had designed the fail-safe measures here.

The security officer wheeled the giant, colorful machine out of the vault, past the tourists, and into an adjoining studio. The tour guide pointed to a pane of glass that allowed them a view. Next door, stagehands in KPHX coveralls assembled the *Jackpot Jack* set. Burgundy carpeting. A runway outlined in bulbs. Blackboard-size sheets of plywood painted to resemble a flurry of overlapping hundred-dollar bills descending from Heaven.

Activity increased as the start of the show approached. Uptight people with clipboards hopped over thick cables and yelled into tiny headset mikes. Red lights winked on and off. White-hot spots illuminated the set. At 6:45 the balls inside the jackpot machine began to churn. At 6:54:30 the chaos in the studio abruptly halted. As the red second hand on the clock above the door swept past 12, Jackpot Jack Sierra stepped onstage.

La Low-tay-REE-yah! Low-tay-REE-yah! Low-tay-REEEE-yah!

The fat man excused himself past people and their children until he stood beside the security officer. He wore a mustache trimmed to regulations, a haircut featuring pale fender wells at the ears. Dark stripes on his pant legs. Matching epaulets on his shirt.

"Hi," Aaron Dodge whispered. "I'm an inventor."

The officer glanced at him. Folded his arms. Redirected his attention to the pane of glass. Jackpot Jack's voice, fed to them through a speaker monitor, seemed unconnected to the actions of the man on the other side.

Fahn-TASS-ti-co!

"I was wondering if I might ask a few questions."

The officer placed a finger to his lips without taking his eyes off Jackpot Jack.

Eees-pay-see-AHLLLL!

The fat man asked his name. What high school. What college. He found out he'd served during the war. That he had a Vietnamese wife. No, he hadn't known any Herschel Wigginses there.

The show only ran five minutes. Aaron Dodge didn't intend to waste it all. He'd noticed the usherette looking their way during his brief interview with the sentry. He moved toward her through the crowd.

"Pardon me, miss. I'm an inventor. I was just wondering if—"

"Robin takes his job kind of serious," she said.

"I've had livelier conversations with instant-access machines."

"Oh, I don't know. Robin's just sort of . . . you know." Her expression obliterated by makeup, she worked over a cud of gum as she spoke, talking and chewing, chewing and talking in a way that reminded the fat man of how snakes can unhinge their jaws to swallow gophers.

"I was just won—"

"You don't have to whisper, sir." She nodded in the direction of the glass. "It's soundproof."

"I was wondering. The machine. Who fixes it if it breaks?"

She shrugged. "Never has since I been here. They precheck it to make sure. Every Wednesday. That way, if something's wrong, there's time to fix it. An inventor, huh? Neat." And then his five minutes were up.

The fat man left KPHX Studios that day with no ideas—only an observation. Call it instinct. Call it two decades of watching people in love—the erratic bounces, the unpredictable combinations. But somehow the fat man knew. That lottery security officer was definitely slipping it to that usherette.

His friend Agent Orange knew electronics. Sound systems, lights, instruments. Maybe he'd be able to supply some straight technical data. When the fat man visited his apartment near the Mill Avenue Bridge in Tempe, he found Brad Moe sitting cross-legged on a pillow in his living room, smoking a Thai stick and dressed in nothing but a t-shirt and a pair of tight-whites.

Several thin, pale, wrecked young men with mutilated hair and spiked bracelets were also present. Aaron Dodge recognized the benign, vacant expressions of people whose lives revolve around recreational drug use and dynamite stereo equipment.

His friend, Aaron Dodge discovered, was recuperating. "Hey, brother. I like don't e-ven believe this, do you?" He carefully lifted the elastic waistband of his underwear and peeked in. "I'm so trashed. Look at me. Shooting blanks, man. A fucking vasectomy. Feels like somebody pumping Twenty Mule Team borax through my plumbing."

The woman Brad lived with brought a pan she was stirring into the living room, bent to accept a toke and a kiss, and returned to the kitchen.

Kids screamed.

The floor vibrated beneath the fat man's feet.

"No, brother. Sorry," Brad told him when Aaron Dodge asked the question he'd come to ask. "I guess minimal. That would describe my knowledge of tv. I don't know *how* it works, I only know *that* it works. Aim it at their little faces and ZAP! Hypnosis. I'm as amazed as anybody."

The fat man had always admired the ability of most drug abusers and some parents to raise themselves momentarily above the chaos around and within them, look you in the eye, and provide at least one lucid response per conversation. He saw Brad Moe manage the miracle now. His friend contacted him through the smoke and noise and said, "I'd watch the program and give you a full report on this machine you say exists. But you're one person I wouldn't shit. Man, take a look around you. You've caught me at an unfortunate time. So don't ask me, ask somebody sane."

The fat man smiled. Nodded.

"How about you fags?" Brad Moe said to his friends. "Any of you fags help my friend out?"

Nobody spoke.

"Stay and relax with us anyway. Be company. Sit down, man."

"You do too, Bradley." The woman reappeared from the kitchen. "You know that one guy. He works at KPHX."

"Listen to this shit. I don't e-ven believe I'm hearing this."

"That camera guy."

"Jesus fucking Christ."

"I know you know him, Bradley. If I do, you do."

"Shit, wait a minute. What am I thinking? She's right, Dodgers. I do know that goofy little fucker. Dude works down at that fucking studio. Fucker's a cameraman."

"Great. What's his name?"

"Drexel."

"Dexter!" the woman yelled from the kitchen.

"Yeah, man. Dexter. Hey, you look this dude up. He put you in touch with the airwaves. Fuckin' A."

"Watch out, though," the woman called. "He's LDS."

"Fucker's crazy," said Brad Moe.

The fat man met Dexter the next afternoon at the Gopher Sports Club—McDowell and 16th Street. Dexter was a tall, lean redhead. Early thirties. He ordered a Pepsi Free and immediately told Aaron Dodge his story. Rock music, drug involvement, shattered dreams. A subsequent conversion to the Mormon faith. Nothing like a little adversity in life to turn a person into a lightweight.

Aaron Dodge responded with his own testimony. I'm a professional inventor. I have this idea. A new lottery jackpot machine. Can't offer you details, naturally. But I'm in the paper. Maybe you've seen my name around? "Aaron's Inventory"? The trouble was, the whole time he talked the fat man knew this Dexter would be a sucker for the real story. The missing little girl. An opportunity to strike down an evildoer. He had to suppress every conversational instinct in him in order to stick to his fabrication.

"I can't condone gambling, Mr. Dodge. I'm sorry."

"Wait. Not so fast. You have any idea what percentage of lottery proceeds go to social programs? It's been proven. The people who buy these tickets can afford them."

Dexter shook his head. Climbed off his bar stool. Extended his hand. "Good luck with your project, Mr. Dodge. But I'm afraid we're at odds on a basic principle. And even if moral values weren't at issue, I don't know all that much about Jack Sierra and his machine. I'm a cameraman, Mr. Dodge."

Max's betrayal.

The security at KPHX.

And now Dexter's religious zeal.

Aaron Dodge was an inventor. Used to aligning the results of failed experiments in new ways until they led someplace. Inside the red delivery truck, at the mini–storage unit, and sometimes at the blue apartment village, underwater, he waited for the correct impulse. Total concentration, continuously susceptible to whim. This was the proper state of mind. If you could achieve it. If you could lock out distractions. Like the weekly increases in the jackpot figure. Like the solutions to totally unrelated mysteries that kept occurring to you during meditation . . .

. . . a childproof flashlight. The switch would have to be twisted or depressed before it could be activated. That way the kids couldn't waste the batteries . . .

. . . a tool—something you could hook to your key ring—for holding open those taps in public restrooms that automatically shut themselves off after operating for three seconds.

He immediately drew up both ideas for his "Inventory" column and mailed them to the syndicate to help cover what by now had become a chronically deficient backlog.

Later in April, when the winter visitors began to migrate, the jackpot grew in noticeably smaller weekly increments, but steadily, to three, then four million. The Lottery Commission hadn't confirmed a winning ticket since the fat man's lunch with Phil Dixon. Evidently, seasonal residents had taken their fortunes with them back to Indiana and Wisconsin. Locally, luck dried up as hot weather threatened.

Inside the mini–storage unit, the scarcity of winners began to worry the fat man. But Mary Vanessa Singer wasn't the only female on his mind. With May close, the fat man thought ahead to anniversaries. An even year since he'd met Kennedy. More time than he'd spent with any woman since Cody. Or, more accurately, the most time one woman had been able to endure him. Lately, pushed by Kennedy's suspicions and pulled by Aaron Dodge's evasions and deceptions, things seemed ready to come apart. They told each other that for Laura's benefit they'd stay together—temporarily. At least till the cast came off. And so far they had—unenthusiastically; with such a complete lack of passion, in fact, that one day Kennedy made an alarming discovery. A certain important bedroom implement had disappeared. Each accused the other of purposely misplacing it, both knowing that more likely one of Laura's six had either flushed it, incorporated it into an outdoor game, or traded it to a friend at school. It would've been a difficult confession to extract from a first-grader. Ginger, honey, sweetheart, have you seen Aunt Kennedy's, uh . . . portable teacup? The boat for her turtle? The pool for her goldfish? The tent for her cricket? So Kennedy made an appointment with the gynecologist.

The prescription waited unfilled in Kennedy's purse. Finally, one night after they'd dropped off two of the children at Ont Hazel's in Sun City, they decided to stop at a Walgreen's on the way back to

Laura's. The pharmacist handed Kennedy a white bag, stapled shut, with the register receipt as a seal.

They'd left Laura alone that night with Anthony, Heather, Holland, and Brett, slipping out unannounced to give themselves a head start and Laura a sporting chance. To the children, their mother's injury represented an advantage they never dreamed they'd enjoy. Unaided, under siege, Laura could only defend herself vocally, altering the volume and pitch of her cries to correspond to the seriousness of the mischief that threatened her. Often her screams sounded to the fat man less like attempts at discipline than responses to unimaginable human-rights violations. They had a toll-free number you could call, 1-800-THERAPY, and Laura kept the phone close by when she babysat. Plus Aaron Dodge left her armed with his squirt bottle. That way she could at least keep them at a distance till reinforcements arrived.

"I like a good contraceptive," the fat man said in the car, and thumped the package in Kennedy's lap. Thwack. Kennedy reached behind her, drew the seatbelt across her waist, and buckled it. "We're late," she said. "Laura's by herself. Hurry."

"I especially enjoy working up slowly to the moment when it's appropriate. Urgently appropriate. Then nobody knows where it's at."

Kennedy switched on the radio. The fat man lowered the volume. "It excites me, you know? First you can't find the case. Then, when you do, it's empty. So there you are, all breathless, searching around with nothing on in that kind of pinkish light you get when you drape a red t-shirt over the lamp."

"Quiet. Just drive, okay?"

"Next we locate the jam. Oh, look, a fresh tube. Find us a suitable implement for rupturing the little tamperproof titanium seal. Try that sometime with a pair of legs wrapped around your chest. 'I want you inside me,' she says. 'Please come inside me.'"

"I do not say that."

"You're sliding off the bed. She's pulling you back. By the neck, by the hair. Fingers in your ears and eyes. You finally get the tube to produce. Grease the stuff around in there with a finger. You know. Warm things up some if it's a cold night. What I like is the way it squirms when you pinch it. The way it jumps out of your hand when you squeeze. 'Hurry,' she says."

"Aaron, we can't."

"You peel her off of you. You untangle her legs. Divide those knees. No parking between signs. But I do. All night long."

"Aaron?"

"You fold it up and aim. Careful now. Cooperation, please. She's heaving from one shoulder to the other. Eating the pillow. Try to find that entrance with the spare hand. Oops, that's the exit, sir. So it is. A second attempt, then. Hold still, now. Halfway in and . . . gulp!"

"Is there someplace we could go?"

The fat man considered, then ruled out the mini–storage unit. His private retreat. And home? Not far, but Kennedy's current condition looked to be a highly perishable commodity. She was holding on to the headrest with both hands, grinding against the seat like she intended to leave a permanent imprint there. The fat man ran a red left-turn arrow at 75th and fishtailed onto Olive Avenue. He attacked the turn into Bob the Brush's trailer park at fifty, barely straightening the wheels in time to avoid striking the first speed bump broadside.

"Where are we going?"

They skidded into Bob's driveway, gravel machine-gunning the undersides of the fenders. No truck. No lights. His friend wasn't home.

"Nobody's home," said Kennedy, climbing out her side. Aaron Dodge located the key on his ring and showed her.

"Who lives here?"

He unlocked the door and pulled it open. Kennedy stepped past him and found the light switch. "One of your friends?"

Bob's living room smelled like it had been cooked in. The kitchen smelled like it had been bathed in. As he escorted Kennedy down the trailer's narrow hallway, he pulled the bathroom door shut, afraid of what he'd find inside, and pointed ahead. "In there."

"What if this person comes home? We can't just . . ."

In the room at the end of the hall, Bob's workshop, sawdust had settled in a gritty layer over the tools and bare floor. "We've got to get back. Relieve Laura. We don't have time for . . ." Kennedy said, ripping into the white bag, snapping open the compact plastic case, then unboxing a miniature free-sample tube of gel.

"Wait," said Aaron Dodge. He returned to the living room for two sofa cushions. On the way back he pulled a sheet from the hall cupboard. He heaved the cushions onto the dirty floor and covered them. Kennedy, her pants off, sat on the platform of a table saw, her knees apart, hurrying her preparations. When she'd finished, Aaron Dodge lifted the hem of her blouse. She cooperated, raising her arms. The cloth stretched taut across her breasts as he worked it past. They spilled from underneath, followed by an avalanche of dark hair. A moment later all their clothes, inside out, underthings twisted into jeans, lay beside them near the cushions.

"Now?" said Aaron Dodge.

"I want to feel you," Kennedy breathed. "Inside."

The heavy, powerful machines surrounded them. And the smell of crosscut pine. And on the walls hung the exact rows of measuring tools, called shrink rulers—each calibrated to allow for the expansion and contraction of fiery metals—that Bob used in his work.

Instruments for miscalculating.

But precisely.

12

Mid-afternoon. The corner stool at Camel-Op. The absolute last place Aaron Dodge ought to have been found, under the circumstances. He should've been at the mini–storage unit. Or on the phone to Dixon or Magdalena. He should've been at home, drawing installments of "Aaron's Inventory." Or at Laura's, helping mind her six. All of which made indulging himself with friends on a Friday afternoon all that much more irresistible.

Lulu carried a flat of clean cups from the kitchen and hoisted it onto its shelf. Distributed saucers full of chilled thimbles of half-and-half along the counter. Squeezed lemon wedges into an empty coffeepot, added crushed ice and rock salt, and swished the mixture in the bottom of the pot to clean it.

"How's the litter?" Wendy Wendy asked.

"Fed," said the fat man. "As of yesterday, fed and accounted for."

"You learned all their names yet?" asked Deli Elope.

"Got 'em memorized. Brett and Sylvia. Ginger and Anthony. Heather and Holland. Anyway, even if I can't always differentiate, so what? That way at least I can't be accused of favoritism."

"Laura out of her cast yet?" Lulu wondered.

"They cut her out of one, stick her into a lighter model. You should see her. Defenseless. Those kids, whenever only her and them are at home, they find where her purse is hid and raid it. Then they bike

down to the mall and come back with these Pound Puppies dolls and
robot transformer kits and all this other crap from Saturday tv."

"Don't be such a grouch, Aaron Dodge," Lulu said. "Playthings are
part of a child's special world."

"So's whooping cough," said the fat man.

"Laura must be so depressed," said Lulu. "You should be nice to
her, Aaron Dodge."

"I know, I know. It's hard on her to delegate away her motherhood
or whatever. She's always talking about the time when they'll all be
together every night in the same house, her and the kids. Reunited.
Like they're refugees or hostages or something. And meanwhile she's
ramming the wire end of the flyswatter down inside her cast, itching
herself. Plus she smokes up all my dope. I mean, don't get me wrong,
Laura's okay. And even the kids. Cute. Sometimes."

"Expensive entertainment, though," said Bob the Brush. "I'll flat
guarantee you. Take my advice, buy yourself a gerbil, a parakeet.
They're plenty of responsibility."

"Hey, look. Check this out," said Deli Elope.

A conspicuous redistribution of dust and gravel announced the arrival in the lot of a silver Ford Bronco, which nosed into a space directly
facing Camel-Op's front window. Aaron Dodge and the others watched
as the driver removed her sunshades, hooked them over the rearview
mirror, and climbed out, leaving behind a large dog occupying the
passenger seat.

She was slender, with casually pinned-up hair, and wore khaki shorts
with cuffs, an oversized oxford-weave shirt with the sleeves rolled, the
tail out, the collar upturned. She edged partway onto a stool, examining
the coffee machine, then the refrigerated display, stocked with juice
drinks, in back of Lulu.

"An iced decaf, I think."

"That to go?"

The way she leaned across the counter, supporting her weight with
her elbows, fussing with some singles she'd taken from her pocket,
demanded the question. She glanced around her; Aaron Dodge and
his friends glanced away. "For here, I guess," she said, and settled
onto her stool, one leg folded underneath her. "And could I also get
something to eat. Something snacky maybe. A scone?"

Lulu pointed to the see-through pastry saver, which in any other diner would've held pyramids of encrusted donuts and tiers of oozing cream pies. The visitor selected a bran muffin—choices were limited this time of the afternoon—which she began to dismantle and butter.

The fat man glanced up at the clock. He had a feeling about today. That it might be his last Friday for a while. Last opportunity to knock off early. Last chance to look forward to tomorrow. To drown disenchantment in coffee and companionship. To read the sports section front to rear, including the articles on bluegill fishing and high school track. Tonight he'd watch the *Jackpot Jack Show*, though he hadn't entered this week's sweepstakes and probably wouldn't next's. A feeling that he was betting against himself and against Mary Vanessa Singer had stopped him soon after Phil Dixon created the monetary equivalent of a deadline. Tonight the payoff would exceed Dixon's limit, unless a lucky winner claimed the prize. Which the fat man didn't expect. He expected a five-million-plus jackpot tomorrow, and along with it a message from Phil Dixon on his machine. But between now and then lay an afternoon. And he planned to waste it. To stay as late as he could, talk as long as he wanted, drink his limit in refills. The bottomless cup versus the boundless appetite.

The fat man waited.

His friends were looking at him. The visitor too.

He allowed what he considered a generous pause. When nobody else spoke, he held out both hands, representing the dimensions of a fresh topic, or its length anyway, and said, "But tell me America isn't a society divided into classes. This to me is not an accurate statement. Because listen. I hear Reagan in his speeches. This family, that family. On welfare and about their VCR's and four-wheel-drive vehicles. The taxpayers' money. So I say, 'Hey, Mr. President. Put me in one of your anecdotes.' "

He addressed this observation directly to the newcomer, who smiled weakly in response and concentrated on her beverage, which she was now sipping through a straw.

"Don't worry," Bob the Brush assured her. He nodded in the fat man's direction. "With an organic menu you don't get the really dangerous types. Somebody who's maybe going to offer you a hostile report on your aura, that's about as violent as it gets here."

She stared out the window at the grille of her Bronco as if she hadn't heard.

"So I'm straight downtown, to the welfare people, to social programs, I should say—Social Services. Get me some of this lucre they're supposed to be handing out, right? I explain how Laura's laid up. I'm here strictly on her behalf. And the behalfs of the children. Myself and Kennedy I don't even mention. By now my butt's like it's been vaccinated with Novocain, I've been sitting so long. I itch where my skin and pants have stuck together. You know. From the vinyl? And what do I get from this person? The huffy-secretary response. Telling me come back later. Sure. Of course. Come back with a crippled woman on crutches and dragging a cast. With children whose attention spans, all six added together, can't be measured without scientific equipment. Believe me, I refused to leave without some assurances. Which turned out to be a case worker. They would send out a caseworker, they tell me. We were now an official case."

He swiveled on his stool to face the visitor. "Our caseworker's name? Lindsay. Her first name. Which I know immediately our odds have been reduced. She shows up wearing this yacht clothing they sell from catalogues. Smelling like a war between fragrance mists. It doesn't take this person five checkmarks, okay, before she's into air-force pensions, insurance policies, homeowner equity. Sounding like an IDS representative more so than her own job. Then she wants to cover *my* finances. To what extent am *I* a contributor to this household? You can tell, no way does she respect our side of the story. A suburban variation on the plight of oppressed peoples? Not in her training, sorry. So she leaves us with the feeling that: Okay, you've wasted my time. Your children with six full bellies, their tidy Sears outfits, and drinking fruit juice from their water pistols. I'm being told, in so many words, Go back to your job delivering pizzas and learn to like it. So what happens next, as a consequence? The person I live with, my girlfriend, Kennedy, she quits school. Cancels all her classes before the final drop period. Beginning now, she stays home and babysits so I can work. It's either that or day care, because her sister, Laura—with the cast? Forget it. This is why on a Friday, like today, you know where you'll find me? Paydays, I'm in line at the bank is where. Me and the illegals. Ahead of me and behind, these Mexican nationals who come across the border, working two, three jobs. They're cashing their pay, buying money orders to take to Western Union and wire south to the family. A little like what I'm doing with my income also these days."

The woman lifted one leg, then the other onto the seat of her stool, hugging her knees to her chest—the kind of incredible balancing act which thin people could make look so easy. Then she surprised Aaron Dodge by asking for another iced decaf. Reading encouragement into these acts, he prepared to go on. But Buzz spoke first.

"I don't know. Maybe it was you," he said to their guest. "That dog of yours out there in the truck. But you know what?" He turned to Aaron Dodge. "I got started thinking about Dennis, and now I can't stop."

"Dennis," the fat man said.

"Dennis who?" said Deli Elope.

"You remember Dennis," Buzz said. "You know. From the park."

"You must've had your head up your ass using your pecker for a periscope if you never seen Dennis," said Bob the Brush.

"The park," said Wendy Wendy. "You're right. He was always there, wasn't he?"

"Which park is this?" asked Deli Elope.

"You don't understand," said Buzz. "He wasn't always in any one park. He was always in every park. During a particular period, I mean. In fact, I'd go so far as to say that any month between March and October, anytime between 1965 and '75, any park between Central Avenue and the Pacific Ocean, Dennis was there."

"I was there too, man. What did he look like?"

"You mean to tell me you never saw this tall, skinny dude. Long hair down to about here," Buzz said, and touched a biceps. "Kind of fox-faced and a scraggly beard? Long pointy nose that the tip of it grew straight down and overlapped his top lip when he smiled? This big, U-shaped smile, and these narrow gaps between his teeth. Never wore shoes. Or a shirt. Belly so flat," Buzz said, and slapped his own, "so lean you could've poured three ounces of water in his navel and collected six ounces runoff. So skinny he could barely keep decent in a pair of Levis. And brown? Bronze, man, he might as well've been a statue. He was already the right color. You saying you grew up in Phoenix and never saw Dennis?"

"I was thirteen. Fourteen, maybe," said the fat man. "And delivering *Pennysavers*. I took a shortcut across the park. You know, the one there on 44th Street and around McDowell?" Aaron Dodge pointed excitedly, then continued to gesture indistinctly in that direction. "And there they were. Him and his old lady and their kid. Oh, and the dog. Dennis owned this half-shepherd, half-Lab named Sheriff. And I remember it was about a thousand degrees out, and me humping these *Pennysavers*. So I stopped at the drinking spout. And I wondered to myself, What the hell are these people doing here every day? Because they were just sitting there on this blanket. The three of them, there under the trees. You remember Dennis's old lady, right? She had this kinky blonde hair that rippled out like petticoats down to about her butt almost. And she'd always be kind of tilting her head to one side and going"—Aaron Dodge demonstrated—"like this and slinging it around behind her. I don't know. I think she wore like those tie-dyed undershirts and long print skirts and thongs. Plus a lot of bracelets. And this kid of theirs, I swear. You saw a million of these kids back then. You know, sexless, uncombed, fudge-faced, and all the time naked. Maybe it was that LSD chromosome breakage they claimed happened. All these kids turned out alike. So, as I said, every day. The three of them. Sitting there on this blanket with nothing but a chewed-up Frisbee and a radio—a transistor wound around and around with black electrician's tape like a grenade—and listening to Bill Compton or Phil Motta or somebody. And you say you never saw these people in the park?"

Deli Elope smiled and shook his head apologetically. "I probably did. If I could just remember."

"And so that's when I hear, 'Hey, kid.' This voice. 'Kid. You. Come over here.' 'Me?' I say. 'What for?' 'Come here, I got something for you.' And when I get over there, guess what? His old lady, with the bracelets and orange fingernails, hands me a soldier. 'Go ahead,' Dennis says. 'Smoke it. It's good for you.' And he grins at me. And his old lady, she smiles too. My first toke. Dennis turned me on. Now you know who I mean. Right?"

"I saw a lot of guys who looked like that. I just don't know."

"You saw him, didn't you?" the fat man said to the woman with the dog.

"Of course," she said, and smiled.

"There you go," said Aaron Dodge.

"Too young," said Bob the Brush, and pointed a thumb at Deli Elope.

The woman asked for a glass of water, no ice, which she took outside to the dog. Aaron Dodge and his friends watched as she drained it a little at a time into her cupped hand for the dog to lap up.

"I guess you have to be a saint," said Buzz. "Be a hero. Be in a war. But if they ever start putting up monuments for all the opposite reasons, I know who I'd nominate first. And like you said, with the kid and the mother and the dog. Sitting. I mean they were always in the park so much anyway, why not?"

"Seems logical," the fat man agreed.

"What happened to him? This Dennis?" Deli Elope was asking as Aaron Dodge climbed off his stool. He didn't wait to find out if Buzz would tell the truth. Just because *USA Today* throws together a collage with spoons and spikes and a roach clip superimposed onto a skull-and-crossbones doesn't mean the definitive word has been uttered. In this goddam world any sane person would prefer to stay high. Dennis, if he had it to do over again, and his options were the same, would do everything exactly the same way.

"No more for me, thanks."

And he sealed his cup with the flat of a hand.

Later, at home, he filled the bathtub.

Climbed in.

They had a toll-free number you could call, 1-800-JACKPOT, and that night, following the lottery extravaganza, the fat man had phoned in to confirm his expectation. Computer terminals assigned to every lottery retailer in the state logged all the number combinations selected there, making a virtually instant tally possible. A cheery recording informed Aaron Dodge that the prize had gone unclaimed, bringing next week's jackpot total to—

He'd hung up—the exact figure of no interest to him.

Now, from underwater, he heard Kennedy arrive, with tonight's consignment of children. Pots and pans collided. He could identify human voices, but not the sense in them. Complaints concerning the menu, probably. Inquiries pertaining to dessert. Somebody tried the doorknob. Knocked. "Uncle Aaron? You in there?" Then the fat man was alone.

Dennis walked in.

Barefoot, shirtless.

Exactly as the fat man remembered him.

Same grin. Same long, unwashed S's of hair swerving in front of one eye. His dog, Sheriff, followed. Dennis greeted the fat man with a hopelessly outdated two-fingered salute.

Joy, brother. Joy, joy, joy.

Aaron Dodge offered the one-fingered response that would always be in fashion.

Dennis grinned. He lowered himself into a corner underneath the towel rack, one knee upraised and a forearm resting across it. Sheriff investigated the tendrils of dental floss overflowing the rim of the trash basket. Sniffed at the toilet bowl. Dipped in for a drink. When he'd finished, he circled, then lay down with a sigh.

Been thinking, Dodgers. Know what about? All about those gypsies. Ones follow the Dead from concert to concert. Ones sell souvenir t-shirts and clay hash pipes and silverwork shells for your disposable Bic lighter. A junior *Wall Street Journal* number, is what I been thinking. Capitalism out of the trunk of a Plymouth. What I mean is, there's people out there doing the exact identical trip on us, man. Identical, only bigger. You noticed that? It seems personal against people our age. First it was Gerber's food in those little blue jars. Then baseball cards and yo-yos and television and Top 40 radio. Don't forget, brother, "Elvis" was an anagram for "Evils." And now what is it? Compact disc and cushiony running shoes and status this and gourmet that. Upscale geriatric care—it's coming, I bet. Somebody out there's singing the jingle to himself already. I don't know. It's the truth, though. I swear it to you, man—on Jerry Garcia's missing digit.

Dennis broke into a stammering giggle.

Sorry, man. I'm stoned.

I'm shit-faced, is what I am. But listen. I read something got me to thinking about you. Right after I died, you know? Deana was all fucked up for the longest time. Moves in with some freak. Asshole knocks her up. So as she's leaving the free clinic these people outside hand her some antiabortion propaganda. Pretty soon she's living in this Christian commune in Washington State. She takes D.J. and also she's about to pop with the other guy's kid. So naturally I started reading the Bible. Who else is going to argue with her? I'd come to see her late at night, after she put the kids to sleep. They kept the kids penned up together in this one big nursery. Like one of these day-care centers you read about in the paper. I don't have to tell you. You don't read about a day care in the news only if it's like this one. So while they slept at night— Rebecca and Jonah and Ruth and Jesse, all these kids with Biblical names, right? Only all from the early books, because I don't think any of these idiots bothered to read past page three hundred. While they slept at night, we'd drag one of the extra baby blankets out under the stars and sit in the grass, the dew, and argue religion. Thomas Merton, Augustine, Saint Paul's Epistle to the Galatians. Anyway, I convinced her. She split the commune. Had her kid on state papers, a girl, and put it up for adoption. Her and D.J., man, they're living right here in Phoenix again. You ought to go see them. Deana married some 'kicker. He's okay. Go see her, man.

Dennis stood.

Sheriff lifted his head.

Dennis faced the mirror, steamed by the fat man's bath, and wrote into the fog. From underwater, Aaron Dodge recognized the letters of his own name.

You were in there, man. In the Bible.

I know. All you ever wanted was to be first in the yellow pages. It's not your real name. But it's the one we gave you. Your friends. It was us claiming you, like.

Dennis climbed onto the toilet fixture and sat on the tank lid, a bare foot gripping either side of the seat, his hands dangling between his knees.

Moses, in the Bible. He was the great leader, not Aaron. Let my people go. The plagues. Parting the sea. Moses up on the mountaintop while Aaron stayed down on the plain and worshiped the golden calf. Okay, but Moses wasn't perfect either. A mushmouth, I guess. A stutterer, tongue-tied, shy. So who did his talking for Moses? Aaron did. Moses led the people out of Egypt, but all he ended up seeing was a glimpse from a distance of the Promised Land. He got corrupted, so somebody else led the people into the Land of Milk and Honey. The whole Greatest Story Ever Told trip—that was Moses. But what about Aaron?

Shit, I don't know what I'm saying. But dig it, okay? Because the thing is, it's been twenty years, and it doesn't look like anybody else is going to do anything. I mean my friends, everybody I ever knew in Phoenix, they're all either in a blank stupor from depression or they're like gentrified or something and can't think except what the tile pattern ought to be in their third bathroom.

And then along comes this photo of the missing girl in the paper.

Okay, so maybe your finding her would be only like a gesture. Like a symbol. And I've never believed in them. It's like, when you do something symbolically, after you strip away all the bullshit, doesn't that really just mean you didn't do it? Okay so then why am I guilt-tripping? So I'm sorry. So I'm asking you to do something I never did. But then again my name's Dennis, right? Not Aaron.

He slid his fingers into the pocket of his jeans and brought out a gray-and-black film canister and a packet of papers. And while he rolled, the fat man, underwater, was remembering better times.

Fox-faced Dennis. Shepherding a J.

Always on the periphery of a small circle.

His friends.

Had all those rooms really been lit by forty-watt bulbs, or was just the memory of them dim? Was the furniture really so green and brown and borrowed? A rug textured with spilled wine and pulverized chips from the bottom of the bag. Frank Frazetta reproductions charging from the walls. Saber-toothed tigers and wild, buxom princesses. Somebody nudges you. Nudges you again. You turn and it's Dennis. Grinning. Choking. Refusing to breathe. He laughs his soundless, wasted laugh. Vocal cords roasted, words congealed in cottonmouth, eyes watery and twinkling, poached. Holding the number between two fingers, nudging you hard with the other three. And the fuse burns shorter. Smoke filling up the ceiling. And you finally understand. And you take it from him. And you inhale.

13

The next morning, awake before the kids, before Kennedy, Aaron Dodge lay in bed. Looked up. Monitored his mental and emotional condition.

Some days you start out with a strength you didn't anticipate. Feeling, after all, like one of those pink-faced, drenched joggers at Encanto Park. Like any of the chunky housewives you glimpsed through the front window of an aerobics spa one dusk when you drove past and it was dark enough out for you to look in. You'd felt silly the whole time. Often unable to continue. It hadn't always been fun. But, like them, little by little, every day, you'd gotten stronger. And now you could use that strength. You could use it any way you wanted.

Aaron Dodge climbed cautiously out of bed.

Testing his stability.

Expecting a collapse.

But Dennis's visit—the companionship, the cannabis—had evidently produced a durable impression. That's what he'd always liked about mood-altering substances. About friends too. In sensible quantities, they disturbed your outlook just enough. At the kitchen table, imagining Dennis at his shoulder, the fat man began a mental list. People he could trust. Preferably, but not necessarily, his own age. Ones who might be persuaded to view Mary Vanessa Singer's situation in the way Dennis had interpreted it—more as a responsibility than an opportunity. He included some he'd met during his recent, haphazard attempts to penetrate the secrecy surrounding the jackpot machine.

The phone rang.

Phil Dixon, he knew.

A year ago, no question, he'd've let his machine answer. A month ago, a week ago he would've. Yesterday he would've.

"You checked the results?"

"I'm not ready, Dixon. I need a few days."

"What do you mean? Like a week? Till the next drawing?"

"I'll try for a week, but . . ."

"How close are you?"

"Not very."

"Look, Dodge. Everything's perfect for this coming Friday. Everything but you."

"I figured."

"Then get with the program."

"Stay off my ass. I'm in touch with some people," he said, and hung up.

"Who was that?" Kennedy. Dressed in a kimono he'd never seen before. Laura's, probably.

"Just a guy. About one of the inventions."

"Good news?"

"We'll see."

Heather and Holland were up. And Ginger. In their cartoon nightshirts, standing on kitchen chairs. Aiming cereal boxes at bowls. Asking for juice. Aaron Dodge noticed the ruptured Lottery Commission seal, given to Heather by the KPHX usherette, affixed to the refrigerator door, near the handle. A little joke directed at the fat man. Ha, ha. He peeled it off and said to Heather: "I'm borrowing this, hon. I'll bring it back."

"Mine," said Heather.

"I know. But share, okay? Please?"

The fat man distributed kisses and left the apartment. Dressed in shorts, a t-shirt, flip-flops, he walked to a phone booth down the street. He called one of the people near the bottom of the list of potentially trustworthy allies he'd composed. Dexter, the KPHX cameraman.

"I've got another little enterprise I'd like to discuss with you, Dexter."

Dexter reacted with the exaggerated calmness that spiritually enlightened people often substitute for anger. "Is that right? Fine, then. How can I help you, Mr. Dodge?"

"It wouldn't exactly be helping me," said the fat man. "That's why I think you'll be interested this time."

Dexter seemed less than enthusiastic, but agreed to a meeting. He named a Häagen-Dazs franchise on the East Side. They met there at lunchtime. As they sat excavating scoops of exotic ice cream with plastic spoons, Aaron Dodge told Dexter his story.

The missing little girl.

The six recurring numbers.

The game, the machine, the jackpot.

Listening to Dennis the night before had decided at least one issue for the fat man. From now on, whenever necessary, he'd tell what he knew in return for the information and assistance he needed. And in case the people on his checklist reacted as Max had, he'd go a step further. He'd exchange the six numbers. A cut of the jackpot.

His story produced a change in Dexter even more startling than Aaron Dodge had foreseen. The fat man, who'd been carefully but discreetly searching Dexter's eyes for evidence of weakening resolve, of compassion, saw something else there instead. The eyes narrowed, their expression hardened, sharpened. "You know the picks?" he said. "Before they're picked?"

"Just for this one drawing I will."

"Listen, man, let's hear the numbers."

"What?"

"The picks. The numbers. Then we'll talk. No, wait. How am I supposed to know you're giving me the real six? You try to screw me on this, you're history, hear me?"

Aaron Dodge replied with an adjustment to his posture, slowly resettling his weight in Dexter's direction.

"Okay, okay. Sorry," said Dexter. "But no kidding. I've thought about this, man. I've thought about it a lot."

"And?"

"Holography, man. We set up a holographic display inside the machine. It looks like all these bouncing balls with numbers on them. But only six are real. The six we decide on. Beautiful, man."

"Too complicated," said Aaron Dodge. "Look, all I need from you—"

"Okay. You're right, you're right. But listen to this. Another idea. We duplicate the whole five minutes, see. We build a set, we hire an impersonator. I know this guy, this Chicano. An impressionist, co-median. He—"

"Come on, Dexter."

"Just listen, okay? At exactly 6:55 we break in on KPHX. We pirate their signal. Then we air our substitute. It's happened before. You read about that one guy, didn't you? The cable hijacker? It's possible, man. I can do it."

"Look, Dexter. All that's way too hi-tech. It'd never work. All I want you to do is one simple thing for me. All I need is you and your camera. All right?"

"Whatever it takes. But I want those six winners. Understand?"

The fat man brought the gummy, lint-covered half-a-souvenir of Heather's from his wallet. It stuck to his fingers, the edges curled, as he flattened it against the tabletop. "Dexter, here's what I want you to do."

By Wednesday night Dexter had processed a videotape for the fat man. He'd shot it by leaving an unattended camera operating and aimed in a strategic direction during the jackpot machine's mechanical trial— the regular mid-week inspection that Holly, the KPHX usherette, had mentioned the day Aaron Dodge visited the studio.

The fat man viewed the tape at the mini–storage unit early Thursday, following his shift at Pizza on Wheels. It featured, in sometimes hazy detail due to the unregulated focus of the camera, the actions of the CPA employed by the commission, and of Robin, the security officer. The unsealing of the vault. The logging of the access. The removal of the jackpot machine and its testing. The precautions surrounding its return to safekeeping.

Aaron Dodge stopped the tape.

Rewound.

Punched the play button.

All for the half-dozenth time.

As the tape again unspooled inside Wendy Wendy's machine, he found a pair of calipers and a millimeter stick in his toolbox. He planned to compare the diameter of the seal, whose dimensions he knew thanks to the half Heather owned, against its size as reproduced onscreen. Using this ratio, he'd be able to determine the actual circumference of the numbered spheres inside the jackpot machine as a function of their televised circumference. But as the fat man watched, his measuring instruments nearby, his finger on the freeze button, something interrupted his concentration. Noises. From outside. The kinds of noises he'd dreaded hearing since the day he'd made the mini–storage unit his workshop.

Voices ricocheting among the cubicles.

Footsteps compressing gravel.

Fists pounding the metal door of his stall.

The fat man switched off the VCR. Waited. The unit couldn't be locked from the inside—a fact that whoever wanted in immediately discovered. A band of light showed at the foot of the entranceway, then widened as the door began to lift. Two figures, tall and short, stood silhouetted against bright sunlight.

"Mr. Dodge?"

Dixon and Magdalena.

"Sorry to disturb you, Mr. Dodge," Magdalena said. "But this couldn't wait."

"Shut the door," the fat man said.

"We'll just be a minute," Dixon said. The two men paced Aaron Dodge's little cell, inspecting, their hands buried nonchalantly in their pant pockets.

"Jesus. You weren't exaggerating were you?" said Dixon. "What a fucking cave."

"How's progress?" Magdalena asked.

"Better," said Aaron Dodge. "Good."

"And you've been keeping all this a secret, right?" Magdalena asked.

"Sure," said the fat man. "I mean I guess. Pretty much."

"A couple of questions, then. If you don't mind."

"What were you doing at 122 South Ash in Tempe on Sunday night, the twenty-seventh?" Dixon asked. "Bradley Clarence Moe. New Wave musician, rock promoter. Arrests for possession of a controlled substance. Possession with intent to distribute. Conspiracy to distribute. Attempted bribery of a federal judge."

"Brad? He's a friend."

Dixon approached the fat man. Suddenly he grabbed the front of his t-shirt and yanked. Maybe he envisioned slamming Aaron Dodge against a wall and muttering threats nose to nose. Some sort of tv-cop maneuver. But after a series of violent tugs, their only effect to stretch shapeless the neckline of Aaron Dodge's t-shirt, the fat man hadn't budged. He looked into Dixon's eyes with an unamused expression.

"Get your hands off," Magdalena said to Dixon. Then to the fat man: "Mr. Dodge, if you've consulted with anybody, we need to know about it."

"I've consulted lots of people."

"I knew it," said Dixon. "I told you, didn't I?"

"I'm sure I don't have to tell you, Mr. Dodge," said Magdalena. "This gets in the paper . . ."

"It won't."

"Names," said Dixon. "We want to know everybody. Anybody you've said one word to."

The fat man glanced around his workshop, at his tools, his plans—odd-looking to him in the strong natural light from outdoors. Again remembering Dennis, again thinking of his friends, he chose to speak directly instead of evasively. "I'm willing to bet," he said to Magdalena, "that both of you—and I'll give odds on this prick," he said, indicating Phil Dixon—"both of you, I'll bet, plan to slip those numbers to somebody in advance of the drawing. I doubt anybody's so much of a humanitarian they'd pass up a chance like this. One friend. Somebody who'll show up at Lottery Headquarters to present your winning ticket. Split the take with you. You want something in return for your time and trouble. Just in case Peter Pander doesn't bite and we never see Mary Vanessa Singer again."

Dixon and Magdalena stared at each other. Neither spoke. The fat man knew then that he'd guessed right.

He'd intended all along to present the six winners to Laura on the eve of the drawing. And evidently Dixon and Magdalena had been contemplating their own particular acts of charity or selfishness. He'd hoped to use the numbers to free himself from his connection to Laura's six—to provide for them till their father's death certificate began the flow of negotiable paper that would pay for their upbringing.

And clearly Dixon and Magdalena had each plotted to end in a similar fashion some private run of bad luck. He could read the evidence in their faces.

Magdalena raised his hands. "I surrender. Don't shoot."

Dixon, though, wasn't smiling. "Shit," he said. "You guys are a couple of . . ."

"Don't listen to that," said Magdalena. "He's guilty too. Both of us— all of us—are."

"Let's take a ride," said the fat man. "If we're going to discuss this. The proprietor here shows up at nine."

They left the El Camino parked beside the Pack Rat office module. In Magdalena's municipal Ford Escort, they cruised the bottom land south of the Salt River. Glass down. At fifty, sixty, seventy. Shouting to be heard over the inrushing wind. The consensus seemed to be that a salvage was possible. They'd risk another two weeks, three maybe. The jackpot would be allowed to grow, the bigger the better, just in case their target, hearing he hadn't won the prize outright, decided that a split didn't warrant exposing himself to possible identification. They agreed to instruct their friends not to cash in till the suspect had been given plenty of opportunity to do so first. They'd also have to invent some sort of connection between the friends they planned to include in the payoff. Call them a bowling team or some-thing. You were always reading about some group of factory hands or boat people who'd banded together to increase their chances of hitting.

None of the three mentioned the obvious possibility.

Leaving the jackpot unplundered.

The bait untampered with.

It bothered the fat man afterward that he'd conspired to double-cross Mary Vanessa Singer. To rob her fund. Compromise what it might purchase. It disappointed him that his imagination had refused to furnish more tolerable choices. In the past, similarly disenchanted, he'd canceled his interest in comparable ventures. Inventions, friend-ships, commitments of every sort. Plenty of worthwhile causes had been treated to a leisurely view of the fat man's back on more fanciful pretexts.

Priorities, idealism, principles—this time he set them aside, maybe temporarily, maybe permanently. He'd have to see. For now he moved on to the next person on his list.

Holly, the usherette. Not the ideal age. Young. But he suspected that through her he could contact Robin, the security officer. At least contact, possibly influence. And the tape of Dexter's had convinced him he'd need Robin's help if he hoped to get closer to the machine than a guided tour would bring him. He stopped by Station KPHX one afternoon during the taping of a local talk show and found Holly welcoming audience members into a dim studio amphitheater. Rows of seats faced a stage occupied by a semicircle of swivel chairs, a scrap of carpet, palms in wooden planters.

"Howdy," he said. "Remember me? The inventor?"

"Oh sure. Hi."

"What's the attraction?"

"A panel discussion," said Holly. "You know. AIDS. Drug traffickers. The Central Arizona Project. Who remembers?"

Instead of locating a seat, Aaron Dodge loitered at the head of an aisle. The chairs onstage filled one by one. Panel members fussed with lavaliere mikes. A moderator in the center chair shuffled pages of notes.

"I guess you better . . . whatever. Sit or something," Holly told the fat man. "I think they're about to . . . you know."

"Restroom?" he asked.

Holly pointed with her flashlight.

When he returned, the taping had begun. Holly was about to draw the lightproof draperies at the entrance. She stood aside to allow him in. The audience, a small one, occupied only the first three or four rows. Holly and the fat man could whisper without causing a disturbance. "I'm still interested in that machine," he told her.

She glanced at him. "You're weird," she said.

"Just persistent," he answered. "Sometimes."

"That how you get to be an inventor?"

The fat man shrugged. "You look around. Observe. You see something's not working right, you figure out your own way of doing it. Little math. Little science. Engineering if you're lucky. It's not hard."

"And the lottery machine doesn't work right?"

"Not as well as I could make it work."

This assessment the fat man hadn't fabricated. Since he'd been asked to doctor it, he'd studied the machine. Compared it with the ultraslick, airtight lotto-trons used in other states. Alongside them, Arizona's bingo box seemed— He didn't want to jinx himself by saying crude. But maybe someplace close in quality to the production under way onstage as he and Holly talked. Glaring spectacles, unorthodox syntax, discolored teeth. Supers arriving onscreen a half-second tardy. In this way the jackpot machine was a little like Phoenix itself. A place where the paper still printed photos of little girls and puppies on the front page of the Sunday edition. Where a neighbor, a stranger, would still offer you space in her refrigerator while you defrosted yours. He was counting on the machine's and the city's innocence to help make the work he was about to do possible.

"So if you mostly observe," said Holly, "tell me. What've you observed? You must've spotted something by now."

"True," said the fat man. "That other time I was here. I saw you. And I also saw that guard. Robin."

Holly pressed the flashlight to her hand. Switched it on and off, on and off. Light showed redly between her fingers, held tightly pressed together. "Robin? We're just friends," she said without looking up. "We both work here. And so we're friends."

During pauses in his and Holly's conversation, the fat man had overheard occasional questions, partial responses, from participants in the staged discussion. By now he'd identified the topic. Also two of the panel members.

". . . exploited children," someone said.

". . . Mr. and Mrs. Singer," said another of the guests.

"What do you want?" Holly said to him. "Are you . . . ? Did his wife send you or something? Hire you?"

"Nothing like that," Aaron Dodge said.

"What, then?"

"How about if we go someplace? When are you off?"

"No." Holly chewed her gum in slow motion. "I mean I don't know if I can."

"My car's out front," he told her. "Yellow. Like a taxi."

The fat man swarmed down the aisle. Canvas tennies, no socks.

Olive-drab bermudas with ammunition pockets. Pink-and-aqua Ha-
waiian shirt. He joined the audience. Watched the council overseen
by tv spots share their opinions with each other and the camera. He
listened with special interest, with sympathy, respect, to the Singers.
He thought he'd've liked them both. The dad, shorter than his wife—
but thick, powerful-looking, red-faced—sat hunched forward in his
chair and gestured excitedly with both hands as he talked, accidentally
batting his tie more than once while reinforcing a point. When he or
someone else on the panel addressed the audience, the mom, a slim
desert blonde, would shift positions in her seat to face the new speaker
and rest an elbow on her chair back, chin cupped in a hand.

Keep accurate medical and dental records.

Plus a sample of your child's hair.

Most victims won't remember their ordeal, or the therapy afterward.

The taping ended and the fat man waited in the El Camino. Watched
the lot empty. Observed the building entrance. Steadily, then less
frequently, groups and loners emerged. Then no one. Finally, after
sitting for nearly an hour, when he'd stopped expecting her, he saw
Holly. He shoved open the passenger-side door. She climbed in.

Aaron Dodge drove them to a place he knew called the Owl Pellet.
Inside, he ordered Corona Extras. They sat at a booth with its own
consolette jukebox and set of antelope horns. Holly rearranged the
sugar shaker, the ashtray, the ketchup as they talked.

Aaron Dodge repeated his story, heavy on the sentiment. Extra vi-
olins. And Holly, perhaps because she'd expected ugly accusations,
threats, cooperated with a display of emotion exceeding anything he'd
hoped for.

"That's so totally sad," she said. "I mean really."

"So you see now why I'm this interested in you and Robin. Nothing
to do with anybody's private behavior."

"That's kind of a relief," said Holly. "I suppose. Not that this other
is any less scary."

"I was hoping you'd mention it to Robin for me."

"Sure I will. But don't expect Robin to . . . I mean he's not always
too sensitive of a guy. He might turn you in. Hell, he might turn
me in."

"I wouldn't if I was him. I might refuse to cooperate but I wouldn't deliberately provoke somebody with floodlights and alarms aimed at a secret of mine."

"Robin's pretty different, though."

"Look. I've got a girlfriend. I know. Women can influence. That's all I'm asking, okay? Influence."

A few days after he talked to Holly, without a suitcase, without a ticket, the fat man sat alone in Sky Harbor, staking out a flight to Dallas. He hadn't slept. After his shift at Pizza on Wheels, he'd stopped for coffee at Camel-Op, changed clothes, and come directly here to observe early departures.

Some people sell their blood. Others panhandle or peddle flowers from five-gallon plastic buckets on the street corner. The fat man had been forced to consider desperate means of his own now that he frequently found himself down and out. From now on, when an unexpected bill of Laura's came due, he planned to drive to Sky Harbor, as he'd done today. He'd investigate, observe, then he'd buy a ticket on one of the flights that seemed most consistently overbooked. When the flight was scheduled to depart, at the last minute—when the airline discreetly paged travelers who might be willing to give up seats—the fat man would make sure he stood at the head of the line. Once in a while he might have to eat twenty-five percent of a fare, and he'd need to demand cash or they'd try to stick him with a free trip to Hawaii or someplace, but if he selected his destinations carefully he believed he could almost always earn money for not going there.

Seven A.M.

Briefcases and *Wall Street Journal*s.

Styrofoam coffee cups and sleepy, disgruntled looks.

The smell of jet fuel.

And Aaron Dodge, disguised in his sportcoat. His tie. His pair of presentable shoes.

They'd announced another delay. Dallas was only a rehearsal, no money invested; still, the fat man was beginning to worry about overhead—the parking voucher in his wallet—when he saw a stewardess struggling by in the crowded thoroughfare with one of those tag-along suitcases you always see uniformed women wheeling behind them through terminals. She and it seemed to have opposite destinations in

mind. She tugged, it veered. Or halted altogether. A violent yank
brought it temporarily back on course, but then a wheel came off and
the suitcase tottered and sank onto its side. The loose caster continued
in Aaron Dodge's direction, ignored or avoided by ungentlemanly pairs
of hurrying loafers and Rockports. He stuck out a foot and stopped it.

"Excuse me. Need help?" He rescued her and her wounded valise
from the middle of the traffic jam they'd created and led her back to
where he'd been sitting. They couldn't find the screw that had secured
the wheel, but the fat man carried a respectable assortment—he'd
activated the metal detector earlier—and was able to provide a mate
after searching his pockets. He fitted the wheel back onto its axle.
Tightened the screw with the edge of a dime.

She offered to buy him a cup of coffee. If Dallas would wait.

He admitted he hadn't purchased a seat to Texas.

"Come to see a friend off?"

"More just to look around. I'm an inventor." An explanation that
seemed to excuse behavior of almost any sort.

Together they passed through the concourse, following the square,
color-coded overhead signs—the internationally understood parallel
knife and fork. They stopped at a busy standup snack grotto. Her name
was Ann, and when Ann opened her purse to treat for the coffee and
pastries she could come up with only sixty cents. The fat man paid
and they joined a circle of rushed travelers bunched at one of the
elevated pods—circular Formica wheels with room for each diner to
wedge in an elbow and stare off into a private nothingness. In the
squeeze, the cologne, the cigarettes, the Muzak, they talked.

Ann about L.A., from where she'd just returned.

Aaron Dodge about his ticket refund scheme.

She about Toronto, New Orleans.

He about "Aaron's Inventory," the Bunkport.

She about bulimia, yeast disorders, herpes.

He about Kennedy.

She had the sad, collapsing face of a middle-distance stew. Disin-
tegration beginning at the margins of the eyes. The mouth in paren-
theses. She seldom smiled as she talked—a neutral expression being,
the fat man supposed, one of her off-duty indulgences.

"You ever fly to Washington?"

"State or the city?"

"D.C."

"All the time."

"No shit?"

Ann suggested a real breakfast. The fat man knew a place, Rumeel's, near the airport—but not so near that they'd gouge you for tourist prices. They ordered dirty eggs. Tortillas. Cakes. Coffee. As they ate, the fat man showed Ann how to synchronize the day, hour, and meridian indicators and shut off the alarm on her digital wristwatch, which despite her every effort had chimed twice on the half-hour, once on the hour, since the day she'd purchased it.

She told him she shared an apartment, a tiny efficiency—not much more than a dishwasher, couch, and shower—with a roommate, also an airline hostess. The arrangement worked out because their schedules rarely assigned them to home on the same night. The roommate's name was Pam. Before Aaron Dodge had even met them both, he'd supplied his two new friends with nicknames.

Pan and Amm.

At the cashier Amm insisted, "I'm getting this," and dug her checkbook out of her purse. "Oops. You know how when you get to your last pad of checks the one on top will be this order form you're supposed to send in?" The fat man paid and dropped her at her apartment.

"Really. Thanks," Amm said. "For everything. Breakfast was scrumptious. And if you'd be interested at all, I could help you out with your ticket redemption idea." Pan's boyfriend, she explained, was a travel agent.

"Great," said the fat man. "And next time you fly to D.C., if it's anytime soon, you could do me an even bigger favor."

"What's that?"

"The U.S. Patent Office is located near there."

He briefed Pan and Amm in their little apartment near Sky Harbor later that week. He included Pan because Pan turned out to be the one scheduled to fly to the capital soonest. He copied out the Patent Office's address in Arlington, Virginia, and listed for the two friends the classifications Pan would need to look under.

Class 273. Amusement Devices.

Subclasses 138–147. Chance Devices.

Consultants at the office would help with the search. Pan would
need only to match the drawing of the machine with which Aaron
Dodge provided her to the corresponding diagram in the Patent Office
files. Pan and Amm didn't ask a lot of questions. They seemed satisfied
with Aaron Dodge's all-purpose excuse: I am an inventor. For now he
didn't offer the rest of the story. He'd do that afterward, when, he
hoped, the time would come to thank Pan and Amm.

On the day Pan was due back, Max Yoder called. A surprise to the
fat man. He'd considered their association over. Minus one patent
attorney. One friend.

"I want to do something, Aaron. I've changed my mind."

"Thanks, Max. But I think I'm set."

"I'd really like to get involved, Aaron."

"Sorry, Max. I appreciate the offer. But . . ."

"There must be something. I'll help any way I can. I shouldn't've
hesitated in the first place. I see that now."

"Can't think of a thing, Max. If I could, I'd tell you."

"Please," said Max. "It's important to me. Genuinely."

"If anything comes up, I'll let you know."

"I could turn you in, Aaron. You know that."

"Max, I'll keep you in mind. I'll call."

"You're being vindictive, Aaron."

"Not at all. It's just that you're too late. I'm sorry."

"Reconsider. Please."

"There's nothing to reconsider. You don't have to feel guilty. Nobody's holding a grudge."

Max didn't respond.

"I don't know what else to say, Max."

"I'll do anything, Aaron. Please call," Max said, and hung up.

He met Pan at the airport that night, late, when he was supposed
to be delivering pizzas, and alone because that afternoon Amm had
departed for Indianapolis.

"It was so easy," said Pan. She carried a vinyl airline handbag. A
nine-by-twelve envelope bearing the same logo in a corner. "They do
practically everything for you."

"Getting out there's the trick," said Aaron Dodge. "Can I drag that
for you?"

"No thanks." Followed by her noisy blue Tourister, she walked with the fat man down the giant, empty concourse. Both of them yawning. Dim yellow light. Echoes. The smell of floor wax.

When she handed over the envelope, he peeked inside. Two, three, four pages. Xeroxes. "Listen," he said. "Let me pick up your cab ride or whatever. Meals. Motel."

"Put me in one of your newspaper stories sometime," she said.

He drove Pan to the apartment of her travel-agent boyfriend, punched in late at Pizza on Wheels, and finished his shift. At dawn, inside the mini–storage unit, he examined the patent application closely for the first time.

A simple electric blower generated air currents, directing a fusillade of numbered spheres toward an upright Plexiglas cylinder. A spring-steel catch at the mouth of the cylinder detained inductees, allowing individual retrieval at the discretion of the game operator. Transparent panels on four sides heightened the illusion of a fair deal. A decorative shell invested the machine with bulk and consequence.

Nothing very complex about the design itself. The machine appeared mostly gloss enamel and camera angle. The elaborate security arrangements, the ritualistic care that accompanied its movements—mainly these intimidated an observer. That and its size. The jackpot machine seemed to have been created or modified to show up impressively on television rather than simply fulfill its primary function. This feature, for reasons Aaron Dodge couldn't yet identify, made it seem vulnerable. Size. Maybe that would turn out to be the game's downfall.

Though rudimentary, the plans confirmed earlier impressions. Added to Aaron Dodge's confidence. Provided enough additional clues to keep Aaron's Enterprises in business. For the first time in years, a project was totally absorbing the fat man. He found himself skipping dinner to work. Leaving breakfast half eaten after stopping to calculate on a napkin. Others noticed the change before he did. He was losing weight.

The fat man was used to stepping onto a scale and propelling the dial nonstop past zero. In friends' bathrooms he always weighed two, ten, fifteen, twenty-seven pounds. Less than the littlest child. But that spring, at Ont Hazel's in Sun City, he enjoyed a profound mechanical and mathematical experience. Waiting while Kennedy swapped

Heather and Anthony for Holland and Ginger, he helped himself to several Lites from the refrigerator, then found it necessary to excuse himself. Hazel's fixture was armored with a fuzzy tank-cover that matched the rugs—a peach-colored set so plush that the fat man had to aim from the side and hold the lid open with a knee. He spotted the scales, also decorated with a peach-fuzz vest, balanced on top of the trash can. Hazel kept it there to discourage her wiener dog, Franz, from raiding it for mementos of personal hygiene Kennedy and Laura sometimes deposited there when they visited. By stepping out of his shoes, emptying the change from his pockets, and removing his wallet and belt, the fat man was able to log in under three ticks—the kind of number he hadn't registered since Martha Reeves and the Vandellas last hit.

Partly, he knew, the heat inside the mini–storage unit was responsible. And worry. But a pursuit he cared about, in the fat man's opinion, represented the crucial difference between before and after. The 90-Day If You Live That Long Help Find Mary Vanessa Singer Diet. He couldn't divulge to friends the source of the willpower he'd suddenly acquired. Couldn't tell Laura or Kennedy why the austerity with which he'd lived his life was finally translating itself into physical terms. But some days lately he was happy. Tentatively happy, but happy. Now that he'd learned to cook for two, for six, for nine, he didn't see how he'd ever be able to go back to cutting his recipes in half.

14

One drawing later, a laid-off copper miner from Eloy wiped out the jackpot.

Dixon, the fat man, and even Magdalena, usually the careful one, met at Ernesto's on a Monday night to complain—bitterly, drunkenly, and without regard for who might be listening, so deep and final was their disenchantment.

"It's over," said Dixon. "We're beat."

"My fault," the fat man said. "Put the blame right here." He prodded the tabletop in front of him.

"Save it," Dixon told him. "We all three of us sold that little girl out."

"I don't know," said Magdalena. "A month, three weeks ago I'd've said: Sure. Let's go again. But now? An unrealistic situation. Wishful thinking."

"We waited too long," said Dixon. "We acted like it was always going to be there. How could we've been so stupid?"

"I say we can still do it," said Aaron Dodge.

"Now you're dreaming," Dixon said. "We'd have to rebuild from square one. Not just the jackpot. I mean the enthusiasm we had. The momentum. The spirit of the thing."

"When the confidence goes . . ." said Magdalena.

"Maybe," said the fat man.

"If this is anybody's responsibility, it's mine," said Magdalena. "I didn't trust you, Mr. Dodge. Caution. Suspicion. It was those friends of yours. The illegal drug activity. And that woman, the mess you got into involving her husband."

"Fighting amongst ourselves," Dixon said, and shook his head unhappily.

"Consequently I didn't encourage you, pressure you like I should have. To go ahead with your contribution. Get on with it. While the opportunity was there."

"I fucked up with no help from anybody. You two did fine."

"What amazes me," said Magdalena, "astounds me, is the misjudgment. What smug assholes we were. How could we sit around and congratulate ourselves on this great idea of ours while the thing itself, the objective, got lost?"

"What about her?" said the fat man. "Let's not forget her."

"He's right," Dixon said. "Here we are feeling sorry for ourselves when it's her who's . . . you know."

"The victim," Magdalena said. "She should be home by now. Back with her family. Instead, thanks to us, some snapshot freak probably has her in his basement someplace. But listen. Fuck it. I just want to forget this. Put it behind me. Get on with other things."

"We'll never forget this," Dixon said.

Uneasy glances crisscrossed the table. A scary recognition that Dixon had found the truth.

"That's why we've got to try," the fat man insisted. "For that one reason alone we can't quit."

"You can't," Dixon said. "I can. I've got to. Look." He touched his forehead. "Falling out in clumps. When I take a bath the tub won't even drain."

"You never had enough to make a respectable clump in the first place," Magdalena told him.

"Fuck you," Dixon said harmlessly, almost gently. "And Snow White and your six buddies too."

They talked through the night. Past ten. Past twelve. Talk kept circling back and back, to that one unequivocal admission.

"We had a shot. We just couldn't get it done."

"We had to cut ourselves in. Had to get rich."

"What a sad sack of shit."

One bought, then another, then the third. And somewhere between rounds the fat man saw Tulane Wiggins come in. He stopped at their table to say hello. In April, Tulane had reported for the last time to Aaron Dodge, ending his probation period. The fat man hadn't seen him since.

"Hey, man. I got me work. And not just a job, I mean a c'reer. They give me like a HMO plan. Desk and shit. You know that community service the judge had me doin'? Otherwise I never a got hired. 'Cause you know what I'm workin'? With 'bused children, man."

Dixon, Magdalena, and the fat man passed a drugged expression around the table.

"And I know I got this here man to thank," Tulane said. He gripped Aaron Dodge's shoulder. "My friend. This here, he got me my first paper route. Man, I wasn't no bigger'n your age," he said to Magdalena. "He done for me. I do for him sometime too, I get a chance."

"Thanks, Tulane. Congratulations."

"I got to book, man. But I call you up, okay? I stay in touch, man. What you done for my old lady' mama, I pay you back."

"Don't worry about it, Tulane."

"Really, man. I owe you. A lease let me invest in some a them gimmicks you always thinkin' up. How 'bout it?"

"Sure, Tulane. That'd be great."

"Abused children," Dixon said, once Tulane had left to join friends at the bar. "I about shit."

"I *would've* shit," said Aaron Dodge, "if he'd been collecting donations for Help Find Mary Vanessa Singer or something."

"We really zipped our dicks in our flies on this one," said Magdalena.

They ordered one more. Shared it silently. And when they'd finished, the three men stood up and shook hands across the table. "Good to work with you two," said Dixon.

"A pleasure," Magdalena agreed.

"Same here," said the fat man. "But listen—"

"Forget it, Edison," Magdalena told him. "My nerves won't take it. I'm going back to standard police work. Slow, meticulous, uneventful."

"Say, you look like you've . . ." Dixon nodded toward Aaron Dodge's midsection. Narrowed his own waist in pantomime.

"Maybe. A little," the fat man admitted.

The three friends stared at the floor. At the television. Everyplace but at each other.

"Well," said Dixon.

"Later I guess," said Magdalena.

"Right," said Aaron Dodge.

No pizzas to deliver. Night off. So the fat man drove to Pack Rat. Parked. Sat outside his rented stall on the front bumper of the El Camino and thought about the hours he'd wasted here. And everywhere. And always. The chance he'd missed.

He almost left without venturing inside. Almost drove home to Kennedy. Wanted to. But he decided to stay. Detoxify. When he opened the door, the sight of his inventions, all his plans, had a definite sobering effect.

The patent application Pan had flown from D.C.

The news photo of Mary Vanessa Singer taped to his drafting table.

And, markered on a wall, two lists of figures.

Not phone numbers but amounts.

One ranking followed the rise of the jackpot total. The other the more gradual increase in the rewards outstanding in connection with Mary Vanessa Singer's disappearance. Whereabouts. Apprehension and conviction. Safe return. He'd labeled none of the lists. From the beginning he'd known that any day his suspicious, probably illegal activity could be reported. The lock sawed off. Contents searched, seized. He inspected those contents himself now. And as he did, an unexpectedly clean, clear tide began to separate itself from the pollution in his brain.

An idea.

Tulane had said something at Ernesto's.

Let me invest in it, man. One a them gimmicks a yours.

The fat man looked again at the reward figures. And squinted. Looked again at the gimmicks he'd devised. And smiled. He locked up. Drove to Camel-Op. Waited with a cup of coffee till nine. Then, instead of calling Dixon or Magdalena, he dialed Max Yoder.

"Max. Listen. There is something you can do. You still interested?"

"Aaron! Wonderful! I'll do it."

He drove directly to Sky Harbor after talking to Max. A busy itinerary confronted Aaron Dodge for the remainder of the day. Denver at ten.

Houston at eleven-thirty. Chicago at two-fifty. Las Vegas at six-oh-seven. Pan had persuaded her boyfriend, the travel agent, to provide a computer printout of crowded flights. The fat man had overdrawn his checking account by more than a thou to gamble on likely bookings.

Faced by a tier of those unified waiting chairs routinely encountered in public areas, heavy people always select a center, never an end seat. Leverage. Aaron Dodge stationed himself accordingly for a day of lucrative inaction.

Denver crapped on him. He negotiated at the ticket counter. Cut his losses. Didn't panic. He saw his luck turn around: Houston paid off Texas-size. That afternoon Chicago nearly doubled his earnings. At six o'clock, up by three hundred, a pair of airline chits totaling that amount in his wallet, the fat man anticipated the departure of his cheapo shuttle to Vegas.

But the page he was waiting for never came.

So he said what the fuck, and boarded with the other passengers.

He landed at the Las Vegas airport, caught a hotel courtesy van downtown, and made a phone call from the lobby of the Mint. In half an hour, an '81 Toyota wagon with '79 Utah plates, snow tires, and a square of cardboard taped over a missing window bullied into the taxi lane in front of the hotel. Aaron Dodge climbed in. His mom leaned across and kissed his cheek.

"The Judge ain't home from work yet. But we'll you and me visit till he gets in."

Several months earlier Esther Dodge had met a man named Judge Meade at the dog track in East Phoenix. They married, he either sold or lost the house on Encantero Drive, and they moved to Las Vegas soon afterward. His mom and Judge Meade lived in a yellow stucco kitchenette located behind an all-nite driving range on Russell Road, its entrance a sliding patio door that derailed when Aaron Dodge tried to open it. They sat at the kitchen table and shared a pint of Black Velvet, sipping it two fingers at a pour from a couple of amber water glasses with a twist pattern.

"The Judge, he's a fine one," said his mom.

"From what you've told me," Aaron Dodge agreed, "I'd say no question."

"You think I done all right then? This time?"

"You seem happy. That's good."

As they talked Esther Dodge smoked Benson & Hedges, withdrawing them from a pack she kept inside a gold, scaly pouch that snapped open like a change purse.

"So tell me. What's Vegas like? You work in town?"

"Oh, you know me. Can't sit still. Got me a job at the Albertsons. They just recently opened up a deli. Serve breakfast and lunch. Don't tell nobody, but the reason their prices is so cheap is because they take all the food that's due to spoil off the shelfs and give it to us to cook."

Later they moved two kitchen chairs outdoors to the uneven blacktop patio and sat facing the parking lot and practice range beyond. Tall banks of stadium lights projected through a low desert haze, illuminating the erratic bounces of the golfers' shots. Occasionally a red-striped ball, particularly well struck, would clear on its first or second hop the chain-link fence dividing the two properties. They'd watch it ricochet off a wall or fender and begin to roll, following swells and dips in the asphalt, finally coming to a stop in the darkness beneath a parked car.

"The Judge appreciates me," Esther Dodge said.

"Good," the fat man said. "He ought to."

"That gal a yours. She appreciate you?"

"She does, Mom. Lot more than I deserve."

"Me too. I think sometimes the Judge, he reads my mind. I say, 'Judge, how come you to guess I was thinkin' that? You read my mind, didn't you?' 'Short book,' he tells me." She laughed. A smoker's laugh. A voice to match.

"We ain't always been on ideal terms like now, though. Not till just lately. At the start he wasn't home much nights, the Judge. His work kep' him out. Which I couldn't blame him. You know how I snore. My ribs, where they got broke that one time, they'll get to achin'. They was this one old boy, I was married to him for a short while. I don't know if you two ever met. But anyways I'll shift over onto my back the way I do, and the Judge, he ain't slow. It didn't take the Judge too many of 'Esther you're snoring, Esther roll over' till he figured out he could make me stop right quick. His voice—that's all it took." She paused to look up at the sky and deliver her startling laugh again— the kind of laugh that made people turn and look in restaurants.

"But so pretty soon the Judge, being creative like he is, got tired of his 'Esther, wake up' and his 'Esther, shut up' and he started in on other topics. It didn't make no difference what he said. The sound of his voice was all I was hearin'. 'Esther, think the Rebels'll make the Final Four?' 'Esther, don't it never rain here?' I knowed what he was saying, 'cause one night I didn't stay asleep, see. Instead of just stopping snoring, I woke all the way up. 'Course you know what happened then.

"After that I ever' night only pretended to snore. I wanted to find out what the Judge was about to say next. It's hard enough to get a man to talk, you don't waste a chance like that.

"So things kept on this way for a while, till I guess finally the Judge figured, Shit, long as I'm talking, I might as well be sayin' somethin' important. So first thing you know I hear one night in this little bashful voice, 'Esther, I lost three hundred today.' 'Esther, I bought a hand job from that blonde-headed waitress down at La Perla.' Things he'd never in his life a said to me awake.

"After that you couldn't shut me up. I'd snore like a opera queen. 'Esther, it wasn't really nothing wrong with the solenoid on the Toyota.' And I'd quieten down for about a minute till curiosity would get the best of me, then I'd snort a couple more times. 'Esther, I give all that money to this guy I owe.' Lordy, I can't even remember all the confessions and revelations. 'Esther, I think maybe I'm puttin' on some weight, girl. Esther, you don't think I'm alcoholic, do you? I got terrible pain sometimes, Ess. Inside, I mean. Esther, babe, I wonder whether I always done the right things in my life.' Aaron, you never know what that person beside you might have on their mind in the middle of the night."

They sat silently a while, then Esther Dodge stood and walked out into the dark. She stooped to retrieve one of the practice balls and with an awkward, girlish throw returned it to its side of the fence.

"And you want to hear somethin' else, Aaron?" she called.

"What, Mom?"

"I think he knows I'm awake."

Later, back indoors, his mom set out a jumbo bag of barbecue chips and unwrapped slices of American cheese, which she melted on bread in the toaster oven. They finished the loaf at half past two in the morning, about the time the Judge arrived. A short, round man of fifty or so, with a deep suntan and full head of undulating silver hair, the Judge wore a thin mustache with a gap in the middle, high-waisted leisure jeans, and a bolo tie fastened by a beadwork thunderbird. He seemed genuinely pleased to see the fat man and brought from the pocket of his sportcoat a leather-holstered flask, which he uncapped and emptied into three glasses.

"Love's a gamble," Esther Dodge said, and they saluted with the Judge's liquor.

At four, Esther Dodge had to report to cook eggs. The fat man and Judge Meade delivered her to the Albertsons. Parked beside the dumpster in back. Followed her into the store. Before she disappeared behind the deli counter, she applied a ferocious hug and whispered against the fat man's neck: "You take good care a that gal, now."

"I'm trying, Mom."

Then she insisted on bagging him a half-dozen day-old donuts for the road. "We throw these out anyhow," she said. "Besides, they never feed you right on them shuffle flights."

On the way to the airport, Aaron Dodge finally brought up the issue he'd come to Nevada with vague hopes of investigating. "By the way, Judge. You wouldn't happen to know anybody who . . . See, I been working on this idea. A new lottery machine. You know—like the state lotteries? I'd hoped I could talk with a few locals. Get some advice maybe. Because I've read there's ways to rig games of chance, and naturally I'd want to build my machine so it couldn't be tampered with."

"Games of chance," said the Judge. "Oh, I've heard of some people. Sure. Let's see, there's this one in peticular." He glanced at a stick-on digital time disk attached to the Toyota's dash. Half past four. "Might be asleep now, though."

The Judge detoured to a night spot in East Vegas called the Velour Club. They entered through the back, by way of the kitchen. Unattended fry stations, deserted dish room, abandoned grill. Dented metal door with a porthole at eye level to prevent collisions. The Judge paused to stare through the cloudy Plexiglas circle, then pushed. The door opened into a cocktail lounge.

The barroom smelled like last night's beer and cigarettes. And the last ten years of last nights. A man who looked like he ought to be named Sharkey, Nick, or Diamond Tony sat at the bar. He turned to inspect them when Aaron Dodge and the Judge walked in. A woman dressed in tight black jeans, a vest, and frilly white blouse—the uniform of a casino dealer—stood at the jukebox, leaning, considering the selections.

"Morning," said the Judge.

No response.

The woman dug in her pocket. Inserted coins. Punched buttons. Mechanical clicks and whirrs, then an Elvis Costello 45 erupted from wall speakers aimed at the center of the room.

Instantly the flimsy metal door the fat man and Judge Meade had just made use of banged open. Through the doorway struggled a small, stocky Oriental carrying an upright vacuum cleaner, performing rope tricks with the cord.

"You pawson! Out!" she yelled.

Short, coarse gray hair. A shamrock bowling shirt. Painter's pants. Circles that hung like swags of drapery under her eyes.

"Out now! You unwaycome! Go! Go!" She pointed with the hand she held the vacuum cleaner cord in, squinting against helixes of smoke from her cigarette. "You stay," she said in a kinder voice to Judge Meade. "Them!" she told the man at the bar. "Go! Boo-shit cocksuckos!"

The young woman at the jukebox retreated from the old Asian lady, who pushed the sweeper at her, attacking her feet, backing her toward her friend. He climbed off his stool. "Relax, Kim. We're leaving, okay?" He hastily guided the startled young woman past Aaron Dodge and the Judge, through the stainless-steel swinging door, still rippling from the impact of Kim's abrupt appearance. Kim reached into the narrow space between it and the wall and killed the jukebox.

"Good mowing," she said.

The Judge introduced her to Aaron Dodge, Kim filled three light, white stackable cups, and they crowded around a tiny table with a sour black ashtray in the center.

Immediately an unmistakable emotion overtook the fat man.

Again he'd found his way here in the dark.

To a place he'd never been. For reasons he didn't understand.

Food, drink, the advice of strangers.

"You fuss visit La Vegas?" Kim asked.

The Judge helped Aaron Dodge explain what had brought him. His plan to replace the jackpot machine with his own design. His concern that the proposed invention be immune to monkeying.

Kim smiled. A gap the width of a nickel separated her two front teeth. "You worry about swindlow, somesing, huh? I no blame you. Not game in town can't be fix."

"Really?" the fat man said.

Kim stood. Shuffled behind the bar. Explored a ravine separating two beer coolers and extracted a broom.

"I pawsonally would love to see. No offense to you profession, Misso Dodge. But lottery in how many state now? Newly all, yes? Many, many lottery, and over much time somebody get wild hair and go faw swindow. Unnastan?"

"Someplace there's a fool," the Judge agreed.

Kim set aside the broom, lifted sets of wooden slats from behind the bar, and stood them on edge. Bottlecaps skated across the floor as she started to sweep.

"I hear pawsons sometime talk about. Skew-ty make them nawvous, though. Still they talk. In La Vegas every way cheating been thought of. And some of it wuck. In La Vegas, always somebody with new, foolproof system. Blockjack, roulette, po-kaw. Swindlow take small bite, maybe okay. Try take big bite, no okay. Always pawsons watching. Obsovaws. With lottery, many, many obsovaw. Big-time. High stake. Unnastan? Lottery like Intunnel Revenue, somesing. Lot of govoment involve. Risky."

Kim climbed with a grunt onto a short stepladder and began to rearrange team pairings on a tote board displaying the day's baseball odds.

"Only one way cheat pawson. Distrack pawson. Unnastan? Whole town La Vegas one big magic trick. Big hotel, lot of young goll stick big knowkas in tourist eye. He here two day, spend thousand dollar. Go home feeling good fawtune. In La Vegas lawn to look for other pawson weakness. Unnastan?"

"And what would the lottery's weakness be, I wonder?" the fat man encouraged her.

Kim returned to her chair. Sat down and lit a cigarette. Parked it in one of the melted notches in the rim of the black ashtray. "Impawtant thing rememo. You invent new lottery, you hand machine over many, many govoment flunky. Pawsons sometime not care. Not smot. They-faw, pawson who try swindow machine have one awvantage maybe. Not have useless pawsons on side. Maybe smot gamblaw, he take awvantage this weakness, somesing. He see chance and go faw swin-dow. Unnastan?"

Kim chuckled. Leaned forward to extinguish her smoke. When she did, the fat man saw that she wore a necklace—a beaded chain, a rabbit's foot dyed bright green. "Not to be agains' you wuck, Misso Dodge. Not to wish troubaw. But I feel much sympathy this pawson. Very bowd, I think. And maybe litto crazy awso. Theyfaw, I be on this pawson side, I think."

"All the way to jail," said Judge Meade.

Kim dismissed the objection with an indignant stiffening of her posture. "Okay to sometime be on side of crimnaw," she said. "Lady sometime unpredictobaw."

They sat together a while longer, scalding fluorescent light unnat-urally illuminating Kim's barroom, never intended to be viewed so directly. Then Kim walked them out the way they'd come in. The kitchen. Stainless-steel prep tables, tall cold ovens.

She accompanied them into the alley. Watched as they climbed into the Judge's Toyota. Before they pulled away, Kim discreetly touched the fat man's arm through the car window. "Faw you," she whispered, and withdrew from the pocket of her bowling shirt a ballpoint the same shade of Irish, the Velour Club's name and address printed on its barrel. "Good-luck chom, somesing. Unnastan?"

He nodded and accepted a kiss on the cheek.

The Judge chauffeured him through Vegas's sunny, canyonlike downtown. Hotel facades, marquees, billboards. Then, nearer the out-skirts of the city, used-car lots and powerboat showrooms. Self-serve gas stations, convenience markets, savings-and-loan branches. The Judge pulled into the drive-thru at a fish franchise. They shared a boxed meal of seafood nuggets, fries, slaw. Drank coffee from throw-away cups decorated with the straw-and-orange silhouettes of weeds or wildflowers. At the airport Judge Meade parked in the busy curbside lane, designated by yellow warning slashes, that faced the terminal entrance. He shook Aaron Dodge's hand. The fat man was already climbing out, almost ready to turn and wave, when he heard the Judge say softly from behind him: "Don't do it, son."

He slammed the car door. Faced Judge Meade. Smiled. "Kiss Mom one more time for me. And tell Kim thanks a million."

The Judge answered with a worried frown. A nod. The Toyota stalled once. Then the fat man watched its crooked license plate disappear in traffic.

On the plane, instead of sleeping, he ate a stale donut and thought about luck. He'd been chasing her for decades now, it seemed. From the '60s through the '70s, into the '80s. She'd eluded him in fast cars. Disguised herself in stylish fashions. Intimidated him with her so-phistication, hiding behind expensive menus and in ritzy nightclubs with dress codes that excluded him. She'd sicced her pit bulls on him. Changed numbers to avoid him. Luck to the fat man had always been a million-dollar idea that somebody else patented the day before he thought of it. About time she switched sides. Or at least declared her neutrality.

But even with all the luck in Vegas with him, Aaron Dodge would've still worried that the game, the machine, controlled the winner's share. In comparison he felt small, and the fat man wasn't used to feeling small in comparison with anything. He'd always taken size for granted. Always brought his influence with him wherever he went. People stared. Got out of his way. He was part of the biggest generation. The one everybody paid attention to. Catered to, wooed, indulged. But now he saw that there'd always been something bigger, more powerful and influential. He hadn't had to face it so directly since he'd eaten his way out of the draft. But now he sensed its presence again. Something large that he was no part of, that was no part of him. And the game was only a fraction of it. The game, with its advertisements, its budget, the agencies associated with it. The awe its hugeness inspired. Its rules and its odds—slim and so tempting. Something about the game and its vast mediocrity reminded you of an endless weekday afternoon, three o'clock, sitting in front of the tv, eating when you weren't hungry, watching when you weren't interested, living when you didn't care. Quiz shows, talk shows, soaps. An incoherent dullness that annihilated every desperate attempt at enthusiasm. The fat man wanted, more than he'd ever wanted anything, to beat that game.

By the time his flight landed in Phoenix, he'd decided on a next step. He'd build a full-scale working model of the jackpot machine. He made the decision without knowing exactly what he'd do with the replica once he finished it, only that he needed to be doing something while Max worked out the arrangements he'd asked her to supervise. Maybe he could find a way to substitute his machine for theirs when the time came. Or could be he'd use his copy simply to guarantee a better understanding of the original. Something about the process of construction always revealed a machine's strengths and weaknesses in a way that no amount of theoretical assembly and disassembly could. Your mind was a third and your imagination a fourth hand, but they couldn't, either separately or in partnership, replace your original two.

Manufacture would be a problem. But he knew people. Friends of his. He'd ask Bob the Brush to help him duplicate certain components with his pattern-making tools. He was thinking particularly of the central chimney through which the payoff sequence would have to pass. He'd already researched the composition of the numbered spheres themselves. Celluloid. Now he'd have to dig through the crammed and disorganized file folders he'd accumulated over the years for an appropriate leaflet or catalogue. Somebody someplace sometime must've offered to press celluloid for him. Jowls, from the eviction squad—thanks to work he'd done customizing bike chassis—knew how to cast Fiberglas. He was sure he could count on Jowls for a reproduction of the big, colorful facade responsible for the jackpot machine's Wizard of Oz theatricality. And he hoped the videotape Dexter had shot for him would supply adequate dimensions and specifications.

But he knew that ultimately the value of his imitation would depend less on its authenticity than on the success of the effort he'd asked Max to oversee. He called her office from an airport payphone to check on her progress. Now that a really important issue was at stake, not just the fat man's dreams and bank account, Max accepted the call without delay. "

"This is so energizing, Aaron! I haven't felt so positive in years. Literally years."

"Then the response has been good so far?"

"I wish I could say it has. But I'm learning fast, Aaron. These people! In the last year they've been approached by every fringe element imaginable. Aaron, the schemes they've had to listen to! They're very skeptical. Justifiably. And at the same time I've been trying to reveal as little of the truth as possible. But I feel so exhilarated! It's such an opportunity!"

The fat man had asked Max to initiate a fund-raising operation. The idea, though basic, contained an element of desperation that Aaron Dodge didn't feel altogether comfortable with, in spite of Max's optimism. Max had been negotiating with the Singers. She'd been trying to convince them to divert the Help Find Mary Vanessa Singer donations, plus the reward money they'd helped raise, into ticket purchases in order to revive the lottery jackpot. Eventually, as soon as Aaron Dodge invented a way to program the system to produce the six numbers he wanted, the accounts administered by the Singers would be used to help inflate the payoff. By itself, the bounty money wouldn't purchase nearly enough tickets, but since it would represent the Singers' endorsement the amount would be indispensable to Max when the second round of her pledge drive began. Max had also volunteered to enlist the help of investors—the local wealth she'd brought in to back ideas of the fat man's in the past. Their millions would provide the transfusion necessary to bring the lottery figure up to size.

"Aaron, they're curious about you. Understandably. Will you speak to them if they keep asking? Don't say you will unless you mean it. I'd rather not look like a fool."

"I always do what I say I will. Eventually."

"Does that mean you'll act sensibly? Dress respectably?"

"I'm always sensible," the fat man said.

"We may have to tell them everything!" Max said. "I want to, Aaron. They deserve to know. They're such wonderful, regular people, and they've worked so hard to bring in those contributions."

"I suppose if we can't trust them . . ." the fat man admitted. But he felt only marginally confident in the judgment. He couldn't help picturing the fragile network of trusts he'd constructed already. The assortment of ungraceful partners he'd have to share the same tightrope with in order to complete this crossing. The friends of friends of friends.

He phoned Holly next.

He'd wait for a more encouraging report from Max before notifying Dixon or Magdalena. When he talked to them, he wanted to be able to present evidence of a campaign so far advanced that they'd have to approve. His conversation with Holly, like the one he'd just had with Max, left him minimally cheered.

"You talk to Robin yet?"

"I . . . sort of. Don't worry, I will."

"Today," he told her. "All right?"

"Look," she said. "I shouldn't suggest this. Not without talking to Robin. But let's meet, okay?" She gave him the address of a motel on East Van Buren. "Tonight. Sometime between, oh, say, ten and midnight. Ask at the desk." She supplied a last name. The fat man wrote it down with the pen Kim had given him. Not until he'd hung up did the fat man fully realize he'd been invited to make a trio out of what most natural human urges would ordain a strictly two-party arrangement.

In the El Camino, on the way home, he remembered that he'd forgotten to call Kennedy last night from his mom's. Shit. He was always doing this. Getting absorbed in some project and neglecting her. Ignoring her feelings. Injuring her pride. Accidentally, of course, but he knew that from her viewpoint—alone, uncertain, worried— intentions hardly counted. The prospect of facing an angry and indignant female triggered a brief adrenaline surge, immediately lost in the vast exhaustion he suddenly felt. He could already imagine the welcome awaiting him. She'd hear the door unlock. He'd hear another door slam someplace inside. Then the apartment—accusations and panicky hormones saturating the air like the smell of skidmarks at the scene of a collision.

Stay away.

Get out.

I don't want to talk to you.

You don't love me.

Then silence. Silence during which he'd be expected to refute those charges. Silence the artificial absence people construct when they're afraid to tinker with the genuine article.

That, the fat man decided as he drove, represented the crucial dif-

ference between him and Kennedy. Between men and women. In the
1980s you weren't supposed to say it. In conversations you had to
argue the reverse. Sound progressive. But there it was—an unhappy
observation that the fat man and all men had to make sooner or later.
Mostly you tried to tell yourself it wasn't so. And when you felt mag-
nanimous you declined opportunities to take advantage of the situation.
But sometimes you couldn't stop yourself. It was like when you're
playing softball and you look out at the other team's fielders and notice
who they've put in right. Street shoes. No cap. Wearing a lefty's mitt
upside down on the wrong hand. In an emergency, down a run, you
know you're going to hit to right, no matter how nice a guy you are.
That's why Aaron Dodge sometimes wished he didn't know, and didn't
callously exploit whenever it suited him, the simple and sad truth that
a woman will endure just about any level of abuse, suffer practically
any amount of frustrated desire, before she'll face life without a male.
And it didn't seem to matter much what male. In fact in women's
minds an inverse proportion seemed to exist between a man's apparent
worth and his subjective value. Feminine logic seemed to supply conflicting messages depending on current circumstances. A happy
woman might think: If I deserve a guy this terrific, I don't see why I
can't find a better one just about anytime. Unhappy, the same woman
could as easily say to herself, If this gourd is the best I can do, I better
hang on to him or else I'll spend the rest of my life alone.

He tried not to acknowledge these inappropriate opinions. Tried to
respect the threats he knew Kennedy would deliver. Wanted to believe
them. To be more afraid of living without her than with her. But he
doubted he'd be able to invent a convincing performance when the
time came.

So the fat man wasn't at all disappointed when he arrived and found
the apartment empty, Kennedy out.

The grocery store, he assumed at first.

Or Laura's.

But then he sensed a difference he hadn't thought to look for right
away. Ions or something. Maybe the almost imperceptible gravities
that accumulated possessions generate, which you don't notice until
additions or subtractions substantially alter their strength. He opened
the closets. Found most of her clothes and other belongings in their

usual places. But what about the decisive items? Toothbrush, book bag, blow-drier, address organizer? All missing. He managed a cynical laugh for the mental inning of softball he'd played between the airport and home.

When you haven't slept for twenty-four, thirty-six, forty-eight hours, a time eventually arrives when you ask yourself how long it's been and your brain won't surrender the information. Or any information. It's become an entirely independent, selfish organ, demanding rest. And if your body refuses to cooperate, your brain rests anyway. When he understood Kennedy had deserted him, that moment occurred inside the fat man's mind. Mentally he couldn't've recruited the strength to find her, plead with her, reason with her, any more than he could've physically climbed into a track suit and high-jumped seven feet. The laws of physics prevented him. Time and mass. Space, distance, the transfer of energy. For now the best he could do was hot water for coffee, cold to douse his headache with. He'd confront Robin later tonight. And Kennedy tomorrow or the day after or the day after that. But first he had two other people to make angry.

Working graveyard eliminates most of your best excuses for showing up late or leaving early. You can't very well claim a root canal and disappear for three hours in the middle of the night. The errands people run after dark they run without camouflage. When Aaron Dodge told his bosses he needed to extend his meal break by an hour in order to attend Open House at Brett's school, Laszlo and Tony stared down at the cheeses they were shredding, the onions they were dicing, and chewed their gum aggressively.

"Oh yeahr?" said Tony. "Well for wants you better be back win you say. 'Cause I hat it wit you."

"And here. Deliver this here on you way," said Laszlo, and handed the fat man a hot double deluxe.

He arrived at the Starlite at just past ten. Inquired at the office. Knocked on the door of the cabin the night clerk directed him to.

"Who is it?" Holly's voice.

"Hi," said the fat man.

The room contained the standard motel grouping. And the odor that went with it. A combination of smells that reminded Aaron Dodge of the black rubber backing on all-weather floor coverings. Robin sat in the room's vinyl armchair, dressed in his uniform pants, no shoes, a t-shirt so white it phosphoresced. Aaron Dodge avoided imagining the scene that had preceded his arrival, though he probably could've come close to reconstructing it word for word just by counting the layers of fury and resentment in Robin's expression, as obvious as strata in exposed rock.

"I'll go out and get a pop or something," Holly offered, and left the two of them alone.

A creaky, straight-backed chair accompanied the combination dresser/desk. Aaron Dodge straddled it. Backward. Arms folded atop the backrest.

"So. I guess I don't need to introduce myself?"

Robin stared at him.

"Holly's probably told you all about me. Why I'm here?"

Still no reaction.

"Listen, Robin. It doesn't have to be this way, man. Why not look at it like you're doing something nice for a lost little girl, not like you're—"

"Being extorted? Blackmailed?"

The fat man let his head drop onto his folded arms. Tried to force his weary brain to cooperate.

"Besides, there's no little girl," Robin said.

"Don't you read the newspaper?" Aaron Dodge asked, without lifting his head.

"You know what I mean. There's a kid, sure. Or there was. Maybe she's alive, maybe she isn't. Probably isn't. But don't try to tell me what you're up to's got anything to do with finding out. I'm not sweet, gullible Holly." He jerked his head in the direction she'd gone. "So forget the little girl, okay?"

He managed enough strength to open his eyes. To rest his chin on a forearm and look at Robin again. "What I told Holly's true. It'll happen. Every bit of it. Just the way I said."

"It won't if I turn your ass in."

"Lookit. I don't blame you. I'd want evidence too. But there's no way I can offer you any. It's taken me months to believe all this myself. It's up to you. You're either a hero, you're helping somebody out, there's this incredibly good thing and you're part of it, or else— Ah, fuck it.

I'm too tired to argue with you. Believe what you want, you're entitled."

Robin wore one of those military-looking, multifunction black wrist-watches that calculate depth, altitude, and time zone. He consulted it now. Maybe for a readout pertaining to his current situation.

"Just exactly how far do you expect me to hang my flag out while I watch you score? Because it won't be far. I'll take my chances at home, I'll take my chances with the old lady, a lot quicker than I'll look at twenty years. You would too."

"I don't expect you to actively assist. Just don't actively obstruct. That's all I'm saying. You'll see. Nobody but me and you'll suspect what's going on. Not unless one of us lets that happen. Listen, you were in the war. You can handle this, man. This'll be nothing compared to then. Nobody's getting killed here. The opposite in fact. If we're lucky."

"I can't talk to you, man, if you're going to drag in what happened back then." Robin stood up. Turned. Appeared to study the list of legal restrictions posted to the door.

When he talked to veterans—of Robin's war, at least—Aaron Dodge felt a self-consciousness he associated with blacks, gays, the disabled. He was sure that any minute he'd say something outrageously ignorant and offensive. Something that might be misconstrued. Might refer in an indirect or bigoted way to obvious, irreconcilable differences. On occasions like this, everything he ever wanted to say seemed to pertain in a way he didn't intend. Like now. He wanted to tell Robin that he knew a little about disenchantment too. But Robin, literally, physically, had already lived through the war Aaron Dodge had up to now fought with only half his mind and a daily fraction of his spirit. So who was he to lecture Robin?

"Show up with your scam," Robin said finally. "Whether I go along or not depends on what I see. But I still don't buy the little-girl part. Okay?"

The fat man shrugged. "Suit yourself."

Robin opened the door. Searched the dark in both directions. Then stepped outside. The fat man heard him call to Holly. Heard Holly answer. Her voice reminded him of what Robin had said. Sweet, gul-lible. She was twenty years old, Kennedy's age. Born when he and Robin were making the decisions that had led them to this night, this

room. No wonder a man could fall so hard for someone younger—
someone equal in years to the distance between him and his mistakes.

Alone, the fat man turned his attention immediately toward bed—
the bed Robin and Holly hadn't had a chance to use. Its white spread.
Soft, pebbled starbursts. Chenille. He could barely keep himself from
touching it. And then he couldn't. The bedsprings gronked, the mattress sank as he applied his weight. He'd lie here a minute. Relax.
Rest his brain. Just till Robin and Holly returned.

He woke shivering, the motel-room door still open.

Daylight.

Traffic noises.

He pulled the covers over him and held them tightly at his throat.
Wasn't waking up in a strange room supposed to leave you disoriented?
Temporarily uncertain as to time and place? He only wished. The fat
man knew exactly where he was. In whose bed. The nature and se-
verity of his recent indiscretions assaulted him as vividly as the white
slash of lightning in the $4.99 reproduction of a desert landscape that
occupied the opposite wall. He blocked the sight of it with a pillow.
But he knew if he lay there any longer, artificially blinded, inhaling
stale foam rubber, he wouldn't move till checkout time had past. So
he heaved a leg over the edge and sat up.

Second to sleep on his list of preferences would've been a bath. But
the room offered only a tilting galvanized stall with a vinyl curtain a
foot too short. After his shower he dressed, pocketed the extra complimentary bar of Cashmere Bouquet, a couple of matchbooks, a picture
postcard. He closed the door behind him. Climbed into the El Camino.
Drove to Camel-Op.

"Did you see your horoscope yet today?" Buzz asked, offering a
section of the newspaper as Aaron Dodge mounted the corner stool.

"Take a look at *The Far Side*," said the fat man. "That's where they
print predictions about my life."

"How could somebody *do* something like that?" asked Wendy
Wendy. She flung the section she'd been reading onto the counter.
Another Mary Vanessa Singer story? Probably, though the remark
could've applied equally well to any of the names he saw mentioned
on the front page. "I don't understand it."

"I do," said Lulu. "And you'll see more and more of it, believe me."

She filled a cup from the instant hot-carob-drink machine, decorated it with a swirl of institutional whipped cream from a silver cylinder, and served Aaron Dodge.

"There used to be monsters," she said. "Horrible creatures of the imagination that embodied people's darkest secret fears. Now actual human beings are out there *doing* all the things people used to only have nightmares about." She brought a tiny jar of lip salve from her apron pocket and without pausing applied a coat with her little finger.

"It's this incredibly paradoxical situation. People are so insulated. You can visit San Diego and find the same Sheraton and Burger King as in Denver and Cincinnati. You can go for months and not see anything unfamiliar or frightening. All the monsters are in hibernation. Banished. So much so that when one of them finally surfaces it assumes some really fiendish, intolerable form. Terrorism, AIDS, thermonuclear holocaust."

Between sips, listening, the fat man stared into his cup, soon empty except for sugary beige webs clinging to its sides and a dark-brown, almost purple carob sludge at the bottom. "It takes these like incredibly powerful manifestations of evil to even begin to break through defenses as strong as Americans'," he heard Lulu saying.

Then, next thing he knew, she was squeezing his arm, shaking him. "—up, Aaron. You can't sleep in here. It runs off the customers. Wake up. Aaron?"

"You okay, buddy?" Buzz was saying. "Man, you look beat."

"The mold-spore count is through the ceiling today, I know that," said Wendy Wendy.

"I'm okay," said Aaron Dodge. "Coffee." He slid his cup across the counter to Lulu.

"You need to go home and go straight to bed, Aaron Dodge."

"You okay to drive?" Buzz asked.

"I just got up," said the fat man. "Make that coffee to go, Lulu. A large. I've got a few errands to run first, but you're right. An hour or two in the sack does sound pretty good."

But Aaron Dodge never got around to his nap that afternoon. Instead he stopped at the hardware store where Bob the Brush worked. He didn't mention Kennedy. Kennedy he didn't want to talk about. He only spoke to his friend about cutting the patterns he'd be needing.

He sketched each feature on the back of a blank invoice with the souvenir pen of Kim's and promised Bob he'd call later with exact dimensions and specifications. Then he drove to South Phoenix and completed similar arrangements with Jowls, who agreed to supply the Fiberglas he required. Jowls couldn't offer the kind of paint job called for, but he knew a tattoo artist who did pinstriping and airbrush and who claimed to be able to copy anything. A Felonious Realist, Jowls called him. "This dude," Jowls promised, "could forge your old lady's snatch on a bowling ball and tomorrow half the guys in Phoenix'd have chipped teeth."

By then it was time to report to Pizza on Wheels and find out if he still had a job. The suspense didn't last long. When he walked through the back door, Laszlo and Tony stopped chewing their gum to glance once at him, once at each other—then it was back to business as usual behind the counter at Pizza on Wheels. Or that's what Aaron Dodge believed. He squeezed into the tiny employees' john to change, and when he emerged, dressed in his uniform, he found Laszlo waiting.

"You check," he said, and handed it to the fat man. "It's like this, see. We got to let you go, okay? You fired, all right? It ain't like we mat at you or nothin', but Tony and me, this is our livelihoots, you know?"

"We hat it wit you," said Tony.

"Come on, Tone. You know how bad I need this job. I got Laura's kids. They count on me."

"I toad you we hat it," said Tony.

"Come on, you guys. Let's talk about this. What do you say, Laz?"

"Me too," said Laszlo. "I stick up for you all those other time. 'Cause I like you, you know? You a nice friendly guy. But you unappendable. We can't append on you, you know?"

"Me? You're joking. I was a paperboy, Laz."

"What you stand around here in my kitchen for?" said Tony. "Waste my time? Don't come in here. I hat it."

"One more chance. Come on, Tone? Laz?"

"No more chance. We already hire new boy. You finish."

"Shit!" The fat man punched the door of the walk-in, leaving a shallow crater in its silver finish.

"You got a bat attitute. You know that?" said Tony.

Aaron Dodge booted an empty pickle pail across the kitchen.

"Look a this guy," said Tony. "Violence. Don't make me call nobody, Aaron. 'Cause I will."

"Screw this place. You guys don't know what good help is."

"Oh yeahr?" Tony opened the oven. Redistributed pies with a pizza paddle. "Well hows about you go fawk youself then?"

The fat man showed Tony a finger, and on his way out attacked the most convenient inanimate object within reach—an open cardboard box sitting on one of the prep tables. The box crashed, and its contents, white disposable forks, a thousand count, cascaded in a satisfying, brittle rush onto the kitchen floor. Backtracking once to enjoy the sound of snapping, shattering plastic, the fat man stomped and crunched through the spill and outside.

He filled up at a Mars station and drove. Not toward home but in the opposite direction. As far north as Paradise Valley. East to Chandler and past. He parked at a rest area on I-10. Stared ahead at the foul graffiti as he pissed. Then stared ahead at the pitted stars in the El Camino's windshield as Blazers, Fleetwoods, and mini-vans pulled into the parking space to his right and waited. Into the space to his left and waited, engines running, for the fat man to announce his intentions and desires. Start the El Camino and follow. Comply with the raunchy contracts drafted on the men's-room wall.

Long after midnight he drove back into Phoenix, crosstown via the busiest arteries. Thomas, Bethany Home, Camelback. That's when he noticed the first symptoms. A head cold. This time an actual, physical virus, not one of the exotic emotional or mental strains he typically suffered from. He drove to a U-Totem and bought capsules, the most powerful-sounding formulation on the shelf, packaged in solid blocks of fine print. Phenylpropanolamine hydrochloride. Do not exceed recommended dosage. Do not operate machinery. He ate three in the car on his way to the mini–storage unit, where he planned to spend the night working on his replica.

15

The fat man stood beside the refrigerator, a clock radio he'd unplugged and brought from the bedroom held to his face. He'd been standing that way, staring at the clock's sweep second hand for a total of maybe half a revolution, when Kennedy, obeying a peculiar instinct mandating the destruction of privacy and concentration, barged into the kitchen and made him lose count.

"Sorry," she said. "I knocked."

"Oh. Sorry. Guess I didn't hear you come in. I was busy."

"I can see that. I should come back—"

"No. Don't go. Really."

"Okay. Sorry."

He hadn't talked to Kennedy in more than a week. Not since the day he'd come home from Vegas and found her gone.

"I've got a diskette in the freezer," he explained.

"No thanks. I already ate."

"When one won't access, sometimes you can revive it if you stick it in the freezer for a minute or so. Just a minute, though. If they freeze solid, there's a chance they'll shatter in your disk drive."

"Sounds bad."

"I thought everybody your age was supposed to be computer-literate. Nobody gets issued their Firebird or Club Med membership, you know, till they learn Pascal."

Silence between them. Rumble of the air conditioner from the living room. It shuddered, the character of its vibration changing as the compressor kicked in, responding to the heat Kennedy had admitted as she let herself inside.

"I just came back to pick up some of my stuff."

"Oh. Okay. I'll help you."

"I think it's been at least a minute, hasn't it?"

"Shit!" He yanked open the freezing compartment and retrieved the diskette. "Fuck!" He held it in the palm of one hand and pressed gently with the index finger of the other. Snap. "Well. I guess it wasn't all that important. Whatever was on there."

"Aaron, you've lost weight, haven't you? You don't look healthy. Are you eating?"

"I'm eating. I've got a cold. That's probably it."

She opened the cupboards, still fully provisioned for the godchildren, and brought out a jar of nut butter. Tuna. A bag of cheese curls, which she tried to hand him. "No thanks," he said. "I never eat anything fluorescent." She unclipped the clothespin holding it shut and started to eat from the bag. They both sat down at the kitchen table.

"You're such an extreme personality, Aaron. Read any book on the subject. Eliminate a thousand calories a day. Lose two pounds per week. It's the safe limit."

"Water weight," the fat man said. "So far I'm just shedding water weight is all. It's deceptive. It won't be permanent."

"You don't even know what that means."

"Water weight? Sure I do. Water weight is—it's like your body retaining fluids. Fluid retention. Adipose tissue. Muscle, you know, weighs more than fat."

Kennedy laughed. But her face looked like it had aged five years in the past five months. And five more since last week.

"How's Laura?"

"Fine. The same."

"Kids?"

Kennedy grabbed the edges of the table and mimed a brief earthquake.

"And him?"

"Oh, him. There is news about him. 'Aggressive treatment.' Ever

heard of that? Her lawyer's accusing the doctors of aggressive treatment. Extraordinary measures. But it probably won't help. Just more
applications to fill out, I'm sure. Since Laura was divorcing him the
doctors are being extra cautious. Malpractice and all that." She looked
at him closely and added with a half-smile: "See what happens when
people move out?"

He glanced away.

"Listen, I'm still planning on doing my share with the kids. Tell
Laura that. I'll still give her money. Loan her, I mean. And I can take
a couple of the kids now and then. Just like always."

"You don't have to do that."

"I will, though."

"It'd be a big help if you would."

"I will. Don't worry."

"You didn't call," said Kennedy. "How come?"

"I meant to. But you know how I am. I get involved in— No, actually
that wasn't it. The truth is, I was going to call but I decided not to.
Purposely. Because, to be truthful, I think you did the right thing."

"By going?"

"Do you realize," said the fat man, "that if you were sleeping with
somebody as younger than you as you are than me, he'd be seven
years old?"

"Why are you always bringing up our ages? I wish you'd shut up
about that. Besides, there's a hell of a lot more difference between a
seven-year-old and a twenty-year-old than there is between somebody
my age and somebody yours. Look at what all happens between seven
and twenty. Adolescence. Puberty. School."

"School? Are you saying nothing happens between twenty and
thirty? How the hell would you know?"

"What are you yelling at me for?"

"Sorry. But that's what I can't stand about people your age. How
would you feel if you were surrounded by a bunch of seven-year-olds
who took it for granted that they knew as much about everything
as you?"

"Okay then. Just tell me what happens to a person when he's thirty
that's so goddam important?"

"You name it. Your parents die. Your teeth rot. That's the whole point. It's different for everybody. Wars, jobs. Marriages, divorces, children. Ask Laura."

"I'll bet you've already forgotten as much as I don't know yet."

"See what I mean? I knew this would happen. This is why I didn't call."

"Sorry," said Kennedy. "You're right. I'm sorry."

"Quit saying that."

"Okay," she said. "Sorry. But hold me, will you, please? Just for a minute."

"You want me to?"

She put her arms around him, pressed an ear to his shoulder. It was the first time in eons a woman had been able to do that. Wholly encircle him. "You feel so different," she said. "You have bones."

He switched on the radio he'd brought from the bedroom. Tuned it till he found a station playing something other than KKGB jingles. "Here," he said. "Like this." Aaron Dodge had never learned to dance. Heavy people seldom try. But today he faked it. The fat man and Kennedy, there on the kitchen linoleum, rocking together foot to foot. Penguin-dancing. A couple of nervous teenagers at a prom.

Don't go.

He wanted to say it. As sincerely as he knew Kennedy wanted to hear it. Come back. Please stay. But the fat man kept it inside.

He helped Kennedy pack. Arbitrarily. Absent-mindedly. Neither of them seemed able to believe in the finality of what they were beginning. Something would happen. A reprieve. One of them would speak up and halt this foolishness. But the war of indecision continued until it had filled the pink Mustang's back seat and trunk. Soon Kennedy sat behind the steering wheel. Tears. Plastic milk crates blocking the rearview mirror.

He promised to call.

She said she was sorry and drove away.

He missed her. More than he'd expected. In ways he'd've never guessed. He remembered how she'd entice him into indefensible positions with her endearing trap-and-pounce maneuver.

Aaron, which pan do you usually make grilled cheeses in?

Doesn't matter. Use any of them.

But which one do *you* use?

I don't know. That silver one with the loose handle, I guess.

Not the aluminum one? Aaron, aluminum cookware has been implicated in Alzheimer's.

The hourly tragedies, traumas, and complications. Luxuries, emotionally speaking. Like owning a tape player instead of a radio, or separating the colors from the socks and underwear instead of washing everything in the same machine. But once you understood what you were doing without, you could get to feeling kind of deprived if you weren't careful.

No doubt about it, Kennedy had exercised a regulating influence on some of his more immoderate tendencies. An effect he couldn't seem to reproduce without her, though he tried with the help of Laura's six. First on weekends, then more frequently, he accepted day-care duty as part of some unspecified debt he felt he owed Laura. Kennedy would call up from Laura's Peoria apartment, her new home, barely able to suppress the panic in her voice. "Laura says you could probably have them today, Aaron. I guess right now would be as good a time as any." As if she were offering the keys to her villa, her Ferrari. And the fat man would go along with the pretense. "Gee, that'd be great. Are you sure?"

More than once lately the thought had crossed his mind—a short commute these days—that Laura's six had come to mean something especially important to him. Suddenly he required their company. Laura was in a walking cast now, more self-sufficient, working again. Money had begun to arrive regularly and in conspicuous sums—evidence that Kennedy had reported the end of their living arrangement to Olivia. Now the kids were his one connection to the chaotic life that had temporarily disrupted his bachelorhood. And his one connection to Kennedy. A fragile, frayed connection he wasn't willing to break but wasn't completely willing to mend either.

He'd take them to Encanto Park. Or to sit by the dry bed of the Salt River. No threat of anybody drowning there, so he didn't have to watch them closely. Not that he minded looking out for Ginger, for Sylvia, for Heather and Holland. Now, some days, they and their brothers actually appeared beautiful to him. Always so healthy in their miniature swimsuits, full of unregulated joy, their summer tans just beginning to show. Sitting, watching them displace the dry bed with their pails, shovels, and tin trucks, he saw in each of the children Mary Vanessa Singer at a different age. A different state of undisturbed innocence. While he watched them play, he'd try to simplify his plan.

When the sun started to sink, one of the younger ones would run to where he sat to demand a towel. Then the others would notice. There'd be quibbling. Tears. He'd drive them home, maybe stay for supper if Laura invited him. Then he'd spend the hours till dawn at Pack Rat, exploiting the brief comfort the desert night offered.

He believed that if he endured enough hours in the company of Laura's six he might finally learn to appreciate them fully. Maybe that's what love was. Accepting obligations that terrified you. Absorbing expenses you couldn't afford. Exhibiting cheer you didn't particularly feel. And even if he was wrong about love—and his track record spoke for itself—he had another reason for spending his Saturdays as he did. In spite of Max's faith in makeovers, he knew the length of his hair and the labels he wore weren't going to impress Mary Vanessa Singer's parents when he sat across the coffee table from them in their living room. Only what he said would make a difference. Only what he felt would show. He'd know the machine and how it operated. The game and where it was vulnerable. But unless he demonstrated a comparable facility where the internal mysteries of children were concerned, why should the Singers entrust their daughter's life to him?

And so, just as he'd grudgingly accepted the responsibilities of guardianship without first experiencing the joys of fatherhood, Aaron Dodge now stoically agreed to the status of divorcee having never served as a husband. This shortage of personal experience led him to rely heavily on the example set by his divorced friends, particularly Bob the Brush.

Sometime between dawn and high noon on the final Saturday of every month, Bob the Brush's ex-wife met him at Camel-Op with the boys. The conclusion of the monthly arrangements created a dismal mood at Lulu's counter—an atmosphere of decayed intimacy that suggested hostage bartering, ransoms exchanged at the crossroads. Regulars often stayed away. Nobody wanted to look so directly on the disfigured face of American family life that early on a Saturday morning. But Bob the Brush was a friend. So on the last Saturday in May the fat man decided to bring Brett along to meet Bob's sons. As they sat at the counter with Bob, anticipating the arrival of his ex-wife and the transfer of custody, the fat man noticed a long waxy thread dangling from the corner of Brett's mouth.

"What's that?"

"Nothing."

"Yes it is. That's dental floss, isn't it?"

"I guess."

"What are you doing with dental floss hanging out of your face?"

Brett stared at his tennies. Bumped his heels against the chrome column supporting his stool.

"I think it's some kind of fad going down in the schools," said Bob. "Mint-flavored dental floss."

"Kids at your school suck on mint-flavored dental floss?"

"I don't know."

Bob and the fat man exchanged a look. Bob shrugged. Lulu refilled their cups.

Brett was still chewing when Bob's ex arrived with the boys, dressed alike in striped knit shirts with pocket insignia, nylon backpacks, and Levis so new they buckled like sheets of cardboard when they sat down. Their names were Noel and Drew and their father introduced them to Brett.

Bob's ex handed him a bottle of orange syrup with a prescription sticker on the front and a spoon taped to it. "Drew gets a teaspoonful before bedtime. And no MTV." Their mother said goodbye, pressing her lips to the tops of their heads. As she exited, Bob patted himself on the ass and blew her a kiss.

Lulu took their orders.

Gathered their menus.

While they sipped coffees and chocolate milks, Brett reached into his hip pocket and brought out his stash. He slid the white dispenser down the counter, past Aaron Dodge and Bob the Brush, to Noel, who copped for himself and his brother. He started to pass the dispenser back, but the fat man intercepted.

"Do a line with me?" he asked.

"Far out," said Bob.

Aaron Dodge unreeled enough for himself and his friend and returned the rest to Brett.

"Righteous product."

"Primo," Bob agreed.

Satisfied, the five of them sat silently.

Chewing.

Waiting for their eggs.

Certain friends the fat man never expected to run into at Camel-Op, or any place on the West Side. Max Yoder was one of them. East Phoenix residents considered Central Avenue a sort of social and intellectual Iron Curtain, separating them from junkies and stereo thieves. So, when he looked up from his breakfast and spotted a showroom-condition ivory Saab in the lot outside, Aaron Dodge didn't think immediately of his attorney. Not until he saw her, standing just inside the door, squarely in the way, and evidently unaware—as smart people often are—of the obstacle she represented. "Over here," the fat man called.

"I tried phoning you at home," she said as she approached. "Your machine was on, so I assumed you must be here. You're always here aren't you? You come here a lot."

"We're regular as baby butts in a diaper ad," Bob said.

Aaron Dodge introduced his two friends. Max slid onto the stool next to Brett's and ordered coffee. "I've made a couple of appointments for you, Aaron. I hope you don't mind."

"For when?"

She looked at her watch. "Today. Soon. Can you come?"

"Max is pimping me to some people," he told Bob. "Says I have to look presentable. Cut the hair. Shine the shoes."

Bob looked puzzled. Even a little angry.

"Did I hear you say 'haircut,' Aaron Dodge?" Lulu arrived with the coffeepot and dispensed refills.

"He's sucking up to some investors," said Bob. "As in 'Bend over, Mr. Dodge, and let us invest in you.' "

"I think it's a terrific idea," said Lulu. "Really. I can easily imagine you in a windblown look, Aaron Dodge." She set the pot down and framed the fat man's face with her hands. "Well, maybe not easily, but I can imagine it."

"And then Aaron's agreed to let me help him update his wardrobe. I'm excited."

"Okay if my friend comes along?"

Max looked down at Brett, who didn't react except to shift his dental floss from one side of his mouth to the other with a spasm of his lower lip.

"Sure. I don't see why not."

Bob the Brush made a point of conferring with his boys, and ignoring the fat man, as Aaron Dodge climbed off his stool. Which surprised him. He wouldn't've expected Bob, with a haircut like his, to begrudge anybody a trim and pair of dress shoes. True, he'd been behaving insanely. Keeping bizarre hours, borrowing money, begging favors. But weren't friends supposed to understand? To tell the truth, he believed they owed him. How many had he helped move? Or helped avoid a move by offering the top bunk of the Bunkport for a night, or several? How many toilet-tank floats had he replaced? How many times, with his tool box and an ad clipped from the classifieds, had he accompanied a friend to the vine-covered, dirt-floored garage of some bandit to inspect a used Renault or Vega? The crankcases full of motor honey, the twirled odometers, the differentials packed with axle grease. The rips and burns they'd've suffered if it hadn't been for him. The least they owed him was the benefit of the doubt. That's the way he figured it. Even if right now he did look a little arrogant. Even if he appeared, perhaps, to be scorning their company. Ducking their questions. Favoring some anonymous congregation of irrecoverable junk that would probably never make it past the door of his workshop.

The fat man pulled a handful of napkins from the holder, honked into one, and stuffed the rest in his pocket. "Ready," he said.

Outside, they climbed into Max's Saab. An argument began practically before they'd left the lot. "Max, you're headed in the wrong direction."

"Where are we going?" Brett asked.

Max glanced in the mirror. "Your Uncle Aaron is going to have his hair cut and styled."

"And I get to watch?!"

"I see a striped revolving pole outside or I don't budge," the fat man vowed. "Copies of *Field & Stream*. The smell of Vitalis. That's my one condition, Max."

"Aaron, please. You never know what kind of shearing you'll take at one of those places."

"Turn around, Max. I'm serious. Look at your watch. We could be in for a long wait if we don't get there early."

"Honestly," said Max. "I hate it when you're like this." She U-turned through the parking lot of a mini-mall on Bethany Home.

A quick visit to a Glendale True Value, and the fat man came out wearing a mesh feed cap, all his long hair bundled inside. He located a diner on the same block, where, safely disguised, he polled customers seated at the counter. The consensus: Dundee's, a shop not far from the courthouse and public library.

Max parallel-parked at the address endorsed by the experts. "This looks like it," the fat man said. By name and by proximity, Dundee's, the barbershop, maintained an affiliation with Dundee's, the newsstand/tobacconist—an adjoining storefront with poster-size La Lotería promotions displayed in its window.

Max unbuckled her seatbelt, but Aaron Dodge stopped her from reaching for the door handle. "Max. Now don't take this wrong. But I think it'd be best if us two, Brett and me, went in by ourselves."

"What on earth for, Aaron? No. Of course not."

"*De facto* segregation, Max. Sexist calendars. It's not 1986 in there." He nodded in the direction of the shop's "Closed Mondays" notice. "Trust me. You'll see a higher-quality result if you let us go in alone."

"Are you telling me that women are excluded here?"

"Cooperate with me on this one and the next stop's all yours. The clothes, I mean. Your call, Max."

A pause and a downcast glance testified to her inward deliberations. "You're a witness to this, Brett," she said.

Brett and the fat man entered Dundee's alone.

When they returned, less than an hour later, Max greeted Aaron Dodge with a smile bordering on a snicker. "It looks . . . okay," she said. "It'll do fine. Let me just . . ." She brought a comb from her purse.

"He looks funny doesn't he?" said Brett.

The fat man twisted the rearview mirror for a close inspection. Dundee had left him with no more than a fig leaf. Neatly parted. Subdued with oil. Trampled, dormant, shocked. A pathetic allotment that reminded Aaron Dodge of the yellowish grass underneath a sheet of plywood that's been lying in somebody's yard all summer. Rubbing his neck, Aaron Dodge felt the breath of the world in unfamiliar places.

"It'll be easier to take care of," Max promised.

Evidently sensing his mood, she stopped at a soft-serve ice-cream stand and bought cones for the three of them before heading east on Camelback. The fat man didn't protest when she turned up Fifth Avenue in Scottsdale. He quietly accepted the parking place she chose—down the street from an exclusive men's apparel shop. On the sidewalk in front of the store, Max attempted a few more refinements. Brushing, patting, straightening. He wore his usual janitorial ensemble. Twill pants and shirt. Work boots with bright-yellow stitching and all-terrain soles.

"Where'd your cap go?"

"I left it on Dundee's hatstand. For a landmark."

The clerk on duty inside welcomed them with a defrosted smile. "Keep that asswipe away from me," the fat man said, not bothering to whisper. "Don't let him start sliming me. Understand? That's my one condition."

The clerk blended into the haberdashery and London Fog, and Max assumed his duties. She led him first to a double tier of sportcoats. She stepped back, regarded him briefly, estimating, then reached for a navy-blue blazer at the far end of the row.

"I've already got a good corduroy sportcoat at home," the fat man protested. "You've seen it. It's gray."

"Green, Aaron."

"Is it really? Are you sure?"

"It's the color of a frog pond. And lapels this wide." She used both hands instead of a thumb and forefinger to illustrate. "I'm surprised you don't take off like an M-16 fighter jet."

"F-15," said Aaron Dodge. "M-16s are rifles."

"Whatever. This is your coat, Aaron. Put it on." He tried several before Max approved one she said could be altered to fit.

An hour later, a stranger to himself, the fat man stood multiplied before the shop's full-length, full-width triptych mirror. The blazer. Chinos and a pink oxford-weave shirt. Rag socks, sailboat moccasins, and a striped tie. Brett stared from behind. Max folded an arm across her stomach, propped the opposite elbow on it and tapped a fingernail against a front tooth, appraising.

Aaron Dodge.

His military haircut.

His uniform.

Max issued one more order before dismissing him. He'd be meeting with the Singers in less than a week, and she wanted him prepared. He should finalize his presentation. Authenticate every detail of the story he planned to tell.

What presentation?

What story?

As late as Monday afternoon he sat on the corner stool at Camel-Op, playing with a length of bonded nylon polyfilament. Thanks to Brett, the stuff had installed itself in his imagination. A bad sign. For an inventor, any impulsive fascination with a new material or a previously unnoticed physical principle usually led to the compulsive need to explore. To discover a useful application. Say you notice that when your windows are open your front door always slams viciously shut on windy days. Most people could accept the phenomenon. Live with a closed door. But an inventor would be up all night trying to reproduce the effect. Placing fluffs of pillow down on the doorsill to ascertain the force of the vacuum created when interior and exterior air pressures differed.

In this same way, dental floss had become a distraction and a nuisance. Its one-dimensionality. How it disregarded width altogether and aimed all its efforts stubbornly in a single direction. He'd been trying to think of ways, stretched, wound, or snarled at a particular location inside the jackpot machine, it might fit into his strategy. To help him visualize, he'd selected fifty yards of unwaxed from alongside the flavorless, gritty toothpastes and scent-free lotions in the holistic-health aisle at Camel-Op, where he'd come looking for cold remedies. He purchased a squat amber vial, with stalks of grain, rays of sun, honeycombs, and similarly potent manifestations of organic black magic congregated on its label, and now he sat sniffling at Lulu's counter, examining a segment of floss he'd unreeled and conducting informal experiments. He wrapped an end around the last three fingers of either hand and pulled steadily, the loops digging in as he applied more strength.

"Hi, Aaron Dodge."

Wendy Wendy climbed onto the stool beside him.

The string snapped.

"Guess what?" She set a camera on the countertop between them.

"Let's see. You ambushed a tourist. Strangled him with his camera strap. And now you've got all these great shots of the Wrigley Mansion and Grady Gammage."

"I'm taking a photography workshop. And I'm absolutely addicted. Already."

"Sounds fascinating. Bowls of fruit? Shadows cast on brick walls by tenement fire escapes? The broken boards of old barns?"

"Actually that's what I wanted to discuss with you, Aaron Dodge. I was hoping you'd consider modeling for me."

He picked the camera up and searched the store through its view-finder. "How much did this cost you?"

"It was Cody's."

The fat man set it down. "Really?"

She'd been going through some boxes Cody had left in the attic of the house Wendy Wendy shared with Buzz and Lulu. "I found it when I was moving," she said.

"You moved out?"

"Bart. He kept calling up and coming over. You know, threatening me again. If you see him, make sure and don't say where I'm living. Okay?"

"Cody," said the fat man. "Couldn't consolidate all her junk alive or dead, could she?"

"I think you have a really interesting shape, Aaron Dodge. Seriously. I wish you'd come over to my apartment with me or something. Because I have these poses I'd like to try out."

"Don't you think the desert would be more appropriate? You know. Juxtapose figural and landscape elements? My butt and El Capitán Pass."

"Aaron Dodge. I asked politely." She crossed her legs and nudged him with a foot. She was behaving like a person elected to coax the guest of honor to a surprise birthday party. The fat man was surprised. And flattered. Prior to Kennedy, he'd never strayed from his friendships for long in favor of anyone else. Evidently this was one of the ways your friends reclaimed you.

"Come on. You have a couple of hours. Don't be such a prude."

For an instant he considered accepting. The offer reminded him of his recent, sudden, and unexpected weight decline. Nothing he'd asked for. Nothing he'd earned. But how fortuitous! Wendy Wendy was a friend, though, not excess meat.

"Maybe next time," he was saying, when a small trim stranger, older, with a leathery suntan and thick gray walrus mustache, slid onto the stool beside Wendy Wendy's. He leaned forward and smiled past her at Aaron Dodge, extending his hand. "Rumor has it you're an inventor?" He nodded toward Lulu, the origin of all rumors.

"Oh, not really."

"Aaron Dodge. I've seen your column in the paper. Lots of times."

"That. Actually I may be discontinued before long. I let myself slip behind a little, I'm afraid."

"That so? You think they'll be looking for anybody to replace you?"

Unfortunately for the fat man, Arizona's sandy soil and shallow water table made basements impractical, and the climate favored carports rather than garages—which meant that all the amateurs who should've been tinkering away in obscurity were walking around Phoenix free to violate his privacy and ruin the prospect of supper.

" 'Aaron.' That's Jewish isn't it?"

"Usually," said the fat man.

"You ever invent anything I might've heard of? Or you just borrow other people's ideas?"

"Mainly borrow I guess."

"He doesn't either," said Wendy Wendy. "He's incredibly clever. You wouldn't believe the amount of close calls he's had. The disappointments."

"I've nailed the armpits, belly button, asshole, and all the dimples. It's just a matter of time now."

"It isn't easy to reconcile your talents with mainstream values," said Wendy. "He tries really hard. But it's the system. People like Aaron Dodge, with integrity, don't have a chance. It chews them up and spits them out."

"It hasn't spit me out yet," said the fat man.

"Listen. I think maybe you'll be interested in this. Just a little gadget I dreamed up." He leaned closer, crowding Wendy Wendy against the fat man's shoulder. "It's this—"

"Normally I would be. But—"

"But he promised me a photo session," Wendy Wendy said, and picked up Cody's camera.

"I'd love to stay and chat. But I did promise."

"It'd just take a second to explain. See, it's a—"

"Good luck with it," said the fat man. He and Wendy Wendy retreated. Escaped together to the parking lot, laughing.

"I really hate to be rude to people," he told her.

"Oh yeah? Then how come you're so good at it?"

She ignored her own car, a green Honda with a seatbelt buckle trailing from one door, and walked with Aaron Dodge toward his. He climbed into the El Camino and opened up for Wendy Wendy from his side because she couldn't from hers. "You don't have to," she said, testing the temperature of the garbage-bag upholstery with a hand before sitting. "It's up to you."

"Don't have to what? What's up to me?"

She smiled, and after slamming it three times finally got the door to stay shut.

She directed him to her new apartment, in a duplex cluster on East Osborn Road. By the time they arrived, she'd stopped pretending to be an art student. In fact, the fat man noticed that she'd left Cody's camera outside in the El Camino. She sat on the couch, an album jacket balanced on her knees, seeding a mound of dope. She filled a pipe, lit it, passed it to Aaron Dodge.

"I might be contagious."

"Your cold?" She shrugged. "When your energy locks are open, Aaron Dodge, when you're in the right place spiritually, you aren't vulnerable to disease." Nothing could make a sick person feel as guilty and soiled as the new, alternative approaches to healing.

Aaron Dodge handed back the pipe. "You plan to divert your womb energy in a nonliteral direction? Or should we use a rubber or something?"

Wendy Wendy stood up. Took his hand and tugged, demanding with her full weight. He followed. In the bedroom he pulled the curtains, though they weren't the lightproof kind, and undressed. He thought he recognized the sheets from nights he'd spent on Wendy Wendy's floor or futon, too obliterated to drive home.

"New cut's cute," she said. "I like it."

He lay on his back, relying on gravity to keep his leaky sinuses from destroying the romance of the situation. Wendy Wendy propped herself on an elbow. Brushed the knuckles of her other hand lightly across his chest. Dark toner from the machine she worked with accentuated her fingerprints. For earrings she wore shiny lids from a set of salt and pepper shakers, each perforated with its initial.

"You're warm." She pressed the backs of her fingers to his forehead. Then slid the hand behind his neck and bent to kiss him. He pulled her as close as he could. Brought as much of her against him as the limits of three-dimensionality would permit. Chemicals surged and changed direction inside the fat man.

According to experts on creativity, inspiration often occurs at unexpected moments. Relaxation, a change of pace, a fresh context can make all the difference. They did for Aaron Dodge. Just as Wendy Wendy announced her readiness with a subtle shift of position, and Aaron Dodge cooperated, a complex series of associations was completed instantly.

"Son of a bitch!" the fat man shouted, rudely disengaging himself.

"Did I hurt you?"

"What a fucking idiot I am!"

Wendy Wendy sat up and observed with a stunned expression as he rolled out of bed and started to gather his clothes.

"I'm really sorry. But . . ."

She sank back disgustedly onto her pillow.

"I like you. You're one of my best friends. I guess that's why . . ." With just his pants on, carrying his shirt and shoes, Aaron Dodge ran from the apartment. Dove into the El Camino. Not even rush-hour traffic, smelly and sullen, could stifle his joy.

He knew now how he'd outwit the machine.

"It's simple," he told the Singers the following Friday night, sitting across the coffee table from them in their living room. "Should've thought of it sooner. Why it took me so long, I can't imagine." He showed them the cardboard cylinder from the center of a roll of toilet paper and brought a Ping-Pong ball from the pocket of his blazer.

"Watch this," he said.

Max had agreed to let him come alone, but not without insisting

that he report to her house in Paradise Valley first, for final approval
and to exchange vehicles. She'd decided that her Saab would enhance
the illusion of respectability imparted by the Harvard Square outfit
she'd chosen for him.

"Try not to say 'you know' all the time, Aaron. Will you please? And
let me see your hands. God! Look at those." She had to trim past the
quick to eradicate the crescents of axle grease that defined the frontiers
of his manicure. Before sending him out the door, Max squared his
shoulders. Plucked imaginary imperfections from his lapels. Hugged
him.

He drove to the Northwest Phoenix neighborhood where the Singers
lived, which he was almost sure had been a date orchard the last time
he passed through the area, and parked Max's Saab in front of their
house. He sat in the driver's seat, nervous, sweating, indecisive. Finally, with a sigh and a grunt, he climbed out of his friend's car,
recalling times when, as a paperboy, he'd dreaded the houses of subscribers slow or unwilling to pay.

Their names were Connie and Dave. Their tv was on, but with the
volume at a whisper. He'd asked to visit on a Friday at this hour so
they'd be able to watch the lottery payoff telecast together. Connie
asked if he'd like something to drink. He remembered Max's coaching.
Coffee, not beer. Connie returned with three cups. Instant, but the fat
man drank it and smiled, while Connie and Dave, Mormons, sipped tea.

La Low-tay-REE-yah! Low-tay-REE-yah! Low-tay-REEEE-yah!

Three transparent chutes affixed to the side of the mixing reservoir
held thirty numbered balls in ranks of ten. Jackpot Jack opened a gate
at the base of the chutes, releasing the multicolored avalanche. Dexter's camera zoomed in. Balls tumbled and swirled, their commotion
produced by the blower underneath, hidden by the machine's gaudy
housing.

LAW-kay WEEEEE-naires! sang Jackpot Jack.

Then a closeup of Jack's hand. The plump brown fingers, bulging
with rings, operating a petcock. A noisy suction withdrew the first
selection from the swarm below, into a clear display chimney that
extended from the lid of the reservoir. Jack announced the result, his
pronunciation conspicuously unaccented for number combinations up
to thirty.

The audio transmitted a constant whirr and hum—the electric

blower. The balls, colliding, glancing off the Plexiglas walls surrounding them, made a clicking sound, like an excited dog tap-dancing across a kitchen floor.

Jack operated the petcock five more times. Five more balls, numbered on all sides for easy identification, rattled into the display chimney. Bilingually, Jack confirmed each draw.

REE-chase on-LEEEEEE-may-teed! Jack teased.

The payoff show concluded with a shot of all six choices, stacked inside the display chimney. Superimposed, the usual scroll of liability clauses accelerated past, as if propelled by the same updraft that had attracted tonight's six costars. Finally a last-second glimpse of Jackpot Jack, smiling, waving, throwing kisses with both hands.

A commercial followed. Dave switched off the set.

"Jesus!" Aaron Dodge, perhaps overstimulated, forgot the Singers didn't know his reputation, weren't yet his friends. "Did you see that?" he accused the blank screen. "Can you believe they allow him on television? The guy's as slimy as a bag of month-old lettuce."

Inappropriate, and he knew it immediately.

Radiating the shade of red, perspiring with the freedom that only a fat man could, he stared down at his regatta footwear and waited for the reaction to dissipate.

Connie recovered first. "Anybody hungry?"

"You bet," said Dave.

"Please. Don't go to any trouble," said the fat man. "On my account."

"Nonsense. No bother at all."

"If you're sure."

"I insist."

"Then thank you."

"Thank *you* so much, Mr. Dodge. For coming."

"You were nice to invite me."

Thank your mother and father for giving birth.

Thank your grandparents. Thank Columbus.

Thank dinosaurs. The Big Bang.

Everybody smiled.

Connie microwaved a dozen eggrolls and brought them out along with a tray of sweets.

"So you're the inventor?" Connie said. "And a columnist, too. Or so we hear."

"Max," said the fat man. "Max is great isn't she?"

"We like her a lot," said Dave.

Aaron Dodge spread out on the Singers' coffee table a schematic view he'd brought along, and withdrew a pen, the green one of Kim's, from his shirt pocket. "Odd isn't it? How our pockets—where we conceal our important possessions—are located at the heart and genitals?"

Grim smiles.

He'd overcompensated. The Singers didn't go for crude, and intellectual didn't impress them either. He hadn't sniffed assholes with a domesticated breed for some time. He'd forgotten about the bland diet. Before referring again to the sketch he'd unfolded, the fat man smiled. Accepted another cup. Sat back and finished it while he and the Singers swapped inoffensive tidbits across the coffee table.

Jobs?

Colleges?

Family?

Dave and Connie, though his age, seemed to have escaped the Vietnam era free of disenchantment. Dave drew a high number. Connie had been lucky too—one of the middle five in a family of seven children whose parents donated so lavishly to Mormon charities that the IRS computer red-flagged their return every April for a full audit. They'd waited to marry until both finished school. Four years at ASU for Dave, at Tucson for Connie. On the strength of their two incomes, they saved, invested, repaid their student loans, and bought a home. They had the second of their children just before Connie turned thirty. Thirty just to be safe. Thirty despite Connie's excellent health. Thirty to avoid all the actuarially significant complications of pregnancy and childbirth.

Right. Tell me about it.

Though evidently little else, he and the Singers had at least that one tragedy in common. If Aaron Dodge could demonstrate a shared concern. Maybe it was the way he talked, or the disgusting cough he'd developed in the last couple of days, but the Singers weren't responding. He couldn't blame them. He wouldn't've trusted anybody wearing these clothes, smiling this much, wheezing and hacking like a chorus of winos waking up in an abandoned boxcar. And now he saw that he'd been undermining his cause in a more sinister way as they talked. While he kept his coffee and tie separate, and censored his conversation, he'd been forgetting to suppress another indiscriminate urge. His eating.

Virtually solo, he'd emptied every plate Connie had been able to furnish between decisive events in her and Dave's past. Nachos, ice cream, pretzels. He'd eaten more than he should've. And he'd continued to eat. If the treats had been homemade, at least Connie might've interpreted his gluttony as a compliment. But to gorge on Sunshine Hydrox? Not even real Oreos. He felt the way anybody would who'd just finished stuffing himself on unnourishing amenities—sick and ashamed for having revealed himself in spite of all his precautions.

"Don't they say 'feed a cold'?" the fat man asked. He shrugged and wiped his mouth, and nose, with a napkin.

Connie smiled and fidgeted.

Dave watched with an uninterpretable expression.

He could see his interview about to conclude, the critical questions unasked. Even the silver leaf-shaped mint dish on the coffee table had been emptied. Also by him? No crazed longhair, brain-dead glue-sniffer, or lethargic Deadhead could've aroused more of the Singers' suspicions. They sensed fraud. Malpractice. A parody of their appearance and etiquette. An invader.

That was when he brushed the crumbs from his knees and produced the cardboard tube, which had been flattened to fit in his shirt pocket, and the Ping-Pong ball. Fuck rapport, he told himself. Time to salvage credibility. "Well . . ." he said. "Here we go. Let me just . . ." He restored the gray cylinder to its original shape. Passed the ball through it and back.

"I'm not sure how much you already know. Besides about the lottery ticket I mean. It and the other messages. And of course the police officer who's involved. Sorry all that was kept from you for so long. But I'm sure you see why it had to be that way."

Dave nodded.

"Then I guess I'm here to talk about the game. Convince you it can be fixed. Which, believe me, it can. I'll show you." He pointed the green pen at the simplified diagram facing the Singers. He circled the mouth of the chimney that pipelined the six weekly winners from the reservoir every Friday. "I won't try to make it sound more involved than it is. Basically, I plan to reduce the width. Here. This aperture."

He brought a stiff rubber O-ring from one of his pockets, fitted it inside the cardboard cylinder, and demonstrated. His unnumbered sample wouldn't fit through. "Then I introduce six undersized balls into the mix. It'll be physically impossible for any of the others to be selected. See?" Connie leaned toward the diagram, her arms folded across her stomach, and tilted her head for a better view. "I know the security guard. The Lottery Commission's caretaker. I can get at the machine."

Dave pinched the underside of his chin, studying the site of Aaron Dodge's alteration. "That's a neat idea. Uncomplicated. I like that. But . . ."

But. The fat man had hoped to avoid technical disagreements. You know. Nit-picky stuff like: How do you get the six oddballs out once you get them in? What keeps the same numbers from turning up next week and the week after? What happens when the lottery people count and discover the extras? What keeps them from finding the roadblock installed in their machine and voiding the drawing before they make the results official? And of course the question that had troubled Aaron Dodge from the outset: This sounds like something that might've been possible once, but isn't it too late now to act on information gathered so long ago?

Dave interrogated, then Connie, then Dave again. And the fat man, for an hour or more, struggled to answer, altering his drawing with explanatory circles. With long, curving arrows. With lines, broken and solid, and faintly blotted intersecting arcs revealing the former locations of his coffee cup. He told the Singers about the plans Pan had flown west from D.C., allowing them to sound a little more detailed than they actually were. He told them about Robin and his contribution, leaving Holly and hers out. And about Dexter's, emphasizing his recent rather than his current status in the Church. And he described his full-scale replica, promising that by the time he finished it he'd know as much about the machine as the people who invented it.

The Singers, though impressed, still weren't persuaded.

The fat man flung his pen down amid the coffee-table clutter and slumped backward in his chair.

"It's not your ability. Or your determination," said Connie. "We don't doubt those, Mr. Dodge. Not so much as the whole . . . I don't know. It's the whole lottery operation, I guess. I mean you can't just go up against the entire state government this way and expect . . ."

"It sounds impossible," said Dave. "To be honest."

"What if I told you it's already been done?"

"What do you mean?"

"Pennsylvania. Mid-'70s or thereabouts. The staff who ran the lottery telecast got together and injected the balls with mercury. All but the crucial six. You know, figuring those six, being lighter, would . . ." He pointed upward with a thumb. "And they did. It worked. The culprits couldn't keep their mouths shut, they ended up in jail, but the point is it could happen. It did happen."

Connie watched her husband's reaction.

"It's just a game. Don't let yourself be intimidated. Because that's exactly what they count on. The bully factor. Loud. Flashy. Listen, I'm an inventor. I see it all the time. The amount of junk out there, it's unbelievable. The lack of substance. Like these hot-air blowers in public bathrooms. So you can leave with warm wet hands instead of cold wet hands. If it says, 'Blade guaranteed for three years,' that means the handle will fall off in three months. You think you ordered a large, then you find out about jumbo, deluxe, and supreme. You won first prize all right, but there were over ten thousand first prizes awarded. What you wanted was the—"

The fat man sneezed. Explosively. The kind of sneeze that fills up your fist so that you have to reach behind you with your left hand and fish your handkerchief out of the opposite hip pocket.

"—the grand prize. Excuse me," he said, mopping up.

"Can I bring you something, Mr. Dodge? Hot tea with lemon and honey? A Tylenol?"

The fat man shook his head.

"Don't think we aren't frustrated, Mr. Dodge," said Dave. "We've been continually frustrated. That's why we hired Mr. Dixon. Why we've endorsed every kind of desperate search and investigation you could imagine. We've listened to the advice of clairvoyants, Mr. Dodge. We've done things we never dreamed we'd do. We just want to be sure. We don't want to get involved with anybody . . . in anything that's—"

"I know. Except listen." He sat forward, surrounding the problem with his big hands. "The very fact that you refuse to believe me ought to tell you one thing at least. Like that this guy, whoever's holding your daughter, he probably thinks the exact same way. He believes in the game too. He sees his numbers come up, one two three four five six, on the screen there, and Jackpot Jack invites him to come pick up his earnings, it won't be possible for him to back out by then. His decision was already made when he bought his ticket."

He saw encouraging signs. In their eyes. They wanted it too. They were hoping. Don't let him be another charlatan, another operator, cashing in on our little girl's misfortune. Witnessing their indecision, Aaron Dodge wished for the confidence he'd displayed in living rooms twenty years earlier. That same ability to change minds. Only pennies a day. The coupons alone will save you the subscription price. Less than you pay now per week for your morning coffee.

"Who sneezed?"

Their toddler, Mary Vanessa Singer's little brother, had appeared in the doorway. He went to his mom, towing behind him a colorful pull toy—one of the approved kind with nothing to stab and nothing to swallow, that teach them all about the world around them.

"Darcy. You're supposed to be in bed."

"Let us think it over, Mr. Dodge," said Dave.

"Yes, please," Connie agreed. "It's such an overwhelming prospect. So much to consider. Not just the release of the reward money, but the question of public reaction. I mean if this were to fail."

"We'd look pretty silly, Mr. Dodge," said Dave. "And without the public's confidence we'd never raise another dime."

"Truthfully, we'd made up our minds to say no before you ever arrived," Connie said. "And now . . ."

"We'd like to discuss it," said Dave.

The fat man brought a pack of gum from one of his coat pockets, already full of balled-up wrappers, and offered Darcy a stick. Darcy watched the fat man shyly, then looked up at his mom.

"It's the kind that rots their teeth. That okay?"

He sensed that it wasn't. But Connie nodded. She released the boy, who avoided the lengthy detour past the coffee table, crawling underneath to accept the fat man's gift.

16

▼▼▼▼▼▼▼▼▼▼▼▼▼▼▼▼▼▼▼▼▼
▼▼▼▼▼▼▼▼▼▼▼▼▼▼▼▼▼▼
▼▼▼▼▼▼▼▼▼▼▼▼▼▼

One morning you check the air pressure in your tires and find it's expanded by forty pounds per square inch overnight. Yours and the cars parked next to it are ticking like sauna rocks. You insulate the driver's seat with today's news and carefully climb in. You find a black fried egg with green yolks on the dash and realize it's your sunglasses.

Summer in Arizona.

One Saturday in June, after working all night at the mini–storage unit and breakfasting at Camel-Op, the fat man drove home to the blue apartment village. Sidewalks deserted. Steaming ponds of irrigation in the yards he passed. Drivers sealed inside their Toyota Crayolas and Pontiac Sunburns. He still hadn't heard from the Singers, but he was hoping for a message on his machine, maybe today.

What a dipshit. He'd forgotten to turn it on when he left the previous night. From the front door he beelined to the window unit and punched the button farthest to the blue end of the spectrum. Then to the kitchen. The refrigerator.

Aaron Dodge rearranged blocks of frozen hamburger. Moved aside antarctic hemispheres of homemade lentil soup preserved in Tupperware bowls. Each item, he noticed, had been labeled with a neat strip of dated masking tape. Further reminders of Kennedy. He found the package he was looking for, a plastic Kopy Korner bag with a thick stack of papers inside. The fat man kept most of his important paperwork here. In the freezer. The one reliably fireproof receptacle the average person could afford. He scraped off a layer of frost. Undid the twist tie. Enclosed he found a copy of the application Pan had flown from D.C. Also many pages of handwritten notes he'd compiled since. He sat down at the kitchen table and dug in.

Earlier that month, after Wendy Wendy provided the inspiration, he'd consulted a friend. A consistent provider of infallible advice. The Handyman. The Handyman hosted *Rocky Mountain Know-How Radio*—a call-in program carried by a local all-nite, all-talk AM station. Aaron's Enterprises had been a consistent contributor since its first broadcast in the Valley, so the Handyman was willing to listen to ideas like the one Aaron Dodge, via a staticky 1-800 connection, transmitted to the region on the night he now sat reviewing in his kitchen.

The fat man remembered hastily inventing a little girl, a niece, who'd suffered eye injuries in a game of lawn darts. He told on the air how he wanted to surprise her with a special gift. Maybe market the idea later if it worked out and use the proceeds to start a get-well fund.

"Table tennis for the visually impaired?" The Handyman had greeted the suggestion with less than his usual enthusiasm.

"Don't you think it's a good idea?" The fat man. Affecting an injured tone.

"Well, sure, Aaron. I mean I guess so. You're talking about, like, large-print books? Something along those lines?"

"Only in this case with oversized balls. Larger paddles. Extra-wide boundary stripes."

"Okay. If you say so. I guess maybe I do recall an item or two of information might be of use to you. Common knowledge for the most part, but . . . You got a pencil ready?"

Aaron Dodge had taped the entire exchange, then transferred the essentials to paper. If he could just find the piece he'd written on. He thought he remembered using the back of a form letter sent by the adjustment company he'd been receiving scratch paper from for the past year. The information provided by the Handyman had included the official USTTA-approved dimensions for table-tennis balls. Size and weight. Also the name of an Ohio manufacturer of athletic equipment. Though he'd told the Handyman larger than standard, he supposed a supplier who could furnish oversized could furnish any size.

Repelled at the switchboard, butterfingered and hot-potatoed at every level of management, voided repeatedly by the company's sophisticated telecom system, his calls to the Midwest eventually aroused the suspicion of an authorized representative of the sales division, who responded lackadaisically to the fat man's inquiries, his enunciation only mildly impaired by the gum he chewed.

"Can you run that by me one more time?" he said after Aaron Dodge finished explaining the reason for his call. "We don't get many inquiries from private individuals such as yourself. Let's make sure I heard you right. Hello?"

The fat man pictured an ex–Ohio State football reserve. Four years on the sidelines. An equally disenchanting tryout with the Falcons or Lions. A return to Ohio and his current position. A guard who'd entered late in the fourth quarter of games already decided, now beer-bellied and bewildered for life.

"Oh, I don't know. I guess we could run you through a special order. Cost you, though."

"How much?"

"What you want with a bunch of runt Ping-Pong balls anyways?"

"I'm an inventor."

The fat man heard paper rustling in Ohio. A tabulator subtotaling. Click, click, click.

Ka-chig.

Click, click, click.

Ka-chig.

Click, click, click.

Ka-chig.

Ka-chig.

Ka-chig.

He'd already touched every friend he had left at Camel-Op. And bumped from so many flights at Sky Harbor that his travel agent had alerted him. He should avoid the courtesy counters of most of the major carriers, where his face, or more likely his width, was becoming well known. Aaron Dodge. A name on a clipboard list like the one the supermarket checker pulls from beside the register and runs her finger down when you produce your two forms of ID.

If Connie and Dave decided to release their Help Find Mary Vanessa

Singer savings, the fat man would be able to deduct the hefty deposit required, call Ohio, and place the order. Most of the Singers' funds needed to be preserved for ticket purchases later, but a loan of a few hundred wouldn't be missed. He'd pay Bob the Brush and Jowls for the work they'd done, and pick up the contributions to the replica they'd agreed to provide, which he'd been too embarrassed and impoverished to claim. Right now the future of his plan depended almost entirely on the replica. Arranging a switch. Either his machine for theirs, or, much more likely, one doctored replacement part from his for the original from theirs. To make an exchange possible, he'd considered posing as a repairman. *The* repairman. The Lottery Commission, according to Holly, maintained a bonded local representative—a service which, so far, they'd never called upon. Robin would have to arrange a breakdown during the weekly rehearsal. Slice a wire maybe. Or damage the spring-steel catch obstructing the top end of the central chimney that fed balls up from the mixing reservoir. Aaron Dodge smiled, picturing the eruption. Painted balls pinging off ceiling girders, ponging across the studio's cement floor, lost, stepped on, crushed. Then Robin would have to place a phony call, clearing the way for the fat man's impersonation.

But Aaron Dodge knew better. Before Robin would sabotage the machine, before he'd initiate a diversion, before he'd agree to anything half as revolutionary, Holly would have to . . . And the fat man pictured a series of pornographic acts, equally degrading to both sexes but a lot more fun for one of them. Robin, with luck, would stand by and watch. He shouldn't expect more.

Which left Aaron Dodge badly in need of a fresh idea. Something foolproof would've been nice. Something simple, efficient, and slick. Or if not then at least reliable. Shit, even possible would've satisfied him tonight. He sat at his kitchen table, a chill on the pages and scraps of pages he shuffled through in search of an option.

In the past, recognizing shortcomings in his work, he'd've simply given up. Quit. Abandoned his mistakes and started over. But some projects didn't offer that alternative. He stood, stalked to the refrigerator, stared inside. He closed the door, returned to the table, sat.

He decided to collate his material. Three piles. Usable, marginal, irrelevant. He finished with a stack as thick as the one he'd started with, alongside it a disenchanted memo or two, of questionable value and arbitrarily selected near the end of the elimination process in order to avoid a unanimous victory for irrelevance. He'd decided to take the survivors with him and run a bath when he noticed, protruding from the discards, conspicuous because of the legal-size paper on which it was Xeroxed, the bottom four inches of his copy of the court agreement he'd signed over a year ago.

COMES NOW Lewis K. Dodge . . .

At ten that night he and Tulane Wiggins sat across a table from each other at Ernesto's.

"I've got to ask you a favor, Tulane."

Tulane wore Ponys. And the uniform of the team he played for. A t-shirt with black, elbow-length sleeves. Pinstriped pants with grass-stained shins. "What you need, man? Like I tole you before, I be pleased to help you out some way."

"That's kind of what I wanted to talk to you about. Before. When you said you'd like to back one of my inventions someday. Was that a serious proposal?"

"Money? Man, I let you have it. No co'ditions."

"I'd just as soon call it an investment. Like a loan."

"Don't matter. Ever' which way you like to say it. You want to tell me 'bout this ideal a yours?"

The fat man stared. At the tabletop. The door. The Nut Hut behind the bar.

"No, man. 'Course you don't. How much you need?"

"I . . . well . . . let's see . . ."

"Never mind, man. Here." Tulane unbuttoned the pocket flap of his team pants and brought out his checkbook. "You got a ink pen, man?"

Aaron Dodge offered Kim's. Tulane started to fill in his signature but lifted the pen immediately and inspected its tip. He slid the cocktail napkin from under his beer bottle and scribbled in circles. Nothing. Then inconclusive wisps. Finally results. He signed and dated the check. Handed Aaron Dodge the checkbook and pen. "Go," he said. "How much ever you need."

"I'd rather you—"

"Uh-uh," said Tulane. "You."

"If it's too much you'll tell me?"

"Man, relax you brown penny and write."

The fat man estimated.

Picked a number.

When he tried to reveal the amount, Tulane looked quickly away. "Juss cash it. I truss you."

"Then at least let me enter the check in your . . ." He flipped to the front of the checkbook. Tulane snatched it away.

"It's just that I hate to run you short."

"Hey, if I don't owe him, I don't know him. This much more ain't gone hurt."

"Thanks, Tulane. Really."

Tulane didn't mention his haircut. The weight he'd lost. His raucous coughing fits or his girlfriend. Aaron Dodge knew he didn't look like a man a few hundred away from a big score. He appreciated the dollars without the insinuations.

They sat together a while, silently. Watching and drinking. Legs outstretched and crossed at the ankles. Arms still except when they unfolded them to reach for their bottles. Letting time go by unexamined, the way men do. If there wasn't potential profit or potential sex in it, why talk?

When the fat man emptied his beer Tulane did the same. Their eyes met briefly and they stood.

"Thanks again for this." He patted his shirt.

"Get some," Tulane told him.

He salvaged and overhauled the fan from a junked evaporative cooler. Ultimately it would furnish the circulation in his simulated jackpot machine, but for now he connected it to his power source and used it to churn the cremated air inside the mini–storage unit, where he chose to continue working in spite of the discomfort. The dirt. The inconvenience. The expense. Conditions that seemed inevitable anyway wherever a bachelor headquartered, so why try to outrun them. At home he'd've been vulnerable. To interruptions. To detection. No telling who might barge in. Kennedy hadn't returned her key yet, and though he could've changed the lock and assured his permanent privacy, he kept postponing the decision.

Kennedy at the front door.

Twisting the key in the lock.

Turning and walking away forever.

He didn't want to talk about it.

The two of them still communicated. Mostly by phone. Mostly fights. The fat man would sit at his kitchen table, doodling on the torn flaps of envelopes. Boxes, borders, mazes, loops. The configurations of their arguments. Unless you counted rushed and chaotic greetings exchanged when he called at Laura's for the kids, they'd seen each other in person only once since her move. One romantic summer evening. A fiasco for them both. The fat man had offered to cook—stir-fry. Even though he hated chopsticks. And the tiny pieces you had to dice everything into. All through dinner Kennedy kept reminding him. He'd never talked to her about his work. Did he think she was too stupid to get it? So much dumber than those friends of his? But not until afterward, when they were cleaning up, did Aaron Dodge finally lose his temper. Following more of her accusations—you always, you never—he turned to her, holding the wok by its two wooden handles between them like a shield. He thrust his chin at her, gritted his teeth, and with one sudden crushing movement brought his fists together, folding the wok in half like a giant tarnished taco.

Which partly explained why he'd felt more comfortable imposing on Tulane for cash than Laura, even though both owed him, both would've staked him, and neither had it to spare. He disbursed their cuts to Bob the Brush and Jowls, then spent the balance on supplies, which he stored at Pack Rat.

During the nights that followed, he worked sundown to dawn—with summer here, the only hours he could endure inside the module. First he constructed an airtight cube from six panes of Plexiglas. Though his budget now allowed it, he couldn't afford the time to accurately reproduce the trio of see-through stacks that should've branched from its side, so for now he sawed up a set of headers he'd rescued from the scrap heap in back of a muffler shop, bent and welded together three tall sections, and sealed the arrangement in place. He bought ten three-packs of Sportco Satellites at an Oshman's, fed them into the lengths of tailpipe, and liberated them with a flue he'd inserted across the tri-channel.

He watched the thirty Ping-Pong balls pile into the reservoir and veer unanimously to one corner.

He trued the box with his carpenter's level until a celluloid layer a sphere deep distributed itself across the transparent floor. Then he cut a narrow window from the cube's underside, installed a metal vent, and below it transplanted the rebuilt swamp-cooler fan. He switched on the blower. The contents of the etherium began to percolate, lifted, batted, and juggled by an inrushing fountain of air.

The next day he phoned Ohio to place his order. That's when he discovered the odd-lot charge. The setup charge.

The handling and shipping.

The minimum order of a hundred dozen.

The fat man said no thanks and hung up. That night at the mini–storage unit he retrieved and examined one of the standard white Sportco Satellites, rotating it slowly, observing the seam at its equator. He soaked a dozen in solvent overnight to melt the bonding agent. Next day, using the band saw at Bob the Brush's trailer, he cut a longitudinal cross-section from each of the separated halves, then joined the resulting quadrispheres. When the adhesive dried he switched on the grinder and shaved the rim of each ellipse. He glued pairs together. Sanded joints. The process split, cracked, or shattered several. Occasionally altered halves refused to mate satisfactorily. But the fat man managed to produce an ensemble of six. Disappointing specimens if you inspected them closely. More ovate than spheroid. But smaller in diameter by a critical quarter-inch than the sextet they'd be asked to understudy.

He kept them at home, afraid of what distortions the daytime temperatures reached inside the storage unit might produce. They fit nicely in the refrigerator-door panel, there among the eggs, a few of which had been X-ed on top to indicate hard-boiled. Kennedy again. He was about to leave for breakfast—for some reason Camel-Op eggs tasted better—when he remembered another responsibility he'd been neglecting.

Near the beginning of May he'd received a letter. Lewis K. Dodge. His name typed directly onto the gray envelope, not computer-affixed to a bulk-mailing sticker. The implication, that knowledge of his existence had filtered through the machinery to actual human beings, encouraged the fat man to leave it sealed. As did the return address, which belonged to a major airline. So he'd filed the letter alongside the month's unopened electric, gas, and telephone statements, between the coffee and sugar canisters on the kitchen countertop.

Tulane's capital supplied Aaron Dodge with the courage for a peek at the batch of bills. He tore into the gray envelope, prepared, he thought, for news of any sort. Even so, its contents ambushed him. Though he could remember leaving the Valley just once during the previous five years, he'd evidently booked enough fraudulent air mileage to qualify for a frequent-flier premium.

Perverse. Uncalled for. He didn't want a voucher like this around. It offered exactly the opportunity he'd been plotting for a year to deny himself. Debts, allegiances, conspiracies. He'd done everything he could think of to maneuver himself into a quandary, and now this. A free ride to any destination in the continental U.S. Nobody was stopping him from tearing it up, of course. But he stashed it in the freezer with his other unredeemed opportunities. That summer the fat man wasted a lot of electricity standing at the icebox with the freezer open, enshrouded from the shoulders up in a cloud of condensation. Staring at the complimentary offer. Reconsidering. Dreaming.

"What I'd really like to do," Wendy Wendy was saying, "is live in South America. Join the Haitian Contra-fighters. You know, strike a blow against tyranny."

"Combat tyranny right here," Lulu said, and pointed emphatically to the linoleum on which she stood.

Wendy Wendy shrugged. "I guess I meant a well-defined tyranny. Guys with uniforms and submachine guns standing on street corners. I don't know. Apartheid maybe."

"Did anybody see *Doonesbury* today?" asked the fat man, offering the funnies to whoever was interested.

"Tyranny is whatever keeps you from doing what you want to," said Lulu. "Period."

"Tyranny is restaurants with no-smoking signs," said Bob the Brush.

The fat man had stopped for breakfast hoping Wendy Wendy would be here. Instead of the corner stool, he'd taken a stool next to hers. Practically an act of contrition by Aaron Dodge's standards.

"Does Kennedy have multiple orgasms?" Lulu asked. Obviously she'd had her turn with the "Lifestyle" section.

"Like a pinball machine."

"Or I guess I should say *did* she?"

"I wish you wouldn't," the fat man suggested.

"That's such a predictable response," said Lulu. "From a type-B personality."

"Incredibly left-hemisphere," Wendy Wendy agreed.

Your friends. Your friends meant well. They'd offer to introduce you to somebody. Or, if you met her on your own: Great. Must be a fantastic girl. But stop smiling just once during the next six months and it's: Aaron Dodge, this is probably none of my business, and I'm certainly not trying to tell you what to do, but . . . It's: You used to be so happy and carefree all the time, Aaron Dodge. What happened? It's: We don't see enough of you around here any more, Aaron Dodge. How come? Your friends knew you before they knew her. They were going to be there to comfort you, even if they had to trash your car or poison your dog to have something to comfort you for.

"If you don't mind my saying so," Lulu said, "I always did think you two were an odd match."

Aaron Dodge didn't want to talk about it. The last thing he needed right now was somebody assuring him he'd done the right thing. What was best for them both. Between his work at Pack Rat and a day with the kids, he'd slept maybe two hours in the last seventy-two. He was in no mood for gossip. Especially gossip that included him.

"Aaron?" said Wendy Wendy. Dipping and redipping a tea bag. "Aaron, have you heard of the Holmes and Rahe Social Readjustment Rating Scale?"

He didn't encourage her. He stared ahead, past the rim of his coffee cup, and sipped neutrally. This was the first time he'd talked to Wendy Wendy since the day he'd vanished from her bedroom.

"It's a really helpful tool, I think. It like rates all the stressful events that can happen in a person's life, you know? And assigns points."

He took another defensive sip.

Reminded himself that he'd come here to apologize.

"Fuck stress," he said.

"This is science, Aaron. There's nothing the least bit ditzy about it. According to Holmes and Rahe, you're seriously at risk."

"Better drop it, Wendy," Bob the Brush advised. He must've seen or sensed something. In the fat man's posture. His eyes. "He looks just this side of an episode today."

"And I started 'way the other side," the fat man warned.

"Three hundred points in a year's time and you're practically guaranteed a catastrophic illness. Here, I'll show you." She climbed off her stool. On a shelf in one of the grocery aisles, among Camel-Op's copies of *Diet for a Small Planet* and *Our Bodies, Ourselves,* she located a book which she brought back to the counter and opened to an appendix. "Will you quit being such a hard-ass, Aaron, and look at this with me?"

"Listen, I'm sick, I'm mad. Leave me alone, okay?"

"Pay attention, Aaron. This is serious. Here. Let's go down the list and I'll show you. 'Fired from work'—forty-seven points. 'Change in family member's health'—such as Laura's broken leg. Guess how much? Forty-four, Aaron Dodge. 'Sex difficulties—' "

"Wait a second. Who said I was having sex difficulties?"

Wendy Wendy answered with a scornful smile. "Okay, never mind. Skip that one for now. But how about 'Addition to family'? A big thirty-nine points. Multiplied by six in your case. And so on down the list. 'Change in financial status.' 'Change in work responsibilities.' 'Revision of personal habits.' 'Change in eating habits.' "

"Hold it. Not all those are necessarily negative."

"Doesn't matter. A change is a change. Any kind of readjustment produces stress. It says."

"Yeah," said Bob. "Look what happened to that one Pope."

"Fuck stress," said the fat man.

"And now this separation," said Wendy Wendy. "A romantic readjustment. See what that does to your total, Aaron? Just look."

"I don't want to look."

"Don't try to ignore this, Aaron. How many? Here. Read it."

Bob the Brush lifted himself partway off his stool for a peek. "Jesus," he said. "You better go home and hibernate till about October, cowboy."

"Did you hear that, Aaron? Aaron, listen to me. I'm telling you—"

The fat man stopped her mid-sentence with a merciless stare that concentrated all the attention he'd been trying to withhold for the last half-hour and said, slowly, quietly, "Wendy, I don't need to listen to you. I've heard everything you've ever thought or said so many times it passes straight through my brain like Muzak."

"Aaron Dodge!" Lulu charged down the counter toward him.

"You can shut the fuck up too," he said to her, pointing a thick finger, climbing off his stool. He slapped coins onto the countertop and turned to go, leaving Wendy Wendy crying into a napkin Lulu had provided.

Later, calmer, he recognized the senseless abuse of a friendship. He wanted to go back and explain. But he also knew that a brief exile from Camel-Op would be prudent. His friends weren't inconsiderate. Or blind. Too little sleep, too much caffeine, a case of the sweaty toilet seat flu. A few days to think about it and they'd understand he hadn't been a hundred percent lately. They wouldn't begrudge him one tantrum, surely. Meantime he had the mini–storage unit, and plenty to keep him busy there.

At that point, mid-June, he still believed he'd be able to talk others into increasing their participation. Maybe divvy up the responsibility some. One memorably disenchanting night, he sat with Holly and Robin and three cups of mechanically vended instant in a staff canteen at Saint Luke's Hospital—a melancholy subterranean cube decorated in ironically festive aquas and oranges, as private and anonymous a meeting place as Robin could've located without CIA affiliations. As they talked, the two men diverted most of their attention toward a disposable gray pepper and matching white salt shaker in the center of the table. Holly listened anxiously, leaning forward, elbows on the tabletop, jiggling the chain of a necklace she wore, its charm clamped firmly between her teeth, except when she held it aside to speak.

Rob?

Listen to him, Rob.

Do you have to be so scrupulous all the time?

Robin slouched obstinately, his arms folded across his chest, and shook his head every time the fat man attempted to raise an issue. No way. Forget it. Fuck that noise. Never happen. Belligerently ruling out any active collusion. Maybe he'd been reading his newspaper. The Walker spy trial, Jerry Whitworth, the Pollards, Daniloff, and Zakharov. Espionage didn't look like a high-percentage roll that summer. The best Aaron Dodge could obtain was a reaffirmation from Robin of the position he'd already stated. As long as nobody else at KPHX noticed the fat man's subterfuge, then maybe he wouldn't either.

In the back of his mind—a short reach lately—he'd known all along this could happen. Machine set to assemble. Help available. No excuses left. He was supposed to be the inventor. The one with the imagination. The ideas. The magic. But his genie, the one the freezer exhaled every time he opened its white-enameled door to look inside, hadn't brought the fat man many of his wishes so far this summer. No temperate days. No Kennedy. No easy shots at the jackpot machine.

Aaron Dodge.

Enraged and humiliated.

His the one contribution lacking.

He didn't want to think about it. But think about it was all he could do that summer. Over coffee. Sleeplessly. Constantly. His eyelids twitched, his hands trembled, his skin prickled with night sweat, and his lips turned chalky dry. A kidney ached. His brain felt packed in Styrofoam, his stomach like a keg of warm beer rappelling down a cliff. At four-thirty one morning that June, punished by caffeine and insomnia, he dialed a toll-free number: 1-800-IGIVEUP.

Busy.

Robin's unfriendly response convinced the fat man. Reluctantly he abandoned the idea of a swap. The machine stored at Pack Rat for the one in KPHX's vault had never seemed entirely realistic. Adventurous, but, without Robin's cooperation, unlikely. He considered new possibilities. His replica as a demonstrator. A display model. Not a lifelike prosthetic advance or history-making transplant, but a cadaver on which useful experiments, directed at skeptics like Robin, might someday be performed. He could complete that kind of toy easily and quickly. But now he had to confront this other rebuilding project. The mental one.

Aaron Dodge knew how far a rubber band would stretch. What a silver strip of duct tape or cloudy trail of Elmer's Glue-All would hold together and what it wouldn't. Nobody had more experience with inadequate materials under desperate circumstances than Aaron's Enterprises. But this invention. This idea. Nothing he scrounged, scavenged, or borrowed proved adaptable. All the usual shortcuts seemed to be sealed off, all the corners he'd've normally cut obstructed by reputations, livelihoods, friendships, careers. Too many other people involved this time. A life was at stake here.

The Singers didn't call and they didn't call. It got to be one of those situations. You're afraid to initiate contact because you sort of have a feeling but then again you'd just as soon keep it vague for as long as you can. He'd endured the same suspense over a million inventions. You know. Ah, Mr. Dodge. Of course. Yes, I did receive your messages and I've been meaning to get back to you. . . . The Singers and everybody else seemed to be waiting for him to act. Lead. Two virtues that had never come naturally to him, unless you considered spearheading a solo retreat authoritative leadership. Aaron Dodge. The only recruit ever promoted directly from deserter to commander.

A cynic, devout and unequivocal, the fat man had ducked responsibility so successfully for so many years that he didn't recognize it at first when he got back a taste of what he'd been dishing out all this time. Insubordination. Somebody questioned *his* authority. One of his troops mutinied. He didn't care to recall it afterward, but the confrontation took place in an unlit, unruly skinhead bar on South 16th. The Crack. Plastic beer pitchers. No air conditioning. Brick walls the color of raw meat.

Dexter was late, so he sat at the bar, soaking up perspiration with bev naps, and talked with a neighbor. Fingerless black gloves. Head shaved in concentric bands. Androgynous but definitely young. She called herself Astrid. Her conversation and demeanor suggested isolation, confusion, alienation. All the torments that Aaron Dodge thought he and his friends had endured two decades earlier in behalf of every subsequent generation. But I don't care, Astrid kept saying. I don't care, you know? I don't care. When Dexter arrived, he squeezed a bar stool between them and addressed the fat man with an insolent sneer, chewing his gum and grinning. "Got your ears lowered, I see," he said to Aaron Dodge, outlining one of his own sideburns with a thumb.

"I see somebody dropped yours off a cliff," the fat man answered. "With you attached."

Dexter's appearance had changed. Dexter hadn't. Enough fuck-you to win him a friend or two in a place like the Crack, enough restraint to keep him his job at KPHX. He wore all-black, an oily spiketop, and one ostentatious accessory. An earring made from an actual fish lure— a number-two spinner, the treble hook dangling from its stern baited with a fresh anchovy.

Dexter fidgeted.

Drummed the bar.

Twirled his keys.

Aaron Dodge recognized the indications. Coke probably. Or speed. Whichever, it probably had something to do with how badly Dexter wanted those numbers. Now, he kept saying. Either the picks or a cash advance to make for a more pleasant wait. Aaron Dodge could've issued him six at random and been on his way. Maybe should've. But it didn't suit his present mood. Besides, in a case like this, inaccurate information could be as damaging as any other kind. If Dexter intended to barter with it, its origins wouldn't remain secret for long.

Dexter threatened. Harassed. Demanded. Drank. The fat man matched him pitcher for pitcher, insult for insult, till finally, out of patience, sick, exhausted, his judgment pinned down in a chemical crossfire between caffeine and alcohol, Aaron Dodge lost control.

He snatched a beer-soaked towel off the bar and whipped it hard against Dexter's jaw, snagging his silver earring. A couple of stout tugs set the hook. He hauled Dexter's ear close to his face and told him in a fierce whisper: "Listen you ugly shit. I'll burn your fucking house to the ground if you screw this up. Understand?" Dexter looked like he might reply. The fat man discouraged him. The agonized cry that resulted drew the attention of onlookers, Astrid among them.

"I've got your video. And you've left some particularly indiscreet messages on my machine. You're conspicuous, Dexter." Dexter watched the fat man fearfully from the corners of his eyes. Aaron Dodge allowed him enough slack to nod his head. The exact terms of the agreement weren't immediately clear, but Dexter's compliance was. The fat man steered Dexter's head toward Astrid and passed her the unbloodied end of the towel. Ignoring protests and accusations, he climbed off his stool and bellied his way toward an exit.

Later, he cooled off in the dark, in his kitchen, in front of the open freezer door, the flight coupon in his hand.

San Francisco, Tampa, Atlanta, Baltimore.

He'd never considered himself a persistent person. But he persevered. He drove to places he knew he wouldn't be interrupted. Withstood the indifferent service, the grease, the onions. The insubstantial toothpicks that splintered prematurely against his tongue. Looking into those cups of coffee was like staring down the throat of a pulsar. A well so black and deep it took his reflection and wouldn't give it back. The first swallow, tarry, acidic, cauldronous, embedded itself like a tomahawk at the base of his skull. Frazzled his nerves, fouled his breath and spirit. The last gulp, bitter as ink, potent as etching fluid, brought with it black flecks of its own residues scoured from the bottom of the pot. But he drank up. Waded through refills till he felt his scalp crawl, bugs on the backs of his eyeballs.

Finally, one impenetrably hot night in July, over the racket the swamp-cooler fan created, he thought he heard a hornblast from outside the mini–storage unit. Shave-and-a-haircut. The universally accepted signal of friendly intentions. He hoisted the door and stood with his arms raised, letting the night air cool the sweat basting his stomach.

Officer Magdalena climbed from his tan compact.

Just passing by. Right. Sure. On a stretch of road familiar to no one but long-haul truckers and black Lincolns with former members of the Bonanno mob jackknifed in the trunk.

"I thought you quit," Magdalena said.

The fat man shrugged. "To a serious inventor, quitting's only the beginning."

He invited the little man inside and shut the door.

"I can't believe you still come here." Magdalena puffed up his cheeks and exhaled forcefully, tugging his shirt collar with a finger to dramatize the message.

"You get used to it. Besides, refrigeration's for leftovers, man. The good stuff comes straight from the oven."

When he updated Magdalena on the progress he and Max had made without him, Magdalena didn't seem surprised. "I had a feeling," he said. The fat man accepted the compliment, though the possibility of surveillance also occurred to him.

He and Dixon had already talked, Magdalena said. They'd been reconsidering. They missed the partnership. He looked around at the scattered elements of Aaron Dodge's redesign. Believe it or not, they hadn't turned up anything as promising since. As intriguing or exciting. As gratifying, he guessed you might say. "Looking for accomplices?" Magdalena asked.

Aaron Dodge knew he must seem like a man in need of some. Eyes inflamed. Several sizes of slack in his wardrobe. Voice constricted by laryngitis.

"I could use help. Volunteering?"

"Guess so. If the Singers are."

And of course the Singers were. Magdalena's brief but conveniently timed visit should've alerted the fat man. Instead he worked unsuspecting through the night, a newspaper waiting on his doorstep, a message from Max blinking on his machine. He heard the story on the radio as he drove home.

Sometime the previous day, large, irregularly shaped rust-colored stains had been discovered on the concrete walls and floor of a low-maintenance racquetball facility in East Mountain Park. Clothing and remains had been recovered later in the vicinity of the ball court. The gruesome incident immediately provoked rumors and speculation, reinstating Mary Vanessa Singer's name in the news. Evidently hearsay had influenced the Singers. They'd notified Max. Obviously Phil Dixon too. And Aaron Dodge was last in line for the information.

That same morning he returned to Camel-Op and immediately apologized, reaching over Wendy Wendy's shoulder—and Bob the Brush's and Buzz's and Deli Elope's—to collect the green tickets from Lulu's receipt pad, which lay face down near their coffee cups.

"On me," he announced, and climbed aboard the corner stool.

His friends. They'd balance one instance of cruelty against decades of harmless insolence, rare but occasionally heroic acts of kindness and intimacy, and they'd dismiss it.

"Hide the steak knives," said Lulu. "The Tonton Macoute is back."

He conserved the effort an argument would've required. Turned his cup right side up in its saucer. Waited for Lulu to pour.

"I used to think of you as a deep person, Aaron Dodge," Lulu said. "But you know what I've decided?"

"It's a mistake to confuse size and substance," Wendy Wendy proclaimed.

The fat man waited for Bob, Buzz, or Deli Elope to say something. Defend him. They sipped expressionlessly. The cup in front of him remained unfilled as Lulu peeled a white corrugated filter off the stack near the coffee machine. Reached underneath the counter for a pump bottle of glass cleaner. Walked to the front door and began to wipe fingerprints.

No conversation. Not even a greeting. Bob the Brush stood, pinned singles under his cup, and departed without a comment.

He'd taken a few rounds close to the heart recently, but he wasn't ready for this. He climbed off his stool. "Well fuck you then," he said. On his way to the door he paused. Elaborated.

"I mean goddam. I'm in this place every day since—when?—ten years at least, I bet. Wait. Correction. I helped *build* this place. And now? I commit one minor social blunder, I violate protocol just once, and all of a sudden I'm a traitor. Is that it? Well listen to this. I don't need assholes like you. You talk about amnesty. You talk about peace. Tolerance. But you see a literal, actual person sitting beside you, and this guy could use a break—forget it. Let the fucker bleed. Well you know what I think? I think you're all nothing but a bunch of bigots. Except worse. Because you don't hate black people, Jews, foreigners. You're against anybody that's *like* you. You hate your*selves*. And that is sad. Truly fucking sad. Didn't you ever hear of a personality? Didn't you ever hear of opinions? Sure you read the newspaper. You're well informed, naturally. But why bother, because you all think exactly the same anyway. You're afraid if you don't you might not sound fashionable. Can't you do anything without thinking about it for a year first? And then spending the next year feeling guilty about it? All you do is sit here and plagiarize other people's suffering. Study American Sign Language. Buy Nicaraguan pity beads at the artisans' gallery. Collect Navajo rugs. Sign up for a blues workshop. Sponsor a whale. But what about me? I thought I was supposed to be your friend? Well look. Just watch this."

And he did.

He walked out.

The fat man banished himself.

Now, eighty-sixed from Camel-Op, bewildered and friendless, he began to frequent his second choices. Mornings, he could barely rally the concentration to follow strings of ellipses across the page from inedible menu item to inexcusable price. His breakfasts arrived on unbreakable dishware bordered with scorchmarks. As he drank he could see the levels at which others who'd been served this cup had surrendered. By now all orifices operated at the disposal of the bug he'd contracted. He croaked when he talked. His stomach impersonated Donald Duck. During what had once been the most meditative moments of his day, he made noises like zippers and kazoos in an oil drum.

One Friday in July he stopped at a place he'd never been before. Air conditioning cranked up to maximum igloo. Squares of linoleum missing from the pattern. Grease-cicles drooping from the exhaust hood above the grill. At the counter a row of backs.

A waitress with hair the length and texture you know you'll find later in your eggs took his order. He watched the one stingy cube he'd been issued drown in his water glass while he waited. Coffee as transparent as whiskey. Limp, wheatless triangles of toast. Eggs gritty with disintegrated shell. Hash-browns so raw they crunched. Sausage links that squirted when he pierced them with his fork. He pushed the plate away. Crossed his arms on the countertop. Let his head drop. He stared down at a gray mop strand snagged beneath the chrome skirt at the base of his stool. Incapacitated.

"Hey. Mister. You okay?" The waitress.

"Just a cold." His breath clouded the chilly countertop. "A miserable summer cold."

"Leave the guy. Can't you see? What does he, have to write his biography for you?"

"All's I asked was if he's okay."

"He's okay. Leave the guy. You're so anxious to get involved in somebody's life? Pay some of his bills why don't you?"

That voice. The fat man thought he recognized it. He lifted his head.

Intriguing how often, when you're running an errand, on your way someplace downtown, you'll pass a certain person on the sidewalk, and then, on your way back, whether it's ten minutes or an hour or two hours later, you'll pass that exact same stranger traveling in the opposite direction. That's the way the fat man felt when he looked up and saw, climbing onto the stool to his right, the other fat man. The one in the striped uniform shirt who'd fixed the refrigeration at Ernesto's a summer ago.

Or was it him?

Or was he climbing off, not climbing on?

"Hold it. Friend. Don't go. Let me buy you a . . ."

Then he thought he heard the woman seated to his left interrupt. Call him by name. He turned and it was Cody.

"Did you think you were through, darling?" Cody was saying. "Sorry. Not quite. You have to hold out a little longer. There's one more thing."

She beckoned with a finger. Leaned closer. Placed a hand gently on his shoulder.

And shoved.

The fat man remembered reaching. But finding nothing stationary to hinder his fall. He grabbed at cups, plates, glasses, silverware. At salt and pepper, sugar, syrup, ketchup. Bringing much of it with him, very nearly clearing the countertop, he continued sideways. He fell, and reaching up the last things he saw he committed to memory. Streaky fluorescent lights . . . the waitress's startled expression . . . the underside of the counter . . . chewing gum.

When he opened his eyes he saw Kennedy.

"Aaron. Look everybody, he's awake."

"Bronchitis. It'll go away."

"Don't talk, Aaron."

"Walking pneumonia. I had this once before."

Other voices. Laura's, Max's. Ont Hazel and Bob the Brush. All talking at once.

"Do you know where you are, Mr. Dodge?"

In bed. But not his bed. Not the Bunkport. He asked how much time had passed, and when he was told, Aaron Dodge understood how serious his condition had been.

Unconscious.

Hospitalized.

Near death.

The only way the fat man would consent to love.

17

You call this food?

You call this a bath?

I just hope you're consistent when you make out my bill. That's all
I can say.

If only it had been true. The fat man thought of plenty more. And
he said it all. And none of it endeared him to the personnel responsible
for his care. His friends petitioned for a sense of humor. But the staff
paramedics must've exhausted the entire summer's quota when they
ambulanced him here. To, of all places, Vets Hospital at 18th and
Indian School—evidently the medical facility nearest the site of his
collapse.

The fat man's convalescence allowed him ample time for calm reflection. An opportunity he despised. Somebody mentioned a cof-
feeshop downstairs, and the minute his legs would hold him up, Aaron
Dodge located it. He sat in his bathrobe among campaigners representing America's three most recent conflicts, who'd come here to
mend or die, and swapped war stories. They nicknamed him the Com-
munist. The Slacker. He retaliated with Baby-Killers, Neofascists.
They became friends.

His ambassadorship among the heroes didn't last. As soon as the
VA staff caught him out of bed, they transferred him to County, 24th
and Roosevelt, where his get-well cards, calls, and visitors caught up

with him a day later. The delay made him wonder how anybody had found him in the first place. None of his friends could supply the entire story, but by combining disjointed recollections provided by visitors and callers Aaron Dodge assembled an explanation.

His wallet couldn't've helped much. Its contents didn't even furnish conclusive proof of his own whereabouts, much less evidence of a loved one's. But the police must've reconciled the conflicting addresses, arrived at a consensus, and pursued their hunch to the blue apartment village. There they could've used his keys to enter, and though he didn't own a programmable phone with friends' numbers electronically memorized, inside they'd've certainly discovered his manually compiled analog to that invention. From the numbers surrounding the wall phone in his kitchen, they'd selected Laura's, and she and Kennedy had initiated the chain reaction. Visitors and flowers had inundated the fat man's semiprivacy ever since.

At County they roomed him with an inexhaustible gust of wind named Nolan Muncie. Nolie kept talking about his "golds in life" and how "sadistics proved" the accuracy of the bigoted and outrageous views he maintained on every subject. Nolie's company was enjoyable. But so was a steam bath. Fortunately, his wife, Babe, relieved Aaron Dodge at regular intervals. Built like a telephone repairwoman, Babe arrived wearing a maternity smock—her third, she told the fat man—and stockings rolled down to donuts at her ankles.

"Shut up, Nolie. The man ain't listening no more. He's answering with grunts. One word at a time. Take a hint."

"Doctor says it's a melodrama," said Nolie, pointing to the top of his head. "They're the dangerous kind, I guess. From what he says. Who'd think? Just from working outside for over the summer. A cancer. I tar roofs, you know? For a living. And besides I'm not from around here. The sun. Who'd think?"

"The bag brain won't admit he's losing his hair," Babe said. "I guess now he'll wear a hat. Huh, Nolie?"

"What do you know about it anyways? Going bald?"

"You don't have to be a turd to smell one."

"How about you?" said Nolie. "What's your . . . ?"

"My medical complaint? Exhaustion."

He stared at the fat man, nodding slowly from the shoulders. As if

Aaron Dodge had announced he'd scalded himself on his cappuccino machine or missed a loop in the jogging trail. "Shit," said Babe. "Most people'd be in bed their whole lifes if they calt that sick."

The nature of the fat man's ailment created a temporary class barrier, promptly eliminated when he and Nolie discovered they were both prospective guests of the taxpayers. Likely recipients of state papers. Indigent. The fat man's destitute status had gone undetected so far— a secret from everyone but Nolie and Babe. He still carried an ancient Blue Cross ID, which he'd neglected to toss after he let his premiums lapse in 1978 or so, presuming it might induce the sort of auspicious mixup that could be counted on to occur in an emergency if you gave it half a chance. The expired policy number had admitted him to the VA Hospital on Friday, the day of his collapse, and since he transferred to County over the weekend, he'd be able to prolong the misunderstanding till Monday, maybe Tuesday if he was lucky. Then he'd officially join Nolie on the list of available stretchers. Candidates for immediate triage. Victims of capitalized medicine.

Meantime he misappropriated benefits to which comprehensive coverage would have entitled him. A nurse assisted on his strolls through the hospital corridors, and during one of these excursions they descended to a subbasement complex near the hospital cafeteria. Aaron Dodge endured a brief consultation on healthful nutrition, featuring properly controlled portions of toy food—hamburger, spaghetti and broccoli rubberized like the realistic lumps and puddles of prank substances available in novelty shops. But the real revelation came when he stepped onto the dietician's scales.

"Jesus. Are you sure this thing's accurate?" he asked, nudging the counterweights.

Over a hundred pounds.

"I lost an entire person," said the fat man.

On Sunday, his second day at County, he told Nolie to go get his doomed ass radiated or chemo'ed or something till about lunchtime. Kennedy arrived soon after visiting hours began.

She wore a gold-and-white rugby shirt and a pair of sweatpants with ESPRIT lettered vertically down one leg.

"Hi," she said.

"Hi."

"How do you feel?"

"Pretty good. I feel okay."

"I brought you some . . ."

He lifted the foil at the edge of the paper plate she held out to him. Oatmeal raisin. He extracted one from the pile and took a bite. "I missed you," he said.

"Really?" She sat beside him on the bed. They both looked across at Nolie's half of the room. "You're alone," she said.

"I slashed his vocal cords and they took him someplace to sew him up. You should meet Nolie. Compared to him, I'm on the ten-best-dressed list. Take a peek in that little cupboard they hung our clothes in. His wardrobe's definitely safe from moths, but if any of those genetically engineered organisms that eat oil spills ever gets loose in his closet, look out."

"I missed you too."

The fat man glanced away. "I think the same dish towel's still hanging on the door of the refrigerator as when you left. It's rigidified into this permanent wedge." He formed an apex with his fingertips. "I spilled a pitcher of juice one morning."

"Gross."

"Pretty incompetent, huh?"

"You're fine."

"I'm lucky you're young. Nobody with any experience would be this understanding."

Kennedy smiled. "You know what they say. People should accept each other the way—"

"—the way they are. I know. Except what if you're never the same for over three minutes at a stretch?"

"I look at it like this. A person who's indecisive can change more easily."

"Listen. Before Nolie gets back. I've been wanting to talk to you. You know how you were always ragging me to tell you more about my work?"

"I was not ragging. I was just—"

"Okay, asking I mean. Suggesting. Well is it all right if I tell you something right now?"

Kennedy shrugged.

"I should've admitted this a long time ago. You'd've understood why I was acting so . . . the way I was."

"If you could explain that, I'd be—"

"I can explain."

And Aaron Dodge told her the story. While he talked he could see Kennedy scrutinizing, searching. Probably questioning her own gullibility. Definitely examining Aaron Dodge's credibility if not his sanity.

"Is that true?" she asked when he'd finished. "That can't be true."

"Absolutely true."

"I don't believe you."

"You will. Soon."

"That's incredible."

"I know."

"Is it really true? If it's true, I'll . . . I mean I'd love to help if I could. Is there anything?"

"Sure. Probably. But you're already helping."

"What're you going to do, Aaron?"

"Well, I guess I'll ask Bob to bail me out with the machine, then—"

"Not about that. I mean just generally. Once you're home, you think you'll be okay? By yourself and all?"

"I guess I hadn't planned as far as that."

"It'll be harder than you think, I bet. At first. You know. By yourself."

"You could be right. I'm still pretty tired. I lost a lot of—"

"—weight. You certainly did. I'm concerned, Aaron. You don't take care of yourself."

"What do you suppose? Maybe you should move—"

"—back in. Just what I was thinking."

"I know."

"You read my mind?"

"Large print."

He stared up at the U-shaped track in the ceiling. A floor-length vinyl curtain could be drawn around the bed for private consultations.

Kennedy finished the thought for him, quarantining them behind the curtain.

"Did you bring the—?" he asked. She quickly worked one leg of the sweatpants past a shoe. Leaving her modesty otherwise intact, she lifted the hem of his hospital gown.

"No, but I have one of these. Borrowed it down in the lobby, from an AIDS-awareness display."

"Clever."

"I know. I used to live with an inventor."

"No shit?"

"He was very imaginative. I guess some of it must've—ooh—"

"—rubbed off?"

"You said it."

The next day, once she'd had a chance to consider his story, Kennedy returned with a cross-examination. Why hadn't he confided in his friends sooner? How come he'd made it so difficult on himself? Why had he insisted on absolute solitude? A gloomy cinderblock cell? The blackest hours of the night and the unappeasable heat of summer? Hadn't he recognized the obvious alternatives?

The fat man shrugged. "The grass is always greener . . ."

He recognized the miraculous healing powers of insolvency at work when his nurses announced later in the day that he'd be sent home tomorrow or Wednesday. He didn't want to be responsible for piling disenchantment on top of worry, so he encouraged Kennedy to believe that her vigil had contributed to his early release. She stayed with him for most of the rest of the day and helped him greet visitors.

Wendy Wendy, in her bright-tangerine smock, stopped by on her way to the Kopy Korner.

"Oh," she said. "Hi. I'll come back later."

"No, please," said Kennedy. "Come in. Really."

They smiled at each other like the last two survivors in a beauty pageant.

"I can't stay," Wendy Wendy said. "But I thought if you had time you might want to read." She handed him a paperback on self-healing, bagged in a see-through envelope along with a complimentary shard of crystal.

"I just wanted you to know, Aaron Dodge. About your . . . you know . . . recent behavior? I'm at a place right now in my life where I can forgive that."

"It was my fault, Wendy. Completely. So let's forget it. Please."

"Do you really mean that, Aaron Dodge?"

"I do. I don't want to hear another word, okay? I insist."

"I'm so glad, Aaron Dodge. The last thing I wanted was to, you know, undermine our dynamic or something."

"What recent behavior?" Kennedy wanted to know later, the minute Wendy had gone. "What 'dynamic'?"

"I was half deranged. Who knows what I might've done? You hungry? There's a row of machines down the hall. And a lounge where you can—"

"What recent behavior, Aaron?"

"Delirium. I was probably delirious, whatever I did. Think these rhinestones really do anything?" He unbagged the crystal and Wendy Wendy's book. "My powers of personal ascension could use a—"

"What . . . recent . . . behavior?"

"Bob! Buddy, come on in! Good to see you!"

Another visitor. This time Bob the Brush. "You know Kennedy, don't you?"

Bob nodded.

"Hi," Kennedy said. "Thanks for coming."

Unaccustomed to enthusiasm from the fat man, and clearly embarrassed by it, Bob stood at the foot of the bed, the ends of his fingers inserted in the front pockets of his Levis, and cautiously inspected the room.

"Where's your balloons?"

"My what?"

"Cost us forty-five bucks. They better get here. We had a choice of a French maid, a harem girl, or a football cheerleader. But we talked them into a— Hell, you'll see. If they deliver. Sorry. Hope I didn't shit on your surprise."

"A man in my condition, they don't allow me surprises."

Bob smiled at Kennedy. "What a fragile guy."

Bob the Brush was another friend he'd made the decision to confide in. And now seemed like the ideal time. He could inform his friend and maybe redeem himself in Kennedy's estimation too. Remind her of his humanitarian intentions.

"What're you guys whispering about over there?" Nolie. "How do you expect anybody to earsdrop with you whispering?"

"Shut your retarded mouth, Nolie." Babe appeared from behind the partition dividing the room. "Excuse him, folks. Nolie's the kind of guy who'd butt-fuck you and wipe the shit on your shirttail. No manners whatsoever."

By now his and Nolie's friendship had progressed—or deteriorated— to something near the status of cellmates, or seat partners on a cross-country bus journey. Politeness was no longer an issue between them. They'd listened to each other snore. They'd each sat on a toilet seat warmed by the other's haunches. His understanding of Nolie's needs, preferences, and personal habits, and Nolie's of his, transcended courtesy.

The fat man told Nolie to fuck himself and suggested a walk.

Holly and Robin. Dexter, Max. Dave and Connie. Mary Vanessa Singer. He told the story as the three of them traversed the hospital's busy corridors. The fat man walked in the middle, addressing excited gestures to either side, occasionally halting traffic to grip Bob's shoulder and affirm a point so crucial he felt they couldn't proceed until he'd clarified it.

Aaron Dodge.

Dressed in his blue bathrobe.

Coming clean.

Bob reacted with an enthusiasm significantly compromised by doubt and curiosity—a delayed reaction familiar to the fat man now that he'd told the story to half a dozen friends and strangers. But by the time they'd completed a circuit of the halls and returned to Aaron Dodge's doorway, Bob the Brush seemed close to believing. Or at least accepting. The fat man retrieved his pants from the cupboard where his and Nolie's street clothes hung, unhooked the key to the mini–storage unit from his ring, and handed it to Bob the Brush. He told him to go see for himself. If the evidence persuaded him, he could haul the replica from Pack Rat to his trailer and finish assembling the machine. By the time Aaron Dodge recuperated, it would be available for simulations. And by then he believed he'd have something to simulate. Because a possibility had occurred to the fat man during his stay at County.

He'd intended to keep the idea to himself for as long as he could. But that night, while Kennedy was downstairs at the grill eating a sandwich with Babe, two more friends visited, bringing with them such good news that he felt he owed them a story in return.

"Here's four-fourteen. Eighteen must be down this way."

He heard them before he saw them. Voices from the corridor.

"Nope, four-twelve. It's that one. Over there."

"You positive?"

"Look for yourself. You think you're the only person on the planet ever learned to read?"

Magdalena peeked around the corner. Knocked on the open door. Saluted. Dixon followed him inside, tilting like a wine bottle too tall to fit on the refrigerator shelf.

"How you feeling, Edison?"

The fat man answered with an outstretched hand, an unsteady gesture.

"You don't look all that great," Magdalena admitted.

"He looks fine," said Dixon. "He'll perk up when he sees this." They'd brought a couple of skin magazines and a newspaper. Yesterday's.

"You see the lottery results Monday?" Dixon asked. He opened the paper to page two of the "Metro" section.

"They wouldn't mean anything to him," Magdalena said. "We haven't told him the—"

"I know that. Just shut up, okay? I'm talking." Dixon pointed to the column listing the six numbers drawn the previous Friday.

Aaron Dodge placed a finger to his lips and nodded in Nolie's direction. He climbed out of bed, put on his bathrobe and slippers, and invited Dixon and Magdalena down the hall to a lounge. Empty bookshelves. Crooked lampshade. Chrome-and-vinyl couches and copies of *Psychology Today.*

"Somebody nailed five of the numbers," Dixon said immediately.

"They what?"

"Jackpot Jack drew five out of the six numbers we've been sitting on. And somebody collected."

"Wow. All but one? That could be good. Couldn't it?"

"Damn right," Dixon said.

"It doesn't necessarily mean anything," Magdalena warned.

It didn't necessarily mean the sixth number would've matched. It didn't necessarily mean the winning player was who they hoped he was. Five of six paid only four hundred dollars, and a payoff that size could be claimed anonymously at any lottery retailer. All it meant, and all Magdalena had been able to confirm, was that a ticket had been redeemed. By somebody. Somebody playing five-sixths of the crucial combination. Him? The odds were against. Astronomically against. They shouldn't get their hopes up. They should retain a professional attitude. Overly skeptical would be preferable to overly optimistic in a case like this.

They looked at each other.

Aaron Dodge was the first to smile. Then Dixon. Magdalena jumped from his chair, leaped into the air, and war-whooped. Dixon laughed and pumped a fist like a linebacker after a third-down sack.

"Shh! Quiet!" the fat man said. "They'll hear us." He reached for a pen and pad, their logos insinuating kickbacks from pharmaceutical giants, and drew a square. The jackpot machine. "Look," he said. "Here's what I was thinking. See if you don't agree it's a perfect idea. I saw this woman the other day, and all of a sudden it was obvious." He pointed the pen vaguely, thinking of Babe, pregnant with number three, sitting with a paperback a few doors away.

"What we'll do, see, is . . ."

Once he'd shared his inspiration with Dixon and Magdalena, they all three returned to his room. There they found, waiting beside his bed, a barefoot young girl wearing a batiked sun top, leather headband, Ben Franklin sunglasses, and a strand of red-white-and-blue love beads.

"Aaron Dodge?" she asked. As if she'd come to serve a summons.

When he nodded, she handed him a flower and a cluster of pillowy foil balloons, kissed him on the mouth, and retreated toward the elevators, leaving the flavor of her gum distinct on Aaron Dodge's lips.

18

The Wednesday before Labor Day, when Robin and the Lottery Commission CPA wheeled the jackpot machine from KPHX's vault for its weekly examination, Aaron Dodge stood close by, so scared you could've dotted "i"s with his asshole. This coming Friday's would be the critical drawing. He'd come to the studio to assure that the machine would deliver the necessary six numbers.

Robin glanced frequently in his direction. The presence of a visitor wasn't particularly unusual. Journalists and, less often, disgruntled or fanatical lottery participants regularly requested or demanded an inspection tour. The Lottery Commission honored all such requests, welcomed all observers. It had to in order to publicly maintain its integrity. Aaron Dodge stood to one side, watching. So far he'd made no attempt to approach the machine or interfere.

Today Aaron Dodge was again, objectively and not just by habit and reputation, a fat man. He weighed three hundred plus. And the excess at his middle felt like the heaviest load he'd ever carried. The weight pulled him forward and downward, off-center, straining his neck and shoulders, compacting his legs like a pair of beleaguered shocks. He wondered how women endured this for nine months at a time. He wondered how he'd lugged around an equal amount of fat every day, every minute for so many years.

Preparations for today had started following his release from County.

Immediately. And even though Aaron Dodge's constitution didn't register "immediate" with the same urgency that perkier metabolisms did, it seemed to him that with his friends' help arrangements had progressed in an unusual hurry. Bob the Brush finished the building of the replica at his trailer, and rehearsals began in late July, with Max, Dixon and Magdalena, Bob, Aaron Dodge, and Dexter attending. The fat man elected to keep Dexter involved, and involved in a major way, in spite of his unpredictability, so that later, when he witnessed the results of the drawing, he wouldn't be able to retaliate without incriminating himself along with everybody else. The fat man did expect to cut Dexter in. He'd earmarked cash from the Help Find Mary Vanessa Singer fund. But the payoff wouldn't be nearly the size Dexter was anticipating. Aaron Dodge had suggested—and Dixon and Magdalena agreed—that this time they shouldn't water down the jackpot unnecessarily. No duplicate winners. Not if they could avoid it. Consequently, the numbers Aaron Dodge issued Dexter would not be the genuine set. Dexter, who evidently didn't suspect this, had been video-camming the rehearsals at Bob's trailer to confirm the photogenic aspects of Aaron Dodge's plan. Every night they'd tape several run-throughs of the operation, screen the results with the help of Bob's Curtis-Mathes and a VCR supplied by Max, then discuss ways to improve subsequent performances.

During one of these critiques, on a night in mid-August—Aaron Dodge's birthday in fact—Magdalena stood up and announced: "We're ready. Let's set a date."

"You think so?" said Aaron Dodge. "I'm not so sure. What do you guys think?"

"Three weeks," said Magdalena. "Definite. The Friday before Memorial Day."

"Labor Day," said the fat man. "Memorial Day's in May."

"Right. The thing is, see, there's more activity with the lottery close to holidays. The figures show it. That's why I say Veterans Day's an intelligent choice."

"Labor Day," said the fat man.

"Correct," said Magdalena. "Then it's settled."

During the remaining weeks, Max continued her negotiations with millionaires. She'd been taking the Singers along to help her plead their daughter's cause to wealthy patrons, and, in spite of the fact that she represented specifics of the rescue attempt with the euphemistic opacity only a lawyer could've, she'd been collecting substantial pledges. It seemed just to Aaron Dodge that the truth could be revealed without caution to thieves like Dexter, who appreciated the limits of their credibility, but had to be hidden from important men like Eelfleet and Dick Banks, on whose say-so the authorities would've taken prompt, direct action. The beans, like any other commodity, made a noisier splash when spilled from high places.

A week early, two weeks prior to the targeted drawing, they voted to collect and wager the proceeds of Max's fund-raiser. Waiting any longer would've created at least two unacceptable complications. Because the last-minute bets wouldn't be publicized, the jackpot might not entice their suspect if he played his sequence intermittently. Also, the kind of instantaneous inflation they planned to produce would likely attract official attention. That week's drawing could be more closely watched. Which made now the proper time. Even so, one obvious, intimidating risk accompanied their decision to buy into a lottery other than the one they planned to rig. If somebody happened to hit, the result would be bankruptcy for Aaron's Enterprises.

Once they'd agreed on when, how to invest became the question. Lottery plays had to be issued one at a time, and the number of plays necessary to significantly raise the prize amount would tie up a lottery terminal day and night for months. Years. Aaron Dodge and Max wrote a program on the PC network at Max's office, based on the various parlays the lottery allowed, and which, according to their calculations, would exhaust their resources in less than a week. But this consolidation of funds didn't answer their second requirement—a cooperative retailer.

You can always count on sound advice from a barber. Back in the spring, when the fat man came to him for a haircut, Dundee had furnished a complimentary item of information with the service. Did Aaron Dodge play the big game? If he did, or if he ever intended to, he could do a lot worse than Dundee's. The terminal at his newsstand next door had dispensed more winning tickets than any other machine in the state.

On Saturday, Aaron Dodge showed up at Dundee's with Max and

Officer Magdalena, prepared to collaborate on one more edition of the story. Dundee welcomed them and invited Aaron Dodge into a tiny office, barely big enough for one, at the rear of the shop. Max and Officer Magdalena waited in the no-appointment-necessary chairs near the front door. Alone with Dundee, the fat man started to explain. He was willing to explain. He wanted to explain. But as he examined Dundee's face—a face like a basketball played with too many seasons on asphalt courts—he saw something familiar there. Dundee was a bachelor. He'd been a bachelor for five decades. You don't survive on your own for that long without developing some basic, reliable philosophies. For instance that life proceeds at a more satisfying pace if you don't insist on understanding every little thing that goes on around you. Partway through Aaron Dodge's appeal, Dundee interrupted, led him next door to the terminal, and instructed the clerk, in English and then in Spanish, to cooperate with the fat man and his friends.

Until that moment a used El Camino and his Commodore 64 had been the most expensive purchases Aaron Dodge had ever transacted. He watched Max present the clerk with a printout of computer-generated number combinations. The clerk's hands quaked as she pressed keys for the first of the entries. The terminal clattered. Ejected a curled receipt.

For the next five days and nights, virtually twenty-four hours, Aaron Dodge or one of his friends stood duty at Dundee's, overseeing the process, systematically wasting the funds that had been entrusted to them.

La Low-tay-REE-yah! Low-tay-REE-yah! Low-tay-REEEE-yah!

That Friday they gathered at Bob's trailer, another potential disaster concerning them as they watched. One of their sequences could pay off. They'd played as many duplicate combinations as discretion allowed; even so, a dreadful prospect—accidentally raking in millions—had to be considered. Her briefcase computer rested on Max's knees, a list of their bets queued in its memory. As Jackpot Jack selected the night's winners, Max reproduced each on the grayish screen, the fingers of her unoccupied hand crossed against luck. Jack announced the final pick. Max entered the series. Waited. Glanced gratefully at the ceiling and exhaled. Everybody else in the room breathed along with her.

"We're losers," Max proclaimed cheerfully.

Afterward, to determine if less well financed speculators had been more fortunate, they dialed 1-800-JACKPOT, repeatedly, until they contacted the Lottery Commission recording. The following Monday the paper confirmed the hotline's preliminary declaration. The fat man's stomach constricted as he surveyed the official results that morning at Lulu's counter. Instinctively he began to invent excuses. But then he checked himself. A deadline. Less than a week.

He drained his coffee cup resolutely.

He'd be there, he promised himself.

And he was.

Aaron Dodge shuffled aside as Robin uncoiled the black cord and plugged into an outlet near the vault door. He unlocked an attaché case that held a set of thirty numbered balls, one of three the commission rotated week to week, and fed them into the chutes adjoining the mixing reservoir. The fat man watched for six in particular.

Twenty-two.

Sixteen.

Eleven.

Eight.

Five.

Six.

The previous night, no sooner than absolutely necessary, Magdalena had finally divulged the sixth number, which Aaron Dodge had then painted onto the last of the oddballs. Now, to avoid more disturbing thoughts, he repeated: Twenty-two, sixteen, eleven, eight, five, and six.

The CPA seemed to be watching him.

Aaron Dodge smiled.

He knew he'd looked fairly authentic when he and Magdalena left the apartment earlier. For weeks he'd been swallowing pills. Salt tablets, cortisone, steroids. They'd encouraged swelling in his face and hands, imparting a plumpness that helped complement the bulky stomach. But maybe something had shifted or slipped since this afternoon. Twenty-two, sixteen, eleven, eight . . .

He staggered to the side of the machine opposite the CPA and said to Robin, "Mind if I take a look back here?"

"Don't touch anything, sir."

The fat man struggled to stoop beside the machine and pretended to inspect its rear panel. The CPA leaned past a corner of the wide façade to keep him in sight. "Just wondering if this shitbox is patented," the fat man said casually. "Ought to be a plate back here if it is." Robin stepped between him and the CPA and touched a red power switch, activating the machine's blower. The balls he'd stocked in the reservoir stirred.

Not as much racket as Aaron Dodge had hoped for. They must mike the machinery during the telecast, he decided. But fuck it, he couldn't delay any longer. In fact he knew he wouldn't be able to stand without first shedding the weight that pinned him in his crouch. He quickly unsnapped his shirt, and as Robin looked on helplessly, amazed, the fat man let Officer Magdalena spill from his waist.

His friend slid efficiently, just as they'd rehearsed the maneuver, beneath the giant machine, into the foot or so of clearance between it and the floor, turning his head aside to accommodate the narrow space. Aaron Dodge yanked the ripcord to an inflatable vest—an airtight bladder, seams reinforced with sealer—that Laura had sewn. It filled with a whoosh. As he refastened his shirt over it and nonchalantly stood, suddenly ninety pounds lighter, he found the CPA staring.

"What's he doing? I heard something."

The balls ticked and rattled. The blower hummed.

"No you didn't," said Robin.

"Look, I'm positive I—"

"Shut up," said Robin. "Do your job, I'll do mine. And you," he said to Aaron Dodge, "get the hell away from there. I told you not to touch anything."

"Sorry," Aaron Dodge said, and complied, innocently showing the palms of his hands.

The CPA looked carefully at them both. Seemed about to say something. Then returned his attention to the logbook in which he'd been recording tonight's access.

Robin switched off the machine. Unplugged it. Coiled its cord. He removed the thirty Ping-Pong balls and ordered them in their compartmentalized valise, exhibiting, Aaron Dodge thought, inhuman patience. Finished, he prepared to wheel the machine back inside the vault.

"Wait. I'll help you," the CPA offered.

"Me too," Aaron Dodge said, and stepped toward the machine.

The CPA reached out to obstruct him. Aaron Dodge stepped back as his hand grazed the stomach.

"I've got it," Robin told them. "Thanks anyway."

Robin secured the vault door and turned to Aaron Dodge. The fat man shook his friend's hand and thanked him, careful to leave the CPA with a distinct impression by suggesting nothing more than his gratitude for having been allowed to watch.

Positive visualization, Lulu called it. And that night, in his tub, the fat man tried it. Magdalena. Successfully implementing the operations they'd been rehearsing at Bob's trailer for a month. Underwater except for his matterhorn of a nose, the roundish islands of his knees—belly mostly submerged now—the fat man wished he could be there himself. Would've been, if not for his size. The best he could do now was hope he'd furnished Magdalena with all he'd need to survive his incubation.

The fat man's friend had a flashlight with him. A wristwatch. Basic tools and simple materials with which to modify the machine. A flask of water and a ration of trail mix to last until his scheduled rescue. And of course, protected by a crushproof metal sleeve, the six doctored balls. Twenty-two, sixteen, eleven, eight, five, and six.

Since he and Wendy Wendy first collaborated on the restricted-aperture concept, Aaron Dodge had refined it considerably. Transported into the vault, alone with the machine, Magdalena was to remove the rear panel and climb inside. There, presumably, he'd face a setup resembling the one his training had prepared him for. His first responsibility would be to insert an opening in the floor of the mixing reservoir large enough to permit him limited access to the process during Friday's drawing. Next he was to install a slender spring, something like the pin that holds the band to a watch, inside the machine's display chimney, at the top of the shaft. The tiny spring would hold in place a length of microfine filament, suggested by Brett's addiction to dental floss but far thinner than floss—invisible, as far as their screen tests had been able to determine. During the drawing Magdalena would control the thread from below. At the moment—the six separate moments—when a rush of vacuum alerted him that Jack had opened the petcock to induct another selection into the display chimney, Magdalena would release one of the counterfeit balls, each drilled to permit the filament to pass through it. The sequence would be channeled unerringly, like a string of beads, directly to its destination.

This was the primary plan. They'd also rehearsed a much cruder contingency measure. But it, and the circumstances that might require Magdalena to consider it, the fat man didn't want to talk about.

After Friday's drawing ended and the lottery program left the air, Robin would operate the petcock and release the six displayed selections back into the mixing reservoir. Using the acrylic filament as a leash, Magdalena would be able to retrieve them easily. Prompt retrieval would be a necessity so that the presence of the six extras wouldn't be detected during the transfer of balls from the machine to storage.

Later, back inside the vault, Magdalena would undo his alterations. He wouldn't need to hurry the procedures. Not till the following Wednesday, during the machine's weekly start-up and test, would he finally be extracted. To create a diversion during the rescue, Aaron Dodge had enlisted his friend Dibadj and Dibadj's Palestinian acquaintance, Fuad. He'd asked them only to show up at KPHX and begin conversing loudly and rapidly in Farsi. In the 1980s, in America, two darkly mustached Middle Eastern intruders could be counted on to provoke an abundance of vaguely founded but instantaneous associations. Shiites. Amal militiamen. Abu Nidal. With Dibadj and Fuad present, Magdalena could blast his way out of the studio with an AK 47 assault rifle and attract only peripheral attention. Holly would be there to umpire if needed, and to provide Dibadj and Fuad with an alibi. She'd volunteered to pose as the central issue in their quarrel— a romantic rather than a criminal trespass.

Sequestered in his tub, Aaron Dodge congratulated himself. He'd assigned a friend to every responsibility, a constant to every variable with an aptitude for calamity only a pure pessimist could've aspired to. Which he was already beginning to regret, since this left him with nothing to do but worry. Thursday, aboard the corner stool at Camel-Op, he wore a pair of weightless jogger's earphones he'd borrowed from Kennedy. At home that night, cooling off underwater, he listened to a pink-and-green Kermit and Miss Piggy portable one of Laura's six had left at the apartment. All day Friday, hourly, he continued to monitor the news. Aaron Dodge. Wondering what had gone wrong. Dreading the hour he'd find out. Begrudging himself even the stingiest crumb of hope or satisfaction.

Friday night, on Bob the Brush's set, he watched the *Jackpot Jack Show*. Watched along with Bob, Max, Kennedy, Phil Dixon. Watched, still unconvinced, as the numbers fell into place—for once understanding the mechanisms, knowing the outcomes, calling the shots.

On Tuesday morning he sat alone in a window booth at a diner across the street from the municipal complex in downtown Phoenix.

And on Wednesday morning.

And again Thursday.

On Friday he still occupied his lookout post, while Phil Dixon staked out a frequently used side entrance, and Magdalena, free since Wednesday, waited inside, loitering in the hallway near the office of the administrator responsible for dispensing jackpot payoffs.

It hadn't been the kind of week people move to Phoenix for. Northerners liked to multiply already extreme winter temperatures by what they called a wind-chill factor. The fat man wondered why nobody had invented a similarly masochistic summer formula. The torpid incineration factor or something. A man approaching the vicinity of the Capitol stopped to remove his sportcoat and sling it over a shoulder, a finger hooked inside the collar.

He existed. The man they were waiting for existed. Aaron Dodge had been positive of him since the night of the drawing, when 1-800-JACKPOT reported an unidentified, unofficial claimant. Monday's paper confirmed him. Tuesday, Wednesday, and yesterday added proof to certainty. Why else would a jackpot winner hesitate to collect? He existed. But where the fuck was he?

The three-day weekend, a vacation for the rest of Phoenix, had felt like triple overtime to Aaron Dodge. First he'd had to appease Dexter, who went absolutely apeshit when he found out he'd been dealt a worthless series of numbers. When they met at the Crack on Saturday, the fat man swore to a foul-up. The numbers hadn't cooperated. They'd all come out losers, not just Dexter. He assured Dexter they'd be trying again. As long as nobody found out about yesterday, what was stopping them? A little patience and he'd only be out a buck. Panic and he'd piss away his share of a fortune. Dexter tugged at his right earlobe with the opposite hand. The logic seemed to penetrate. He followed Aaron Dodge into the alley behind the Crack, where the fat man distributed the dregs of the Help Find Mary Vanessa Singer fund.

Once he'd settled with Dexter, Aaron Dodge expected to spend the rest of the weekend sedated by bathwater, tranquilized with coffee. No way. On Sunday, as he and Dixon reviewed a videotape of the drawing, they began to notice incongruities. A microscopic search produced no evidence of the cobweb-fine filament that ought to have been present at the center of the display chimney to channel selections inside. Either an inspired camouflage job, or Magdalena had been required to improvise. Extensive scrutiny wasn't necessary to determine which. Balls swarmed and hesitated at the mouth of the tube. A sickening pause preceded each induction. Worse, any observant viewer could've counted extras—thirty-six, then thirty-five, then thirty-four balls cycling in the crucible as the drawing proceeded.

If obligated to switch to their alternate strategy, Magdalena was to have inserted a thin glass halo at the mouth of the display chimney in order to exclude all but their own candidates. This seemed to be the effect the fat man witnessed as Dixon forwarded, froze, reversed, and restarted the video. But they couldn't spot the transparent halo Aaron Dodge had supplied. After his rescue on Wednesday, Officer Magdalena confessed. He'd rolled over on it while he slept. The microfilament had ruptured when subjected to previous and similarly unforeseen stresses. Magdalena, stiff and hungry, still suffering from claustrophobia, confirmed what a review of the video had suggested. He'd installed a substitute for the fragile glass halo. The fat man cringed, remembering the instant Phil Dixon, fiddling with the reception on Bob the Brush's set, had produced an image. The obstruction? A lump of Magdalena's chewing gum.

The diner where Aaron Dodge was stationed called itself the Kettle, though he'd yet to see a bowl of soup, stew, or chili consumed here. The Kettle served its sandwiches in red oval baskets lined with sheets of wax paper, its coffee in flimsy white cones fitted into reusable brown plastic pedestals. The last, late-for-work, shell-shocked commuter stumbled out with his Danish at around nine-fifteen. After that you could idle with the newspaper or your own thoughts till nearly eleven-thirty, when they'd start denying you refills. Which Aaron Dodge understood. Clearly the Kettle's survival depended on the daily noon-hour crunch.

The fat man relinquished his position cordially and promptly to patrol the Capitol plaza on foot. He'd return to the Kettle at one o'clock to reclaim his window and order lunch. A deluxe bacon cheeseburger or maybe a tuna-salad sub. They gave you chips and a pickle spear on the side, and coffee came with. Not a bad deal.

Daydreaming the wide, white Plexiglas menu displayed above the counter, the fat man almost spaced off the Brillo-gray Toyota. He'd plugged his meter and was rolling down the El Camino's windows a crack so the upholstery wouldn't disintegrate in the heat, when he saw the gray compact maneuvering into a spot across the street. He squinted, trying to identify its driver through the dark glass. As he climbed out, Aaron Dodge saw that he was sizable. A fat man.

Astonishingly, he'd brought her with him.

She climbed out his side.

The fat man wanted to stare, to examine every detail of her appearance, but he forced himself to look away. He opened the El Camino's glovebox and pretended to search.

Aaron Dodge glanced up frequently to keep track of them. Holding her by the hand, he walked a block in the wrong direction, then doubled back. No accident, the fat man thought. Arriving just as lunch hour ended and the government returned to the Capitol.

He continued to ransack pointlessly. The console hutch. Under the seats. He came across the camera Wendy Wendy had left in the El Camino weeks ago, when they'd almost terminated their friendship. He picked it up to see if it was loaded.

Aaron Dodge adjusted the angle of the door until he could watch in the El Camino's side mirror. Dark hair. Fastidious mustache. Numerous chins. Red, out of breath, sweating. And her. Bedraggled hair, caved-in eyes, rigid posture. Only somebody who knew her as completely as Aaron Dodge did could've recognized her from the outdated likeness they kept reproducing in the news.

As the two of them approached, Aaron Dodge stepped directly into his path. He stopped. The two of them looked at each other. Aaron Dodge lifted the camera and snapped off six quick shots. The fat man turned and ran.

There's nothing more comical, futile, or extravagant than a fat man trying to run. Aaron Dodge could've overtaken him inside fifty yards. But an instinct urged him not to. He looked down at Mary Vanessa Singer. She reached for him.

"Don't go," she said.

Aaron Dodge watched the fat man retreat up Washington Street. He knelt on the sidewalk beside Mary Vanessa Singer and embraced her.

19

Laura's husband died that October. Or rather he'd been dead, and in October everybody finally started admitting it. Judicial-review panels. Medical-ethics boards.

The air force buried him with full military honors, judging from the length of the ceremony, and afterward Aaron Dodge bummed a ride back to Phoenix, leaving Laura, Kennedy, and the kids in Tucson to absorb the condolences and endure the food. You know. Brisket, three-bean salad, yellow sheet cake, coffee from a spigot.

"I really appreciate the lift," Aaron Dodge told Anita Fuentes, the woman with the available vehicle, and her friend Lunes Montoya. Anita Fuentes wore eye makeup the color of the recently renovated Statue of Liberty and carried a pair of glasses she never put on, but, from the looks of them, sat on regularly.

"This friend of mine," said Aaron Dodge, "this waitress, we're throwing a sort of a farewell bash for her. I'd've hated to miss it." Anita Fuentes' companion was closer to Aaron Dodge's age, robust, with dignified Indian features. Lunes Montoya wore her plain sweater like a shawl, buttoned once at the neck, her arms free of the sleeves. Both of them had on the practical white shoes identified with their profession. Either they were being polite to Aaron Dodge, or Anita Fuentes and Lunes Montoya didn't recognize him. Polite probably. Aaron Dodge doubted there was anybody left in Arizona that fit into the other category.

During the weeks since, the rescue had monopolized the entire state's attention, and Aaron Dodge's contribution didn't remain secret for long. Dexter, when he found out about Mary Vanessa Singer's safe return, sold or gave away a sensational interview—his method of getting even for his exclusion from the payoff. Dexter's revelations produced a scandal. Rumors of indictments. An immediate shutdown and total reorganization of the lottery. The commission refunded the contributions of the investors Max had enlisted. Tightened security. Adopted tiresome internal regulations. Dismissed Robin. Dismissed the CPA. Dumped Jackpot Jack, his show and his machine, and selected fully automated replacements. A less controversial, more constrained and respectable five minutes of air would've been difficult to imagine. No telling how the predicted drop in state revenues would be compensated for.

Besides offending every taxpayer in the state and implicating most of his friends in a criminal conspiracy, Aaron Dodge owed for another failure. Some—the Singers, Dixon and Magdalena—said he ought to have chased the kidnapper when he'd had the chance. The suspect still hadn't been captured, even though police were able to impound his gray Toyota. With the car, plus the snapshots Aaron Dodge had taken, they'd easily determined his identity—information Aaron Dodge could've provided without a vehicle registration check if they'd asked him. He'd figured out who the fat man was as he'd watched him escape. Cody helped, and the camera he'd held at the time. The association seemed obvious when he thought of all the cameras Cody had faced while she was alive. Always the same number series, printed in legible increments surrounding the lenses she'd looked into. F-stops. Twenty-two, sixteen, eleven, eight, five-point-six. The owner of the gray car was the school photographer who'd taken the photo of Mary Vanessa Singer that had appeared beside every story written about her since the day of her disappearance.

When they arrived at Camel-Op, Aaron Dodge assumed the corner stool and introduced his new friends. Bob the Brush and Wendy Wendy scooted down one to make room.

"How'd it go?" Bob asked.

"This guy comes up to me afterward," Aaron Dodge said. "A pall-bearer. In his parade uniform and all. White gloves. Cap with the patent-leather visor. And you know what he says to me? How he'd like to stretch razor wire across the barrel and shoot me out of a cannon."

"That a public or a private sentiment?"

"Would you've stuck around to find out?"

The new waitress reported to take their orders. "Our special today is the shiitake-mushroom-and-snow-pea omelet."

"Just coffee," said Aaron Dodge.

She brought the pot and poured. Somebody's acupuncturist's fiancée, Wendy Wendy had called her. Stone-washed jeans. Fingernails and a tan that ruled out any serious work for the past ten months, minimum. Lulu's replacement.

Lulu, if you accepted her account, had given her notice in order to protest a member-council vote that lifted prohibitions against the sale of red meat on the premises. The real issue, though, had nothing to do with cholesterol or antibiotic silage. For Lulu, the move was over-due. Like so many of Aaron Dodge's friends, she'd taken ten years off to reduce her life to ruins, and now she was going back to school. Creative writing. Feminist studies. Counseling. Today's celebration would acknowledge not just her farewell to Camel-Op's lunch counter but the dissolution of her marriage to Dibadj. Her friends seemed to share a conviction that, in calling off her arrangement with the fa-natically good-natured Iranian, Lulu was also divorcing a much larger and more destructive element in her past—the impulse that obligated her to compromise her own happiness in order to bring satisfaction to others. For her customers, this realization brought mixed feelings. The tendency they saw Lulu abandoning was the same one that had made her such a perfect waitress.

Wendy Wendy blinked. Shifted her eyes to the left. To the right. Reached up and recentered one of her contacts with a fingertip. "So you two must've been friends of his? The deceased's?"

Aaron Dodge set down his coffee cup to listen. On the way from Tucson he'd asked, and Anita Fuentes' responses had been lengthy and animated, but he still couldn't've told you what exactly had brought the two friends to the funeral of Laura's husband. He'd been able to determine that both were on staff at the VA Hospital in Tucson. Which implied certain possibilities but raised additional questions. He could see developing attachments. A hydrocephalic infant, a godforsaken leukemia victim, okay, maybe. But Laura's husband? A personality defined by the glowing red indicator of a life-support apparatus? He preferred to think they'd befriended Laura over the course of her many visits.

Aaron Dodge knew that Anita Fuentes and Lunes Montoya were planning to move to Phoenix. That they'd been shopping for houses here on weekends. He knew all about Billie Jean King, and why Camel-Op couldn't keep turkey basters in stock in the housewares aisle. He wasn't born yesterday and he was no prude. But it shocked him just the same to hear Anita Fuentes, during her haphazard exchange with Wendy Wendy, speak so casually and ruthlessly of Laura's husband and patients in a condition similar to the one he'd recently been delivered from. "Surge protectors," she called them, referring to the inexpensive gray boxes installed between electrical outlets and expensive pieces of machinery to intercept voltage spikes that might otherwise damage sensitive circuitry.

Aaron Dodge, a snob when it came to disenchantment, doubted that this whippersnapper could possibly have earned the pleasures and privileges of cynicism. Even so, her jolly contempt for the authority of suffering tempted him. 'Eighty-six had been a hilariously eventful year if you took your comedy black, no sugar. The AIDS epidemic. Leon Klinghoffer. The space shuttle *Challenger*. Begging the pardon of Lunes Montoya in advance, Aaron Dodge performed a few favorites concerning recent tragedies. Which he regretted instantly. Because Anita Fuentes knew jokes too. More, and more offensive ones than his, it turned out.

What does Mary Vanessa Singer call her bedtime story?

Foreplay.

What's Mary Vanessa Singer's earliest memory?

Virginity.

What do you get when you cross Mary Vanessa Singer and a chocolate sundae?

A cherry and permanent psychological damage.

Aaron Dodge made a choked sound approximating laughter. Stared down at Camel-Op's freshly laminated and revised nouvelle-cuisine menu. He'd always mistrusted those hesitant to reduce calamity and affliction to comedy. Always considered such people morally ostentatious. As phony in their own way as the pious consumers who escaped for bed-and-breakfast weekends to Sedona. But if this kept up, his conscience would be craving mushroom-and-snow-pea omelets right along with theirs.

He turned to Lunes Montoya. He wanted to say something. Apologize maybe. Or atone. Take some of it back if possible. Finally he could do no better than admit: "Actually, I was always afraid of him. I never believed they'd really let him die."

Lunes Montoya nodded sadly. And crossed herself.

"Anybody else hungry?" Anita Fuentes reached for a menu and her glasses. She reconfigured their frames. Tightened with the tip of her butter knife the miniature screws securing the stems. Put them on. "What's good here?" she asked, looking up. "Aaron Dodge! Lunes!" She grabbed her friend.

"*Mira!* It's him! Aaron Dodge!"

"Are you Aaron Dodge?" the waitress asked. "I've got a note here someplace for an Aaron Dodge."

The napkin carried a tiny indentation where it had been pushpinned to the bulletin board in the kitchen. And the Singers' phone number.

Following the previous month's disclosures, with reporters waiting to ambush him at the blue apartment village, with congratulatory and other messages blinking on his machine, with a representative of Sportco after him for Ping-Pong ball endorsements, he'd shut down Aaron's Enterprises' home office. He and Kennedy had been hiding out at Ont Hazel's in Sun City. Not an ideal situation but preferable to daily harassment. They slept apart, out of respect for Hazel, who discreetly rewarded their nocturnal propriety with frequent and prolonged daytime visits to the bank and grocery store. Kennedy had re-enrolled for the fall semester, and, afternoons when she was away at class, Aaron Dodge wandered the subdued and immaculate neighborhoods alone—streets named for famous golf courses, treacherously curved to discourage invading speeders. His one consolation during those aimless excursions was that people forget. Backgammon. The U.S.S. *Pueblo*. Grand Funk Railroad. The havoc he was responsible for would rattle around in public opinion like a shampoo lid dropped in a sink and then subside. Meantime he had his one consolation. His one consolation was Kennedy. His one consolation was Laura and her six. His inventions and his friends. And Mary Vanessa Singer.

Aaron Dodge.

Retired at thirty-five.

Part of what permitted this retreat was an unaccustomed degree of financial security. Or if not security then at least breathing room. Laura's leg strengthened and she went back to work at the fabric outlet. And Aaron Dodge—finally—had patented an invention. Predictably, somebody else did most of the work. A competitor had marketed ahead of him a nearly exact duplicate of the Bunkport. Max spotted it in a trade publication. Under U.S. patent statutes, in the event of conflicting claims, legal protection falls to the inventor able to furnish earliest documented evidence of the invention, and Aaron Dodge, naturally, had published a sketch of the Bunkport in his "Inventory" column the minute the inspiration struck, more than a year before. Now that he'd patented his bed, though, he didn't plan to sleep in it. Not any more. For the near future, he was thinking double, maybe even king. Something an ex–fat man and his partner could lose themselves in. That is if he and Kennedy could ever get near their apartment again and resume a life there. That a safe return didn't seem imminent wasn't bothering Aaron Dodge in the least. For a man whose figure had offered as easy a target as his had for so many years, disappearing represented an edifying experience.

He vanished so thoroughly that the Singers had trouble locating him to request his assistance. They'd finally contacted Max and left it up to her. Max knew most of the holes Aaron Dodge would be likely to emerge from when he decided to reappear, and issued appropriate bulletins. Dave and Connie, he learned, wanted to talk to him about their daughter.

According to the psychologist who'd been assigned her case, none of the usual approaches had helped. Puppet therapy. Anatomically correct dolls. Re-enactment. Hypnosis. But she'd mentioned Aaron Dodge by description on several occasions. The Singers wondered if he'd consider attending a session. Maybe with him there she'd talk.

Aaron Dodge resisted. Instead he thought maybe something less institutional. A burger? A matinee? Encanto Lagoon or a reach of sand along the dry Salt River? Mary chose Encanto Park.

He'd brought along donuts, and offered her one as they walked, following a slender gravel path near the water. "Go ahead. They're good. Eat one. If you don't like it, you can feed it to the ducks."

"They're messy."

"What're you, royalty? Here."

"Okay." She reached into the bag. "Thanks."

He watched her as she walked beside him. Maybe what he'd heard was true. Maybe after something this horrible she'd never be the child she'd had the chance to be, or ever enjoy the happiness a pretty girl from a prosperous family in a sunny suburb was supposed to be entitled to. A happiness that would belong to her friends. But Aaron Dodge wasn't ready to predict incurable disenchantment. There was, he'd heard, an ecstatic, pure, uplifted, and unconditional happiness in the world. And then there was another kind. And Aaron Dodge believed in that other kind of happiness.

He sat with her in the grass beside the lagoon. She took off her shoes. Wiggled her toes in the water. Aaron Dodge ate the donuts. Together they stared out over Encanto, quiet at first. He waited, and when she was ready Mary Vanessa Singer talked. Simply, with little anger, few tears, she told her story.

Where she'd been.

How she'd survived.

And what it felt like to be alive.